Sarah M. Anderson may live east of the Mississippi River, but her heart lies out West on the Great Plains. Sarah's book *A Man of Privilege* won an RT Reviewers' Choice Best Book Award in 2012.

Sarah spends her days having conversations with imaginary cowboys and American Indians. Find out more about Sarah's love of cowboys and Indians at www.sarahmanderson.com and sign up for the new-release newsletter at www.eepurl.com/nv39b.

HIS SON, HER SECRET

BY
SARAH M. ANDERSON

To Joelle Charbonneau and Blythe Gifford,
who took me under their wings when I was new and
clueless, held my hands when I stumbled, and who
even became friends with my mom. Thank you
for being guides on my journey, ladies!

One

"This place is a dump," Byron Beaumont announced. His words echoed off the stone walls, making the submerged space sound haunted.

"Don't see it as it is," his older brother Matthew said through the speaker in Byron's phone. It was much easier for Matthew to call this one in, rather than make the long journey to Denver from California, where he was happily living in sin. "See it as what it will be."

Byron did another slow turn, inspecting the extent of the neglect as he tried not to think about Matthew—or any of his older brothers—being happily engaged or married. The Beaumonts hadn't been, until recently, the marrying kind.

Yet it hadn't been so long ago that he'd thought *he* was the marrying kind. And then it had all blown up in his face. And while he'd been licking his wounds, his brothers—normally workaholics and playboys—had been pairing off with women who were, by all accounts, great for them.

Once again, Byron was the one who didn't conform to Beaumont expectations.

Forcibly, he turned his attention back to the space before him. The vaulted ceiling was arched, but the parts that weren't arched were quite low. Cobwebs dangled from everything, including the single bare lightbulb in the middle of the room, which cast deep shadows into the corners. The giant pillars supporting the arches were evenly spaced, taking up a huge amount of the floor. Inches of dust coated the low half-moon windows at eye level. What Byron could see of the outside looked to be weeds. And the whole space smelled of mold.

"And what will it be? Razed, I hope."

"No," Byron's oldest half brother, Chadwick Beaumont, said. The word was crisp and authoritative, which was normal for Chadwick. However, the part where he lifted his daughter out of his wife's arms and onto his shoulders so she could see better was not. "This is underneath the brewery. It was originally a warehouse but we think you can do something better with it."

Byron snorted. Yeah, right.

Serena Beaumont, Chadwick's wife, stepped next to Byron so that Matthew could see her on the phone. "Percheron Drafts has had a great launch, thanks to Matthew's hard work. But we want this brewery to be more than just a craft beer."

"We want to hit the old company where it counts," Matthew said. "A large number of our former customers continue to be unhappy about how the Beaumont Brewery was sold away from our family. The bigger we can make Percheron Drafts, the better we can siphon off our old customers."

"And to do that," Serena went on in a sweet voice at direct odds with a discussion about corporate politics, "we need to offer our customers something they cannot get from Beaumont Brewery."

"Phillip is working with our graphic designer on incorporating his team of Percherons into all of the Percheron Draft marketing, but we have to be sensitive to trademark issues," Chadwick added.

"Exactly," Matthew agreed. "So our distinctive element can't be the horses, not yet."

Byron rolled his eyes. He should have brought his twin sister, Frances, so he would have someone to back him up. He was being steamrollered into something that seemed doomed from the start.

"You three have *got* to be kidding me. You want me to open a restaurant in this dungeon?" He looked around at the dust and the mildew. "No. It's not going to happen. This place is a dump. I can't cook in this environment and there's no way in hell I would expect anyone to eat here, either." He eyed the baby gurgling on Chadwick's shoulder. "In fact, I'm not sure any of us should be breathing this air without HazMat masks. When was the last time the doors were even opened?"

Matthew looked at Serena. "Did you show him the workroom?"

"No. I'll do that now." She walked toward a set of doors in the far back of the room. They were heavy wooden things on rusting hinges, wide enough a pair of Percheron horses could pull a wagon through them.

"I've got it, babe," Chadwick said as Serena struggled to get the huge latch lifted. "Here, hold Catherine," he said to Byron.

Suddenly, Byron had a baby in his arms. He almost dropped the phone as Catherine leaned back to look up at her uncle.

"Um, hey," Byron said nervously. He didn't know much of anything about babies in general or this baby in particular. All he knew was that she was Serena's daughter from a previous relationship and Chadwick had formally adopted her.

Catherine's face wrinkled in doubt at this new development. Byron didn't even know how old the little girl was. Six months? A year? He had no idea. He couldn't be sure he was even holding her right. However, he was becoming reasonably confident that this small human was about to start crying. Her face screwed up and she started to turn red.

"Um, Chadwick? Serena?"

Luckily, Chadwick got the doors open with a hideous squealing noise, which distracted the baby. Then Serena lifted Catherine out of Byron's arms. "Thanks," she said, as if Byron had done anything other than not drop the infant.

"You're welcome."

Matthew was laughing, Byron realized. "What?" he whispered at his brother.

"The look on your face…" Matthew appeared to be slapping his knee. "Man, have you ever even held a baby before?"

"I'm a chef—not a babysitter," Byron hissed back. "Have you ever foamed truffle oil?"

Matthew held up his hands in surrender. "I give, I give. Besides, no one said that starting a restaurant would involve child care. You're off the hook, baby-wise."

"Byron?" Serena said. She waved him toward the doors. "Come see this."

Unwillingly, Byron crossed the length of the dank room and walked up the sloping ramp to the workroom. What he saw almost took his breath away.

Instead of the dirt and decay that characterized the old warehouse, the workroom had been upgraded at some point in the past twenty years. Stainless-steel cabinets and countertops fit against the stone walls—but these walls had been painted white. The overhanging industrial lighting was harsh, but it kept the room from looking like a pit in hell. Some cobwebs hung here and there, but the contrast between this room and the other was stunning.

This, Byron thought, *had potential.*

"Now," Matthew was saying as Byron looked at the copper pipes that led down into a sink that was almost three feet long, "as we understand it, the last people who used this brewery to brew beer upgraded the workroom. That's where they experimented with ingredients in small batches."

Byron walked over to the six-burner stove. It was a professional model. "It's better," he agreed. "But this isn't equipped for restaurant service. I can't cook on only six burners. It's still a complete teardown. I'd still be starting from scratch."

There was a pause, then Matthew said, "Isn't that what you want?"

"What?"

"Yes, well," Chadwick cleared his throat. "We thought that, with your being in Europe for over a year…"

"That you'd be more interested in a fresh start," Serena finished diplomatically. "A place you could call your own. Where you call the shots."

Byron stared at his family. "What are you talking about?" But the question was a dodge. He knew *exactly* what they were thinking.

That he'd had a job working for Rory McMaken in his flagship restaurant, Sauce, in Denver and that not only had Byron been thrown out of the place over what everyone thought were "creative differences" but that Byron had left the country and gone to France and then Spain because he couldn't handle the flack McMaken had given him and the entire Beaumont family on his show on the Foodie TV network.

Too bad they didn't know what had really happened.

Byron's contact with his family had been intentionally limited over the past twelve months—his twin sister Frances notwithstanding. Nearly all of the family news had filtered down through Frances. That's how Byron had learned that Chadwick had not only gotten divorced but had then also married his secretary and adopted her daughter. And that's how Byron had learned Phillip was marrying his horse trainer. No doubt, Frances was the only reason anyone knew where Byron had been.

Still, Byron was touched by his family's concern. He'd more or less gone off the grid to protect them from the fallout of his one great mistake—Leona Harper. Yet here they were, trying to convince him to return to Denver by giving him the blank slate he'd been trying to find.

Chadwick started to say something but paused and looked at his wife. Something unspoken passed between them. Just the sight of it stung Byron like lemon juice in a paper cut.

"You wouldn't have to get independent financing," Serena told Byron. "The up-front costs would be covered between the settlement you received from the sale of the Beaumont Brewery and the capital that Percheron Drafts can provide."

"We bought the entire building outright," Chadwick added. "Rent would be next to nothing compared to what it would be in downtown Denver. The restaurant would have to cover its own utilities and payroll, but that's about it. You'd have near total financial freedom."

"And," Matthew chimed in, "you could do whatever you wanted. Whatever theme you wanted to build upon, whatever decorating scheme you wanted to use, whatever cuisine you wanted to serve—burgers and fries or foamed truffle oil or whatever. The only caveat would be that Percheron Drafts beer would be the primary focus of the beverage menu since the restaurant is in the basement of the brewery. Otherwise, you'd have carte blanche."

Byron looked from Chadwick to Serena to Matthew's face on the screen. "You guys really think this will sell beer?"

"I can give you a copy of the cost-benefit analysis I prepared," Serena said. Chadwick beamed at her, which was odd. The brother Byron remembered didn't beam a whole hell of a lot.

Byron could not believe he was considering this. He liked living in Madrid. His Spanish was improving and he liked working at El Gallio, the restaurant helmed by a chef who cared more about food and ingredients and people than his own brand name.

It'd been a year. A year of working his way up the food chain, from no-star restaurants to one-star Michelin establishments to El Gallio, a three-star restaurant —one of the highest-ranked places in the world. He had made a name for himself that had absolutely nothing to do with his father and the Beaumonts, and he was damned proud of that. Would he really give all that up to come home for good?

More than anything, he liked the near total anonymity of life in Europe. There, no one cared that he was a Beaumont or that he'd left the States under a swirling cloud of gossip. No one gave a damn what happened with the Beaumont Brewery or Percheron Drafts or what any of his siblings had done to make headlines that day.

No one thought about the long-running feud between the Beaumonts and the Harpers that had led to the forced sale of the Beaumont Brewery.

No one thought about Byron and Leona Harper.

And that was how he liked it.

Leona...

If he were going to move back home, he knew he'd have to confront her. They had unfinished business and not even a year in Europe could change that. He wanted to look her in the face and have her tell him *why*. That's all he wanted. Why had she lied to him for almost a year about who she really was? Why had she picked her family over him? Why had she thrown away everything they'd planned—everything he'd wanted to give her?

In the course of the past year, Byron had worked and worked and *worked* to forget her. He had to accept the fact that he might not ever forget her or her betrayal of him—of them. Fine. That was part of life. Everyone got their heart ripped out of their chest and handed to them at least once.

He didn't want her back. Why would he? So she and her father could try to destroy him all over again?

No, what he wanted was a little payback.

The question was how to go about it.

Then he remembered something. Before it'd all fallen so spectacularly apart, Leona had been in school for industrial design. They'd talked about the restaurant they'd open together, how she'd design it and he'd run it. A blank slate that was theirs and theirs alone.

It'd been a year. She might have a job or her own firm or whatever. If he hired her, she would work for him. She would have to do as he said. He could prove that she didn't have any power over him—that she couldn't hurt him. He was not the same naive boy who'd let love blind him while he worked for an egomaniac. *He* was a chef. *He* would have his own restaurant. *He* was his own boss. *He* was in charge.

He was a Beaumont, damn it. It was time to start acting like one.

"I can use whomever I want to do the interior design?"

"Of course," Chadwick and Matthew said at the same time.

Byron looked at the workroom and then through the doors to the dungeon of the old warehouse. "I cannot believe I'm even considering this," he muttered. He could go back to Spain, back to the new life he'd made for himself, free of his past.

Except...

He would never be free of his past, not really. And he was done hiding.

He looked at his brothers and Serena, each hopeful that he would come back into the family fold.

This was a mistake. But then, when it came to Leona, Byron would probably always make the worst choice.

"I'll do it."

* * *

"Leona?" May's voice came through the speaker on her phone.

Leona hurriedly picked up before her boss, Marvin Lutefisk, head of Lutefisk Design, could hear the personal call. "I'm here. What's up? Is everything okay?"

"Percy's a little fussy. I think he might have another ear infection."

Leona sighed. "Do we still have some drops from the last round?" She could hardly afford another hundred-dollar trip to the doctor, who would look at Percy's ears for three seconds and write a prescription.

But the other option wasn't much better. If Percy got three—now two—more ear infections, they would have to talk about putting tubes in his ears, and even that minor outpatient surgery was far beyond Leona's budget.

"A little bit…" May sounded unconvincing.

"I'll…get some more," Leona announced. Maybe she could sweet-talk the nurses into a free sample?

Just like she'd done nearly every single day since Percy's birth, Leona thought about how different things would be if Byron Beaumont were still in her life. It wouldn't necessarily solve her health care issues, but her little sister May treated Leona as if she had the means to fix any problem, anytime.

Just once Leona wanted to lean on someone, instead of being the one who took all the weight.

But daydreaming about what might have been didn't pay the bills, so she told May, "Listen, I'm still at work. If he gets too bad, call the pediatrician. I can take him in tomorrow, okay?"

"Okay. You'll be home for dinner, right? I have class tonight, don't forget."

"I won't." Just then, her boss walked past her cubicle. "Gotta go," she whispered and hung up.

"Leona," Marvin said in his nasal tone. Unconsciously, he reached up and patted his comb-over back into position. "Busy?"

Leona put on her best smile. "Just finishing up a client phone call, Mr. Lutefisk. What's up?"

Marvin smiled encouragingly, his eyes beaming at her through thick lenses. He really wasn't a bad boss—that she knew. Marvin was giving her a chance to be someone other than Leon Harper's daughter, and that was all she could ask. That and the chance to get her foot in the door of industrial design. Leona had always dreamed of designing restaurants and bars—public spaces where form and function blended with a practical application of art and design. She hadn't really planned on doing storefronts for malls and the like, but everyone had to start somewhere.

"We've had an inquiry," Marvin said. "For a new brew-pub on the south side of the city." Marvin tilted his head to the side and gave her a look. "We don't normally do this sort of thing here at Lutefisk Design but the caller asked for you specifically."

A trill of excitement coursed through her. A restaurant? And they'd asked for *her* by name? This was good. Great, even. But Leona remembered who she was talking to. "Are you comfortable with me being the primary on this one? If you'd rather handle it yourself, I'd be happy to assist."

It hurt to make the offer. If she was the primary designer instead of the assistant, she'd get a much bigger percentage of the commission and that could be more than enough to cover Percy's medical costs. She could pay off some of May's student loans and...

She couldn't get ahead of herself. Marvin was very particular about the level of involvement his assistants engaged in.

"Well..." Marvin pushed his glasses up. "The caller was very specific. He requested you."

"Really? I mean, that's great," Leona said, trying to keep her cool. How had this happened? Maybe that last job for an upscale boutique on the Sixteenth Street Mall? The owner had been thrilled with the changes Leona had made to Marvin's plan. Maybe that's where the reference came from?

"But he wants you to survey the site today. This afternoon. Do you have time?"

She almost said *hell, yes!* But she managed to slam the brakes on her mouth. Years of trying to keep her father happy when he was in one of his moods had trained her to say exactly what a man in a position of authority needed to hear. "I need to finish up the paperwork for that stationery store..."

Marvin waved this away. "That will keep. Go on—see if this is a job worth taking. Charlene has the address."

"Thank you." Leona gathered up her tablet computer—one of her true luxuries—and grabbed her purse. She got the address from Charlene, the receptionist, and hurried to the car.

A brewpub. One that was on the far south side of the city, she noted as she programmed the address into her Global Positioning System. There wasn't any other information to go with the address—like which brewery this was for—but that was probably a good sign. Instead of doing an upgrading project, maybe this would be a brand-new venture. That would not only mean more billable hours but the chance to make this project the showcase she'd need when she started her own firm.

The GPS estimated the pub's location was about forty minutes away. Leona called May and updated her on her whereabouts and then she hit the road.

Thirty-seven minutes later, Leona drove past a small sign that read Percheron Drafts as she turned into a driveway that led to a series of old brick buildings. She looked up at the tall smokestack in awe. White smoke puffed out lazily, but that was practically the only sign of life.

Percheron Drafts…why did that name sound familiar? She'd heard it somewhere, but she didn't actually drink beer. She was going to have to fake it for this meeting. She'd have time to do the research tonight.

The GPS guided her underneath a walkway, around the back of the building and told her to park on a gravel lot that had weeds growing everywhere. Ahead she saw a ramp that led down to an open door.

Okay, she thought as she turned the car off and grabbed her things. So maybe the building was old, but this certainly wasn't an already established restaurant. Heck, she didn't even see another car parked here. Was this the right place?

She got out and put on her professional smile. Then— like something out of a dream—a man walked through the doors and up the ramp. The sunlight caught the red in his hair and he smiled at her.

She knew that walk, that hair. She knew that smile— lopsided and warm and happy to see her.

Oh, God.

Byron.

Percheron Drafts… It suddenly clicked. That was the name of the brewery the Beaumont family had started after their family business had been sold—and she only knew about that because it was her father who'd forced the sale.

Panic kicked in. He was coming toward her, his lean legs closing the distance rapidly. If he got too close, he'd see the baby seat in the back of her car.

Her head began to swim. She wasn't ready for this. He'd walked out on her. He'd believed her father over her and simply disappeared—just like her father had said all Beaumont men did. Beaumonts took whatever woman they wanted and when they were done, they simply abandoned them—and kept the children.

She'd known she'd have to confront him eventually. But now? Right freaking *now*?

She wasn't ready. She hadn't lost all the baby weight and, as a result, she was wearing the only kind of business-casual attire she could afford—the kind from discount stores. She couldn't even be sure that Percy hadn't spit up on her blouse this morning.

When she'd imagined facing the man who'd broken her heart and abandoned her, she'd wanted to look her very best to make him physically hurt. She hadn't wanted to look like a rumpled single mother struggling to get by.

Even if he was the reason she was exactly that.

But she couldn't let him see into the back of the car. If he didn't know about Percy, she wasn't going to tell him until she'd had time to come up with a plan. Because what if he did the Beaumont thing and demanded her child? She could not lose her son. She couldn't let Byron raise the boy to be yet another Beaumont in the line of Beaumont men. She had to protect her baby.

So, against her better judgment, she walked toward him.

Oh, this wasn't fair. It just wasn't. Byron's hair had gotten a little longer and he wore it pulled back into a low ponytail, which took all of the natural curl out of it—except for one piece that had come free. His lanky frame had filled out a little, giving him a more muscular look that was positively sinful in the white button-up shirt he wore cuffed at the sleeves.

He looked good. Heck, he looked better than good. And she looked…dumpy. Damn it all.

They met in the middle of the parking lot, stopping less than two feet from each other. "Leona," he said in his deep baritone voice as he looked at her. His eyes were a deeper blue now—or maybe that was just the bright sun. God, he was *so* handsome.

She would not be swayed by his good looks. Those looks lied, just like he did.

"Byron," she replied. Because what else could she say here? *Where have you been? I had your son after you left me? I don't know if I want to kiss you or strangle you?*

This was no big deal, she tried to tell herself. It was just the former love of her life, the father of her son—suddenly back after a year's absence. And apparently hiring her for a job. A flash of anger gave her strength. If he was back, why hadn't he just called her? Why did he have to hire her?

Unless…he hadn't come back for her.

He'd left without her, after all, jetting off to Europe. That'd been as much information as Leona had been able to get out of Byron's twin sister, Frances. Europe—as far away from Leona as he could get without leaving the planet. Or so it had felt.

And now he was back and hiring her. For a job she desperately needed. This was not him sweeping back into her life and making everything right. This was not him needing her.

So she did not flinch as he looked her up and down as if he expected her to fall into his arms and tell him how damned much she'd missed him. She would not give him the satisfaction. Yes, the past year had been the hardest year of her life. But she wasn't the same silly little girl who believed love would somehow conquer all. The past year had shown her how tough she could be. It was time for Byron to realize the same thing.

But it was difficult to keep her head up as his gaze traveled over her. He'd always done that—looked at her as though she was the most beautiful woman on the planet. Even when they'd worked together at that restaurant and the cream of the high-society crop had come into the restaurant every single night—even when other women had thrown themselves at his Beaumont name—Byron had always had eyes only for *her*.

She shivered at the memory of the way he used to look at her—at the way he was looking at her right now.

"You cut your hair," he noted.

Her mouth opened, the truth on the tip of her tongue—she'd cut it because Percy liked to yank it while he was nursing. She clamped down on that impulse. The words sat in the back of her throat, a lead weight that held her tongue still. She would give him absolutely nothing to use against her. She would not let him hurt her again.

"I like it," he hurried to add when she couldn't think of a single reasonable thing to say in response.

She blushed at the compliment. Her fingers itched to tuck the short bob behind her ears, but she held fast to the straps of her bag. She was not here for Byron, just like he hadn't been there for her. She was here to do a job and that was final. "Do you really need an interior designer or did you call me away from my job just to note I've changed my style?" *Since you left.*

She didn't say those last words out loud, but they seemed to hang in between them anyway.

Byron took another step toward her. He reached up. Leona held her breath as he trailed the very tips of his fingers over her cheek. It was almost as if he couldn't believe she was really here, either.

Then he reached down and picked up her left hand. His thumb rubbed over her ring finger—her bare ring finger. "Leona…" he murmured, his voice husky with what she recognized as need. He lifted her hand to his lips and kissed it.

Everything about her body tightened at the sound of her name from his mouth, his lips on her hand—tightened so much that she had to close her eyes because if she looked into the depths of Byron's beautiful blue eyes for one second longer, she'd be lost all over again.

It'd always been this way. There'd been something about Byron Beaumont that had pulled her in from the very beginning—something that should have sent her running the other way.

After all, her father had been drumming his hatred of all things Beaumont into her head for as long as she could remember. She knew all about Hardwick Beaumont, her father's nemesis, and his heirs. How the Beaumonts were dangerous, how they seduced young and innocent women and then cast them aside as if they were nothing.

Just as Leona had been seduced and cast aside.

So she did not give. She ignored her body's reaction to Byron, ignored the old memories that the mere touch of his lips brought rushing back to her. She kept her eyes closed and her focus on the job.

The job she needed because she was raising Byron's son on her own. A son he did not know about.

She needed to tell him.

But she couldn't. Not yet. Not until she figured out what he was doing here. Not until she knew where she stood with him. She was no longer young and innocent and she was not someone who would forget a year's worth of heartache and loneliness with the whisper of her name, thank you very much.

God, what a mess.

A tense second passed between them and then Byron dropped her hand. She felt him step away from her and only then did she open her eyes.

He now stood several feet away, looking at her differently—harder, meaner almost.

Another flash of panic hit her—did he already know about Percy? Or was he just mad that she wasn't falling at her feet in gratitude for being acknowledged?

"I need a designer," he said quietly. He didn't sound angry, which was at direct odds with the way he was looking at her. "I'm going to be opening up my own restaurant."

"Here?"

"Here," he agreed, sounding resigned to it. "It's a massive job and I—" she saw him swallow "—I wanted to see if it was the kind of thing you were still interested it."

"You're going to stay in Denver?" The question came out with more of an edge than she meant it to, but that was the thing she needed to know. If he were going to stay in Denver, then...

Then he'd have to know about Percy. They'd have to figure something out, something involving child support and visitation and...

Well, not their relationship. There was no relationship. That part of her life was over now.

And if he were opening up his own restaurant—her mind spun around the facts. Her father, Leon Harper, would find out that Byron had come home.

Oh, *God*. Her father would get out his old axes and grind them all over again. Her father would shove his way back into her life, ignoring all the ways she had tried to extricate herself from her parents. Her father would do everything he could to destroy Byron—again.

Her father would do everything to punish *her* again.

"Yes," Byron said, turning away from her and looking up at the old buildings. "I've come home."

Two

Byron walked into the darkened room that, somehow, would become a restaurant. Somehow. "Here we are. The dungeon."

Behind him, he heard Leona cough lightly. "Is that the theme you're working with?"

"No."

What the hell was he doing? Touching her face? Kissing her hand? That was not part of his plan. His plan was to hire her, get his restaurant going and kick her right back out of his life—this time, on his terms. She hadn't needed him. He didn't need her. Except for design purposes.

But that's not what had happened because something as simple as seeing Leona Harper again—and seeing that she wasn't wearing a wedding ring—had blown all to hell his simple plan to get simple answers.

There was nothing simple about Leona. A fact she'd made abundantly clear when she'd closed her eyes—when she'd refused to even look at him.

"Pity," she sniffed. "You wouldn't have to change a thing."

He grinned in spite of himself. Leona had always been something of a contradiction. She was, in general, a quiet woman who avoided confrontation. But when she'd been alone with him, she'd let out the real her—snarky and sarcastic with a biting observation ready at all times. She'd made him laugh—him. He'd thought he was too jaded, too cynical to laugh anymore, to feel much of anything anymore. But he'd laughed with her. He'd had all these feelings with her. For her.

He'd loved her. Or thought he had. But maybe that'd all been part of the trick, a Harper trapping a Beaumont. She hadn't told him who she was, after all, until it was too late.

"So if you're not going with torture chamber," she went on, "what do you want?"

"Whatever."

"Be serious, Byron." If he hadn't been looking at her, he wouldn't have seen the tiny stamp of her foot that set off eddies of dust.

He paused. "I am being serious. You can do whatever you want. I can cook what I want. The only caveat is that the beverage menu has to feature our beer. The restaurant can be whatever it wants."

Clutching her tablet to her chest, she gave him a long look that he couldn't quite make out in the dim light. "You have to have some idea of what you're interested in," she finally said in a soft voice.

"I do. I've always known what I wanted." He turned away from her. This was a bad idea. But then again, it was Leona—she'd always been a bad idea. "But I'm used to not getting it."

She gasped, but he kept walking back toward the soon-to-be-kitchen. He couldn't let her get under his skin. He never should have asked her here. He was safer in Spain, where she was nothing but a memory—not a flesh and blood woman who would always push him past the point of reason.

The reasonable thing to do was to keep as much space between the Beaumonts and the Harpers as possible. That's the way it'd always been, before he'd unwittingly crossed that line. That's the way it should have stayed.

He dragged open the doors to the workroom and flipped on all the lights. "This needs to be upgraded considerably," he said. He couldn't fix the past, couldn't undo his great mistake. But he could stop making it over again. He just had to focus on the job—it was the reason they were both here. He needed to find a way to be Byron Beaumont in a place where his last name permanently branded him, and he needed to make sure that Leona Harper knew she would never exert any power over him ever again.

She followed him into the cleaner space. "I see." She took several pictures with her tablet. "Do you have a menu yet?"

"No. I only agreed to do this yesterday. I thought I'd be on my way back to Madrid by now."

"Madrid? Is *that* where you went?"

Of course she wouldn't know. She probably hadn't bothered to look him up at all.

But there was something in the way she said it—as if she couldn't believe that was the answer—that made him turn back to her. She stared at him with big eyes and this time, there was no hiding that look. She was stunned—confused? She was hurt.

Well, that made two of them "Yes. Well, I spent six months in France first. Then Spain."

Her eyes cut down to his left hand—his ring finger. "Did you…"

He tensed. "No. I was working."

She exhaled. "Ah." But that was all she said. He was about to turn away when she added, "Where did you work?"

"George, you remember him?"

"Your father's old chef?"

For some reason, the fact that she remembered who George was made Byron relax a little. It wasn't like she'd forgotten him. Not entirely, anyway. "Yes. One of his old friends from Le Cordon Bleu gave me a job in Paris. Then I heard about an opening at El Gallio in Madrid and took the job."

Her eyes widened again. "You were at El Gallio? That's a three-star restaurant!"

He relaxed more. She remembered. Even though her reaction was probably all part of the same ruse to undermine the Beaumont family, he couldn't help himself.

For months, he and Leona had talked about restaurants—how they'd love to travel and dine at the world's best establishments and then open up their own. She'd design everything and Byron would handle the food, and it'd be so much better than working for Rory McMaken, the egotistical bastard.

Leona spoke, pulling him out of the past. "You're leaving behind El Gallio to open your own restaurant *here*?"

"Crazy, right?" He looked around the workroom. "Don't get me wrong. I loved Europe. No one there knew or cared that I was a Beaumont. I could just be Byron, a chef. That was…" *Freeing.*

He'd been free of the family drama, free of the longstanding feud between the Beaumonts and the Harpers.

"That must have been amazing," she said in a wistful tone. Which was so at odds with how he remembered the way things had gone down that he turned back to her in surprise.

"Yeah. I wasn't sure I wanted to come back to all of this. But this is an opportunity I can't pass up. It's a chance to be a part of the family business on my terms."

"I see. So you've decided to be a Beaumont, then." Her voice was quiet, as if he'd somehow confirmed her worst fears.

He would not let her get away with using guilt on him. Guilt? For what? He was the injured party here. She'd lied about who she was—not once, but for almost a year. And then she'd cast him aside the moment her father asked her to. Hell, for all he knew, that had always been the plan. It'd only been after he'd left the country that Leon Harper had managed to sell the Beaumont Brewery out from under the Beaumonts. Maybe he'd told Leona to split one of them off—divide and then conquer.

Right. If anyone should be feeling guilty here, it was her. He'd never lied about his last name or his family. He'd never made promises and then broken them. Thank God he hadn't actually asked her to marry him before she betrayed him.

"I've always been a Beaumont," he answered decisively. "And we are not to be trifled with."

He shouldn't have said that last bit, but he couldn't help it. He was the boss here. She worked for him. Emotionally, he didn't need her. If she was getting any ideas about turning the tables on him, she'd best forget them now.

She looked away.

"Anyway," he went on, focusing on the job. *His* restaurant. "I'm starting from scratch and I wanted…" Unexpectedly, his words dried up. He wanted so much, but like he'd said, he'd gotten used to disappointment. "I know there was a time in our past when we talked about a restaurant."

Even though she was studying the tips of her shoes very closely, he still saw her eyes close.

He remembered that look of defeat—he'd only seen it one other time—when her father, Leon Harper himself, had shown up at Sauce and gotten Byron fired and demanded that Leona come home with her parents right now or else. Leona had looked at the ground and closed her eyes and Byron had said "babe" and…

Well. And here they were.

"If you don't want the job, that's fine. I know that Harpers and Beaumonts don't work well together and I wouldn't want to make your father mad." He didn't quite manage to say *father* without sneering.

He watched her chest rise and fall with a deep breath. "I want…"

Her words were so quiet that he couldn't hear her. He stepped in closer and took a deep breath.

Which was a mistake. The scent of Leona—sweet and soft, roses and vanilla—was all it took to transport him to another time and place, before he'd realized that she wasn't just someone with the last name of Harper, but one of *those* Harpers.

He leaned forward, unable to stop himself. He'd never been able to stay away from her, not from the first moment she'd been hired at Sauce as a hostess. "What do you want, Leona?"

"I need to tell you..." Her words were still little more than a whisper.

He touched her then, which was another mistake. But she took what control he had and blew it to bits. He cupped her face in his hand and lifted her chin until he could look into her hazel eyes. "What do you need?"

Her eyes widened again as his face moved within inches of hers, and she exhaled, something that sounded a hell of a lot like satisfaction. His gut clenched. Despite her lies and betrayal, the messy ending to their relationship and the long year on a different continent—despite it all—he wanted her.

"The job," she said in a voice that didn't even make it to a whisper. "I need the job, Byron."

She didn't kiss him, didn't tell him she was so sorry she'd picked her family over him. At no point did she apologize for lying to him. She just stood there.

"Right, right." She couldn't be clearer. She was here for the job.

Not for him.

Her heart pounded and she wasn't sure she was still breathing.

Byron had dropped his hand and turned back to the stove, leaving her in a state of paralysis.

If he was going to stay in Denver, he had to know and the longer she didn't tell him—well, that would just make everything worse.

Somehow. She wasn't sure how things could get much worse, frankly. Byron hiring her to design a restaurant—and then switching between unbridled lust and a cold shoulder?

That thought made her angry. Why did he have to hire her to see her? He could have called. Sent a text.

The anger felt good. It gave her back some power. She was not a helpless girl at the mercies of the men in her life, not anymore. She'd gotten away from her father and had a son and done just fine without Byron. So what if all he had to do was look at her and her knees turned to jelly? Didn't matter. He'd left her behind. She was only here for the paycheck. Not for him.

She could not tell him about Percy, not when she couldn't be sure what version of Byron she would get. She'd spent the past year carving out a life that made her as happy as possible—a job she liked and a family she loved, with May and Percy. She'd spent a whole year free to make her own choices and live her own life. She'd stopped being Leon Harper's wayward oldest daughter, and she'd stopped dreaming of being Byron Beaumont's wife. She was just Leona Harper and that was a good thing.

Now she had to remember that.

"Well," she started, then cleared her throat to get her voice working properly. "I guess what I need is a menu. It doesn't have to be specific, but are you going to serve burgers and fries or haute cuisine or what? That will guide the rest of the design choices."

"Something in the middle," he replied quickly. "Accessible food and beer, but better than burgers and fries. You can get that anywhere. I want this to be a different kind of restaurant—not about me, but about the meal. The experience." He looked out at the depressing room that she was somehow going to transform into a dining hall. "A different experience than *this*," he added with a shake of his head.

"Okay, that's a good start. What else?"

"Fusion," he added. "I was cooking things in Europe that I didn't cook here. Locally sourced ingredients, advanced techniques—the whole nine yards."

She took notes on her tablet. "Any ideas for the actual menu items?"

"A few."

She waited for him to elaborate, but when he didn't, she looked up again. "Such as?"

He didn't look at her. "Why don't you come by the house tomorrow and I'll make you a tasting menu? You can tell me what might work and what doesn't."

She should say no. She should insist that their interactions be limited to this dank building. "The house?"

"The Beaumont Mansion. I'm staying there until I get my own place." He pivoted and fixed her with a look that she'd always been powerless to resist. "If you can tolerate being in the lair of the Beaumonts, that is."

"I tolerate you, don't I?" she snapped back. She would not allow him to make her the bad guy, and she would not let him paint her as the coward. He was the one who'd run off. She was the one who'd stayed and dealt with the fallout.

She didn't know how she'd expected him to respond, but that lazy smile? That wasn't it. "Shall we say six, then?"

Leona mentally ran through her calendar. May had class tonight—but tomorrow night she should be able to stay with Percy.

"Who else will be home?" Because no matter what had happened between Leona and Byron, that didn't change the larger fact that the Beaumonts and the Harpers got on much worse than oil and water ever had.

He shrugged. "Chadwick and his family live there full-time, but they eat on their own schedule. Frances just moved back in, but she's rarely home. A couple of my younger half siblings are still there—but again, everyone's on their own schedule. Should be just us."

For a brief, insane second, she entertained the notion of bringing Percy with her. But the moment the thought occurred to her, she dismissed it. The Beaumonts were notorious for keeping the children from broken relationships. That's what her father had always told her—Hardwick Beaumont always got rid of the women and kept the babies, never letting the children see their mothers again. That's what Byron had said happened to him and his siblings. It wasn't until later in his life that he'd gotten to know his mother.

At the time, that story had broken her heart for him. He'd been a lost little boy in a cold, unloving house. But now she knew better. He hadn't been looking for sympathy.

He'd been warning her. And she was more the fool for not realizing it until it was too late.

She was done being the fool. No, she would not bring Percy. Not until she had a better grasp on Byron's reaction to the idea of having a five-month-old son. Not until she knew if he would decree that the boy would be better off a Beaumont instead of a Harper.

Byron had to know about his child eventually, but she could *not* lose her son.

"All right," she finally said. "Dinner tomorrow night at six. I'll draft a few ideas and you can provide feedback." Her phone chimed—it was a text from May, reminding Leona about her class tonight. "Anything else?"

The question hung in the air like the cobwebs hung from the ceiling. Byron looked at her with such longing that she almost weakened.

Then the look shifted and anything warm or welcoming was gone and all that was left was an iciness she hadn't seen before. It chilled her to the bone.

"No," he said, his voice freezing. "There's nothing else I need from you."

That was an answer, all right.

But not the one she wanted to hear.

Three

"Your sauce is going to burn."

This simple observation from George made Byron jump. "Damn." He hurried over to reduce the heat under the saucepan, mentally kicking himself for making a rookie mistake.

George Jackson chuckled from his perch on a stool—the same place he'd been sitting for the past thirty-five years. Mothers and stepmothers came and went, more children showed up—being a Beaumont meant living in a constant state of uncertainty. Except for the kitchen. Except for George. Sure, his brown skin was more wrinkled and, yes, more of his hair was white than not. But otherwise, he was the same man—one of the very few, black or white, who didn't take crap from any Beaumont. Not even Hardwick. Maybe that's why Hardwick had kept George around and why Chadwick had kept him on after Hardwick's death. George was constant and honest.

Like right now. "Boy, you're a wreck."

"I'm fine," Byron lied. Which was pointless because George knew him far too well to buy that line.

George shook his head. "Why are you trying so hard to impress this girl? I thought she was the whole reason you left town."

"I'm not," Byron said, stirring the scalded sauce. "We're working together. She's designing the restaurant. I'm preparing food that might be on the menu in said restaurant. That's not trying to impress her."

George chuckled again. "Yeah, sure it's not. You Beaumont men are all alike," he added under his breath.

"I am absolutely not like my father and you know it," Byron shot off, checking the roast in the oven. "I've never married anyone, much less a string of people, and I certainly don't have any kids running around."

George snorted at this. "Be that as it may, you're exactly like your old man. Even like Chadwick, sitting up there with his second wife. None of you all could be honest with yourselves when it came to women." He seemed to reconsider this statement. "Well, maybe not Chadwick this time. Miss Serena is different. Hope your brother doesn't screw it up. But my point is, you all are fools."

"Thanks, George," Byron replied sarcastically. "That means a lot, coming from you."

From a long way away, the doorbell rang. "Watch the sauce," Byron said as he hurried out of the kitchen.

The Beaumont Mansion was a huge building that had been built by his grandfather, John Beaumont, after prohibition and after World War II, when beer had been legal and soldiers had come home to drink it. The Beaumont Brewery had barely managed to stay afloat for twenty years, and then suddenly John had been making money faster than he could count it. He'd built several new buildings on the brewery campus as well as the mansion, a 15,000 square-foot pile of brick designed to show up the older mansions of the silver barons. The mansion had turrets and stained glass and gargoyles, for God's sake. Nothing was ever over-the-top to a Beaumont, apparently.

Byron had always hated this house, the way it made people act. The house was toxic with the ghosts of John and Hardwick. This was not a house that had known happiness. He couldn't understand why Chadwick insisted on raising his family here.

Byron hadn't even bothered to unpack the rest of his

stuff because he wasn't going to be here long enough to settle in. He'd get a nice apartment with a good kitchen close to the Percheron Drafts brewery and that'd be fine. In the meantime, he'd spend as much time in the one room that had always been free from drama and grief—the kitchen.

He almost ran into Chadwick, who was coming downstairs to answer the door. "I've got it," Byron said, sidestepping his oldest brother.

Chadwick made no move to go back upstairs. "Expecting company?"

"It's the interior designer," Byron replied, happy to have that truth to hide behind. "I've prepared a sampling of dishes for her so we can build the theme of the restaurant around them."

"Ah, good." Chadwick looked at him, that stern look that always made Byron feel as though he wasn't measuring up. "Anything else I should know?"

Byron froze and the doorbell rang again. "George is making apple cobbler for dessert tonight," he said.

Then—weirdly—Chadwick smiled. It wasn't something Byron remembered happening when they were growing up. Back then, Chadwick had been imposing and their father's clear favorite, and Byron had been the irritating little brother who liked to play in the kitchen.

"If you need another opinion, let me know," Chadwick said, turning to head back upstairs. But that was all. No judgments, no cutting words—not even a dismissive glance.

"Yeah, will do," Byron said, waiting until Chadwick had disappeared before he opened the door.

There stood Leona. Something in his chest eased. It wasn't as if she was dressed to kill—in fact, she looked quite businesslike with a coordinating skirt and jacket. For the first time, he realized how much she'd changed in the past year—something that went much deeper than just her hair. *Maybe*, an insidious voice in his head whispered, *she's moved on and you haven't*.

Perhaps that was true. But there was no missing the fact that he was glad to see her. He should hate her and all the Harpers. Not a one of them were to be trusted.

He needed to remember that. "Hi. Come in."

She paused. Despite their year-long relationship, he'd never once brought her back to the mansion nor had she ever asked to visit. That had been part of what had attracted him to her—she had no interest in the trappings of Beaumont wealth and fame.

He hadn't realized her disinterest was because she had her own money. Maybe George had been right. Byron *was* a fool.

"Thank you." She stepped into the house and he closed the door behind her. "Oh," she said, staring up at the vaulted ceilings and crystal chandeliers. "This is lovely."

"Not my style," he admitted. "This way."

He led her down the wide hallway that bisected the first floor, past the formal dining room, the receiving room, the men's parlor, the women's parlor and the library. Finally, they reached the hallway that led around the back of the dining room and down the six steps to the kitchen.

The whole time, they walked silently. Byron didn't know much about the Harper house—it wasn't as if Leon Harper would invite him over—but he was sure this level of wealth wasn't unfamiliar to Leona and he had no desire to rehash old memories of his parents slamming doors after yet another disastrous meal.

Byron opened the door to the kitchen. "Here we are," he said, holding the door for Leona.

She stepped into the warm room. Early-evening sunlight glinted through the windows set above the countertop. The room had an impressive view of the Rocky Mountains. The light reflected off the rows of copper pots and pans that hung from racks, bathing the room in comfortable warmth.

Leona gasped. "This is *beautiful*." She looked at him, her eyes full of understanding, and in that moment, he nearly forgot how she'd lied and broken his heart. This was *his* Leona, the one he'd shared his deepest thoughts and feelings with. "Oh, Byron…"

"And George," George said, straightening from where he'd bent over to check the oven.

"Oh!" Leona took a step back in surprise and ran right into Byron. Instinctively, his arm went around her waist, steadying her—and pulling her into his chest. Heat—and maybe something more—flowed between them and he suddenly had to fight the urge to press his lips against the base of her neck, in the spot where she'd always loved to be kissed.

She pulled away from him. "George! I've heard so much about you! It's wonderful to finally meet you in person."

Then, to Byron's surprise—and George's, given his expression—Leona walked right up to the older man and hugged him.

"Yeah," George said in shock, shooting Byron a look. "I've heard—well," he quickly corrected when Byron shook his head. "It's good to finally meet you, too."

Byron exhaled in relief. George was the only person who knew the entire story about Leona—he hadn't even told Frances the whole thing. God only knew what the older man might have said to Leona.

"George is advising on the menu," Byron told her when she finally released George from the hug. "He'll be dining with us tonight."

"Oh. Okay." For some reason, Leona looked…disappointed?

Had she been thinking this would be an intimate dinner for two? She wasn't dressed for it—she looked as though she'd come directly from work. There would be no hot dates. Not now, not at any time in the future. If that's what she was angling for, she was in for a surprise.

A timer went off and Byron pushed that thought from his mind. He had food to prepare, after all. "This is going to be a tapas-style meal—all small plates," he explained, directing Leona to a stool across from George's normal perch. "Chadwick has all the current Percheron Drafts in stock so we can pair them up." He opened up one of the three refrigerators in the room, the one with all the beverages. "Which would you like to start with?"

Leona blinked at him. "I don't drink."

He stared at her. This was a new development. They'd always shared wine with a meal. Odd. "All right," he said slowly, snagging a White Horse Pale Ale for himself. "Then I'll get you some water."

Then he got to work. He plated the braised lamb shoulder, the *croquetas de jamón serrano*, the coq au vin, the ratatouille, the herb-crusted swordfish and the duck confit. He ladled the vichyssoise soup into a small bowl, and did the same with the bowl of Castilian roasted garlic soup and the gazpacho. George sliced the French bread and the homemade root vegetable chips fried in truffle oil.

Leona took a picture of every dish and made notes as Byron explained what the dishes were. "I don't know if I should have a hamburger and fries on the menu," he told her as he spooned the hollandaise sauce onto the asparagus spears. "What do you think?"

"It's a safe dish," she replied. "If you can handle having it on the menu…"

Byron sighed. "Yeah, yeah. Food for the masses and all that."

They all sat down. Leona looked at him. Was she blushing? "It's been a long time since you cooked for me."

Before Byron could come up with a response, George said, "Yeah, same here." He took a bite of the duck confit. "I'll give you this, boy. You've gotten better."

"Oh?" Leona said.

"When he started in my kitchen," George went on, "he could barely make cereal."

"Hey! I was what—five?"

"Four," George corrected him. He turned his attention back to Leona. "He wanted more cookies and I told him he had to work for them—he had to wash dishes."

Leona beamed at George. Then she shot a reproving glance at Byron. "He never told me that."

"Oh, he didn't do it at first. But the boy always had a weak spot for my chocolate chip cookies. He came back a few weeks later, after…" George trailed off thoughtfully.

Byron knew what the older man was thinking about—that Byron's parents had fought horribly at dinner, screaming obscenities and throwing dishes. A plate had nearly hit Chadwick in the head and Byron and Frances had ducked to avoid flying soup. He and Frances had been crying and their father had yelled at them.

Byron had run away from the noise. Frances had come with him and they'd wound up in the kitchen. It was the safest place he could think of, somewhere his father would never go. Frances had no interest in working for a cookie and a glass of warm milk, but Byron had needed…something. Anything that would take him away from the stress and drama, although that's not how he'd thought of it at the time. No, at the time, he'd just wanted to feel like everything was going to be okay.

Washing the dishes required enough focus that it had distracted him from what he'd seen at dinner. And then he'd gotten a cookie and a pat on the shoulder and George had told him he'd done a good job and next time George would show him how to bake the cookies himself. And that had made everything okay.

"I washed the dishes," he told Leona. "The cookies were worth it."

"You did an absolutely lousy job, I might add," George said with a chuckle.

Byron groaned. "I got better. Here, try the gazpacho." He ladled a few spoonfuls into Leona's bowl. "It's not quite as good as it was in Spain—the peppers aren't as fresh."

George scoffed as Leona tasted the soup. "Boy, don't tell them what they don't know. She never had the stuff you were making in Madrid."

"Mmm," Leona said, licking her spoon. Byron found himself staring at her mouth as her tongue moved slowly over the surface of the spoon. She caught him looking and dropped her gaze. He swore she was blushing as she cleared her throat and said, "He's right. As long as we can say 'locally sourced ingredients'—preferably with the name of the farm where you get your vegetables—that's what foodies value."

"We can do that. There's enough space around the brewery that I could also have some dirt hauled in and grow my own herbs and the like."

Leona's eyes lit up. "Would you? That'd be a great selling feature."

Byron liked it when she looked at him like that, even though he knew damned well that he shouldn't. But sitting here with her, talking about a restaurant they were going to open within months...

He'd missed her. He'd never stopped missing her. And as much as he knew he couldn't let himself fall under her spell again—couldn't risk getting his heart broken a second time—he just wanted to wrap his arm around her shoulders and hold her to him.

She would burn him. That he knew. That was the nature of the Harpers whenever they were around the Beaumonts.

But watching her savor the meal he'd cooked for her, talking and laughing with George...

He wanted to play in the flames again.

<u>Four</u>

Everything was, unsurprisingly, delicious. Leona especially liked the *croquetas*—she'd never had them before.
Yes, the evening was full of good food and comfortable
conversation. It should have been relaxing—fun, even.

The only problem was, she still hadn't told Byron about
Percy. And, as George regaled her with story after story
of Byron learning how to cook the hard way, she couldn't
figure out how to break the news to him without running
the risk of losing Percy.

Byron served three desserts—an almond cake that was
gluten-free, peaches soaked in wine and yogurt, and a
flan flavored with vanilla and lavender. She looked at her
notes. A vegetarian dish, gluten-free options—with the
hamburger, he'd have a menu that met most dietary needs.

"You like peaches, right?" he said as he set half of a
peach in front of her.

"I do," she told him. Seemingly against her will, she
looked up at him. Byron stood over her, close enough that
she could feel the warmth of his body. He remembered that
peaches were her favorite. There'd been a time when he'd
cooked for her, peach cobblers and grilled peaches and
peach ice cream—anything he could come up with. Those
had been things he'd made just for her.

"Thank you," she told him, her voice soft.

"I hope the wine sauce is okay." He didn't move back.
"I didn't know..."

"It's all right." She used to drink wine, back when he'd

make her dinner and pick out a bottle and they'd spend the evening savoring the food and the rest of the night savoring each other. But she hadn't drunk a thing while pregnant and then she'd been breast-feeding and pumping and who had the money for alcohol anyway?

He stood there for a moment longer. Leona held her breath, unable to break the gaze. All of her self-preservation tactics—clinging to the memory of being cast aside by a Beaumont, just like her father had warned her, and the very real fear that Byron would take her son away from her—they all fell away as she looked up at him. For a clear, beautiful second, there was only Leona and Byron and everything was as it should be.

The second ended when the door to the kitchen flew open with a bang. Byron jumped back. "George!" a bright female voice said. "Have you seen— Oh, *there* you are."

Leona looked over her shoulder and her heart sank. There stood Frances Beaumont in a stunning green dress and five-inch heels. "Byron, I have been texting you all... day..." Frances's voice trailed off as she saw Leona. They'd met a few times before. Frances had liked her then. But that felt like a long time ago.

Byron cleared his throat. "Frances, you remember—"

"Leona." Frances said the word as if it were something vile. Then she grabbed Byron by the arm and hauled him several feet away. "What is *she* doing here?" Frances added in a harsh whisper that everyone in the room had no trouble understanding.

Leona turned her gaze back to the luscious desserts. But her stomach felt as if a lead weight had settled into it.

"She's helping with the restaurant," Byron whispered back in a quieter voice.

"You're *trusting* her? Are you insane?" This time, Frances made no effort to lower her voice.

Leona stood. She did not have to sit here and take this assault on her character. Byron was the one who'd abandoned her, not the other way around. If anything, she shouldn't trust *him*. She didn't.

"I'll show myself out. George, it was a pleasure meeting you. Byron, I'll look over my notes and come up with some suggestions." She met Frances's glare as she gathered her things. "Frances."

"I'll walk you out," Byron offered, which made Frances hiss at him. But he ignored his twin and held the door for Leona.

"Good meeting you, too," George called out after her. "Come back anytime."

Which was followed by Frances gasping, "George! You're not helping…"

And then Leona and Byron were down the hall, the sounds of the kitchen fading behind them. They walked in silence through the massive entry hall. The evening had been, up to this point, an unmitigated disaster. Byron's cooking was amazing and, yes, George was just as sweet as she'd always pictured him.

But Byron had this habit of looking at her as if he wanted her, which didn't mesh with the otherwise icy shoulder he'd given her. He confused her and after everything he'd put her through, that seemed like the final insult.

She could not let him get to her, just like she couldn't let Frances's undisguised hatred get to her. Byron had left. He'd done exactly what his father had done and simply walked away. He didn't care for her—certainly not enough to fight for what they'd had.

She simply could not allow herself to care for him. It was not only dangerous to her heart, but also to Percy's well-being. She had to protect her son.

Thus resolved, she expected to say goodbye to Byron at the front door and call it a day. But Byron opened the door and stepped outside with her, pulling it shut behind her.

She walked past him, shivering in the chilly autumn air. She would not lean into him and let his warmth surround her. She did not need him. She did not want him. She could not let him ruin everything she'd worked so hard for and that was that.

Once the door was shut, he took a step into her. He wasn't touching her, not yet. "I'm sorry about Frances," he said in a quiet voice. "She can be a little…protective."

A part of Leona—the old part that cowered before her father—wanted to tell Byron it was all right and she'd smooth things over. But that part wasn't going to save her son. So she didn't. "Obviously." He looked confused, as if he couldn't guess that his sister would have been less than helpful in tracking Byron down. "I have no interest in re-living the past. That's not why I'm here."

She didn't know what she expected him to do—but lifting his hand and cupping her cheek like she'd said something sweet wasn't it. "Why are you here, then?"

"For the job." To her horror, Leona felt herself leaning forward, closer to his chest, to his mouth. "Byron…"

But before the words could leave her lips, a noise that sounded like a herd of elephants came through the door. Byron grabbed her by the arm and led her away. "I'll walk you to your car," he said.

As they walked, his hand slid down her arm until his fingers interlaced with hers. It wasn't a seductive gesture, but it warmed her anyway. He'd always held her hand whenever they were alone, whether they were watching a movie or watching the sun set over the mountains. She leaned her head against his shoulder as they walked. If only things had been different. If only…

She jerked to a stop less than five feet from her car. And the telltale car seat in the back.

"What?" Byron asked.

"I just..." She fumbled around for something to say and came up with nothing.

So she did the only thing she could think of to distract him.

She kissed him.

It wasn't supposed to be sexual, not for her. It was supposed to distract him while it bought her enough time to think of a better exit strategy.

But the feeling of Byron against her drove all rational thought from her mind. She melted into him. His hands settled on her waist and, as the kiss deepened, the pads of his fingertips began to dig into her hips. He pulled her into him. Her bag dropped to the ground as she looped her arms around his neck and held him tight.

She hadn't allowed herself to think about this, about how he used to make her feel. She'd made herself focus on how much she hated him, hated how he'd abandoned her—she hadn't allowed herself to remember the good parts.

Heat flooded her body and pooled low in her stomach as she opened her mouth for him. She wanted this, wanted him. She couldn't help it. She'd never been able to stay away from him. Some things never changed.

"I missed you," he whispered against her neck before he kissed the spot right under her ear.

Her knees wobbled. "Oh, Byron, I missed you, too. I—"

Suddenly, he pulled away from her so fast that she stumbled forward. His hand went around her waist to catch her, but his attention was focused on something behind her.

The car.

"What's that?" he demanded, taking a step toward the backseat of the car.

"What?" Again, her voice was wobbly. Everything about her was wobbly because this was the official moment of reckoning.

"That's a baby seat." He let go of her. "You have a baby

scat in the back of your car." This statement seemed to force him back a couple of steps. He cast a critical eye over Leona.

She wanted to cower but she refused. She was done cowering before any hard gaze, whether it was her father's or her former lover's. So she lifted her chin and straightened her back and refused to buckle.

"You—you've changed."

"Yes."

"You had a *baby*?"

She had to swallow twice to get her throat to work. "I did."

Byron's mouth dropped open. He tried to shut it, but it didn't work. "Whose?"

Leona couldn't help it. She wasn't cowering, by God, but she couldn't stand here and watch, either. She closed her eyes. "Yours."

"Mine?"

She opened her eyes to see that Byron was pacing away from her. Then he spun back. "I have a baby? And you didn't tell *me*?"

"I was—I was going to."

"When?" The word was a knife that sliced through the air and embedded itself midchest, right where her heart was. "And what? You had to kiss me? This I have to hear, Leona. I have to know the rationale behind *this*." He crossed his arms and glared at her.

No cowering. Not allowed. "I— You— You left me. I can't lose him."

It was hard to tell in the dim light from a faraway lamppost, but she swore all the color drained out of Byron's face. "Him?"

"Percy. I named him Percy." She bent over and retrieved her tablet from her bag. After a few taps, she had the most recent picture of Percy up on the screen. The little boy was sitting on her lap, trying to eat a board book. May had taken the photo just a couple of weeks ago. "Percy," she said again, holding the tablet out to Byron.

He stared at the computer, then at her. "I *left*? I left you pregnant?"

She nodded.

"And you didn't think it was a good idea to let me know you were pregnant? That you had *my son*?" His voice was getting louder.

"You left," she pleaded. Now that he knew, she had to make him see reason. Why hadn't she assumed he'd be this mad at her? For a ridiculous second, she wanted to beg for forgiveness, say whatever it took to calm him down—whatever it took so that he wouldn't take her son from her.

But she wouldn't beg. Not anymore. She'd fight the good fight. "You were gone by the time I got away from my father and I was afraid that your family would take Percy away—"

Byron froze midturn. "Wait—what?"

"I got away from my father. I took my little sister with me. May. She's watching Percy now."

Byron moved quickly, grabbing her by both arms. "Your sister? Is watching *my son*?"

"*Our* son, yes—"

He half shoved her, half lifted her up and carried her to the car. "Take me to him. Right now."

"All right," she said, retreating to grab her bag and fishing her keys out of the pocket.

They drove in painful silence. Her apartment was out in Aurora, which meant a solid thirty minutes of feeling Byron's rage from the passenger seat.

She was miserable. Just when she had a moment of hope, thinking maybe there was still something between them, something good—and it hadn't lasted. It would never last with Byron. It would always be like this—the two of them straddling the thin line between love and hate.

If only she wasn't a Harper. If only he wasn't a Beaumont. If only they'd been two nameless nobodies who could fall in love and live happily ever after in complete obscurity.

But no. It wasn't to be. He hated her right now because she'd kept quiet.

They pulled into the apartment complex parking lot. "You live here?" Byron asked. She could hear the confusion in his voice.

"Yes. This was all we could afford."

"And your parents? Your father?"

She got out of the car. "Please don't mention my father around May. She's…still nervous about him."

"Why?"

"Just…don't." Because she didn't want to go into why her parents were terrible people right after she'd finally told Byron about the baby. She grabbed her bag and locked the car. "This way."

Byron followed her up the two flights of stairs to the third floor of the apartment complex. "Here we are," she told him, unlocking the door.

"Oh, thank goodness you're home," May said from the couch, where Percy was crying. "I really think he's got another ear infection and—oh!" She recoiled in horror at the sight of Byron.

"It's all right," Leona told her little sister. "I told him."

May stood, cradling Percy in her arms. "He didn't come to take Percy, did he?"

"No," Byron said a little too loudly. "I just came to meet my son."

May's gaze darted between Leona and Byron like a rabbit trapped between a fox and a rock. And Byron was definitely the fox. "It's okay?"

Byron stepped up next to her. "Hello, May. It's nice to meet you. I'm Byron Beaumont."

Percy looked at Leona and held out his chubby little arms. May couldn't seem to do anything except stare in openmouthed horror at Byron.

"Let me have him," Leona finally said. She laid her bag on the kitchen table and took Percy from her sister and whispered, "It's going to be okay."

May attempted a smile and failed. "I'll just go. To my room." She all but sprinted down the hall. Seconds later, her door clicked shut.

"Hey, baby," Leona said, hugging Percy tight. "Aunt May says you have another ear infection. Do your ears hurt?"

Percy made a high-pitched whine in the back of his throat.

"I know," she agreed. "No fun at all." She looked over at Byron, who was gaping at the two of them. "I'm going to go find his ear drops. Do you want to hold him while I look?"

If possible, Byron looked terrified at this suggestion. "He has red hair."

Leona smiled down at her son. He had his fingers jammed into his mouth and he was getting drool all over her work blouse. "Yes, it's coming in redder. He takes after you."

Byron took a step back. "He takes after me," he repeated in a stunned whisper. "How old?"

"Sit down. I need to get his drops. Then we'll talk."

Almost robotically, Byron walked over to the couch and sat heavily.

"Percy, baby, this is your father," she whispered to her son as she sat him on Byron's lap. "Just hold him for a second, okay?"

"Um…" came the uncertain reply.

Leona moved quickly. She hurried to the bedroom and stripped out of her suit. She grabbed a clean pair of yoga pants and a long-sleeved tee and then rushed to Percy's room. "May?" she called out. The walls were thin enough that her sister should have no trouble hearing her. "Where are the drops?"

"I couldn't find them," May replied through the wall. "Are you sure he's okay?"

"He's Percy's father," Leona replied quietly. "He has a right to know."

There was a pause. "If Father finds out he's back…"

Yeah, that was a problem. Leon Harper would not take kindly to Byron's return any more than he'd taken kindly to Leona leaving with May. They'd reached an uneasy truce in the family since Percy had been born, but Leona didn't want anything to set off her father. She didn't even want to think about how low he might sink to get even with the Beaumonts.

She did a hurried check of the medicine cabinet and then checked her bedside table—ah. There they were—on the floor. They must have gotten knocked off and rolled under the bed. Leona fished the bottle out and held it up to the light. The little bottle was only one-fourth full, but that would have to do for now.

When she got back to the living room, Percy was leaning back against Byron's chest, starting up at him with curious eyes. "Here," she said, sitting down next to them. "I need to put the drops in."

She tilted Percy onto her lap. "Mommy's going to count to ten, ready? One…" She put the drops in and counted very slowly.

Byron rested his hand on Percy's feet, and then picked up one foot and held it against his palm. "This is really happening, isn't it?" he asked in a shaky voice.

"…Ten," she said in a happy voice. "That's such a good boy! Let's roll over." She lifted Percy so that he faced her.

"Yes," she told Byron, "it all happened." Then she began to count brightly again.

All of it—finding out Byron was exactly like all the other Beaumonts, realizing her father was right, keeping Percy far away from any Beaumont, long nights worrying how she was going to make it all work—it'd all happened.

Without Byron.

When she got to ten again, she sat Percy up. He was half on her lap, half on Byron's lap, safely stuck in the space between them. He looked up at Byron and smiled a drooly smile.

Byron managed a weak grin and then stroked Percy's hair. "How old?"

"Almost six months. I was three months pregnant when..." She couldn't bring herself to say, "when you left." At least, not out loud.

"I don't— You didn't—" He took a deep breath. "Why didn't you tell me? I mean, I could have helped out. I could *know* him."

She sighed. She'd long since put the events of that night behind her—or so she'd thought. But the pain felt as fresh as it ever had.

"He's a good baby," she said, desperate to avoid the hurt of remembering. "He's teething and that leads to a lot of ear infections, but that's about the only problem. He's happy and he eats well. And we...we do all right. He's got his own room here." Which was why they were so far out on the edge of Denver. The rents were cheaper, so they could afford a three-bedroom apartment. "I work for Lutefisk Design and May is finishing up college. She watches him when she doesn't have classes, but when she does, we have him in a day care. He likes it there," she added.

Percy squirmed against them. "It's his bedtime," Leona explained when Byron tensed. "You could help me get him ready for bed. If you want."

"Yeah," Byron said. "Sure."

She picked Percy up and carried him into the small bedroom. They'd found most of the furniture at resale shops. They had a crib, a glider and an old dresser that doubled as a changing table.

Leona laid Percy out on the changing table. With Byron watching, she changed the baby's diaper and got him into a clean set of footie jammies. Then she lifted him up. "Sit," she told Byron. To his credit, he sat in the glider and held out his hands for the baby. He didn't look less shell-shocked, but she appreciated the effort.

Leona leaned over the small basket that held the books. "How about…" Percy reached his hands out for the worn copy of *Pat the Bunny*. "All right," she agreed. "Can you read to him while I wash my hands?"

"Yeah. Sure."

She hurried to the bathroom, which was on the other side of May's room. In the distance, she heard Byron's deep voice read the simple story.

May's door opened and she popped her head out. "He's not staying, is he?"

"May," Leona said in a quiet whisper. "No, I don't think he's staying."

May shot her a disbelieving look. "You don't *think*? Leona, you know what he's like. He's a Beaumont. What if he wants to take Percy with him?"

Leona washed her hands in the bathroom. That was the question, wasn't it? Byron had the weight of the Beaumont name and family fortune behind him. And what did Leona have? She had May and Percy. She knew what lawyers could do to a woman. Her own father had regaled the family with tales of how he'd left his first wife penniless after she'd been seduced by Byron's father.

"I don't think he'll do that," she told May, who hovered in the doorway as if she expected to have to bolt at any second. Once, Leona would have said yes, Byron would take the boy and she'd never see her baby again.

But now? At dinner tonight he'd been the Byron she'd once thought she'd known. Caring, attentive, thoughtful. Heck, he'd even apologized for Frances's behavior. Those were not the actions of a man out to destroy her.

Of course, that had been before he'd seen the car seat. She had absolutely no idea what he was thinking now.

"I'm sorry," May said. "I'm just worried."

"I know." Leona dried her hands and gripped May by the shoulders. "I won't let him take Percy. I promise."

May's eyes watered. "I don't want him to hurt you again."

Leona pulled May into a tight hug. "I won't let him," she promised.

"Leona?" Byron called out. "We're done. Now what?"

At the sound of Byron's voice, May hurried back to her bedroom and shut the door.

Leona paused to take a deep breath. She couldn't let Byron break her heart again. She couldn't lose her son. And if they could keep her father out of it, that'd be great, too.

Sure. No problem.

Byron was rocking Percy, whose eyes were half closed. "Hi," he said when she entered the room.

Despite it all, she smiled at him. To see him holding Percy—she had dreamed of this moment.

This was what she'd wanted before that horrible night when it'd all fallen apart. For the months they'd been seeing each other, she'd thought about Byron being a father— being a husband. Helping with the babies, because of course they'd have children together. She and Byron were different than their families. Better. Electric. They were going to love each other for the rest of their lives.

Then he'd left before she'd gotten the chance to tell him she was pregnant and Leona had put those old dreams away.

She couldn't help it. Part of her still wanted those dreams, even knowing how much of a Beaumont he was.

But that vision of them growing old together was just that—a vision.

It could never happen.

Five

Byron's head was a mess as Leona took the boy—his son!—from him. No, *mess* was too generous a word for the muddle of emotions and thoughts all struggling to be heard.

He had a son—that was the first thing he had to make sense of. He had a son and Leona hadn't told him. She had lied to him again—maybe he shouldn't be so damned surprised. After all, she'd had no problem hiding her family from him before. Why was it so shocking that she would hide his son from him now?

It was obvious she loved the boy. She'd been sweet and gentle with him and this thing right now—nursing—was obviously something they did every night.

Byron walked back into the main part of the apartment. The place wasn't fancy—a standard apartment with beige walls, beige carpeting and beige countertops in the kitchen. A set of patio doors indicated that there was a small deck outside. There were a few pictures on the wall, all of May and Leona and Percy. Mostly of Percy. None of Byron. But then, why should there be?

He realized he was standing in the kitchen, opening the cabinets, drawers and the fridge, looking for something to cook. He always retreated to the kitchen when he was upset, even when he'd been a little kid.

Cooking was predictable. There was comfort in the routine. If he followed the recipe, he knew how the dish would turn out.

Leona had apples. Byron could make applesauce. There—

that was a good plan. That was him taking care of his son. Everyone had to eat.

He peeled the apples and got them simmering in the pot. Then he debated the ingredients—would Percy like cinnamon or would it be too strong for him? Would Leona want the applesauce to be unsweetened? In the end, Byron went with a little lemon juice to brighten the flavor.

As he cooked, he tried to think. Why hadn't she told him? It wasn't as though he'd gone off the grid. Yes, he'd been in Europe but he'd been findable. Frances, at least, had always known where he was. He'd kept his email address. He hadn't disappeared. Hell, even a birth announcement would have been okay, but there'd been nothing. Just another lie.

He needed answers—and while he was thinking about it, he still needed to know why she thought he'd left her and what did she mean, she and her sister had "gotten away from" their father?

She'd *gone* with her father. Leon Harper was her father and she hadn't told Byron that truth. And when Harper had demanded Leona come with him, she had. She'd left Byron standing on the sidewalk, in the rain, his heart in shards at his feet.

If she'd dumped him, he could have dealt with it. He might have still wound up in Europe, but if she'd said "Gee, Byron, this just isn't working, we should see other people, it's not you, it's me and we can still be friends" or whatever, he'd have moved on.

But she'd lied to him. She was the daughter of the man who was hell-bent on destroying Byron and his entire family. By all accounts, the man was doing a hell of a job at it, too. The brewery—a hundred and sixty-six years of Beaumont history and ownership—was gone, all because of Leon Harper. And his daughters.

Byron knew what betrayal looked like. He knew his father had cheated on his wives. He knew that at least one of the ex-wives had cheated on Hardwick. Byron knew there was always a risk that any relationship could go wrong. The Beaumonts didn't have exclusive rights to dysfunctional marriages.

But when he'd been with Leona, he'd managed to convince himself that he was different. That they were different. Byron and Leona had loved each other.

Or had they?

She'd lied to him before. Twice. Was she lying again? Even if she was, would he be able to tell the difference?

Apples were not going to solve that mystery. He had more pressing issues to deal with.

Percy was his son. Byron wanted to be there for the boy, to let Percy know that Byron loved him in the big ways and the little ways. All the ways Byron's own father had never loved Byron.

But how was that going to happen? He was still living in the mansion—he didn't even have his own place. And getting a restaurant off the ground wasn't a nine-to-five job, that was for damned sure. Not now, not ever. How could he make sure he was a part of Percy's life?

The sauce was halfway done when Leona came into the kitchen. She was wearing leggings and a T-shirt but there was still something about her. There'd *always* been something about her.

"Ah," she said when she saw the bubbling apples. She gave him a small smile. "I should have known."

"Applesauce. For Percy," he explained. "Just apples and a little lemon. I didn't know if cinnamon would be too much for him."

"It smells wonderful. He loves apples."

They stood there silently for a minute.

"It's not a big batch. Do you have a container for it?"

Leona dug out a plastic bowl and Byron moved all the

dirty dishes to the sink. Yes, he needed answers. But honestly? He had no idea where to start. So he didn't. He did the dishes instead.

The uncomfortable silence lingered for a few more minutes as he washed the knife and the cutting board. Leona dried. Finally, she broke the silence.

"We should come up with a plan, I guess."

"A plan?"

"Yes. If you're really going to stay—"

"I am," he interrupted, stung by the insinuation that he'd bolt.

"Then we need a plan." She swallowed, her gaze focused on the sink. "A custody plan. I know I can't keep Percy from you, but I'm not going to just give up custody."

"You already kept him from me." She winced but he refused to feel bad for her. "And I didn't say you had to give up custody. But why didn't you tell me?" he demanded. "Why did you keep this from me?"

"I thought…" She dropped the dish towel on the counter and turned away from him. "I thought you didn't want anything to do with me. Your phone was disconnected and you were in Europe—pretty damned far away from here."

That was true. But it was the way she said it that confused him. He looked at the back of her head as if he could peer inside and find the answers he was looking for. "You could have sent an email."

"I could have," she agreed. Her shoulders heaved with a massive sigh. "I should have. But I was afraid."

"Afraid? Of what?"

She turned to him, her wide eyes even wider. "Of you, Byron. Of all the Beaumonts."

He gaped at her. Before he could remind her that he was not the one who'd lied, she went on, "And we left home with only as much as we could carry, and I had to get a job. Being pregnant wasn't as fun as it seems on television and

May had classes and…and you weren't here. And I guess I convinced myself that you weren't coming back and it was just me and May and Percy on our own. It was better that way. We didn't need anyone else."

He dried off his hands and placed them on her shoulders. "I could have helped. Even if…even if I didn't come back, I still could have helped. Child support or whatever. You shouldn't have had to do this on your own."

She dropped her head and he heard her sniff. "Well, you're here now. I can't change what happened in the past but if you're going to stay—"

"I am," he told her again.

"Then, yes. Child support and custody visits. But I can't lose him, Byron." Her voice broke over this last bit. "Please don't try to punish me by taking him."

The anguish in her voice—her assumption that he'd exact some sort of twisted revenge… He spun her around and lifted her chin until she had no choice but to look him in the eye. Child support and custody visits were all very clinical-sounding things, like the few hours a year that he was shipped off with Frances and Matthew to visit their mother, who'd then spend most of the visit trying not to cry.

That's not what he wanted. He was not his father, for God's sake. He was better than that.

Except, was he? He'd gotten a woman pregnant and then left her in the lurch, completely alone with no other resources. Yeah, he'd thought her father would still be paying the bills and yeah, she'd rejected him, but when the facts of the situation were laid plain, he'd left her alone just when she'd needed him most.

She was right. That was exactly what Hardwick Beaumont would have done.

"I'm not going to take him away from you," Byron told her, feeling the certainty of the words. "Because you're both going to come live with me."

* * *

Leona's mouth fell open in shock. *"What?"*

Byron's grip tightened on her shoulders. "I don't have a place yet. You can either move into the mansion with me or help me pick something out—whatever you think is better. But you need to move in with me as soon as possible."

Maybe this wasn't happening. Maybe none of it was happening—not Byron returning, not him kissing her, not him reading a bedtime story to Percy. She could be hallucinating the whole kit and caboodle.

Sadly, the way he was holding her, the look in his eyes? She knew she wasn't hallucinating a damned thing. And that was a problem.

"You want me to pack up and come with you?"

The tendons in his neck tightened. "I want my son with me. And if that means you have to be with me, then so be it."

Ah. So he didn't want her, not really. He would put up with her if that got him what he wanted, though. His words cut like a dull butter knife—painful and ragged.

She'd promised May she would not let Byron hurt her again.

She hated lying to her sister.

Still, Leona was making remarkable progress. She didn't agree to Byron's demands just to keep the peace, and she didn't dissolve into useless tears and, most important, she didn't do both of them at the same time. Those days were done. She might not be able to be strong enough to protect her own heart, but she had to protect Percy.

So she cleared her throat. "What if it's not a good idea for us to live together?"

His eyes narrowed. "Why not?"

She couldn't look at that hardness, couldn't bear to feel the pain again. So she closed her eyes. She couldn't help it. "Look, I know we had something once but it fell apart."

"But—" he started to interrupt.

She cut him off. "And it doesn't even matter who did what. If we live together…we'll have to face those choices every single day."

Every day she'd have to wake up knowing that Byron was mere feet away, not oceans and continents. Every single day she'd have to look him in the eye to discuss what Percy had done and every single damned day, he'd probably cook her a meal and she'd love it.

And every day—every minute—she'd wonder when it was all going to end.

Byron pulled her in closer and she felt his hot breath on her ear. "You listen to me, Leona Harper." Panic blossomed in her stomach at his cold tone. "Maybe it doesn't matter who did what, maybe it does. That doesn't change the fact that I have a son and I am *not* going to stand aside a moment longer because you think it might be awkward around the breakfast table. You *will* move in with me and, until further notice, we *will* raise our son together."

An unspoken *or else* hung in the small space between his lips and her ear.

She would not cry, by God. She wouldn't do it. Not in front of him. Not in front of any man. Not anymore. She was an adult responsible for her sister and her son and she would *not* give.

"I can't afford very much. That's why we live here."

"I will pay for it," he replied firmly.

"But—"

"No buts, Leona. You've had to cover everything for a year. It's my turn to step up to the plate. It's the least I can do."

God, that sounded so good. She could live with him, let him take care of her, of Percy, with his part of the Beaumont fortune. She wouldn't be teetering on the edge of genteel poverty anymore. Things like doctor's visits and ear drops wouldn't be monumental mountains she struggled to climb. Byron had the ways and means to make that part of her life easy.

Of course, if she'd wanted easy—if she'd wanted to step back and let someone else call all the shots in her life— she'd still be living under her father's roof. She'd still be subjected to his rantings and ravings about the Beaumonts in general and Byron in specific.

Yes, that was easier. But it was not better.

She couldn't allow herself to be dependent on a man again, especially a man who'd already left her high and dry once. Byron could not be trusted, not on a kiss and a promise. Because this time it wouldn't just be her heart in danger. It'd be Percy's, too.

"May," Leona managed to say without her voice cracking. "She watches him. I can't just leave her." It was the best defense she had. May was twenty, yes—but she was a fragile young woman who was not ready to be thrown out on her own because a billionaire's son demanded it.

"Percy loves her," she offered, hoping that would help.

It didn't. Byron sighed wearily. Then, unexpectedly, his grip loosened. He didn't lean back, though—he just skimmed his hands up and down her upper arms. "Is that the deal? I have to provide accommodations for your sister before you'll move in with me?"

Once, they'd talked about moving in together. She'd been staying over at his place more and more—which had run the risk of drawing her father's attention to her activities. She'd known then that when her father found out, it would be a problem. But Leona hadn't cared because waking up in Byron's arms was worth the risk.

Of course, once she'd been sure that he'd marry her right away, when she told Byron she was pregnant. It wouldn't have mattered who her father was because Byron loved her and she loved him. She'd been sure that once she told him the truth he'd realize she hadn't been trying to hide anything. She'd just wanted someone who didn't care about her last name. She'd thought she'd found that man.

She was still paying for that mistake. She couldn't afford any more.

"I won't move into the mansion."

"Fine. I was going to look for a place close to the restaurant anyway." His hands were still moving up and down her arms and dang it all, she was leaning into his touch. "Is that all right with you? Or do you need to be closer to your job?"

She leaned her forehead against his shoulder. It wasn't much of a choice, not after he'd demanded that she uproot her whole life to be with him for the sake of their son. But he'd still thrown her a small bone. "The office is downtown. As long as we're not too far out, it should be about the same travel time."

"I'll make some calls in the morning. We'll move as soon as possible."

What was she going to tell her sister? *No, I'm not going to let him break my heart again, but by the way—pack up everything you own because we're all going to set up house together.*

May would be furious.

Still, Leona didn't think she could refuse. What were the alternatives? Byron was not interested in coming by to visit Percy here and, as far as she could tell, the only other possibility was Byron suing for custody. She couldn't let that happen—where would she get the money to defend herself? Lawyers weren't cheap, that she knew. She couldn't ask her parents for help, either. If her father knew Byron wanted the boy... It'd be an all-out war.

And if she lost? Once, she'd thought she knew Byron. But he'd turned out to be more of a Beaumont than she ever would have guessed. She had no idea what lengths he would go to, and she didn't really want to find out the hard way.

It was a risk she couldn't take. It'd be a short-term solution, she tried to tell herself. Just until they could get a formalized custody agreement arranged.

Byron's arms went around her, holding her to his chest. "I don't want to punish you, Leona," he said. None of the coldness was left in his tone. "But he's my son, too."

"I know." That's what she wanted to believe.

"It won't be bad, will it?" He swallowed. "At least, better than living with your parents?"

She shuddered at the thought. "We'll have to have rules. No fighting or anything in front of the baby."

"Okay," he agreed. "But I'm not looking for a fight."

If only she could believe that. There was one other important detail that had to be settled before she agreed. "We'll sleep in separate bedrooms. Just because we're living together doesn't mean I want you back."

His hands stilled and then he snorted. "This is for Percy. You can have your own bedroom. I don't expect you to sleep with me." There was a brief pause. "It'd probably be best if we keep things simple between us until we decide on what to do next."

"Agreed," she said. Which completely disregarded the fact that, at this very moment, he was holding her in a highly not-simple way. Could she really expect either of them to maintain a respectable distance? "Simple is better."

"And you'll keep helping me with the restaurant?"

"Yes." The absolute last thing she could do now was quit her job. Even if Byron was covering the rent, she still needed to maintain her independence. He might not be looking for a fight—and she wasn't exactly spoiling for one, either—but if things went wrong, she needed to be able to pick up and start over again.

Again.

He swallowed. "And your parents? Don't take this the

wrong way, but I don't want my son anywhere near your father."

"They're not a part of this. I cut ties when we left."

He leaned back and looked her in the eye again. "Why did you leave? I mean, we'd talked about getting our own place or you moving in with me—but you wouldn't do it then."

The corners of her mouth turned down as she pushed back against tears. She hadn't moved in with Byron before because moving in would mean telling him who she really was and she hadn't wanted to risk it. Looking back, she should have. But instead, she'd convinced herself that once she finished college and got a job—that would be the time to leave home. But she didn't explain any of that. Instead she said, "May and I had to get out. My father was... unbearable." She shuddered again at the memory of her father's completely unfiltered rage.

"Did he hit you?" Byron demanded, a fierce look in his eyes.

"No." But there are other ways to make a person hurt. "He threatened to have me declared unfit and to take the baby after he was born."

"He did *what*?"

"Because it was you." This time, she couldn't push the tears back. "Because of who you are. He wanted to make sure you'd never get the baby."

For years, her father had berated Leona, her sister, her mother. All of them bore the brunt of his rage. And she'd put up with it for far longer than she should have because she hadn't known any better.

Until she'd met Byron. Until he'd shown her that there was a different way to live, that people could actually care for each other. If only she'd been brave enough before...

But then again, now she knew Byron's true colors. She

could have escaped her father only to be stuck with a man who'd abandon her anyway.

Still, it had been those times with Byron that had given her the courage to leave home, single, pregnant and with May. She'd realized then that she had to get out while she could, before Leon Harper got ahold of her son.

Byron was staring at her in total shock. "He would, wouldn't he?"

She nodded.

A moment passed as he gaped at her. "Then there's only one thing to do," he finally said in a shaky voice.

No, she wanted to say, even though she didn't know what that one thing was. She knew she wasn't going to like it, wasn't going to want it.

"We have to get married."

Six

This was his life now, he realized. Proposing marriage in whispers to a woman who was crying, all so they wouldn't wake the baby. "Why hasn't he done it yet? Why hasn't he taken Percy away from you?"

"I don't know."

"It's the only way to keep Percy safe, Leona, and you know it."

If they weren't married, what was to stop her father from charging in like a bull elephant at any second? Byron had been out of the picture for a year. He didn't know the specifics of family law, but he was pretty sure his absence would count against him. He would beat Leon—he was the boy's father—but it would be a long, exhausting battle.

Memories of his mother mixed in with all the current confusion—not just the screaming fights, but how his father had had all of her things loaded into a moving van before he'd served her with divorce papers. How his mother had never quite recovered from being kicked out, from being steamrollered in court and losing her children.

Could Byron let that happen to Leona? Could he live with himself if she was the collateral damage in yet another Beaumont-Harper legal battle?

He should. She'd lied to him—twice. And not about whether or not she'd spent too much money or hated his cooking or any of those petty things other people lied about. She'd lied about who she was and the fact that she'd given birth to Byron's son.

And yet… He couldn't do it. Because Leona was right about one thing—it didn't really matter who'd done what a year ago. He couldn't bear to think of her being destroyed like his mother had been. That was a risk he wasn't willing to take.

He could barely think right now. Babies and apartments and a wedding. A ring. And a restaurant. Couldn't forget that.

And applesauce. He turned to the stove—yeah, it was done. He shut the burner off to let it cool. For some insane reason, he wondered if Leona had chocolate chips. If ever there was a time for cookies, this was it.

He turned back to Leona. She stood there looking as if he'd threatened her to within an inch of her life. Maybe he had. But what were his options? He could not let Leon Harper get his claws into Percy. Everything else was secondary.

"At least until we're sure your father can't take over," he rationalized. "And you can still have a private bedroom. I…" He took a deep breath. "I cared for you a great deal. I hope that we can at least be friends."

She dropped her gaze and he had the distinct feeling that he was making things worse. "Friends."

"For Percy's sake."

"Can I…think about it? Tomorrow's Friday. We probably couldn't get an appointment to get married for a week or two anyway."

"Sure." He tried to sound friendly about it, but he didn't think he made it. "But I'll start looking for places tomorrow." Because even if she didn't marry him, they still needed to live together.

But she'd marry him. She had to.

He should go. He'd just asked her to move in and marry him within the space of a few minutes, and the pull to make cookies was only getting stronger. She needed to think, too. "When will I see you tomorrow?" he asked.

"I have to go to the office and update my boss on the project and draft a few ideas for you. I promised," she added with a watery smile.

"Lunch, then? I'll have something ready for us."

"Not at the mansion, right?" Another small shudder went through her.

"No," he readily agreed. He didn't want another run-in with Frances. "At the restaurant."

"All right. Tomorrow around noon."

He transferred the applesauce into the container and sealed it. "For Percy," he said, holding out the still-warm sauce.

"For Percy," she agreed.

She didn't sound happy about it.

Byron went straight to the kitchen. It was late, though—George was already gone. The normally warm, bright room was dark and quiet, except for the echo of his footsteps off the tiled floors.

He flipped on the lights and assembled ingredients. Chocolate chip cookies were a must. For lunch tomorrow, he told himself. And he could try a few sandwiches. It was reasonable to think that he'd want to have a simple lunch menu.

He fell into the familiar routine of creaming the sugar and folding in the chips while the oven preheated. He didn't even have to think about this recipe anymore.

Had he really asked Leona to marry him? Because she'd given birth to a son—*his* son, the one with matching red hair?

He needed a ring. He hadn't bought one the first time around. A ring would show her he was serious about this.

"There you are."

Byron spun to see Frances standing in the doorway. Instead of the gown she'd been wearing earlier, she was in a pair of pajamas—thick, fleecy ones with a bright turquoise plaid pattern. She looked fifteen years younger than their twenty-nine years.

"What's wrong?"

"Nothing," he lied. "Does something have to be wrong?"

Frances gave him a knowing smile. "You're baking cookies and God only knows what else at ten at night? You and I both know that something's wrong." A shadow darkened her face. "It's Leona, isn't it? I can't believe you hired her, Byron. Do you enjoy getting jerked around?"

He slammed a bowl down on the island countertop.

"Jeez," Frances said, giving him a long look. "Spill it."

He didn't want to but Frances was his twin. They couldn't keep secrets from each other if they tried. "You're going to tell me why you suddenly moved back home?"

An embarrassed blush raced over her cheeks. "I made a bad investment."

"You're broke?"

"Don't tell Chadwick. You know how he is," she pleaded. "I can't stand to hear another 'I told you so' from him."

"Frannie…"

"Whatever," she said, brushing away his concern with a cynical shrug of her shoulders. "I'll be fine. Just getting back on my feet. But that's neither here nor there. Now spill it. You're baking cookies because…"

He took a deep breath. If he did it fast… "I have a son."

Frances's cynicism fell away. "You *what*?"

"Just like our old man, huh? Get a woman pregnant and then bail on her," he said bitterly. "Leona has a baby boy named Percy. He's got red hair." That probably wasn't the most important thing to know about the boy, but Byron felt it was the thing that sealed the deal.

"Who else knows?"

"Her family." Frances made a face of revulsion. "She

lives with her sister, who watches Percy. They don't have anything to do with their father."

"Oh, I see. And this is what she told you? Because we all know how very trustworthy she is. Do I need to remind you that this is the woman who didn't even see fit to tell you she was Leon Harper's daughter, even after you'd started sleeping with her?"

"No, you do not need to remind me of that," he snapped. "It doesn't change the fact that Percy is my son." He realized he was whisking the cookie batter with more force than was required. He made himself set the bowl down.

"And you're sure," Frances asked.

"Yes."

She shook her head in some combination of disbelief and pity. "God only knows what she's been saying about you. And her father? You have to get that kid away from her."

"I told her we had to get married. Immediately." Frances gasped in true horror.

"Are you nuts? You want to marry into that family of— vipers?"

"That's why I have to marry her—to make sure Harper can't take Percy away from us."

"Listen to you. *Us.* There is no *us.* There's you and a woman who broke your heart and then hid a baby from you." Unexpectedly, her eyes watered. "I already lost you for a year. You weren't here because of *that* woman. No one else understands me like you do. I missed having my twin here."

The last thing he needed right now was more guilt. "I missed you, too. But I'm back now," he told her.

Frances sniffed. "Isn't there another way? Do you have to marry her?"

"Yes." He got out the scoop he used for the batter and began to dish it out onto the baking mats. "It's the only way to make things right."

Or more right. After all, he hadn't spoken of undying love, of treasuring her forever. This was a marriage of necessity. They would have separate rooms. Her sister was going to live with them.

"You need to be careful, Byron."

He wanted to say, when was he not careful? But he knew what Frances would say to that—if he'd been careful the first time, he'd have realized that Leona Harper was Leon Harper's daughter. And, of course, if he'd been careful, he wouldn't have had a child he never knew.

But he hadn't been careful. He'd just wanted her. It hadn't mattered whose daughter she was. It hadn't mattered that every time he tried to ask about her family, she changed the subject. What had mattered was that they were together.

Well. He was finally going to make that come true. They would be together—for the sake of their son, if nothing else.

"I'll call Matthew. He'll get the lawyers going on it." There. That was a perfectly reasonable thing to say. After all, if he'd learned anything from his father, it was that marriages were temporary and a man with a fortune should *always* have a prenup.

"That's not what I meant."

"I know." He scooped out the second-to-last cookie's worth of dough and then offered the bowl to Frances. That'd always been her favorite part, licking the bowls. "Look, I just found this out tonight. I'm still trying to get my head wrapped around it."

She took the bowl and sat on a stool, swiping her finger through the batter. "Is he cute? Your son?"

Byron thought about the pale blue eyes, the shock of red hair and the drooly smile. "Yeah. Really cute."

Frances shook her head, but at least she was grinning as she did so. "You should see the smile on your face. Congratulations, Byron—you're a father."

Seven

"We're *what*? You're *what*?" May stared at Leona.

"I'm going to marry Byron." *I think*, she mentally added.

May's mouth opened, closed and opened again. "When? Oh, to heck with when. Why?"

"He's Percy's father. And no one wants Father to get involved in a custody battle. If I'm married to Byron, Father can't take Percy from us." These were all perfectly rational reasons for this sudden change of course. But rational had nothing to do with the way Leona's stomach was in a knot that might never get untied.

"And what about me?" May demanded, her eyes flashing.

It was, hands down, the angriest Leona had ever heard her little sister. Any other day, Leona might celebrate this development—May was speaking out instead of meekly taking whatever life dished out.

But it wasn't helping Leona's unmovable knot. "You can come with us. We'll get a bigger place—more than enough room for you to have your own space." May looked at Leona as if she'd grown a third head. Leona decided to change tactics. "Or you can stay here. I know this is closer to your college…"

"What about Percy? I don't want to live with a Beaumont, but I'm the one who takes care of him."

Leona winced at the dismissive way May said *Beaumont*. "I know. We'll find a way to make it work."

May looked doubtful, but she didn't say anything else. Instead, she turned and headed back to bed.

Leona went to her room and lay down on the double bed, but she didn't sleep. Her mind raced through all the options. Marrying Byron. Moving in with him. Being a family, at least during the day. Sleeping in separate bedrooms.

What other options did she have? Every time she asked herself that question, she came back to the same answer. None. But she kept asking it, just to be sure.

The separate bedrooms thing was nonnegotiable. It had to be. Even now, she could feel his lips on hers, feel a year's worth of sexual frustration begging to be released by his hands.

Sex with Byron had been fun and magical and wonderful. In his arms, she'd been special.

Was it wrong to want that back in her life? No, that wasn't the right question. Was it wrong to want that with Byron—again?

But separate bedrooms it was. Because she could not confuse sex with love. Fool me once, shame on you. But fool me twice...

She was no fool. Not any longer.

Finally, exhausted, she turned her attention back to the only thing that could possibly distract her from Byron—the restaurant. She needed some ideas for tomorrow.

She drifted off to sleep thinking about Percherons.

Byron shook the tablecloth out over the small metal bistro table he'd snagged off one of the mansion's patios. Then he set up the matching chairs around it. He'd brought a candle because...well, because. Once upon a time, he'd planned a romantic candlelit dinner where he would ask for her hand in marriage. The ring he'd picked out this morning felt as if it was burning a hole in his pocket.

But he'd finally decided that the dungeon was too musty

to eat in and it was far too windy outside to have a flame burning, so he let it rest. Candles were not required.

He had a picnic basket filled with three kinds of sandwiches, potato salad and gazpacho. He'd packed the almond cake from last night and had two bottles of iced tea. This wasn't his ideal meal, but as he was quickly learning, he had to go with the flow.

Just another tasting, he tried to tell himself as he set out the silverware. No big deal.

Except it was huge. He'd called Matthew—this situation seemed too important to discuss over a text—but Matthew hadn't picked up, which wasn't like him. So Byron had been forced to leave a vague, "Something's come up and I need to talk to you," message.

Byron had also called a Realtor and laid out his specifications. And he'd even called the county clerk to find out what he needed to get married.

Now he had to wait. He and Leona could get married next week, but he needed the prenup first.

Finally, after what felt like a long wait but was actually only a few minutes past noon, Leona's car rolled up. She sat behind the wheel for a few moments. Byron got the feeling she was psyching herself up.

Then she got out of the car. She was wearing another suit—the consummate businesswoman. But there was something more about her, something that had attracted him to her from the very first time he'd laid eyes on her. After all this time, he still couldn't say what that something was.

Whatever it was, he wanted to pull her into his arms and not let go. He'd hired her for a very specific reason— to make sure she knew she couldn't hurt him. But instead? He'd found out just how much he couldn't trust her.

He would not give in to the physical temptation that Leona represented. This marriage proposal wasn't about sex. It was about doing whatever it took to make sure his son was safe.

"Hi," she said. She looked at the outdoor table.

Was she nervous? Fine. Good. He didn't want her to think she held all the cards. The sooner she realized he was calling the shots, the better.

He stood and put his hands on her shoulders. She tensed and he swore he felt a current of electricity pass between them. But he wouldn't give in and pull her into his arms. He couldn't let her affect him. Not anymore. "Have you given any more thought to my question?"

Leona notched an eyebrow at him. That was better, he thought. He loved it when she was snarky and sarcastic—not shell-shocked. "I don't remember your asking me anything. I seem to remember more of a direct order."

Byron pulled the small, robin's-egg-blue box out of his pocket. Leona gasped. "Ah. Yes. That was a mistake." He opened the box. The sunlight caught the emerald-cut diamond and threw sparkles across the tablecloth. "Leona, will you marry me?"

If only he'd asked her a year ago...but even as he thought that, he remembered how she'd hidden her name, her family from him. Would she have said yes, if he'd asked her then? Or would she have laughed in his face? Would it have changed everything—or would it all still have happened exactly the same way?

Anything snarky about her fell away as she gaped at the ring, then him, then back at the ring. She reached out to touch the box but pulled her hand back. "We need to discuss work," she finally said in a firm voice. "Mr. Lutefisk is very particular about his employees having personal conversations while they're on the clock. He'll be calling to check in about an hour from now. He's letting me handle this project on my own, but he keeps close tabs on all of his employees' projects."

What a load of crap. She was stalling and he didn't like it. "Leona. This isn't just a 'personal conversation.' This is our life—together."

She gave him a baleful look that, despite all of his best intentions to not let her get to him, made him feel guilty. Then fire flashed through her eyes. "I work. This is my job. You can't think that hiring me and proposing means you get to control every minute of my life, Byron. Because if so, I have an answer to your question. I don't think you'll like it."

In spite of himself, he grinned. "When did you get this feisty?"

"When you left me," she snapped. "Now are we going to discuss the job for which you hired me or not?"

The accusation stung. "That's not how I remember it going down," he said, frustration bubbling up.

She shrugged out of his grasp and sat down at the table as if she was mad at the chair. "I'm not talking about it now. I. Am. Working."

"Fine. When can we discuss nonwork stuff?"

"After five."

"When can I see Percy again?"

She looked up at him, her jaw set. "Ah, now *that* was a question. Lovely. You can see him tonight, after five. I assumed you'd come visit him." Byron gave her a look and she rolled her eyes. "As you can see, I'm not trying to hide him from you. Can we please get to work?"

"Fine." He'd let it go for now. But he left the ring on the table, where it glittered prettily.

Leona pulled out her tablet and handed it over. "We have three basic choices for the interior—we can try to lighten it up, keep it dim, or go for broke and make it very dark."

Byron looked at the preliminary colors she'd chosen. One was a bright yellow with warm red accents. The next was gray with a cooler red and the last choice was a deep red that would look almost black in the shadows. "I like the yellow. I don't want the restaurant so dim that people have to use their cell phones to read the menu."

"Agreed," she said. She flicked the screen to the next page. "I thought we'd want to play off the Percheron Drafts in the name—Percheron Pub?"

"No."

"White Horse Saloon?"

He gave her a dirty look.

"No, I didn't think so." She grinned back. This was better—this was them as equals. This was what he'd missed. He had the sudden urge to lean over and kiss her like he'd kissed her last night, right before his world had changed forever. "I also considered bringing in the European influences. What do you think about Caballo de Tiro?"

"That's—what?" He thought for a second. "Workhorse?"

"Draft horse, literally. Which fits the brand and also highlights the Spanish influences you're bringing."

He glanced at her and saw she wore a satisfied smile. "You like that one, don't you?"

"It is my favorite, it's true. I wasn't sure if you'd get the translation."

"I picked up enough French and Spanish to get by." He gave her a look. "At least, enough to cook and fend off advances."

She glanced back at the ring. "Oh?"

He could hear that she was trying to sound disinterested, but she wasn't quite succeeding. "It was…well, I guess the good news was that no one cared that I was a Beaumont. That was great, actually. But a lot of people were intrigued by the American with red hair."

Which was a huge understatement. In Paris and then Madrid, not a week went by when he didn't leave work to find a beautiful woman—or occasionally a beautiful man—waiting for him.

"I guess that was probably fun." Leona was now staring at her plate, pushing the potato salad around with her fork.

"Actually, it wasn't."

She opened her mouth to say something but then changed her mind. "Right. We're working. What do you think of the name?"

He sighed. "Right. Working." Besides, he didn't exactly want to tell her that, at several points during his self-imposed exile, he'd decided to take a particularly lovely woman up on her offer, just to get Leona out of his system—only to back out before they got anywhere near a bed.

He forced himself to focus. This restaurant was his dream, after all. Caballo de Tiro—it had a good ring to it, and wasn't too complicated to pronounce.

"I thought we could bring in touches that suggest a draft horse—wagon wheels that are repurposed as chandeliers, maybe a wagon set up outside—it's reasonable to think parents might bring their children," she added. "A wagon could be both decoration and something to distract kids."

He flipped back to the colors. "So you'd paint the walls this color yellow, have red accents—"

"The tablecloths, napkins, that sort of thing, yes."

"And accent with weathered wood?"

"And leather," she added, leaning over to flick to another screen, which had several chairs pictured. "Rich brown leather for the seating. And maybe a few harnesses that will serve as picture frames on the walls. The whole experience would be warm and comfortable—formal without being stuffy."

"I like it. Let's go with that. Caballo de Tiro."

Leona looked pleased. "That was easy. I have some other ideas…"

Byron tried not to sigh. The restaurant was important, but he felt as though he was spinning his wheels. He wanted to get back to everything else—how Percy was, if she'd marry him or if she'd fight him every step of the way—and what, exactly, she'd meant by saying *he'd* left *her*.

She shot him a look. "You hired me, after all."

"I know," he groaned. "But five o'clock seems like a long time off."

"Byron, focus. I need the specs of the kitchen and then I need to call contractors and get a timeline set up, and my boss wants that as soon as possible. I'll formalize the sketches of the interior and exterior a bit more and…"

Byron's phone rang. "The Realtor," he said with relief. At least one thing was happening quickly. "You eat and then we'll talk ovens."

"Deal," she said.

The rest of the afternoon passed in a blur. The Realtor had a list of single-family homes ready, and she wanted Byron to come in on Saturday. Leona wanted to discuss kitchen appliances and table placements.

It was enough to give a man whiplash. It'd only been a few months ago that he'd settled into his cramped Madrid apartment, working late nights cooking for a world-famous chef and wandering the city alone, trying to lose himself in another culture.

Trying to forget about Leona Harper.

Now he would be running his own restaurant and living with Leona while they raised their son.

For a brief moment, as Leona talked about bathroom sink options, Byron wanted to go back to Madrid. Right now. This was insane, that's what it was. Proposing to Leona so he could ensure he'd never lose custody of his son? Going to look at houses tomorrow? Debating what "message" bathroom faucets "communicated" to customers?

Living with Leona—the woman who'd nearly destroyed him? Whose father had done everything to ruin his family?

But a Beaumont would not cut and run or admit defeat.

His father had not been much of a father, but Byron remembered the last conversation he'd had with Hardwick Beaumont. His father had been sitting behind his massive desk, a look of disgust on his face as he took in Byron's flour-dusted pants. "Son," he'd intoned as if he were passing a death sentence, "this cooking thing—it's not right. It's not what a Beaumont does. It's servant work."

It hadn't been the first time Byron had considered running away. He'd just wanted to cook in peace and quiet, without being constantly harassed about how he wasn't good enough. He'd been all of sixteen and thought he'd known how the world worked.

But, being sixteen, he hadn't. Instead, he'd mouthed off. "You want me to go? Then I'll go. I don't have to stay here and take your insults."

He'd expected to be disowned, frankly. No one talked back to Hardwick Beaumont, especially not his disappointment of a son. Hardwick's lips had twisted into a sneer and Byron had braced himself.

Then, to his everlasting shock, Hardwick had said, "A Beaumont does not cut and run, boy. We know what we want and we fight for it, to hell with what anyone else says." He'd leaned forward, his hard gaze locked on Byron. "If I ever hear you talk about giving up again, I'll make sure you have nothing to give up. Do I make myself clear?"

"Yes, sir." Byron had been pissed at the threat, but underneath, he'd also been confused. Had his father—what? Given him permission to keep rebelling?

He had turned and started to walk out of Hardwick's office when his father had called out, "The rack of lamb last night—was that you or George?"

It'd been a huge success, as far as Byron had been concerned. Even his half siblings had enjoyed the meal. "I cooked it. George supervised."

There'd been a long pause and Byron hadn't been sure

if he'd been dismissed or not. Then Hardwick had said, "I expect you to present yourself as a Beaumont in the rest of the house. I don't want to see flour anywhere on your clothes ever again. Understood?"

"Yes, sir."

And he hadn't left home. He'd stayed and put up with his father's crap about how he did servant's work and gotten better and better at cooking. Every so often, his father would look at him over the dinner dishes and say "that meal was especially good." Which was as close to a compliment as Byron had ever gotten out of him.

He hadn't thought about that chat, such as it was, in a long time. Not too long after that, Hardwick had keeled over dead of a heart attack. Frances scolded Byron about the flour in his hair, but no one had accused him of embarrassing the Beaumont name by insisting on doing servant's work. He hadn't had to fight for what he wanted anymore.

He'd *stopped* fighting for what he'd wanted.

Including Leona. Instead of fighting for her, he'd run away to Europe.

Well. Things had changed. He was in charge now and he knew what he wanted. He wanted Leona to marry him and he wanted to be a part of his son's life.

It was high time to start acting like a Beaumont.

Finally, it was five o'clock. Leona had made him look at color samples and shaped plates and steak knives and he didn't even know what all. Whatever was her favorite was what he went with—she was the designer, after all. What he cared about was the food.

He rinsed the lunch dishes in the sink and packed everything back into his car—except for the ring. That he put in his pocket. She'd left it on the table, and it made him nervous to have a twenty-thousand-dollar piece of jewelry sitting around.

She would wear it. She would accept his proposal.

This thought was followed by a quieter one, which barely whispered across his consciousness.

She would be his.

And why not? They were going to live together. They were going to get married. Why shouldn't he reclaim what he'd once had? As long as he could have her without letting her get under his skin like she had the first time. He'd always loved being with her. They were good together. He wanted to think they still could have that same magic in bed.

He could enjoy Leona but this time, he would not let his feelings for her blind him to the truth. She was still a liar. He had to keep his guard up, that was all.

She walked to her car door. "You want to follow me out? Assuming you're coming home with me…"

The ring was going to burn him clean through. "Yes, I'm coming home with you."

She looked at him then, her lips curved into a small smile and again he had to fight the urge to kiss her.

Oh, to hell with fighting that urge.

He closed the distance between them in three strides and pulled her into him. She made a small squeaking noise when he kissed her, but he didn't care.

He kissed her like he'd dreamed of kissing her for a long, cold year—like he'd kissed her last night. She might not be good for him—not now, not ever—but he couldn't stay away from her.

After a moment, she kissed him back. Her arms went around his neck and her mouth opened for him and he swept his tongue inside, tasting her sweetness.

He broke the kiss but he didn't let go of her. "Since we're off the clock," he whispered against her ear.

Her chest heaved against his for a moment as she clung to him. Then, apparently with great effort, she pulled away.

"Byron," she said in a warning tone. "You can't keep kissing me like that."

"Is there another way you'd like me to kiss you?"

"No—I mean—it's just—you made it pretty clear that you only wanted to marry me for the baby's sake. And we are going to have separate rooms and…" She took a deep breath. "And you cared for me once. But not anymore."

He pulled the ring out of his pocket. "Would it be bad? Between us, I mean."

"I just need to know what to expect, that's all. One minute you're mad at me and the next you're cooking for me and saying I'll have my own room and then you're kissing me and offering me a ring—is it a family ring?"

He slipped the diamond out of the case and held it in the palm of his hand. "No. I bought it this morning." Something that wasn't tainted by her family name or his. Something that was theirs and theirs alone.

"Oh, okay. I guess it doesn't matter."

That made him smile. "It matters. I don't even know what Percy's full name is—is it Harper or Beaumont?"

"Percy Harper Beaumont. You're listed on the birth certificate as his father. But I gave him my name as a middle name."

She'd given the boy Byron's name. For some reason, that made him happy. He stepped back into her and lifted her head up so he could look her in the eye. "Thank you for that."

Her eyelids fluttered. "You're doing it again," she murmured.

"Leona." He cupped her face in his hands and waited until she looked him in the eyes. "You know what I want. The question is, what do you want?" As he recalled, she was the one who'd asked for a separate bed yet had also kissed him back twice now.

"We need to get going," she replied, completely ignoring

his question. "May will worry." And with that, she turned and walked back to her car.

Byron stared after her for a moment and then shoved the ring in his pocket.

Beaumonts fought for what they wanted…to hell with what anyone else said.

Leona was about to learn how far he'd go to get what he wanted.

Eight

Leona fumbled with the keys in the lock of her apartment door. She didn't know why she was more nervous bringing Byron home with her this time, but she was. Even now, he stood too close to her, watching her. Waiting, no doubt, for an answer to his question.

If only she knew what she wanted.

"May?" She called out when she finally got the door open. "We're home."

Percy made a shrill noise. "Hi, baby," Leona said, walking into the living room and picking him up. "Did you miss me?"

May stood and said, "The doctor prescribed more drops. They're on the changing table."

"Thanks," Leona said.

There was an awkward pause as May glared at Byron without actually looking at him. "Right. I'll be back late."

"Have fun," Leona called after her as May grabbed her jacket and her purse.

That only got her a dirty look. Then May was gone.

Byron sighed. "I actually asked the Realtor if she could find us a place with a nice one-bedroom close by. I get the feeling May might not want to look at me every day."

"I'm not sure if she's going to move or not," Leona told him. If she didn't, Leona would have to keep paying rent on the apartment. Which might not be a bad plan—if it didn't work out with Byron, she could come back. "Here, hold Percy. I've got to change."

Byron sat down on the couch again and took the baby. Today, he looked slightly more confident. Or, at the very least, he looked less panicked. "How's my boy today?"

Percy made a face at him.

Leona hurried back to her room and changed into one of her prettier casual tops and a pair of jeans. She was not dressing for Byron's approval, not really. She was just being…comfortable.

Yeah, right.

When she got back to the living room, she found Byron and Percy stretched out on the floor together, both on their tummies. Byron was smiling at Percy, encouraging him. Leona wanted to stand there and watch them. This was what she'd dreamed of before Byron left her—having him all to herself, with no Beaumonts and no Harpers around to complicate things. They were going to have a family one day—they'd talked about it.

And then he'd gone and proved himself to be a Beaumont just like all the rest. He'd left her, like her father had always warned her Beaumonts did. And now he was back, issuing orders and expecting them to be followed to the letter.

She couldn't trust him. All this stuff he was doing—the ring, the apartment, talking about being a family—all of it was because he thought he wanted it. It had nothing to do with what she wanted. And the moment he changed his mind, it could all be taken away from her again.

She wanted to tie herself to a man she could count on, a man who would not treat her as if she were a ball and chain around his neck like her father treated her mother, and yet would also not treat her as if she were disposable and forgettable like all Beaumonts treated women.

She wanted stability and happiness and safety for herself, her son and her sister.

There'd been a time when she'd thought Byron was all of that and more.

She could not make that mistake a second time.

She focused on the safety and happiness of her son because right now, that was the thing that drove every other action. She would sacrifice her own heart to save his. "Having fun?"

"I was curious to see if he'd roll over," Byron replied, propping himself up on his elbow.

"He hasn't gotten that far yet." She sat down on the floor on the other side of Percy. "How are your ears, baby?"

Percy made a grunting noise as he tried to push himself up. "I know," she told the baby. "It's so hard to look around when you're on your tummy."

She rubbed his back and looked at Byron. He was staring at her as if he'd never seen her before. "What?"

"You haven't answered my questions—any of them."

"Ask me again," she told him, steeling herself to making it official.

"Will you move in with me?"

Letting Percy have this—a loving relationship with his father? Even if it meant torturing herself with her greatest love and her greatest mistake every single day for the rest of her life?

It was no contest.

"Yes."

"Will you come with me tomorrow to look at places? You can bring Percy, too, since he's going to be living there. He might have an opinion."

She couldn't help but grin. It was a thoughtful thing to say. If only everything he said and did was that thoughtful. "Yes."

He stared at her for a moment longer. There was something in his eyes, something deep and serious. "Will you marry me?"

She needed to say yes. For Percy. But… "I need to know what this marriage will actually be before I agree to it."

He raised an eyebrow. "Like what?"

"Will you see other women?"

"No." He didn't hesitate at all, which was good, she guessed. There was a pause. "You?"

"No. I have too much on my plate to even think about dating."

That got her a nice smile. "So we're agreed. No seeing other people. What else?"

Just the small matter of the facts. And the fact was that Beaumonts always cheated. Hardwick Beaumont always took the kids. Beaumonts were not to be trusted, no matter what.

"If it doesn't work out," she asked in a quiet voice as she picked up Percy and held him to her chest, "you won't take him away from me, will you?"

Byron sat up, as well. He leaned forward and kissed the top of Percy's head and said, "I am not my father, Leona."

She didn't reply. The silence seemed to stretch, pushing him away from her.

"And what about you?" His voice had turned colder. "If it doesn't work out, you won't take him and disappear? I will not stand for another lie, Leona. Because if you betray me again..." The words trailed off, but there was no give in his voice.

A cold chill ran up her spine. The threat was implicit. If she did something he didn't like, he would make her suffer for it.

"I never lied." It sounded weak to her own ears. "I told you my last name."

"Is that what you tell yourself? It wasn't a bald-faced lie, therefore you're completely innocent? How touching." He held out his arms for Percy.

She held her baby so tightly that he started to fuss. Byron sighed, the only acknowledgment of her feelings. "I want things to be different, you know. I don't want to be my parents." He came and sat beside her. Percy squirmed in her arms and she had no choice but to hand him over to Byron. "I know exactly what my father did to my mother," he went on in a quiet voice. "I would never, ever do that to you or to Percy."

She shouldn't believe him, shouldn't trust him. But he said it with such conviction that she couldn't help it. She looked down at her son, who was happily trying to suck on all his fingers at once. "I need help with him. If May doesn't move down with us, we'll have to find a day care for him and that's not cheap. The drops for his ears aren't cheap, and I didn't know how I was going to pay for Percy's surgery to get tubes, either. For the ear infections."

"I'll take care of it. All of it." He said it in an almost dismissive way, as if he'd never had to worry about money.

Well, maybe he hadn't. After all, she hadn't, either—not until she'd walked away from her father and his fortune. There'd been a very real price for her independence, but it'd been one she was willing to pay to keep Percy happy and safe.

Would she really give up that hard-fought independence and let Byron call the shots just because it was best for her son—even if it wasn't anywhere close to what was best for her?

No, she would not panic. She forced herself to breath and keep her head on her shoulders. "What about your family?"

"What about them?"

She gave him a hard look. "You saw how Frances reacted to me. If we get married, are they going to be...difficult about it?"

He grimaced. "Things have changed. It's almost like we all finally figured out that Hardwick is really and truly dead and we don't have to be what he thought we were anymore. Even Chadwick is different now. He smiles and everything."

"I wish my father realized that, too," she said wistfully. If only they could all just go on with their lives without a decades-old feud to haunt them.

Percy made the high whining noise that signaled he was getting hungry. "Oh, I should be making dinner."

She started to get up, but Byron was quicker. "Let me. What else does he eat?"

"He liked the applesauce," she called after him as he headed for the kitchen. "And yogurt and cereal. But it's still mostly baby food at this point."

Byron ducked his head around the kitchen door, a jar of what looked like green beans and mashed potatoes in his hand. "This stuff?" He made a face.

"Yes, that stuff," she replied, trying not to be defensive about it. "That's a good brand—all organic, no added anything."

After giving her a dismissive look, Byron disappeared back into the kitchen. Leona stood and checked Percy's diaper. "I have a feeling," she told the baby as she carried him back to the changing table, "that he's going to start from scratch."

She wasn't wrong about that. By the time she got Percy changed, Byron had peeled potatoes boiling and a can of green beans heating. "I don't like using the canned stuff," he told her in his chef voice. "I'll pick up some fresh or frozen ones for him."

"You don't have to…" He cut her off with a look. She sighed in resignation. "Fine. Go ahead."

In forty minutes, they sat down to mashed potatoes and green beans—Percy's being slightly more mashed together than theirs—and pan-fried chicken in a parmesan crust. "This is delicious," she said in between spooning Percy's dinner into his mouth and taking bites of her own. Percy agreed by thumping the top of his high-chair tray with both hands and opening his mouth for more.

"Good," Byron said, watching Percy swallow another mouthful. "I used to cook for the new kids, you know. When my dad would remarry and his new wife had babies. Dad expected us all to like the same things he did, but it was hard for a four-year-old to really get into steak au poivre, you know? George always had something else for us, but we had to eat it in the kitchen so neither of our parents would catch us." He looked at his plate. "That was a long time ago."

"That sounds a lot like dinners in my house growing up."

Byron looked at her. "We never really did discuss your past. You always changed the subject." He stabbed at his chicken viciously. "And I never caught on."

She couldn't tell who he was madder at—her or himself. "I knew who you were—it was hard to miss that last name. But I..." She sighed. "I wanted something different than Harpers versus Beaumonts. I wanted to see if you were really what my father claimed you were. I wanted to know if you liked me for me, not because I was heiress to a fortune."

She'd never gotten the chance to say those words out loud to him. Everything had happened so fast that night... "I just wanted to be something more than Leon Harper's daughter."

Byron set down his fork. "You were." He stood, picked up his plate and headed back to the kitchen. "You were..."

Leona leaned forward to catch the end of that sentence because it seemed important. But when she didn't hear the ending, she got up and followed Byron into the kitchen. "What?"

"Nothing," he said gruffly, scraping his plate into the trash and running hot water into the sink.

"Byron." She stood next to him and put her hand on his

shoulder in an attempt to turn him toward her. He didn't budge. *"What?"*

"You should have told me," he replied, grabbing his plate and scrubbing it furiously. "It wouldn't have mattered if you'd told me yourself. Instead I had to learn it from your father."

Guilt, which had been creeping around the edges of their conversation for the past few minutes, burst out into the open. "I wanted to. But I didn't want to risk ruining the best thing that had ever happened to me."

For a second, she thought he was going to give her that smile, the one that always melted her. But then his face hardened. "You didn't trust me."

She stared at him as a new emotion pushed back at the guilt—anger. "First off," she snapped, "I'm not the one who bailed. I was right here, dealing with the fallout of you abandoning me. I went on with my life when all I wanted to do was run and hide, too. I did not have that luxury, Byron."

Byron opened his mouth to protest, but she cut him off. "Secondly, this is exactly why I haven't said yes to your marriage proposal. At least this time it wasn't an order, but I simply do not know when you're going to switch from doting father to angry ex-lover."

Percy began to fuss, no doubt unhappy about being left behind while everyone else was in the kitchen. However, for the first time in her life, Leona didn't rush off to pick him up.

"And finally, you didn't trust me, either. Four days, Byron. That's how long it took to get away from my father—and you were gone. *Gone.* You couldn't even stick around for a damn week to wait for me." Unexpectedly, her throat closed up, but she would not crack. "So you'll forgive me if I want a little more reassurance that you're not going to up and disappear again, that you're not going to marry me only to dump me and take my son."

"You need me," he said in a quiet voice.

Percy let out a wail of impatience. Leona heard a spoon clatter to the ground.

"I need child support," she corrected him. "I need a job. You have yet to prove to me that I need *you*."

And with that, she turned and walked out of the kitchen.

Nine

It was hard to focus on bathing Percy with Leona's words ringing in Byron's ears. Wasn't offering to marry her enough reassurance that he wasn't going to disappear and take the baby? Marriage was… Okay, maybe it wasn't a permanent legal bond, but it was not something to be taken lightly. Once they were legally wed, it wasn't as though he could just walk off with the boy. Didn't she see that?

Besides, where were the reassurances *he* needed? The promises that she wouldn't lie to him again? Or that she wouldn't sic her father and his horde of lawyers upon Byron and his family? The reassurance that she wasn't just waiting until he let his guard down all the way to hit him where it would hurt the most—Percy? She'd already lied to him twice. Even if that had been a series of massive misunderstandings, it didn't change the fact that she had lied to him for months and months. How could he trust her, really?

Of course, he didn't get far in these thoughts because Percy slapped at his bathwater, splashing it into Byron's face. The baby made a trilling noise as a toy boat floated past him. There was more splashing. Byron's shirt was getting soaked and Percy was not getting any cleaner.

Just then, Percy twisted to reach the boat and Byron lost his grip. "Whoa!" he cried as Percy's head dunked under the water.

Immediately, Leona was next to him, pulling Percy upright. "I'll hold him," she said and amazingly, she didn't sound panicked. "You wash."

"I'm sorry," Byron said as Percy sputtered and coughed. He let out a disgruntled cry but stopped when Leona nudged the boat back in front of him.

"It's okay," she said softly and Byron was surprised to see she was smiling. "It'll get easier."

"If you say so," he said, scrubbing Percy's legs as fast as he could.

The argument—well, it wasn't quite an argument, but it'd certainly been more than a discussion—hung in the air between them. As they finished Percy's bath and got him ready for bed, Byron thought about what Leona had said. That she hadn't told him who her family was because she didn't want to be a Harper.

Did he believe her?

For the past year, he'd been operating under the assumption that she'd misled him on purpose, that she'd intentionally withheld the information so she could use her family name against him at the right time. And hadn't the right time been that awful night?

But maybe...maybe that's not what had happened.

He ran through his memories again—of Rory calling him out and, when Byron mouthed off, firing him. Of taking a swing at Rory because, damn it, he'd put up with enough of that man's crap over the year and a half he'd worked there and that was not how it was supposed to end.

And then Bruce—the pastry chef Byron had counted as a friend—had grabbed him from behind and physically hauled him out of the restaurant and thrown him down on the sidewalk, just in time to see Leona getting into Leon Harper's chauffeured vehicle.

Except...had she? Or had Leon shoved his daughter into the car? It'd been dark and rainy and Byron had thought...

Had it been part of the lie? Or was she now telling the truth? Was she being truthful about the lies she'd already told? Was that even a thing?

This was what she did to him. She spun his head around and around until he didn't know which way was up anymore.

While Leona nursed Percy, Byron furiously washed and dried the dishes, trying to remember exactly what Leon Harper had done in the minute before he'd gotten up into Byron's stunned face and taunted him.

That's when Leona came back into the kitchen.

"He go down okay?" Byron asked, because it seemed like the thing a parent would ask about.

"I gave him something for his ears. Hopefully he'll sleep for at least a couple of hours."

"Hopefully?" A couple of hours did not seem like enough.

Leona gave him a tired smile. "That's why we were looking at tubes."

"Yeah, I guess." He dried another dish. "How many ear infections has he had?"

"I've lost count. May gets up with him sometimes, but he usually just wants to nurse."

Byron's gaze dropped to her chest. She wasn't wearing a bra and he could see the outline of her nipples poking through the thin fabric of her shirt. Lust hit him hard and low as his mind chose exactly that moment to remember the kiss from earlier this evening and the one from last night.

"A-*hem*," she said, crossing her arms.

"Sorry," he replied, focusing all his attention back on the pots and pans.

Leona sighed. "Are you sure we should live together?"

He tensed. Damn it, this was going from bad to worse. "As opposed to what?"

"As opposed to a regular custody agreement where we each have Percy for a week or two and then trade, with child support and the like." She paused. "It might be better that way."

"Better for who? Not better for Percy—not when your father can take him. No way."

She grabbed a towel and one of the few remaining pots. "Byron, I don't want this to be hard."

"Hard?" He snorted. "I hate to burst your bubble, but nothing about this is easy."

"Fine," she snapped. "All I'm saying is that you're obviously still mad at me and I don't want Percy to grow up in a household where his parents are constantly sniping at each other. That doesn't make me the bad guy here."

"I didn't say you were the bad guy. And I'm not mad at you." He was, however, getting pretty pissed at himself. He couldn't be doing a worse job fighting for what he wanted if he tried. His father was probably rolling over in his grave.

If Hardwick Beaumont were still here, he'd slap Byron on the shoulder and say, "Stop screwing around. She's just a woman, for God's sake. You're a Beaumont. Act like one."

Except Byron didn't want to be a Beaumont if it meant bending Leona and Percy to his will just because he could. He didn't want to rule by force and fear.

She glared at him. "No, but you don't have to say the words, Byron. Your actions speak quite loudly."

"Oh, yeah? Then what does this say?" He grabbed her by the arms and hauled her to him. The kiss was not sweet or gentle—it was hard and unbending. He might not be able to get her to say yes to his proposal, but he was damned sure she wasn't going to say no.

After a moment, she bent. Her head slanted sideways and she opened her mouth for him with a sigh. He deepened the kiss. Could he kiss her like this without getting lost in the soft sweetness of her body?

Because that's what she was now, all soft and warm in his arms. His pulse beat out a faster rhythm. When she broke the kiss, he let her. "What are we going to do, Byron?"

"We'll do a trial run. I'll get us a place and you and Percy can come stay for a little while—say a week or two. You won't have to pack up all your things here. And if it doesn't work…" He paused and swallowed. He didn't want to admit it might not work. He didn't want to be wrong. But he had to give her something, a fallback to prove that he wouldn't hold her hostage once he had her and Percy with him. "If it doesn't work, then we'll go to your plan."

He could do that. He could trust her enough to bring her under his roof. And once he had her there, then he could figure out which part of her story was the truth—or if she was still lying to him.

For some reason that could only be described as self-destructive, he wanted to take her at her word.

She leaned back to look at him. "And if it does?"

Her eyes were wide—but not with fear. Instead, she looked hopeful. And hope looked good on her. He lifted his hand and stroked her cheek. "If it does, I'll ask you to marry me again."

She leaned into his touch and exhaled through slightly parted lips. He'd kissed her to end the argument and remind her that he was in control, but instead of it dampening his desire for her, it'd only ramped it up. He needed her—only her. No one, not even sensual European women, could satisfy him like this woman did.

"Two weeks?" she said softly, staring into his eyes.

He could get lost in her light brown eyes. As corny as the sentiment was, it was true. "Yeah," he said, his head dipping to meet hers. "That sounds good."

"Mmm," was all she could say because by then, Byron was kissing her and she was kissing him back and there weren't any more words, any more negotiations. There was just him and her, the way it had been. The way it should still be.

The kiss deepened when she touched his lips with her

tongue. It was a hesitant touch, as though she wasn't sure what would happen next.

Byron knew what he wanted to happen. He wanted to sweep her off her feet and carry her back to the bedroom and spend the rest of the night remembering what they'd once had. He didn't want to think about betrayal and lies. He just wanted *her*.

He swept his tongue into her mouth and felt her body respond. Old memories—good ones of the first time he'd kissed her—came rushing back. She'd been hesitant then, too. Now he knew it was because he was a Beaumont but back then he'd thought it was because she was sweet and innocent and afraid he'd push her too far. So he'd just kissed her good-night against the side of her car before she drove home alone.

Which was what he should do now. He should kiss her long and hard and then remove himself from the apartment. He should go home and take care of business himself instead of burying his body into hers over and over again. He shouldn't push his luck. Hell, he didn't have much luck left to push.

But Leona ran her fingers through his hair and leaned back, exposing her neck as she moaned, "Oh, Byron," and he was lost. He would always be lost to her.

He kissed her on the spot just under her ear and was rewarded with a shudder of pleasure. "Tell me what you want," he whispered. "Do you want me?"

She didn't answer right away, so he kissed her again. Their tongues tangled as heat built between them. Every moment he spent holding her made it that much harder to walk away and soon he would barely be able to walk at all. But he didn't care. If she brought him to his knees, so be it.

"Tell me," he demanded again. This time he took a step forward and pivoted, leaning her up against the counter. He slid his hands under her bottom and lifted her. Her body felt *so* good in his hands. "Tell me you want me." As he said it, he tilted his knee forward and pushed her legs apart.

She hadn't let go of him, hadn't pushed him away. Instead, she trailed her lips over his jaw and down his neck.

He stepped into her and tilted his hips so his straining erection rubbed against her very center. Leona gasped at the contact. She jolted upright, her eyes even wider as she stared at him.

This was it—the absolute last moment he could walk away from her tonight.

He thrust against her a second time without taking his eyes off hers. Her mouth dropped open into a perfect O and he couldn't help himself. He kissed her, unable to restrain the passion that was driving him forward over and over again.

She wrapped her legs around his waist, holding him tight. "You," she whispered in his ear. "I want you."

That was all he needed. He lifted her off the counter and carried her down the short hallway to her bedroom. Each step drove him against her, harder and harder, so that by the time he managed to kick the door shut behind them, she was moaning in his ear. "Byron—oh, Byron."

He all but threw her onto the bed. "Babe," he groaned as he covered her body with his. A nagging thought in the back of his brain told him it'd be a good idea to take this seduction and bedding slowly—that he should do it right.

But then Leona dug the tips of her fingernails into his back and the sensation drove any lingering rational thought from his mind.

He sat back on his knees and pulled her up enough that he could strip off her shirt. Then he traced the pads of his fingers over her skin and around her nipples. The little pink buds stiffened at his touch and he grinned.

Leona lay back, her hands over her head. "It's not— You're not weirded out, are you?"

"Nope. Your breasts are amazing. Your body is *amazing*." He flicked his fingers over the hard tips.

"It's not the same," she said and he heard the concern in her tone. "Everything changed. I'm not the same girl you remember."

"I know." He snagged the waistband of her pants. "You're better. You're a woman now." With that, he pulled.

Her pants peeled right off her legs and then she was in nothing but a pair of white cotton panties. Keeping one hand on her breast, he moved down. He pushed her legs apart and lowered himself onto her. He pulled the panties aside and kissed her on her sex. "Not so different," he murmured. He inhaled her scent deeply and everything he'd tried to forget for a year came crashing back on him. "Oh, babe," he said before he licked her.

Leona's body shook at his touch as she moaned. Her legs tried to close around him but he used his free hand to hold her open as he worked on her body. "Yeah, that's it," he whispered against her skin as her back arched. "You're so beautiful."

"Need...more," she ground out through clenched teeth.

"All you had to do was ask." He released his hold on her breast and trailed his hand over her stomach until he got both hands into the elastic waistband of her panties. He pulled them down and Leona kicked free.

She was completely open to him now. She held her hands over her stomach but he pried them away. There, permanently etched into her skin, were pale pink lines that hadn't been there before.

"Byron," she said in a trembling voice, as if she were waiting for pain to hit.

"Beautiful," he murmured as he kissed the stretch marks. She'd brought his son into this world with her body and he wanted to show her just how much he appreciated that.

So, even though he was about to bust out of his jeans, he

took the time to kiss all of her stretch marks before moving lower a second time. He pressed his mouth against her again. This time, he didn't do tender or gentle. This time, he was hell-bent on bringing her right up to the edge and then pushing her over. He looped his arms around her legs and pulled her up so he had a better angle.

She tangled her fingers into his hair, pulling it loose from the low ponytail. "Oh, Byron," she gasped quietly.

"You still need more?"

"Please," she got out in a high voice filled with need. "*Please*, Byron."

He couldn't help but grin. "*This* is how much I missed you," he murmured as he slipped a finger inside of her. She moaned in pleasure as he stroked her and licked her and kissed her.

"Yes," she whispered. She let go of his hair and pulled his face up so she could look him in the eye. "More. Need *more*."

"This?" he asked, slipping a second finger into her. "Is this what you want?"

Her mouth dropped open again, but she shook her head no.

"Tell me what you want, Leona. I need to hear the words." He didn't know why, but he did. No misunderstandings this time—just the truth between them. The truth he'd never been able to deny.

"I want you—all of you," she whispered. "Make love to me, Byron. *Please*."

He hopped off the bed to shuck his jeans. He had a condom in his wallet. He dug around until he found it, which took a few minutes because Leona had leaned forward and pressed her lips to his tip. He groaned in the small space between the pleasure of her mouth on his erection and the pain of needing to hold back his climax. "Babe, please."

As she lifted her eyes to look at him, her other hand

cupped him. Too much—she was too much. "Babe," he said in warning. He didn't want to lose it before he'd shown her how good it could still be between them and he didn't know how much time they had before the baby awoke or her sister came back. "Let me do this for you."

With his last bit of self-control, he pushed her away—at least, far enough away that he could roll the condom on. Then he climbed back onto the bed, back between her legs, and lowered himself to her. "You still like it like this?" he asked as he tucked her knees under his arms and pinned her to the bed.

"I think so. I'll let you know." Then she licked his lips and he couldn't hold back any longer.

He fit himself against her and plunged into her body. She was so wet and ready for him, as though she'd been waiting for just this moment, too. He buried himself in her and kissed her and thought, *I've finally come home.*

"Yes," she hissed as he drove into her again and again. "Still like that. Harder."

"Yes, ma'am," was all he could say. He had to focus on holding off his climax until she'd come. He had to show her how good he could be for her—to her.

So he thrust in harder and harder until the bed was squeaking and she was moaning and all he could see and feel and hear and taste was Leona. His Leona.

"Oh—oh!" she gasped as he gave her everything he had. Her body clenched down on his and her head came off the pillow and as the climax took her, he kissed her and kept thrusting while she rode it out.

Then she fell back onto the bed and his climax began to roar through his blood. Then—unexpectedly—something changed. The sensation surrounding his erection shifted. Deepened.

He tried to pull out but it was too late. He'd come—and the condom had broken.

Oh, hell.

"What?" Leona panted when Byron pulled away from her.

"I lost the condom," he said in a state of shock.

"Oh." Leona hopped out of bed and basically ran for the bathroom.

Byron sat down heavily on the edge of the bed and threw the remains of the useless condom into the trash. For the love of everything holy—he'd barely gotten used to the idea of being a father to one. Was he already on his way to being a father of two?

Stupid. He shouldn't have used an old condom, shouldn't have kept it in his wallet. He shouldn't have taken Leona to bed, not yet.

But this was how it always seemed to happen with her—he couldn't help himself. He'd wanted to show her how good they could be together and instead?

He'd set them both up for another pregnancy scare. What a freaking mess.

Maybe she was right. Maybe they shouldn't live together, shouldn't get married. Because this was how it was going to be. They'd always be walking the thin line between love and disaster.

The only difference was that, at least this time, he knew when they'd crossed that line.

Leona walked back into the bedroom, head down, arms crossed over her bare breasts. "Come here," he told her, pulling her onto his lap.

She sucked in a shuddering breath. "Might not be anything, after all."

"Might not," he agreed, trying to sound optimistic.

"This doesn't change the plans," she added. "Two-week trial."

"Are you sure?" He kissed her cheek. "Because, right up until the end there, I was… Well, I don't know if I'm going to be able to keep my hands off you." That got him a small smile. "I don't know if I'll *ever* be able to keep my hands off you, Leona," he said in all seriousness as he stroked her hair. "Not even for two weeks."

"I wish…"

"Yes?"

She leaned into him and sighed. "I wish I knew if that was a good thing or bad thing."

"Parts of it were very good. Great, even."

She giggled, but just then a small cry came from the other side of the wall. "Oh— the baby!" Leona said, shooting up and gathering her clothes. She was dressed in seconds and rushing out of the room.

Byron grabbed his shorts and his pants and pulled them on. He didn't know if he was staying here tonight or not. Not, he decided. He didn't have another condom and he couldn't risk the temptation of Leona again, not when there was still a chance that the condom failure might be nothing, after all.

He finished dressing and then peeked his head into Percy's room. The only light spilled into the room from the hallway. Leona sat in the dark, holding Percy to her breast. This time, he noted the things he'd need to get for his new place—the crib, the dresser, the glider.

But he also watched Leona and Percy. One of Percy's hands lazily waved around in the air, as if he wanted to grab on to something but was too sleepy to know what. Leona smiled down at him, her eyes full of love as she offered her finger for him to grip.

Byron had missed so much. The whole of her pregnancy, the delivery, Percy's first smile—all of it was gone into the past. But starting right now, he could make up for that. He could be here for the first time Percy rolled over, the first time he stood and took a step.

He wanted to be a better father than the one he'd had. That's all there was to it.

Behind him, the front door opened. May walked back into the apartment, already glaring at him. "You're still here?" She looked him up and down and sniffed in distaste.

Byron shrugged his shoulders at Leona and then walked over to where May was standing. He kept his voice low so he wouldn't wake Percy. "We're going to look at some real estate tomorrow. You're welcome to join us."

"I'm not going to uproot my life for you," she spat at him. "Not after what you did to Leona."

He kept his calm. Mostly because he didn't want to upset the baby. "I could find you a place of your own nearby if you wanted to stay close to Percy."

At this, May softened a little bit. "Why would you do that?"

"Because he loves you and your sister loves you," Byron replied. "And I want them to be happy."

Whatever small foothold he'd gained with May disappeared. "Then just stay away from them. From all of us," she hissed.

"I wish I could," he muttered as May sidestepped him and headed for her room. "I wish I could."

But he knew he couldn't.

Ten

They met outside the brewery. Leona was exhausted. Between the three times Percy had gotten her up in the middle of the night and the wild dreams she'd had about Byron, she'd gotten very little rest.

But here she was anyway, picking Byron up at the restaurant site instead of the Beaumont Mansion so his family wouldn't see him leaving in her car.

"How are you?" he asked as he climbed into the passenger seat. But before she could answer, he'd pulled her into a light kiss.

In the back, Percy shook his rattle.

"Sorry," Byron said, clearly not sorry at all.

And that, in a nutshell, was her problem. If she were to find herself pregnant again, she'd *have* to marry him.

An insidious voice in her head that sounded a lot like her father whispered, *Maybe that was his plan the entire time. Get you pregnant again to force your hand.*

She shook that thought out of her head. "Tired. He woke up a couple more times last night."

Byron frowned. "How long do those drops take to work?"

"A couple of days. Where are we going?"

Byron gave her the address and they headed out. "Do I take it May's still not interested in relocating to stay closer to you two?"

"No, not particularly." Which was the diplomatic way of saying it. At breakfast, May had been quite upset that

Leona was spending the day with Byron—and was taking Percy with her.

They drove in silence. The weight of what had happened between them last night hung heavy in the air. She could always buy the plan B pill, just to make sure she didn't get pregnant—but she didn't want to do that without discussing it with Byron, and she had absolutely no idea how to begin that conversation.

So, instead, she would look at real estate with a man she still wasn't convinced she should live with. Because last night he'd told her in all seriousness that he wouldn't be able to keep his hands to himself.

She liked to think she was no fool. Oh, sure, she had made some foolish choices. But this?

Living together meant sleeping together, no matter what either of them said about separate rooms. If she agreed to this trial, they'd be together in every sense of the word.

Part of her thought that was a grand idea. It's what she'd wanted, after all, back before she got pregnant the first time and Byron abandoned her and it all blew up in her face. The other part of her couldn't get past the part where Byron had abandoned her.

Even though Byron had laid her out last night and made her orgasm like no time had passed between them, she wasn't sure what she wanted to happen next. She wanted Byron but…she had to put her son first.

Of course, Percy should know his father. That was non-negotiable.

God, her head was such a mess. Maybe if she'd gotten more than four hours of nonconsecutive sleep she'd be able to think.

They arrived at the Realtor's office, and she came out to greet them. "Hi! I'm Sherry!" the woman said in a way-too-bright voice. Leona winced. It was still far too early for this level of enthusiasm. "I don't want you to have to unstrap that little cutie so we'll just head out, okay?"

"That's fine," Byron said. "We'll follow you?"

"Sure!" Sherry said with a blindingly white smile.

Leona turned to Byron. "What did you tell her?"

"Nothing." He gave her a sly grin. "Just that I was a Beaumont and I expected a high level of service. That's all."

"Oh, Lord," Leona muttered, following Sherry's car out of the parking lot. "Let the upselling begin."

Byron chuckled.

They drove into Littleton, which was not a town that Leona had spent a lot of time in. Her family lived in Cherry Hills in an old mansion behind a gated fence.

Although Littleton looked like a nicer place than the section of Aurora where she and May lived, it didn't come close to Cherry Hills. At least, not until the Realtor made a couple of turns and May found herself driving past a country club. "Byron?" she asked. "I thought you were just going to get us an apartment or something."

"Or something," he agreed as the Realtor pulled into the driveway of a truly stunning house. From the outside, it looked as if it was maybe half the size of her family's mansion—and easily five times the size of her current apartment, if not more.

Leona opened her car door and gaped. The house was built to look like a log cabin, but this was no primitive home. The red tile roof gleamed in the morning sunlight and the foundation plantings were lush—obviously well watered despite the lingering drought conditions.

"Here we are!" said Sherry with an even bigger smile.

"How much?" Leona demanded.

Sherry blinked and said, "It's $1.3 million, but it's been on the market for a few months so I think there's negotiating room."

"No."

Sherry's megawatt smile faltered. "I'm sorry?"

"No," Leona said, ignoring the Realtor and turning back to Byron, who had the nerve to look innocent. "This was supposed to be a temporary thing, a three-bedroom apartment—not a—" She turned back to Sherry. "How many square feet?"

"Nine thousand, if you account for the maid's room over the garage."

Nine thousand square feet of luxury. Not a cozy little apartment. This place had a maid's room, for God's sake. This felt wrong. Everything about it was off. She'd spent the past year scrimping and scraping. She didn't want this situation to even suggest that she could be bought—that her affection was for sale. That's what her father would do if he admitted he'd screwed up. He'd throw an insanely expensive gift at her and expect that to make everything okay.

Well, this was not okay. Her affection could not be bought and that was final. Yes, she wanted stability for Percy but this was so far beyond stable that it wasn't funny. "*No*, Byron. This isn't what we agreed on."

She started to get back in the car, but Percy began to fuss and before she could do anything, Byron had the back door open and was unbuckling the baby. "You want out? This place has a swing set in the back," he told the boy. "And a big lawn where you can run around and we could even get a puppy! Would you like a puppy, Percy?"

Percy squealed in delight, although Leona was sure he didn't really grasp what *puppy* meant. She glared at Byron. What the hell was he trying to do here—bribe a six-month-old?

"Come on, little man," Byron said. He shut the back door and walked to the front of the car. "Let's wait for Mommy."

Leona had several choice things she wanted to say, but Percy squealed and clapped his hands and he looked... happy. She was stuck in a very real way. She couldn't drive off without her son—but she didn't like this bait and switch. It felt as though Byron was steamrollering her and she didn't like it. If she wanted to be steamrollered, she'd go home and her father would be happy to run roughshod all over her.

"We're only looking," Byron said. He turned to Sherry, who was not wearing any kind of smile at all. "We have other places to look at that are at other price points, correct?"

"Yes!" Sherry replied enthusiastically.

Byron leaned down and kissed the top of Percy's head while he kept his eyes fastened on hers.

"Fine. But I don't have to like it," Leona snapped as she got out of the car.

"Duly noted. I want to see the kitchen."

Sherry unlocked the house and led them inside. The place had a grand feeling to it, but it wasn't the same sort of cold, sterile feeling Leona's parents' mansion had given her— or, for that matter, that the Beaumont Mansion had given her, kitchen notwithstanding. Instead of severe colors and harsh lighting designed to make everything look as expensive as possible, this entryway was filled with the warmth of the early-morning sun.

"Oh," she couldn't help but whisper.

"Beautiful," Byron agreed. "Which way's the kitchen?"

Sherry went on and on about the specifications of the house—the number of bedrooms and bathrooms and the view and so on. All Leona could do was trail along behind them, trying to take in the magnitude of the place.

She hadn't allowed herself to be disappointed with her apartment because she'd been desperate and only had so much money. It was the best she could do on short notice and, for that, she was grateful for it.

But for the first time in a year, she allowed herself to think about living in a place that was above good-enough.

Byron spent twenty minutes in the kitchen, examining the appliances and discussing a "work triangle" with the Realtor, who was back to full-on perkiness. While they talked, Leona held Percy and they walked through the living room again. Wide French doors opened onto a tree-lined yard. And, as Byron had promised, there was a swing set—although this was closer to the equipment one would find in a park.

They toured the four bedrooms, including a master suite that had a huge whirlpool tub, and then they looked at the office. "This would be yours," Byron said in a low voice as he opened the door for her.

Leona couldn't help but gasp. The room was mostly windows and looked out onto the green expanse of the golf course. Behind that, the mountains broke rank and raced up to the sky. The morning light gleamed deep purple off the mountains' sides. There wasn't a parking lot or Dumpster in sight.

"It's beautiful," she whispered.

"I thought that, if you ever quit working for that Fish guy—"

"Lutefisk," she corrected, staring at the built-in bookcases and filing cabinets that made up the interior wall.

"Yeah, him. If you wanted to quit working for him, you'd need an office space for your business."

She'd always talked about opening her own design firm—how she'd design his restaurant and then build her clientele from there. She turned to face him. "You remembered."

"I never forgot. Not you," he replied, holding his gaze with hers. "I want to make it up to you."

She wanted to believe that—to believe him. But Percy squirmed in her arms and she thought of all the long months without Byron, of being completely on her own.

"By buying me an extravagant house?" She forced herself to walk back out into the hall, away from the beautiful office and the stunning views.

"I've got to live somewhere—somewhere that doesn't involve my extended family," he replied, following her out. "And you requested your own space, did you not?"

Sherry gave them a sideways glance. "Let's go check out that playground!" she said, leaning forward to speak directly to Percy.

"I requested separate bedrooms. Not a freaking nine-thousand-square-foot mansion, Byron. It feels like you're trying to buy my loyalty. Or at least my complicity. And I don't like it."

He stared at her. "What on God's green earth are you talking about?"

"It just feels like this is something my father would do. Throw a lot of money at a problem—"

"You are not a problem," he interrupted. "Percy is not a problem."

"No? Maybe not right now, but how long before you remember you're still mad at me? Or when Percy has a rough day, a rough night and won't stop screaming? Then it'll be a problem, all right. *Mine.* When the going gets tough, you'll get going."

Sherry poked her head back around the corner. "Everything all right?" she asked.

Byron fixed Leona with a hard glare. She fought the urge to step back, to agree with him—to go along to get along. Those days had passed. She had to stand firm—this was her life, too. So what if the house was beautiful? So what if it had everything she could ever want in a home?

It would still be bought and paid for by Byron. He'd control the money, the house—and her. She was only useful as long as Percy needed her. Oh, Byron could dress it up with a pretty office or whatever, but still—she'd be dependent on him. And after she'd left home, she'd vowed to never be dependent on another man for as long as she lived.

After all, if it was his house on his terms, what would happen to her if it didn't work out? Would he show her the door? He might not disappear into the night again—but there were other ways to be abandoned. Wasn't that what his father had always done? Hardwick had never gone anywhere, but as soon as he'd tired of his wife, out she went without a penny to her name. If that wasn't abandonment, she didn't know what was.

She couldn't handle the rejection, not a second time. So she stood firm. She didn't back down and she didn't apologize for having an opinion. She was in control of her destiny, damn it all. If only destiny would stop throwing her curveballs.

Byron turned to the Realtor, who waited with an expression that made Leona think of a golden retriever.

"We'll take it," he said decisively.

Another freaking curveball.

Destiny had a funny sense of humor.

Eleven

The next thing Byron knew, Leona was stomping away from him. Why was she being so damn stubborn?

He had the entire buyout from the sale of the Beaumont Brewery sitting in a bank account, completely untouched. Seventeen million dollars—plus compounded interest—was waiting for him and if he wanted to buy himself a nice house, then damn it, he *would*.

He thought Leona was just going to cool off in a different room—but then he heard the front door slam.

"Leona!" he yelled, running after her. He got the front door open as she was belting Percy into his seat. "Leona, wait!"

She shot him an incredibly dirty look, but she did not wait. She got into the car and fired it up.

Before Byron could give chase, his phone rang with the tone he'd selected for Matthew. What the hell… He had to talk to Matthew. If anyone could fix this mess that Byron kept making worse, it was his older brother. So, with a groan of frustration, he let Leona go.

"Yeah," he said.

"For the love of God, tell me you're *not* backing out of the restaurant." Byron could almost see Matthew pinching the bridge of his nose in frustration.

The Realtor poked her head out. "Is everything okay?" she asked, as if the answer wasn't obvious. "Did your wife change her mind about the house?"

"Hang on," Byron said. Then, to Sherry, he said, "No,

we'll still take the house. But I have an important—and private—call to take, if you don't mind."

The Realtor's eyes lit up with commissioned dollar signs. "Oh, of course! I'll be inside."

Byron waited until the door shut. "No, I'm not backing out of the restaurant. And hello to you, too. Where the hell have you been? I called you three days ago!"

"You didn't say it was an emergency and Chadwick didn't call in a panic, so I figured it could keep. I unplugged for a couple of days."

"Since when do you unplug in the middle of the damned week? I thought you were always working."

"Not always. Not anymore." Something in his voice changed. "I took a trip with Whitney. We got married."

Byron was almost too stunned to speak. "Seriously?"

"Yes," was the terse reply.

"Well, congratulations, man. I would have come out for it."

"I know. But we wanted to keep it quiet."

Byron snorted. Usually, Matthew was all about maintaining the family image—public relations was his thing. But he'd gone and fallen in love with former wild-child star Whitney Wildz who, in real life, was a very private woman named Whitney Maddox. Matthew would do anything to protect her from the paparazzi. Including, apparently, getting married in complete secrecy.

"Did you at least tell Mom? You know she'll be heartbroken if you got married without telling her."

There was a short pause before Matthew said, "I flew her out for it. She was our witness."

"Good." And it was. Their mother had had enough heartbreak in her life. Byron didn't want to add to it. Still, the fact that Matthew had seen fit to invite their mother but not Byron or Frances stung, if only a little.

"So, yes," Matthew went on, "I am capable of unplugging for a little honeymoon with my wife. She's working with a horse, and I've got an hour to deal with the priority issues. If you're not bailing on the restaurant, what's up?"

Okay, so even if Matthew had gotten married without telling Byron, at least he was still a priority. "I have a problem."

"I'm listening."

Was there any good way to say this? Probably not. "You remember how I wanted you to invite Leon Harper to Phillip's wedding reception?"

"And his family, if I recall correctly. A request that struck me as so odd that I looked into Harper a little more. Apparently he has two daughters." Matthew sounded as if this were no big deal.

"And you remember how I went to Europe for a year?"

"Paris and then Madrid, yes. Are you telling me these two facts are connected?"

Byron kicked at a pebble in the driveway. He just had to get this out. It was his mess, but he needed help cleaning it up. "Three days ago, I discovered that Leona Harper— Harper's oldest daughter—gave birth to my son about six months ago. His name is Percy."

There was a stunned silence on the other end of the line—a silence that lasted more than a few moments.

Byron couldn't take it. He plunged ahead. "I've asked her to move in with me and—"

"Into the mansion?" Matthew spluttered. "Are you *insane*? A Harper living in the Beaumont Mansion?"

"As I was going to say before I was interrupted," Byron said, trying not to snap at his brother, "I'm buying a house for us. And I've asked her to marry me. For our son's sake."

Again, there was another painful silence. "Jesus, Byron," Matthew finally muttered. "I'd have thought, after our father left bastards scattered to the four winds, that you would have been a little more careful than that."

The condom failure from last night popped into his mind. "I was careful. But sometimes things don't work like they're supposed to. I need a prenup. We have to get married as soon as possible to make sure her father can't declare her incompetent and take my son away."

"No," Matthew replied flatly. "You absolutely *cannot* marry her. She's Harper's daughter for God's sake! Frances didn't tell me the details, but she made it pretty clear that someone had broken your heart and that's why you left."

"I am well aware of what happened. But I am not leaving any bastards to be scattered to the winds. He's my son and I'll do whatever it takes to keep it that way. Even marry a Harper."

"Are you into pain or something? You enjoy being Harper's punching bag? Because if you tie your horse to his wagon, that's all you're ever going to be," he groaned in exasperation again. "I don't think there's a prenup in this world strong enough to stand up to Harper's sharks. He could use you to take down the entire family. He already took our business from us, Byron."

"I know that," Byron snapped.

"Oh, for God's sake. Just take the boy. Legally, I mean. She didn't tell you about the baby, I take it?"

"No, but I'm not going to—"

"So we'll sue for full custody on the grounds that she's unfit to be a mother. And for the love of everything holy, do *not* sleep with her again."

Byron winced. He couldn't bring himself to deny it, but he couldn't confirm it, either.

"You already have, haven't you?"

"Yes."

Matthew let out a long, low growl of pure frustration. "Did you at least use protection?"

"We did. It failed. Again."

There was a noise in the background that could have

been Matthew kicking or throwing something. "You have *got* to be freaking kidding me. Come on, Byron! Stop thinking with your dick for once!"

"I am not thinking with my dick, damn it. I am trying to make things right. I thought you'd appreciate that—isn't that what you do? I got her pregnant. I wasn't there when the baby was born. I missed the first six months of my son's life. I'm trying to make up for lost time. I don't care what you think about her—Leona and Percy are already my family. I want to make it official. And if you won't help me, then I'll do it myself."

Another long silence. Byron would bet money that Matthew was now rubbing his temples and grimacing comically.

"Does Harper know you're back?"

"I don't think so. Leona took her sister and basically ran away from home after I left. They don't have any contact with their parents. But she was worried her father would try to take the boy."

"He wouldn't win," Matthew said decisively. "You're the boy's father." Then, a moment later, he added, "There's no doubt about that?"

"None. The boy looks like me. Red hair and everything."

Matthew sighed heavily. "There'd need to be blood tests to confirm, but you must realize Harper wouldn't win. You're the child's father. You don't have to marry her to protect the baby."

"But he'd try," Byron insisted. "Harper would sue anyway and that would be almost as bad. He'd drag Leona through court and smear her name in every patch of mud he could find. Not to mention how much it'd cost to defend against him." When Matthew didn't immediately respond, Byron added, "You know what Dad did to Mom."

"Yeah, I know."

"I'm not saying the situation is ideal," Byron went on. "But I can't let that happen."

"And—despite all the facts of the matter—you trust her not to turn you over to her father? Not to use this kid to bankrupt the entire Beaumont family?"

Byron hesitated. Deep down, he believed that she wouldn't turn back to her father again. But…did he really trust her not to rip his still-beating heart out of his chest and hold it up for him to see? Especially after the way she'd driven off and stranded him here with the Realtor, all because he wanted to buy a nice house?

"That's not a good silence over there," Matthew observed.

Byron started pacing. "We're still working through a few issues." There. That was something that Matthew would understand.

"A 'few issues,' huh? And you want to marry a 'few issues'? Man, you are nuts."

"It runs in the family," he shot back. "You're the one who wanted me to get arrested to distract the press so you could canoodle in private with an actress."

"That's not exactly what happened, but that's neither here nor there," Matthew replied calmly. "So what do you want me to do?"

"I want a prenup that protects the rest of the family from Leona's father and guarantees that she and I will always have joint custody of Percy."

"You always did act impulsively," Matthew said in an offhand way. "Running off to Europe, now getting married. What's the kid's full name?"

"Percy Harper Beaumont."

Matthew sighed heavily. "And her middle name? I assume she's still Leona Harper at this point."

Byron had to think about that. "Margaret. And before you ask, mine is still John."

"I hadn't forgotten. Okay, fine. I'll talk to the lawyers and get them working on something. But for the love of God, don't marry her until the prenup has been signed, sealed and delivered, okay? If I were you, I'd think long and hard about marrying her at all. Even if you think this is a short-term solution and even if you have a prenup, the divorce would be a huge mess." Byron swore he heard Matthew shudder. "The press would eat this for breakfast, lunch and dinner. We need to keep the whole thing as quiet as possible."

Byron looked back at the house, where no doubt the Realtor was on her phone. "Understood. But I'm buying the house anyway."

"Fine. Dare I ask how the restaurant is coming along?"

"Uh..."

"Byron," Matthew said in warning.

"No, it's coming along fine. I hired Leona to do the interior design."

There it was again, that noise that sounded like Matthew was breaking something. "Are you *kidding* me?"

"That's what she does," Byron quickly defended. "That's what she went to school for. She's got a lot of really good ideas—we're going to call it Caballo de Tiro, which is Spanish for draft horse. I've been testing out menu options and we've started lining up contractors. It's going to be great. Really."

"Caballo de Tiro?"

"It plays off the Percheron Drafts name but pulls in the European influences," Byron explained.

"Yes, I get it. So let me see if I have this straight—you hid in Europe for a year to get away from a woman, only to come back and hire her, move in with her, and marry her—all at once?"

"Don't forget the baby."

"Oh, no—who could forget the baby?" Matthew scoffed.

"Got any other surprise children hidden anywhere? Didn't leave anyone knocked up in Spain, did you?"

"No."

"You're sure?"

"Didn't sleep with anyone, if you must know. So yes, I'm sure. No more surprises."

"Fine," Matthew huffed, making it plenty clear that it was anything but. "I'll deal with the lawyers. Stay out of the headlines, Byron."

"Thanks," Byron said, but Matthew had already hung up on him.

He stared at his phone. Well. That had probably gone as smoothly as possible.

Now he just had to convince Leona that this house and a wedding were all for the best. No matter what Matthew said, Byron knew that marrying her was not only the right thing to do, but the best for all parties involved. And he had to do it all without letting her break his heart again.

No problem, right?

Yeah, right.

If there was one valuable lesson that Byron had learned growing up as a Beaumont, it was that money talked. Loudly.

He told Sherry that he'd pay full price—and full commission—if everything was settled within two weeks and she kept quiet about both his new address and the people with whom he'd be living. Within a week, he was the proud owner of a fabulous family home. Now he just needed the one thing that money couldn't apparently buy—a family.

His life was a strange dichotomy right now, and he wasn't having much luck merging the two halves back into a recognizable whole.

During the daylight hours, he worked side by side with Leona. They met with contractors, finalized design plans and ate, of course. Byron kept tweaking the dishes or trying something that might work better—something that Leona might like better. They had long discussions about rotating menu items, which local sources to use for beef and herbs and exterior landscaping. She had no problem talking to him during the day.

But at night? At night she kept the distance between them. Even when he came over to the apartment to play with Percy, she made sure she was far more than an arm's length away.

"I can move into the house next week," he told her a week later. He was lying on the floor of her living room, rolling a ball to Percy and making happy noises when the baby got anywhere near it. He could hear music coming from May's room, where she'd basically locked herself every time Byron came over. "I've got some basic furniture, but I wanted you to pick out what you liked."

From where she sat at the kitchen table, staring at her computer she glared at him. "I am not moving into that ridiculous house."

"And you have yet to give me a good reason why not," he shot back at her. "I don't see what the big deal is. You already agreed to move in so that we could raise our son together. I provided an adequate living space."

She snorted and continued to scroll.

"And I'm basically giving you a blank check to decorate it any way you want. Explain to me again how this makes me the villain here." When she said nothing, he sighed.

She shut her computer with a bit more force than was necessary. "You want to know what the problem is? Aside from the fact that I already told you once and you didn't pay any attention?"

"I am not trying to buy your complicity," he replied, trying mightily to keep his voice calm. "I'm not trying to buy your loyalty. I'm trying to provide for my family. I thought that's what you wanted."

She dropped her head into her hands. "Byron..."

Percy squealed as the ball went rolling wide to the right. "Whoa, buddy—now what are we going to do?" Byron asked him.

Percy flopped over and tried to crawl toward the ball, but when it turned out to be only unproductive wiggling, he howled in frustration.

"You can do it!" Byron said encouragingly to the baby. Then he looked back at Leona. Her head was still in her hands. Was she crying? "Leona?"

He got up off the floor and gently kicked the ball closer to Percy. Then he went to her. She *was* crying. Damn.

"I just want to know that you're going to be here," she whispered, her voice muffled by her hands. "And I don't."

Oh, come on. He fought this sense of frustration. "Leona. We have a child together. I'm buying a house for us—not even a rental. And in case you've forgotten it, we're working on this restaurant that will keep me in the greater Denver area. Are these the actions of a man who's going to bail?"

"No," she sniffed. "But that's not what I asked for, none of it is."

"I asked you to marry me. What other reassurances do you want? Do I have to open a vein and sign my name in blood?"

As if on cue, May's music got louder. Leona's shoulders tightened in response. But she hadn't answered yet.

He found a knot in her muscles and began to rub it. "I don't mean to add to the stress. You know that, don't you?"

"I do." Her voice, however, wasn't terribly convincing. But then she tilted her head to the side, stretching her shoulders for him. He found another knot and began to rub that one. "Oh, that's good."

It'd be better if Byron could lay Leona out on a bed.

Then he could give her a proper massage, one that would work out all the knots. Maybe that was what she needed—to know that he would take care of her in every respect, not just the material ones.

Her body started to relax under his touch and, as he focused on the base of her neck, she let out a low moan of relief. That moan took all of his noble intentions and did something less than noble to them. A full body massage was just what she needed, complete with candles and massage oil. Yeah, it'd be better if he could take his time and get her body nice and relaxed and then...

No, stop it. The last time he'd thought with his dick, he'd wound up using a compromised condom. Plus he'd sort of promised Matthew he would keep his damned zipper zipped until the prenup was signed.

Besides, there was that little issue of her making him guess what the hell was holding her up. What did she mean, she wanted to know he'd be there? How was he not showing her that? He didn't get it.

Percy fussed and she got up to get him. One thing was clear. Byron was going to have to figure it out—and fast.

Twelve

Leona tried to focus on choosing a font for the restaurant's name while Byron got Percy changed and read him a story, but it didn't work. Byron had figured out the bedtime routine in only a few short days, really. He could probably handle Percy on his own now, except for the nursing part. Which was great. Really, it was.

But whenever she thought that, it made her sad, too—and she wasn't sure why. All she knew was that the words on her computer screen kept blurring together.

Byron was involved. Byron was helping out. Byron was making all sorts of wonderful-sounding promises.

But did he really need her? Would he keep his word or would he disappear again? Could she trust him—or any Beaumont—not to take her son and leave her behind?

She kept thinking back to the way Frances had reacted to finding Leona in the kitchen. Was it a huge stretch of the imagination to think that, when Byron wasn't with Leona, his family was trying to convince him not to marry her—to just take the baby instead?

She didn't think so. And that made it hard to take Byron at his word. Once, he'd believed her father and his poisonous lies instead of trusting that Leona would come to him.

He could be perfect right now and she'd still be afraid that he'd kick her out of his life a second time.

Her head was such a wash of emotions that she couldn't form a single, rational thought. The house was huge and lovely, it was true. By any objective measure, it was perfect. So what bothered her about it?

She'd once dreamed of Byron asking her to marry him, of settling down with him and raising a family. A year after she'd given up on that dream, it was suddenly happening. She wouldn't have to worry about money or doctor's bills or making rent. Moving in with Byron would solve so many problems. She should be happy.

And yet, what price would she pay for stability? Or even just the illusion of stability?

She would have to give up her independence to a man who didn't want her—who only wanted a mother for his son.

It was a damned high price to pay.

She wiped her eyes again when she heard Byron finishing his story. This part of the nightly ritual—and the morning companion—was something that had always been hers and hers alone, and right now she needed the reassurance of the routine.

She walked into Percy's room and stood there, watching. Byron hummed something low as he rocked Percy back and forth. The whole thing—the baby boy with bright red hair in his father's arms, a look of peace on both of their faces—it was almost too much for her. Her eyes began to water again.

"Ready?" Byron asked in a quiet voice.

"Yes." She had to be, after all. This was for her son.

Byron stood and Leona took the glider. He carefully lowered Percy into her arms. "Good night, little man," he whispered. "I'll see you tomorrow." Then he looked at Leona. "I'll wait for you, if that's okay with you."

She nodded. He had never left while she was nursing Percy—usually he did something in the kitchen, even if it was just the dishes.

She lifted her shirt and Percy latched on. For the next

few minutes, she didn't have to think about moving and marriages and work and Byron. This was her time with her son. He still needed her. She hoped Byron realized that, too.

She might have dozed off while Percy was nursing because the next time she looked down, he'd fallen asleep with a trickle of milk running down the side of his face. She wiped him up and carried him over to his crib.

Surprisingly, Byron was not in the kitchen. And he wasn't in the living room. He wasn't in the bedroom, either, and she highly doubted he'd gotten anywhere near May's room.

Then she realized that the door to the patio was open. He was outside? She grabbed a cardigan to fight off the evening chill and headed out.

Byron was in one of the two sad little deck chairs that May had found at a thrift store, staring out at the night sky. The apartment faced the east, so they could actually see some of the stars over the Great Plains. "What are you doing out here? I'd have thought you'd be elbow deep in a soufflé or something."

He grinned and held out a hand. "Just thinking."

"About?"

"About how it could have been different. Between us."

She should sit down in the other chair. She shouldn't take his hand, not when she was mentally and physically exhausted. She should try to keep some kind of distance between them, some layer of protection from his considerable charms.

But she took his hand and he pulled her down so she was sitting across his lap. "Different how?"

Byron swept her short hair away from his face and rested his chin on her shoulder. She curled into him, into his warmth. "When I first asked you out—almost two years ago—you knew who I was, right?"

She nodded. She didn't want to revisit what had gone

wrong before. Not tonight. But the sky was beautiful and Byron was warm and one of his hands was tucked around her thigh and the other was rubbing against her back and the moment was…peaceful.

"But you went out with me anyway."

"After you asked me three times." Their voices were quiet, their heads close together. It felt intimate to sit like this.

"And…" He took a deep breath. "And if I'd asked you to marry me before *that* night, would you have said yes?"

The corners of her mouth pulled down. "Saying yes would have meant having to face who I really was."

"And it would have been a problem, it's true. Not a deal-breaker, though. But that's not what I'm asking. I'm asking if you would have said yes."

She stared at the stars. A plane from the airport cut across the sky, rising higher and higher. *Not a deal-breaker.* Was he being honest? Or would he have accused her of trying to trap him, when she told him she was *that* Harper and pregnant with his child?

"If you'd known who my father was from the beginning, would you have asked me out three times?"

He shifted, cupping her chin in his hand and lifting her head until he looked her in the eye. "I don't think I could have stayed away from you."

Even though the angle was awkward, she hugged him to her. That was all she'd wanted—to be Leona, and to be good enough. She'd almost had it, too—before it'd been torn away.

"And I can't believe you would have spent a whole year making me fall in love with you if it'd been a trap set by Harper."

She looked up at him. Their faces were close, so close. But he didn't kiss her and she didn't kiss him. "I *made* you fall in love with me? Is that what you thought?"

The last time he'd brought feelings into the conversation, it had been the extremely noncommittal "I cared for you once." Nothing about love, not then and not now.

This new confession, at least, was something that felt less like an evasion. Even if it was still a slight.

He touched his forehead to her, a sweet touch that made her lean into him even more. "All I'm doing is asking you now. I know a lot has happened in the past year but..." He pulled his keys out of his pocket. She was surprised to see that the ring was on the key chain. That didn't seem like the best place for a diamond. "I'll admit that I haven't done the best job of it."

She snorted, but she couldn't tear her eyes off the ring. It was a stunning piece—the emerald-cut diamond was huge. When he'd first pulled it out, she'd been too surprised to do much of anything but gape at it. He'd dropped a fortune on it, that much was clear. Just like the house, it'd seemed like *too* much. But now, flashing only occasionally, it didn't seem as overwhelming.

"I'd been planning on asking you for a few months before... Well, I'd been waiting for the right moment. And I missed my window then. But now? Now is the right time."

He jostled her from side to side as he worked the ring off the key chain. Then he settled her back on his lap and held the ring up for her.

"I thought you said I could decide after we made it through two weeks," she said in a breathless voice.

"Oh, don't worry," he chuckled. "If you want to wait the two weeks, I'll ask again."

This time, she physically picked up the ring. It was the first time she'd touched it. It felt warm in her palm—Byron's warmth. She closed her fingers around the ring. It was a heavy thing, but it didn't feel like a lead weight dragging her down. The corners of the rectangular stone dug into her fingers. She swallowed nervously. "And what if the two weeks don't go well? Then what?"

"I'm still going to live in that house. I like the kitchen," he said with a grin. But then the grin faded. "If we can't live together, I hope you'll consider letting me get you a place closer to me. I don't want to waste time I could be spending with my son in traffic."

She thought about this. She had no attachment to this apartment. And if Byron was helping with the rent, she'd love to get a place that had a yard for Percy to play in. She didn't need a mansion, no matter what Byron said. But she'd like to raise her son in a house.

"I guess that sounds reasonable." She wrinkled her nose at him. "But not a palace." Because if it fell apart, she wanted to try to keep things the same for Percy, and that meant keeping him in the same house as long as Leona could afford it.

"Does that mean you'll come to the house for the two weeks? You'll give it a shot?"

She uncurled her fingers and handed him back the ring. "I'll come to the house. Ask me again in two weeks."

Byron hugged her fiercely. His one hand moved up and down her back while the other did the same on her thigh. She twisted against him because her one shoulder was being compressed by the strength of his embrace—but that brought her chest in contact with his. Her nipples—unencumbered by a bra and sensitized by the cool night air—responded with far more enthusiasm than was strictly proper.

He brushed her short hair back from her cheek and looked at her tenderly. "Whatever happens, I'm here for you. I'm here for the long haul. You know that, don't you?"

She desperately wanted to believe that, wanted to believe all the pretty promises he'd made her. But she didn't know if she could. Not yet, anyway. He was here for the long haul, for Percy, that she believed. After all, the Beaumonts always kept the kids. He'd never desert their son.

She just wished she could believe that he wouldn't desert her—again.

She should have already bought a pregnancy test, but she just couldn't bring herself to do it. Another unplanned pregnancy was something she didn't have time for and she'd made a conscious decision that she wasn't going to think about it until it became apparent one way or the other. She simply did not have the time or energy to waste on what-ifs at this point.

Something about the way he was rubbing her back shifted and instead of just stroking her, he was pushing her toward him. It wasn't as if there was a lot of distance between them to begin with—she was sitting on his lap—but every millimeter closer to his lips felt more intimate—more sexual—than it had before.

She knew she was going to kiss him. She knew she wanted him to kiss her back—wanted all the things that she hadn't allowed herself to dream of for the past year.

She wanted him. She always had. Even when he'd first asked her out and she knew exactly who he was and knew exactly why she should steer clear of him—she'd wanted him then.

There was only one problem.

"We can't," she breathed. "Percy—May…"

"Shh," he said in a gentle voice. His hand slid over the outside of her thigh and down the inside. "Let me take care of you."

His fingers dipped down, rubbing against the seam of her yoga pants until she jolted in his arms. "Byron…"

His other arm circled her waist even tighter, pinning her to him. A single finger moved down farther, testing and pressing lightly until she gasped when he hit just the right spot.

"Shh," he said again, rubbing small circles over that spot. "You have to be quiet, babe. Let me do this for you."

She tucked her lower lip under her teeth and nodded. With a wicked grin, Byron pressed harder.

Leona tried not to make a sound, but Byron used his chin to tilt her head back and then he was kissing his way down her cheek, her neck—right to that place below her ear that had always made her shiver with need, even before she'd been able to name what that need was.

She must have made a noise because the hand around her waist squeezed tighter and the hand between her legs stopped moving and Byron whispered against her skin, "Are you being quiet?"

She bit down even harder on her lip and nodded.

"If you can't be quiet," he went on, his words little louder than a breath, "I'll have to stop. Do you want me to stop?"

Before she could shake her head no, he scraped his teeth over that place. She managed to keep the moan locked down in the back of her throat, but there was no stopping the way her body shook for him.

She clutched at his forearm, the one that was moving against her. The muscles in his arms, thick and corded, moved under her hands. He'd always been so strong, moving with a coiled grace both in the kitchen and out of it. Whether he was handling his knives or handling her, he knew exactly what he was doing.

Her hips shifted down onto what was quite clearly a growing erection. "That's it," he murmured. His single finger made lazy little circles over the seam in her pants, which rubbed against her.

She could feel her muscles tightening, feel him bringing her closer and closer to an orgasm. She clung to Byron as his finger moved faster. Her legs started to lift in response to the strain of trying to keep quiet, but Byron used his elbow to keep them down. "Do you need to come?"

he whispered against her neck, his breath caressing her bare skin.

She nodded, struggling to breathe without uttering a sound. She wanted him inside of her, wanted to feel the weight of his body pinning her to the bed. She wanted to be his. God, how she wanted to be his.

"Say it," he said, and for the first time she heard how ragged his breathing was. "Tell me you need to come."

"I…" He pressed against her and held firm. Her body pulsed around his and she was afraid if she tried to talk, all she'd do was scream.

"Say it," Byron said again. "Say how much you need me to let you come."

"I need to come. *Please*."

Her words came out as a garbled moan, but at least Byron understood the gist of it. Without hesitation, he pressed and rubbed harder and faster until Leona came apart in his arms. Her back arched so far that, if he hadn't been holding her, she would have fallen right off his lap.

But Byron held her close as the waves of orgasm rolled through her. His touch against her sex slowed and then the pressure lightened until he was gently stroking her. When she fell forward against him, he curled both arms around her as she struggled to get her breathing back to normal. Byron stroked her hair, his arms strong around her. She could still feel his erection hard against her bottom. "You're so beautiful, babe. I want to do that to you every night."

"*Just* that?"

He laughed. "I'll get some new condoms or whatever you want to use, I'll cover it. Because *that*," he added, pausing only to kiss her on the lips, "was only the beginning."

Thirteen

Byron didn't have much to pack. He'd only taken a few suitcases with him to Europe. Everything else had gone into storage and it had stayed there when he'd moved back into the mansion.

The beds had been delivered yesterday. For some reason that was beyond his grasp getting mattresses only took a matter of days but the rest of the furniture Leona had ordered would take a couple of months. The baby furniture had also come quickly, but that was because Byron had refused to take no for an answer.

He'd arranged for the rest of his things to be delivered on Monday—his pots and pans and his knives—things that wouldn't have exactly cleared security for the flight over to Paris. He had some basic furniture that would fill the gaps until the rest was delivered.

He was loading his T-shirts into a bag when someone knocked on his bedroom door. He cringed—he didn't want to go around with Frances again. "Yes?"

But it wasn't Frances who poked her head into the room—it was Chadwick. "Hey," he said, looking stern. "Got a moment?"

It was hard to see how this visit would be a good thing. Chadwick had always been the cold, serious favorite of their father, so Byron hadn't even tried. He'd been George's favorite and that was what had mattered. As long as Byron didn't screw up any of Chadwick's plans, they existed in relative harmony.

Harmony that looked like it was about to be broken. "Sure. What's up?"

Chadwick shut the door behind him before he pulled out the chair at the antique writing desk and sat. *Not good*, Byron thought.

Chadwick watched as Byron tried to keep packing his bags. They'd never been close. Byron was eight years younger and Chadwick and Phillip—Byron's other, older half brother—had always been locked in a battle of wills with Matthew. Byron and Frances had been an afterthought, if anyone had thought of them at all.

Finally, Chadwick spoke. "Is there something you need to tell me?"

Damn. The only real question was who had talked— Frances or Matthew? Byron would put his money on Matthew. He ran the new Percheron Drafts with Chadwick. "Actually, I'm planning on getting married."

Chadwick's eyebrows jumped up, but he didn't say anything. He just waited.

Damn it all. Byron forced himself to keep a casual tone. "And I bought a house, so I'm going to be living there from now on." He tried to smile in a jokey manner. "I appreciate the hospitality, though."

Chadwick waved his hand dismissively. "Anytime. This will always be your home as much as mine."

Byron shrugged and started loading his socks into another bag. "So, the future bride," Chadwick went on. "Anyone we know?"

"Frances met her once. She's an old girlfriend. We broke up before I went to Europe but now that I'm back, we're together again." Which was true, in the strictest sense of the word. He was not lying. He was just omitting. Big difference.

A guilty thought hit him. That was what Leona would have thought—what she *had* thought.

Hell.

"I see," Chadwick said in a severe tone that made it clear he was disappointed with Byron's answer. Damn it, someone had squealed. "So the fact that our lawyers want to run a prenup with a *custody* agreement past me has no bearing on the situation?"

Oh, hell—the lawyers. On the bright side, at least Matthew hadn't ratted Byron out. But that probably just meant that he, Matthew and Frances were all in the doghouse for holding out on Chadwick.

"I didn't think it was relevant. I was merely taking steps to protect the family business."

"Ah." Chadwick lounged casually in the chair. He was wearing a suit, of course. Byron had trouble remembering a time when Chadwick hadn't worn suits. He probably even showered in the damn things. "Forgive me, but I fail to see how the fact that you've fathered a child is not relevant. For that matter, I don't see why you felt it was necessary to protect the family without actually telling any of us about it. Forewarned is forearmed."

Byron slumped onto the bed in defeat. "Fine. I didn't want to tell you because I knew you'd freak out on me."

"I do not 'freak out,'" Chadwick replied. "We're not children anymore. It's not like I'm going to ground you. If you have a situation and you think it might affect the family, you can tell me."

Byron had his doubts on that one. "I'm planning on marrying Leona Harper. She had our son six months ago. I only found out about him when I hired her to design the restaurant."

Byron wasn't actually sure what Chadwick freaking out would look like. As it was, he sat in the chair without moving—without even blinking. The only change was that the blood drained out of his face.

Byron waited. He supposed this was always going to happen—sooner or later Chadwick would have found out.

But he'd kept this part of himself secret for so long—with only Frances knowing anything about his entire relationship with Leona, both the good and the bad—that to announce it felt wrong.

"*Leona* Harper?" Chadwick actually sounded a little shaky. "As in, *Leon* Harper?"

"She's his oldest daughter. She has a younger sister, May."

Chadwick began to tap one finger against his pant leg faster and faster. "You're marrying into the Harper family?"

"I knew you'd freak out."

"I am absolutely not freaking out," Chadwick announced in a too-loud voice. "I'm just— She's an old girlfriend of yours?"

"We saw each other for about a year," Byron admitted. "She knew who I was, but I didn't make the connection until her father showed up at the restaurant where we both worked. I thought it was over. That's why I left."

"And the baby?"

"I didn't know she was pregnant when I left. She didn't know if I was coming back."

Chadwick suddenly leaned forward and dropped his head into his hands. "And just so I'm clear on the situation, this is the same woman who's designing our restaurant?"

"Yes." Byron had to make this sound better than it did, so he added, "She cut ties with her father shortly after we broke up. But she's concerned—legitimately, I think—that Harper might pull some stunt to try to get custody of the baby. That's why I want to get married as soon as possible—as soon as the ink is dry on the prenup."

"Harper," Chadwick muttered. "Of all the people in the world, you had to go fall for the old goat's daughter." His head popped up and he glared at Byron. "Do you have any

idea what that man will do when he finds out you're back?"
He shuddered.

"That's why we needed the prenup and that's why I
didn't tell anyone. We need to get married as quietly as
possible so Harper can't screw it up."

Chadwick gave him a mean look. "You haven't told anyone?"

"Well, Frances and Matthew. But that's it." Chadwick
continued to glare. "And Leona's sister, May. She's been
almost like a second mother to the boy. Percy."

Chadwick looked hurt. "I see. And you're sure about
this marriage?"

Byron had learned his lesson with Matthew. He didn't
pause. Pauses were dead giveaways. "I am."

Chadwick thought for a moment. "She didn't tell you
who she was? The first time?"

"No."

"And you trust her?"

Byron hesitated, but only for the blink of an eye. "That's
irrelevant. This is about making sure my son is never taken
away from me by anyone—especially Harper." And that?
That was the truth.

"I want to meet her and this child." If Chadwick had
freaked out—and Byron was sure that he'd deny it until his
dying breath—he was back to his normal, authoritative self.

"Not yet."

Chadwick gave him another harsh look. "Not even a
family dinner, with Serena and Catherine? I wouldn't try
to scare her."

Byron appreciated the sentiment, but he didn't miss the
way Chadwick said *try*. He explained, "She grew up listening to her father tell horror stories about Hardwick—how he
always took the children and left their mothers penniless.
She was afraid I would do the same thing to her."

"Have you considered that option?"

"No," he said forcefully. "She's *not* her father. She has no interest in the old feud and I have no interest in using our child as leverage. Whatever happened between Harper and our father is ancient history, as far as we're concerned. We just want to get on with our lives without Leon or Hardwick's ghost watching over our shoulders." Man, that sounded great. He wished he believed it 100 percent.

But he couldn't help thinking of the fact that, while Byron was making all sorts of truthful promises that he was here for the long haul, Leona had done very little in the way of reassuring him that she wasn't hiding anything else from him. First, she hadn't told him about her last name. Then she'd kept his son a secret. What else would she be willing to hide?

Unexpectedly, Chadwick cracked a smile. "We're all trying to exorcise Hardwick's ghost, aren't we?" He shook his head. "First Matthew gets married in secret, and now you. At least make sure your mom is there, okay?"

Byron felt himself deflate with relief. His mother had never been sure exactly where she stood with Chadwick, but the fact that he was thinking of Jeannie was kind, bordering on sweet. "Are you giving me your blessing?"

"It's not mine to give, really." He stood and put a hand on Byron's shoulder. "You always were the independent one, going off to do whatever you wanted, whenever you wanted to. I have to admit, I was jealous that you never got wrapped up in the family drama."

Byron stared up at his brother. Chadwick had been jealous of him? "Seriously?"

"Seriously. Trust me, trying to be like Hardwick was nothing but a recipe for disaster. You've got to do what you need to be happy." He grinned. "I think you might have figured that out sooner than the rest of us."

"What about you? Are you happy now?"

Chadwick gave Byron's shoulder a squeeze and then turned to the door. Before he opened it, he said, "I am. If you marry her—"

"I will."

"—then we'll stand behind you. You, Leona and the baby will have the full support of the Beaumont family if Harper tries anything."

Byron let out a breath he hadn't realized he'd been holding. Out of all his siblings, he'd figured Chadwick would have pushed the hardest to take a Beaumont baby away from anyone Harper. After all, Leon had come after Chadwick the hardest.

"Thanks, man. I appreciate it."

Chadwick gave him another uncharacteristic grin. It was so weird to see that man smiling regularly. "You're welcome. That's what family is for. And make sure we have your new address." He opened the door but paused. The smile fell away and once again, Byron was looking at a stone-cold businessman. "But don't make me regret it."

"I won't," Byron promised.

This time, there would be nothing to regret.

Leona was in a constant state of anxiety. The contractors were ripping apart the future kitchen of Caballo de Tiro, plumbers were roughing in bathrooms and the electricians were pulling old knob-and-tube wiring out of everything. Leona was in charge of overseeing all of it and every ten minutes someone had to ask her about something. While it was nice not to have to defer to Mr. Lutefisk all the time, the sheer weight of being responsible for every single decision wore her down.

Normally, when she got off work, she'd head home, change and do the mom thing with Percy. But this week she went to pick Percy up from either day care or from May and then she and the baby and Byron went wandering around cavernous furniture stores, where Byron deferred to her judgment in every instance.

When she was done with *that*, Leona headed back to the apartment where May would give her the coldest of cold shoulders. Safe to say, May did not approve of a single choice Leona was making at this point.

And of course, Leona was still getting up with Percy every night. He should have been over his ear infection by now, so Leona tried letting him cry himself back to sleep—only to have May burst into her room in the middle of the night and demand she do her job, accusing her of forgetting about her child in this rush to a new life with Byron.

By the time another two weeks had passed, Leona was little better than a high-functioning zombie. She had no idea what clothes she'd packed for her two weeks at Byron's house and if someone had asked her, she couldn't have told them what she'd packed for Percy, either. She wasn't even all that sure what day it was.

But what made it worse was that there hadn't been another time when she and Byron could be completely alone. The best she'd gotten was holding his hand while they debated the merits of this sofa versus that one.

She'd gone a year without having him in her bed on a regular basis. She should be able to handle another two weeks without him bringing her to orgasm.

But she couldn't. Not when she kept looking up from her work and catching him watching her with a small, suggestive smile on his face. Not when he'd brush a hand over her shoulder or across her lower back whenever he passed her. And certainly not when he'd lean in close and whisper in her ear how pretty she looked today, how much he was looking forward to the day she moved in.

He'd always watched her, always *seen* her in a way that no one else had. And that hadn't changed. And, just like it always had, knowing Byron was watching her—thinking of her—made her want him.

But desire was not love. It wasn't. Just because Byron had gone a couple of weeks without suddenly turning into a Beaumont and blaming her for everything didn't mean it wouldn't happen again. So what if he was being sweet and attentive? So what if he was helping out with Percy? So what if those little touches and glances sent her pulse pounding with need?

Her selfish physical wants were the least important thing going on right now. She wanted to believe this was the real Byron, the one she'd loved once. She wanted this to be a snapshot of what their lives together would be. She wanted more than a marriage in name only with separate bedrooms and separate lives.

She wanted to love him. Even more than that, she wanted him to love her.

And that was exactly the kind of thinking that had gotten her into this mess in the first place. She'd wanted a storybook love for the ages, one that ignored the distinctive realities of Harpers and Beaumonts and birth control.

So what she wanted did not matter. What she needed was a happy, stable home for her son and a viable backup plan for when Byron lost interest in her. She'd had a year with him the first time.

She didn't know how she was going to make it to Saturday without collapsing. Saturday was the day she would load Percy into the car and head for the big house in Littleton.

Somehow, Saturday arrived anyway. Leona wasn't completely sure how she'd held out this long. The fact of the matter was that she'd been too damned busy working to do much of anything but collapse into bed when she could. Even then, Byron haunted her dreams, always kissing her and touching her yet still leaving her unsatisfied. She didn't know what the female equivalent of blue balls was, but she had a *bad* case. The only thing that kept her from losing her mind was the fact that she'd probably already lost it and just didn't remember when.

They had separate bedrooms for a reason. A very good reason. She could not let him break her heart again and she especially could not let him break Percy's heart.

But did that mean she couldn't let him relieve a little of her tension? Or was that the shortest path back to pain?

She had the bags loaded into the car and a snack of raisins packed for Percy. All that was left was a final look around to make sure she hadn't forgotten anything.

And, of course, dealing with her sister. "I can't believe you're really going to *him*," May said from the couch where she was pouting.

Leona sighed. She didn't want to fight with May, but she was tired of being made to feel like a traitor. "You don't know him like I do, May."

"That's the understatement of the year."

Leona almost smiled at the sarcasm. "It won't be bad. I promise."

May looked sullen. It was not a flattering look on her. "But he already left you once. What happens when he bails again?"

"He won't." Leona said it with confidence, but she couldn't ignore the little voice that insidiously whispered the same doubt in the back of her head.

What would happen if he left again?

May shook her head. "Well, I guess I'll be here, waiting to help you pick up the pieces *again*."

Even though she had Percy on her hip, Leona impulsively hugged May. "I know, honey. That's why I love you." May sniffed and hugged her back. "You're going to be just fine."

"Sure." She did not sound enthusiastic about this pronouncement.

"Come out next week. Percy will want to see you. And so will I."

"Will *he* be there?"

"It's a big place. You won't have to see him if you don't want to."

May nodded and then kissed Percy's head. "All right."

And that was that. Leona walked out of the apartment that had been her home for a year without another look back. She loaded Percy into his car seat and began the long drive. For all her apprehension and resistance to the idea that she and Byron should live together, now that she was actually doing it, she had the oddest feeling of...

Of coming home.

That feeling only got stronger when she pulled into the drive. Percy had fallen asleep during the car ride. Byron came out to greet them.

"You're here," he said as if he didn't quite believe she'd actually made the trip.

"We're here," she agreed, getting out of the car. "He's just waking up."

"That gives me time to do this, then." The next thing Leona knew, Byron had wrapped his arms around her and kissed her so hard that it nearly bent her backward. There was nothing slow or sensuous about this kiss—this was pure heat. God, how she'd missed this.

When the kiss ended, Byron grinned down at her. "Been waiting to do that for weeks."

"Oh, my." She blinked in the bright sunshine and gave him a lazy smile. "You're the one who insisted on ordering furniture, you know."

"Don't remind me." He gave her a slightly less passionate kiss and then stood her back up on her feet. "Have you decided?"

She fought the urge to rub her eyes. "About what? I'm here."

Byron reached over and caressed her cheek. "About where you're sleeping tonight."

Her skin flushed hot under his touch. "Oh. That."

"Yeah, that." He grinned. He picked up her left hand and kissed it.

This shouldn't be a huge deal. After all, she was physically moving in with him at this exact moment in time and they'd already done *things*. And it would be a relief to have him take care of her. But could she do it? Could she resume a physical relationship with him without losing her heart a second time?

Byron stepped in closer and slid his hand around the back of her neck. The touch was possessive—and hot. "Tell me," he said, his voice dropping an octave, "that you want me in your bed tonight."

There was nothing between them except some easily removed clothing. Heat, languid and powerful, built between them and her body ached for his. As tired as she was, she couldn't wait to be awake in bed tonight. There were no contractors listening to every word they spoke, no siblings to cast judgment. Now, finally, it was just Leona and Byron and this need between them. Figuring out if she could trust him again would have to wait until the morning.

And Percy. The baby fussed sleepily. But Byron didn't let go of her, not just yet. Instead, he leaned forward and pressed a kiss right below her ear. "Tell me you want me, Leona."

"I do," she said breathlessly. His lips brushed against her sensitive skin and her whole body screamed out for his. She couldn't say no if she wanted to. "I want you in my bed. After Percy goes to sleep."

Byron released his hold on her, trailing his fingers down her neck and her shoulder. She shivered under his touch. "I'll get your bags. Welcome home, Leona."

Fourteen

For the first time in what felt like weeks, Leona took a day off. She did not think about supporting beams or color schemes. She did not have discussions that revolved around which toilet seats were more pleasing to the eye or which kind of leather made better chairs and couches. She didn't even defend her relationship to anyone.

Instead she spent the day playing with Percy on the playground set and eating the delicious lunch of roasted broccoli, sweet apple sausage and macaroni and cheese—homemade, not from a box—that Byron had fixed for them.

The afternoon nap didn't happen—Percy was far too excited by the new playground and the big house and Byron to even think about lying down for an hour and missing out on all the fun. Which meant that, by dinnertime, he was a tornado of unhappiness. Anything or anyone who touched him only made things worse.

"Is he sick?" Byron asked, the concern writ large on his face as Percy screamed and tried to twist out of his arms.

"No, just tired," Leona said, dodging a handful of applesauce. "He skipped his nap. This is what happens with no nap." She tried to grin at Byron, but the exhaustion and the screaming were wearing her down. "I've dealt with worse."

Byron paled as he looked down at the raging ball of adorable fury in his arms. "It gets *worse*?"

A flash of fear hit her. Was this it? Would Byron change his mind? Up until this point, he'd only seen the mostly calm, totally cute side of Percy. He hadn't been getting up at all hours of the night because Percy wouldn't stop crying and he'd never seen an epic meltdown like this.

She tried to steel herself. If he was going to back out, better to do it now. She hadn't even unpacked her bags. They could pick up and be gone inside of fifteen minutes.

The thought made her ache. Byron had made a promise and she couldn't bear the thought of him breaking another one. Especially not this one.

"Okay, yeah," Byron said, looking at her with wide eyes. She thought he might be on the verge of panic, but at least he was doing an admirable job of keeping it contained. "Naps. Every day. Got it."

She felt a real smile taking hold of her lips. "If we can get some food into his tummy, I can nurse him and he'll go to sleep early."

Byron's eyebrows lifted. "Will he sleep all night?"

"Probably not," she admitted. "But hopefully for a couple of hours."

Byron exhaled heavily, which momentarily distracted Percy from his howling. "And you've been doing this alone for *how* long?"

"Five months," she replied. "But I had May with me."

Despite the squalling baby, the flying baby food, the fact that she was exhausted—Byron gave her the kind of look that seared her with heat. "And now you have me."

She was really too tired and coated in too much applesauce to feel this attractive. But that's what Byron did to her. That was why she'd eventually agreed to go out with him, why she'd never been able to call it off despite knowing that it couldn't end well. He made her want to melt into his arms and let the rest of the world fall away.

And he knew it, too. His gaze intensified and he leaned forward. "An early bedtime, you say?"

The warmth spread from her lower back all the way up

to her face because she wanted to have him in every way possible. "Very early."

"Come on, Percy," Byron said, enthusiastically scooping up another spoonful of applesauce. "Yummy, yummy!"

An hour later, Percy had eaten enough applesauce to count, had a soothing bath with only minimal screaming, and was sleepily listening to Byron read him a story. Leona decided to try out the new shower—it was hard to feel sexy with sauce in her hair. The bathroom had a huge two-person whirlpool tub and a separate shower. Byron had gotten some thick white towels and the basics of toiletries. Good enough.

Leona shaved her legs and let the hot water run. Today had been much better than she had expected it to be, but still, a few hours of Percy screaming had taken its toll.

She knew she wasn't going to fall into a deep slumber the moment her head hit a pillow. All day long Byron had been giving her that look—the same look he'd been giving her for weeks now, only a hundred times more potent. That look said he couldn't wait to rip all her clothes off and do bad, bad things to her.

And truthfully? She wanted—needed—to have some bad things done to her. For a year, she'd locked down her sexuality. She'd been so danged busy—untangling her life and May's life from her parents' nose-to-the-grindstone rules, being pregnant, getting a job and being a mother. She hadn't had time to even think about sex. And who would she have had sex with, anyway?

A year's worth of sexual frustration threatened to swamp her. Being touched by Byron every two weeks or so was simply not enough.

But what was he going to do tonight? Somehow, she didn't think it would be a quick and satisfying coupling before they both passed out. As tired as she was, the anticipation was more than enough to keep her awake. Before, he'd been patient with her, kind and loving and he'd never pushed her to do anything wild or kinky—all of which had made her feel very safe.

But since he'd come back? Since he'd held her still on his lap and whispered into her ear that she couldn't make a noise until he demanded she tell him she wanted him to let her come?

That was something new. Something *bad*. And, God help her, it excited her.

She hurried through the rest of her shower and threw her clothes back on. She didn't even get her hair dried. When she got back to Percy's room—which was across the hall and down one doorway from the master suite—Byron was just finishing up another story. Leona smiled at the small pile of books that had grown next to the chair. "Sorry," she murmured. At the sound of her voice, Percy twisted and started to fuss.

"We're fine," Byron assured her as he stood. "Have a good shower?"

She nodded, feeling the water drip off the ends of her short hair. When she took her seat, Byron placed Percy back in her arms and whispered, "I'll be right back."

Which turned out not to be the entire truth. The minutes passed slowly as Percy nursed himself into an epic milk coma and she continued to think.

What was she doing with Byron? She'd made this big fuss—this promise to herself—that there would be separate bedrooms. That she would not fall into his arms again.

And yet, Byron had basically reduced her to a quivering mass of need in the middle of the driveway. There'd been a time when she'd coveted the overnights in Byron's bed. It had felt like the ultimate act of rebellion—not going home to her father's house at the end of a date, but curling up under the covers with Byron and knowing she would have to come up with some kind of believable lie to cover the fact that she was sleeping with a man—and a Beaumont at that.

Oh, the lies she'd told to be with Byron. She'd claimed she'd had to work late, that a friend of hers had asked her out to the bars and gotten too drunk to get home safely, that the roads were bad. Whatever she could make sound believable so her father wouldn't start sniffing around.

Maybe she'd known it wouldn't last. Byron would find out, or her father would—it was only a matter of time. She wanted to think that she'd been preparing for the confrontation, that she would have stood up for herself and for Byron and finally shaken her father off.

But then Percy had happened.

She looked down at her sweet baby boy, touching his face. She could marry Byron. It wouldn't guarantee that they'd live happily ever after, necessarily, but it was an important step in cementing their status as a family. And it'd make it that much harder for her father to steamroller his way back into her life.

Yes, she could marry Byron. That wasn't the question. The question was, did she want to?

Would you have married me, if I'd asked a year ago?

That's what Byron had wanted to know. And she hadn't answered him.

But deep down, she knew. She knew that, had he asked—if she'd been carrying his child and he'd asked her to be his forever—she would have said *yes*.

When Byron appeared in the doorway, Leona startled and glanced at the clock. It'd been over twenty minutes since he'd left. She started to get up—Percy was pretty passed out—but Byron motioned for her to sit. Grinning, he stood and watched as Leona finished up and patted Percy on the back. What a change from the first time he'd seen her do this, when he'd fled to the kitchen to make applesauce.

She carefully put Percy into his new crib. The baby was

so passed out he didn't even stir. *Sleep, sweetie*, Leona prayed. *Sleep for Mommy and Daddy.*

Byron came in to stand next to her, his arm around her shoulders. There was an intimacy to the moment. For the first time since Byron had walked back into her life, she truly felt they were in this together. It was such a relief that she wrapped her arm around his waist and held him tight.

Byron checked to make sure the baby monitor was on and then whispered in her ear, "Come with me."

Desire spiked through her. Only Byron could to that to her—turn her on with three little words.

He led her out of the bedroom and up the hall to their bedroom. How weird was that? *Their* bedroom. She'd slept over at his place, a small apartment in an exclusive downtown complex, back when they'd been dating. But that'd been his. She'd always had her own room, her own bed to go back to.

Then the room registered. Byron had been busy while she'd been with Percy. The drapes were closed and the room was alight with the soft glow of candles, easily fifteen or twenty. Where had he gotten so many candles? They were on the mantel over the fireplace, on the dressers, and contained in tall glass jars on the night tables. The whole room glowed. It was one of the more romantic things she'd ever seen.

"Wow," she said. "This is beautiful."

"I'm glad you like it. Turn around."

She gave him a look, but it had no effect on him. Instead, he leaned in close enough to kiss her. But he didn't. He waited, his gaze searching her face.

The anticipation sending spikes of need through her body ratcheted up another notch. She turned around.

"I wanted to do this the other night," he said, pulling her shirt over her head and pushing her pants down so quickly that she barely had time to register that she was in nothing but her panties.

"What?" she asked, nervousness and excitement fighting for control over her stomach. The fact of the matter was, she didn't know what he was going to do to her. But she was pretty sure she was going to like it.

Then the piece of black silk slipped over her eyes.

Fear flashed through her, temporarily pushing the anticipation into panic. "Byron?"

The tips of his fingers traced the contours of her back, soft and gentle. "I just want you to feel this," he said, his voice right against her ear. His breath warmed her skin. "I won't do anything you don't want me to," he promised as he brushed her damp hair away from her neck. His fingers moved over her shoulder—the lightest of touches that held so much promise. Her skin broke out in goose bumps. "If you want me to stop, I will."

She felt exposed. She couldn't see what Byron was doing and she wasn't sure what, exactly, he wanted to do. Essentially, she was at his mercy.

He seemed to know what she was thinking. "Do you trust me?" She heard rustling.

Did she?

Before, when they'd become lovers, he'd taken his time with her. She'd been the kind of inexperienced that only virgins could pull off, but Byron had never rushed her. Once, they'd been making out hot and heavy on his couch. He'd gotten her top off and his shirt, too and Leona had finally decided to go through with it—right until he'd unbuttoned her pants. Then she'd had this moment of terror that he was a Beaumont and she was a Harper and what the hell was she thinking?

So she'd put the brakes on. Byron had hovered over her, his eyes closed and his chest heaving with effort and she'd panicked because she'd never allowed herself to get into this kind of situation, never before been this vulnerable with a man, especially not a Beaumont. Beaumonts were known for their womanizing ways—would that include forcing the issue?

And then he'd sat back and put on his shirt. And when she'd gotten dressed again, he'd pulled her into his arms and kissed her sweetly and asked what she wanted to do tomorrow night. There'd been no guilt, no pressure. She'd felt warm and safe and loved then.

Just like she felt now.

"Yes," she told him. "I trust you."

"Good," he said. He led her over to the massive king-size bed and said, "Lie down on your stomach."

Even though she couldn't see him behind her blindfold, Leona cocked an eyebrow at him. "Please," he added. She did as he requested. "Scoot a little more toward the middle," he instructed. But he didn't get on the bed, either.

"When do I get to know what it is you've got planned with all these candles and this blindfold?"

He chuckled. Then she felt the mattress shift as Byron kneed onto the bed. She could feel him getting closer, feel the warmth of his breath against her ear. "Very soon, babe. Don't tell me the anticipation isn't driving you crazy."

She shifted her hips, trying to take the pressure off the one place in particular where the anticipation was, in fact, driving her completely nuts. "All right, I won't tell you then. I will tell you, however, that you're being a tease."

She felt the bed shift under him as he moved. She couldn't help it—she tensed. "I consider it turnabout for fair play. Do you know what it did to me to watch you for the past two weeks?" He straddled her legs and said, "Lotion," which her brain hadn't quite made sense of when suddenly there was warm liquid being slicked onto her bare back.

She tensed. "Just massage lotion," Byron repeated.

There was a pause, then his strong hands began to work over her body.

"*This* is what you wanted to do the other night?" she murmured into the pillows as he found a knot in her shoulders and began to rub. "Oh, that feels good."

"I did," he said, his voice thick. "You've been pulling some long days and long nights and a three-minute shoulder rub didn't seem enough. I wanted to take care of you.

"You've changed," he went on. "You were always so quiet, back when you started at the restaurant. For a hostess, you always seemed almost…afraid of people. Like you had to force yourself to smile at them. It was like you didn't want to be noticed."

Leona relaxed under his touch. "I didn't, at first. But you noticed me anyway."

"I did," he agreed, attacking a particularly tight knot in her shoulders. She heard the click of the cap, then he applied more lotion. "I could see then that there was something else going on with you, under the surface. And these past few weeks? Watching you manage the construction and juggle everything? It's been like…" Unexpectedly, he leaned forward and kissed her in the middle of the back. "It's been like watching the woman I always knew was there finally emerging. You're strong and confident and decisive. And I like it."

Oh, my. Even though she still had the silk tied around her eyes, she turned her head to look back at him. "You do?"

This time, when he leaned down, his whole chest pressed against her back. He'd taken off his shirt, she realized when his bare skin came into full contact with hers. "I do. You were always different with me—you relaxed and you were sharp and snarky and I liked it. I liked you." His hands moved over her arms, stretching them out against the bed. "But after a while, it hurt me to watch the woman I loved retreat behind that wall of willing invisibility. I wanted…"

He sighed and pushed himself into a sitting position. This time, instead of kneading her shoulders, he trailed his fingers up and down her back in long, sure strokes. "I wanted you to be free enough to be yourself in the daylight, not just at night with me."

She had no reply for that. None at all. Was that how he'd seen her? Someone trapped behind a wall of subservience, someone dying to break free? She'd never thought of herself in those explicit terms—but had Byron been wrong? He'd been her first love, her first rebellion—and the reason she'd left behind a toxic home life when she couldn't bear the thought of her father treating her baby like he treated everyone else.

"I didn't have to *be* anyone else when I was with you," she said in a quiet voice. "That's why I couldn't stay away from you."

Byron's strong hands were suddenly stroking down until he found the waistband of her panties. He traced the edge for a moment before his hands moved to her thighs. Then he pushed his fingers under the thin cotton fabric. "I'm glad you couldn't," he said as he gripped her bottom.

Leona sucked in air as he massaged her. There was something else in his touch, something that bordered on possessive. *"Oh,"* she moaned as he dug the pads of his fingers into her skin.

She wasn't sure she could relax, not with him working on her like this. The more he loosened up the muscles in her back, the more tense other things seemed to get. The tension inside of her coiled down, tighter and tighter, until she was having trouble keeping her hips still.

Just when she was sure she couldn't take much more, he scooted up. She could feel his erection now, pressing into her bottom, hot and hard and for her. She thought he'd do something else, but instead he went back to work on her shoulders.

All she could do was moan when he hit a particularly tense spot. She let go of the stress of the past few weeks. Her body felt warm and limp under his touch.

He moved again and she expected more oil, but instead he leaned down and kissed her in the middle of her upper back. "How are you doing?"

"Better," she whispered as his mouth moved lower and he trailed kisses down her spine.

She didn't know what he would do next and he was clearly in no hurry to do it. By the time he sat back up and his hands left her body again, she was on the verge of begging for release. Anything he wanted—loud, quiet—anything, as long as he made her come.

When the oil dripped onto the backs of her legs, she jumped. "Easy," he murmured, spreading the oil up her legs and under the edge of her panties. "I'm taking care of you."

"Byron," she moaned, but she didn't know if she was begging or not.

His slick fingers moved in, stroking her sex until this time, she couldn't lie still. She writhed against the bed, the release she needed so close but not there yet. "Please," she moaned.

"You like that?" he asked, his voice ragged as he stroked in and out.

"Yes," she whispered. He slipped a second finger inside of her and her hips bucked from the pressure. "Oh, *Byron*."

He pulled her panties to one side and kissed the skin he'd exposed. She couldn't help the low moan that escaped her lips as he stroked and kissed her. She fisted her hands in the covers, desperate to hold herself down. "I can't—I can't," she gasped out when he hit just the right spot. A sensation of light and heat shivered through her. The pressure was so good, so intense—she couldn't take it. "Please, Byron. *Please*."

"Yeah," he said gruffly. "You tell me what you want and

let me do everything else. Let me take care of you." Then he bit down on her bottom—not hard, but more than enough to send spikes of pleasure and pain crashing through her body. She moaned as her body writhed under his touch.

"Tell me," he said in a sterner voice.

"I need you." It came out almost as a squeak.

She felt his teeth on her again, pushing those spikes of desire higher into her stomach. "Be specific."

If she hadn't been so turned on, she would have laughed. Who could be specific at a time like this? But as it was, she could barely speak enough to say, "I need you inside of me."

Even though she couldn't see him, she could feel his grin against her skin. "Wait a second—don't move."

Then he pulled away from her—his body, his fingers, his hands. She didn't want to lose his touch. But he'd told her not to move, so she didn't.

Then she heard a crinkle that she guessed went with the opening of a condom. "That's a new one, right?"

"Bought them yesterday. The massage lotion is compatible."

That made her smile. "You planned ahead."

"I can't help it if I can't stop thinking about you. Here." The pillows around her head were pulled away. Then he guided her hips up and shoved the pillows underneath. His hands lingered on her skin. "Okay?"

She couldn't speak—she could only nod. He had her so turned on that it took everything she had to lie still and wait for his next touch.

It came soon enough. He grabbed her panties and roughly yanked them down. Then he was against her. "I'm going to take good care of you, Leona," was the last thing she heard him say before he thrust into her.

She hadn't allowed herself to miss this when he'd been gone. She hadn't had the time to think back to the days when Byron would make love to her and it would take her away from everything—the stress of the late-night job, the tension at home, the fact that she was sleeping with the enemy.

But now that she had him back, she turned those memories loose. They wove themselves around her, mingling with how Byron was gripping her hips, how he was thrusting in with hard, sure strokes. "Leona," he groaned over and over again. "*My* Leona."

"Yes, *yes*," was the only sound she could make. The noise hissed out of her with every thrust as Byron took her again and again. She was his—she always had been and she saw clearly now that she always would be.

She couldn't see him, but she could feel every single thing he was doing to her. The way his fingers dug into her skin, pulling her back into him. The way he filled her over and over, pushing her to the brink of orgasm without letting her fall down the other side. The grunting noises that built in pitch until he was nearly shouting her name.

Then he relinquished his hold on her hips and fell forward onto her. His teeth scraped along her back but that feeling was quickly blotted out as he reached around and pressed against the hot little button of her sex. "Come for me," he ordered, thrusting and pressing and nibbling until the tension in her body finally, finally snapped. Her muscles tightened almost to the point of pain as she screamed her orgasm into the bed.

"Oh, God," Byron grunted, slamming his hips against her twice more before freezing. "Oh, *babe*."

The orgasm left her completely wrung out and panting. Byron collapsed onto her, his chest hot against her back.

"I want to see you," she said in a shaky voice.

The blindfold was pulled away. Even though the candlelight was dim, she still blinked. Then Byron slid off and pulled her into his arms. "Wasn't too much, was it?" he murmured into her hair.

"Just right," she replied, curling against him and tracing small circles against his chest. Now that the orgasm and anticipation and massage had all run together, she was having trouble keeping her eyes open. They lay there for a few moments, the only sounds in the room the beating of their hearts and the occasional pop of a candle burning.

He'd put her first. He'd taken care of her, just like he'd said he would. He hadn't run screaming earlier when Percy melted down.

Maybe…maybe this would work. Maybe she could marry him and they could be a family and he would love her. Maybe she should allow herself to hope that she'd get everything she ever wanted.

And then he spoke and ruined it.

"If only you'd been honest with me from the start," he said with a heavy sigh, "it could have been like this for the past year. We would have found a way to make it work."

The insult was worse than any slap in the face. "If *I'd* been honest?"

She was up and moving, off the bed and out the door before he could blink. "Leona? Hey—Leona!"

But she was already out of the room, heading down the hall. "If *you* hadn't left, Byron, maybe we could have made it work," she said, knowing he was right behind her. "But you keep making this all my fault, and I'm not going to take it anymore. You're always going to hold that over my head like a sword, aren't you? Because God forbid I try to make up for my mistakes. God forbid we try to get past it. I'll always be the Harper who lied to you, won't I?" With that, she slammed the door to her room and locked the lock.

"For God's sake, Leona," he growled from the other side of the door. The door handle jiggled. "Damn it, Leona!" No doubt he thought that, because he'd bought the house he could walk right into any room he chose.

"It's fine. I'm fine. Thank you for the massage. Good night, Byron."

"I'm not done with you yet," she heard him say on the other side of the door. "But we can talk in the morning. Get some sleep."

No, of course he wasn't done with her.

Yet.

But he would be. Sooner or later, he would be.

Fifteen

When Leona's phone rang, she was juggling an extremely fussy child, a fever-relieving liquid, some electrolyte solution, her wallet and...a pregnancy test.

She was late. Byron hadn't asked about her "schedule" since she'd moved into the house, but she was officially, seriously Late with a capital _L_.

She glanced at her phone and saw that it was Byron. For the past few days, he'd been trying to apologize to her, but she wasn't listening. She sent the call to voice mail, where it could join all the other messages he'd left her.

Percy kicked it up to eleven and began to howl. The other people in line were giving her dirty looks, as if she'd made the baby cry on purpose. Ugh. She needed to get him home.

She paid for her stuff, ignoring the clerk's smirk between her, the pregnancy test and the screaming child, and then got Percy buckled into the car. At least they were only a few minutes from home, she thought as she got stuck at a light. Percy was not a happy camper back there. "Baby, it's okay," she tried to say in a soothing voice over the screaming. "We'll go home and watch Grover and have something to drink, okay?"

Percy screamed even louder.

Leona made it home in record time. Somehow, she got the baby and her things out of the car on the first shot. "Poor baby," she soothed, setting everything down just inside the door. "Let's get you into some comfy jammies."

Percy let her change him. At some point, he quieted

down. His eyelids began to drift shut. Leona felt his head—warm, but not dangerously hot. "Poor baby," she whispered again, settling into the glider to nurse him. He wasn't feeling good and now he'd exhausted himself with all the crying. If she got lucky, he'd fall asleep for a long time. And if she wasn't lucky, well—he'd be up in an hour, screaming because his ears hurt.

From deep inside the house, she heard her phone chime again. If she'd had the damn thing on her, she would have glared at it. There was no way in heck she was going to jostle Percy just to check her messages.

After five minutes, Percy was out. All that screaming, she thought as she lowered him into the crib. She'd have to wait until he woke up again before she'd be able to dose him.

Closing his door behind her, she hurried downstairs. She knew she couldn't keep ignoring her phone—especially not if it were Mr. Lutefisk, wanting an update on the restaurant project.

But she desperately wanted to take the pregnancy test now, before Byron got home. She needed to know. The past month she'd spent forcibly not thinking about the chance that she was pregnant again? Those days were gone. Suddenly, she needed to know right now.

After all, she reasoned as she hurried to the bathroom, it was only a few more days until Saturday—the official end of the two-week trial run of living with Byron. He'd promised he'd ask her to marry him after those scant fourteen days and she still had no idea what she'd say. They were barely speaking. Percy was thriving, though, and watching Byron and the baby together made her wonder why she was fighting this so hard.

And then Byron would attempt another apology that always seemed to hit upon the fact that she hadn't told him about her father and she was mad all over again.

But if there were other factors at play, she wanted to know before she told him yes or no. If she were pregnant again, she would have to say yes. They would have to work harder to be a family, even if they couldn't love each other like they used to.

She carefully peed on the little stick and set it aside, then washed her hands. The instructions said she had to wait five minutes. After all this time, five minutes felt like way too long.

She got her phone. Sure enough, Mr. Lutefisk had called. She had to tell him that she might not be on the job tomorrow, if Percy didn't miraculously recover.

She called her boss while pacing the length of the first floor. She informed him of the situation and paused in front of the room that was now known as her office. She hung up and just stared at the space.

Her office. If she wanted to start her own design business.

Maybe after she got this job finished and things were settled with Byron, she'd strike out on her own. If she were expecting again, working from home might be just the thing. After all, she'd been completely in charge of this restaurant design. She had what it took to be her own boss now. And that prospect was thrilling.

But...that would mean she'd agreed to stay with Byron. Marry him.

Not necessarily, she thought. She could always hang out a shingle somewhere else. Sure, the rent for an office would put a strain on her finances, but she wouldn't be dependent on Byron.

She checked the time. Close enough to five minutes had passed. She hurried back to the bathroom and grabbed the stick.

Pregnant, it said in an impersonal digital font.

"Oh, God." She leaned against the sink as confused

emotions ran roughshod over her. There was the momentary panic that was familiar—the feeling that she'd messed up again.

Why couldn't she keep her hands off him? Why couldn't she stay away from the one man who seemingly could impregnate her just by looking at her? God, this complicated everything. Now Byron would push even harder for her to marry him and for them to live as a family—and if he abandoned her a second time, then where would she be?

She forced herself to breathe. She'd figured it out once before, and that had been without Byron. This time, she had no intention of letting him slip off into the night without at least paying child support. She was not the same scared girl she'd once been. She was an independent woman who could take care of her family. She could be a little freaked out by being pregnant—that was her prerogative. But she could do this. Alone, if she had to.

The doorbell rang, jolting her out of her thoughts. She mentally cursed at the bell, the phone—all the things that seemed hell-bent on waking up her sick child. Quickly, she shoved the pregnancy test into the box and the box to the bottom of the trash can. She would tell Byron, she decided, but she needed a plan for how to handle the marriage proposal she knew he'd make when she did. Until then, that little stick did not exist to the rest of the world.

"Yes?" she said, quickly throwing open the door in the hopes that whoever was out there wasn't about to ring the doorbell again.

"And hello to you, too," May said, taking a step back.

"Oh! May! You're here!"

"Clearly." She looked around again, as if she expected Byron to jump out of the bushes. "Is he home?"

"No, he's still at the restaurant, probably for another hour. Why didn't you call? Percy's fighting off another ear infection. I just got him down."

May looked guilty. "I'm sorry, Leona. I know I said I'd come out on the weekend, but I wanted to make sure you were okay." She shot Leona a weak smile. "I've been worried about you and Percy."

Leona sighed. "Come in, hon. I'm glad to see you. How have classes been?"

She showed May around the house and made tea. They discussed May's classes and what she was going to register for next semester. It was nice to talk to her sister without the entire conversation revolving around Percy's ear infections or why Byron was a bad idea.

"This is really nice," May said, looking out the kitchen windows. She looked wistful.

"There's plenty of room here for you." Maybe it wasn't the best idea to make the offer. But she couldn't deny that she still wanted to make sure that her baby sister was okay. May might not approve of her relationship with Byron but Leona couldn't turn her back on her sister—not after what they'd been through.

"I know." For once, she didn't sound pissy about it. "You've done so much for me…I think it's time for me to try and be on my own, you know?"

"I'll always be here for you," Leona said, squeezing May's hand. "This thing with Byron doesn't change that."

Then May turned to her, a tight look on her face. "Are you going to marry him?"

"I think so," Leona said. "I think he's going to stay."

She just wished she felt more confident about that—about all of it. She just wished he could look at her, touch her, without thinking about how she'd withheld her family's name from him.

May decided she wanted to be gone before Byron got home so, after using the bathroom, she hugged Leona and snuck into Percy's room to press a kiss to his little head. "I'll see you soon," she said as she walked out the door and Leona couldn't help but think there was something odd about May's voice.

The bathroom? Leona hurried to check the trash can, but the pregnancy test was still safely hidden in the bottom. She dug it back out and hid the little stick in her bedroom, where Byron wouldn't accidentally find it.

The weight of the day hit her hard and she sagged onto her bed. She was pregnant again. She had Percy to think of. She could not hide this pregnancy from Byron—she wouldn't.

They would work harder to get past what had happened a year ago, that was all. She had to do it for the children. And if they couldn't get past it...

No. They would. They had to. Otherwise, she'd be entering into a marriage that guaranteed pain and heartache and she couldn't do that, even if it might be best for the children. He was so good with Percy. She knew Byron would be a great father with the new baby, too.

Yes, he would be a wonderful father—loving, hands-on, full of laughter and stories. But what about her? He wouldn't take her children away from her, would he? He wouldn't make her love him only to use that against her time and time again—would he?

She couldn't believe that he would. She was going to have to take it on faith that he was not one of *those* Beaumonts, just like she wasn't one of *those* Harpers.

The next time he apologized, she'd listen. And she'd apologize, too. She would tell him about the pregnancy test. And she would accept his ring.

They had to find a way to make this work.

Leona still wasn't talking to him, but that wasn't anything new. What was new was how he'd look up from playing with Percy and catch her staring at him. Instead of the simmering anger he'd come to expect from her, there was something different in her eyes. It almost looked like fear.

For the life of him, he didn't know what she was afraid of. Yes, he'd said the wrong damn thing after the last time they'd had sex. Their messy past was not good pillow talk.

But where were his reassurances? Where were her promises that she wouldn't lie to him again—not even by omission? Where were his guarantees that she wasn't keeping her father up-to-date on his every move?

Nowhere, that's where. Instead, there was just silence.

That didn't matter, he told himself. So what if she rebuffed his apologies? So what if she rebuffed his advances? What really mattered was that every night he came home to his son. Every night, he made dinner and helped bathe his son and read bedtime stories and got up in the night with him. What mattered was that they'd scheduled an appointment with the doctor for getting tubes in Percy's ears.

Byron could live without Leona. He'd done so for a year. But he would not allow her to guilt him out of Percy's life. He was here to stay and the sooner she accepted that, the better it'd be for all of them.

Yeah, right.

That night, after he handed Percy off to her so she could do the nightly nursing, Leona said, "I need to talk to you," in a quiet, serious voice.

He looked at her but she didn't elaborate. "I'll be in the kitchen?"

She nodded.

His heart sank. The fear in her eyes, the serious voice—this wasn't a good thing.

He started making the cookies before he even realized he was doing it. What would she say? That she'd decided this wouldn't work? That she was leaving in the morning? Was that why she'd looked so afraid?

He almost couldn't bear it as he creamed the sugar. She'd decided this trial wouldn't work. What else could it be?

By the time she slipped into the kitchen, he was angry. "What?" he demanded, bracing himself for the worst.

"It's—" Here she paused. "It's been two weeks," she finished. He could tell how nervous she was and that fact only made him more upset.

He slammed the bowl down. "I knew you wouldn't stay. Just tell me why, okay? Because it can't have been what I said after we had sex. I've tried to apologize and you won't have any of it."

"That's not—"

"Then what is it?"

She exhaled hard, her eyes narrowing to little slits. "Why does this have to be so hard, Byron?"

"I don't know, Leona. Why don't you tell me?" When she didn't have an immediate response, he said, "You can go if you want, but I won't let you take Percy."

The words hit her like a body blow—he saw her curl forward, as if he'd physically hit her in the stomach. For a second, he thought she was going to start crying.

But then she straightened up, her eyes watery but mad. So damn mad—at him. "You promised me you weren't going to punish me by taking him away from me."

"I can't live without my son."

"I can't live without *our* son," she shot back. "You can keep trying to get rid of me so you can claim you didn't abandon me a second time, but it won't work. I'm not leaving my baby."

At least, that's what he thought she said as she turned and stomped off. But it almost sounded like she'd said something else there—babies?

No, he'd heard wrong. She hadn't said anything else about the one night the condom had broke.

Unless she was lying to him.

Again.

Byron was going to beat these damned pot racks into submission. He was also going to put together the storage racks and if things went according to plan, he'd have all of those things done before the sous chef candidate he was supposed to interview arrived at four.

The kitchen was taking shape. They'd kept the commercial-grade six-burner stove, but the rest of the appliances—the ovens, the stoves, the refrigerators and freezers—were all on order and scheduled to be delivered within the next three weeks. Once they had those and the rest of the furniture, it'd really begin to feel like a restaurant.

It was nice that something in his life was coming together. The fight with Leona from last night was still fresh in his mind. He had to go home and face her today—she'd stayed home with Percy—and he didn't know how he was going to do that.

He had been an idiot to think that he could live with her without being able to trust her. More than that, he was an idiot for thinking that, somehow, living with her without complete trust would be different for them than it'd been for his parents.

This experiment had failed. They were broken as a couple and there was no putting them back together.

But even thinking that made him hurt. Damn it all, he didn't want to give up on her, on them.

Finally, after some rather loud cussing, Byron got the pot rack screwed to the wall. He was just about to grab the second one when he heard, "Hello?" from the front of the restaurant.

"Hello!" he called back. "I'm in the kitchen!" He grabbed a rag to wipe his hands and glanced at his phone—

3:45 p.m. Either the sous chef was early or the landscapers had an issue.

The moment he crossed the threshold from the kitchen into the restaurant, he sensed something was wrong. The sous chef would have come alone. The landscapers had all been wearing matching work outfits emblazoned with their company logo.

Instead, two very large men in very tailored suits stood just inside the restaurant so they blocked out the afternoon sunlight that filtered through the open door. With their thick necks, matching buzz cuts and wraparound sunglasses, they looked like what they probably were—hired muscle.

In front of them stood a thin man in an even nicer suit. His long face and hunched shoulders made him look small, at least compared with the bruisers standing behind him.

Byron came to a quick halt. Out of the corner of his eye, he saw the landscapers' shadows moving in front of the casement windows. Hopefully, if there was trouble—and that's exactly what it looked like was about to happen—the crew would come to his aid. Otherwise, his best hope was to get back to the kitchen and grab the hammers and screwdrivers. A man could do a lot of damage with a hammer.

"Help you?" he asked warily.

"Byron Beaumont?" the smaller man said with obvious distaste.

"Who wants to know?"

One of the bruisers behind the smaller man made a snorting noise.

"Is he here?" The thin, reedy voice came from behind the muscle. The small man stepped to the side just as a gleaming silver-and-black walking stick poked between the bruisers, shoving them aside.

And there he was, Leon Harper in the flesh. He looked older than Byron remembered him, especially when he leaned on the walking stick. The lines around his eyes were deeper. But there was no mistaking him for any other elderly man in a natty suit.

Byron blinked, hoping and praying that he'd fallen off the ladder or dropped the pot rack on his head—anything that could produce a hallucination as unwanted as this.

But no. He knew this was no nightmare—especially not when Leon Harper got a good look at him and smiled viciously. It was the exact same smile he'd given Byron when he'd placed Leona into the family car and announced that Byron would never have his daughter. It was the smile of certain victory.

It was the smile of evil.

"Oh, that's him, all right. I'd recognize the Beaumont spawn anywhere," he said to the thin man. "I hear you're back—and with *my* daughter."

The way he said it—emphasizing *my* so heavily—made Byron's skin crawl. There was no love in the old man's voice. Just ownership. "And that's your business how?"

Harper clucked. "You should have stayed away from her, boy. I was content to let her have the child just so long as you didn't have it—or her."

It? Was this shell of a man seriously referring to Byron's son as an *it*? Oh, hell, *no*. The hairs on the back of Byron's neck stood at attention. Yeah, a man could do a lot of damage with a hammer.

But he knew better than to rise to the bait. Growing up in Hardwick's household had taught Byron how to not get sucked into a fight. When a blowhard old man desperately wanted you to fight back, the only way to win—and drive him nuts—was to stay silent.

So that's what Byron did. He still had the rag in his hand, so he casually wound it around his knuckles. There was no way he could take out the bruisers, but if he could get a good shot at Harper...

Well, either Harper would sue him back into the Stone

Age or Byron would be locked up for involuntary man-slaughter. Possibly both.

But it might be worth it, he decided, if it kept his family free from the clutches of this vindictive old rat.

Harper waited for a moment. His eyes hardened in displeasure at Byron's lack of engagement, but then he smiled widely again. He nodded to the thin man, who moved toward Byron and held out a thick envelope.

"Since my daughter has sought to further blemish the proud Harper name by continuing her association with the likes of *you*," the old rat went on as Byron refused to take the envelope from the thin man, "I have come to the unavoidable conclusion that she must not be operating in her right mind. I'm having her declared unfit to be a mother and petitioning the state for custody."

"You're insane," Byron sputtered before he could keep his mouth shut.

The response was exactly what Harper was looking for. "Me?" He tried to look innocent, but he clearly didn't know how to do that. He probably hadn't been innocent in a good eighty years. "I'm just a concerned father worried about his daughter and the environment in which she's raising my grandchildren."

"You can't claim custody of Percy. I'm his father. And I only have one child with Leona."

Harper clucked. "Do you, now? An absentee father who shows up only long enough to impregnate her again? That doesn't give you a particularly strong leg to stand upon, you realize." He buffed his fingernails on his suit jacket and looked at them as if they were by far the most interesting things in the room.

"She's not pregnant."

"Isn't she?" Harper smiled, revealing graying teeth that matched his graying hair. Byron's gut clenched. She *had* said *babies* last night. "Or maybe she's just not telling you about it. Because she is most certainly pregnant. And I give you my word—you'll never see that child. Never." He motioned toward the lawyer. "My counsel has prepared an airtight case."

The thin man held out the envelope again and this time, Byron snatched it irritably. "You won't win."

"There's where you're wrong," Harper intoned in all seriousness. "I *always* win, boy."

He shouldn't—but he couldn't help himself. He knew there was one chink in Harper's self-righteous armor, and a huge, gaping chink at that. If the old rat was going to make Byron suffer, the least he could do was return the favor. "I'll be sure to pass that along to your first wife."

Harper stiffened, murder in his eyes. One of the bruisers took a step forward, but Harper whipped his cane up and held the man back. "Flippant, boy." Hate dripped off his every word. "Very *flippant*."

It felt good to score a hit against the old man. Leon Harper had once taken everything Byron held dear. No way Byron would let the old man win a second time. No way in hell.

"Trying to take my son away from me won't even the score, Harper. And when you lose, you'll never see the boy again."

Harper's thin lips twitched in satisfaction. "I might say the same to you. You're holding a petition to sever your paternal rights." Byron's glare bounced uselessly off the old man. "Unless you sign," Harper went on, clearly enjoying himself, "your *flippant* little tale of impregnating my daughter and then abandoning her will be front-page news. Doctors testifying to her mental state will give lengthy interviews and as for you?" His grin sharpened. "By the time I'm done with you, boy, I'll have run you, the entire Beaumont clan and this godforsaken beer company into the ground. You have a week. Good day." He turned, the bruisers parting for the old man to pass.

"I won't let you anywhere near her or my son, *old man*." Byron put as much into those words as he could because, as far as he was concerned, that's all Leon Harper was. An impotent old man with too much free time and too many lawyers kowtowing to him.

Harper paused and then slowly turned around, a smug smile distorting the features of his bitter face. "Is that so? And just who do you think called me in the first place?" He chuckled to himself and damn it all, Byron was too stunned to even come up with a stinging parting shot.

All he could do was stand there and watch as Harper and his various lackeys shuffled out.

No. He couldn't believe it—he wouldn't. Even if she'd decided that she was better off as a single parent living with her sister, she wouldn't have gone crawling back to Leon Harper. She might hate him, but she cared too much for Percy to let her father do her dirty work. Especially if she were pregnant again.

He stumbled back into the kitchen and leaned against a counter, trying to breathe. She couldn't be pregnant again, could she? No, that wasn't the right question. The condom had failed. She could be pregnant.

The question was, how could she be pregnant again and not have told him?

It didn't matter how much he apologized. It didn't matter what he did to take care of her. It didn't matter one damn bit how much he loved her—her and only her.

None of it mattered.

He was done. This was just like the last time, he realized. She would always withhold the truth and she would always hide behind her father so she didn't have to do the dirty work herself. She would always hurt him.

He had to stop letting her—them—win. He was a Beaumont, for God's sake. He would protect his son—his children—from the Harpers. Always and forever. And if that meant he had to take Leona to court, then so be it.

If the Harpers expected him to turn tail and run again, they'd soon find out—no one messed with a Beaumont.

Sixteen

Talking to Byron wasn't working, so Leona decided to take a different approach—when Percy fell asleep for a nap, she started writing him a letter.

"Dear Byron," she started, "I'm pregnant and I don't want to fight about raising our children. I want us to be a family and I want us to be as happy as we can be."

Okay, she thought, good start. She had to get that pregnant part out there first. She'd tried to tell him last night, but he'd cut her off and done everything in his power to make her feel two feet tall.

She put the pen back to the paper and wrote…nothing. What else was she supposed to say? She was tired of being made to feel like a bad person because she hadn't disclosed her father's identity on the first date? She was sorry she hadn't contacted Byron when she had Percy, and she was sorry she'd assumed he'd rejected her again—like it felt he was doing right now.

No matter what, she wasn't going to leave her children—and what she really wanted was the reassurance that he wouldn't take them from her and he wouldn't abandon her again but it was hard to see how he wasn't going to do just that when she couldn't even have a face-to-face conversation with him without it going off the rails.

Dang it. Writing it down—without having to say it to Byron's face or being interrupted—was supposed to make this easier, not harder.

The doorbell rang and she glared at the clock. If this

were May, back again without calling, Leona was going to be pissed. It was Percy's nap time—she should know that.

Leona opened the door and was stunned to see that, instead of the slight form of her sister, a weaselly-looking man in a suit was standing there. A *familiar* weaselly-looking man. "Leona Harper?"

Lights began to pop in front of Leona's eyes and for a second, she was afraid she was going to faint on the feet of her father's favorite lawyer. All of the emotions coursing through her—worry for Percy, exhilaration about the pregnancy—all of them smacked headlong into the wall that was Leon Harper.

"Mr. York?"

The lawyer stepped to the side and there her father was. His face was twisted into something that made a mockery of joy. Leona's stomach lurched again.

One thought bubbled up through the misery of the moment—she should have married Byron already. She'd told him that this was the very thing she'd lived in fear of for a year—her father deciding to make her life his business again.

She clung to the door for support. It was tempting to slam it in their faces and throw the bolt, but damn it all, she couldn't overcome years of subservience to this man.

"Father," she said, her voice a shaky whisper.

"My dear," he replied in his most acid tone. She was not now, nor had she probably ever been, *his dear* and they both knew it. "I must say, I'm disappointed in you."

What else was new? She'd always been a disappointment to him. Her name said it all. If she'd been Leon Harper, Jr., things would have been different. But no. She was Leona. A disappointment with an *a*.

"I gave you a chance," her father went on, mocking condescension in his voice. "Your mother convinced me that I should let you move out—as long as you didn't cause any more trouble than you already had."

Oh, *God*—she could not believe this. This was not happening. He was still talking *at* her—not *to* her—as if she were a messy girl of six again.

No. She couldn't stand here and take whatever he felt like dishing out. Things had changed. She was a mother, soon to be twice over. She owed it to her son, to Byron—and to herself—to be well and truly free of the blight that was Leon Harper.

"As I recall, Father, you didn't 'let' me do anything. I left without your permission."

Anger flared in the old man's eyes—dangerous anger, as she knew from too many years of experience. But she wasn't afraid of him, not anymore. Not much, anyway. So to make herself feel brave, she added, "And I'd do it all over again. What do you want?"

Any pretense of happiness at seeing her vanished off her father's face. He'd never been good at pretending he cared, anyway.

"I must admit," her father said in a calm, level voice that only amplified his rage, "that I was surprised when *he* called me."

"He who—*Byron*?"

Her father shrugged in what, on any other human on the planet, would have been an innocent gesture. "He made his intentions clear—he'd won and I had lost. He said he was going to take the child and that—and I'm quoting here—'No Harper would ever see it again.'"

"You're lying," she gasped. So what if Byron had said almost that exact thing last night? She *couldn't* believe that he'd call her father. "You always lie."

"You can, of course, believe what you want. You always did. You're the one who convinced yourself that he could love you—that any Beaumont was capable of love—when we both know that's not really possible, is it?" He managed a pitying smile.

"No," she said again, but she didn't sound convinced, even to her own ears. Her mind flitted back to the positive test still safely hidden in her bedroom. What would her father say—what would he *do*—if he knew that she was expecting again?

Her knees began to shake and she knew that if she didn't sit down, she really would pass out. But she couldn't show him weakness. She couldn't let him think he'd won.

"He's going to take the child," Father went on. "Both of them."

Leona gasped. How did he know about that? Not even Byron knew. Then it hit her—May. May was the only other person who could possibly know. She'd been in the bathroom while the test had still been in the trash. Leona had thought May hadn't seen it—but she'd thought wrong.

"Sadly," her father continued, "I can't help you—that is, unless you help me, my dear."

If there was one thing in this world that Leon Harper did not need, it was help. "How?"

"It's easy," he said. "Turn legal guardianship of the child over to me. Come back home. Let me protect you from *them*."

Mr. York handed her a thick envelope. "Just sign these," he said in an oily voice, "and it'll all be taken care of."

She stared at the envelope that was suddenly in her hands. She'd always thought that when—not if—her father came after her, he'd do it the hard way and try to destroy her credibility, her job—destroy her.

But this? This offer of *protection*…

Was he serious?

No. Leona knew she could not trust a single word that came out of Leon Harper's mouth. He never did anything that wasn't completely self-serving.

If Byron had decided that marriage wasn't truly in the cards, he would have told her himself.

But then her father said, "I do hope you'll sign the papers before he disappears—*again*," and all of her doubt came crushing back.

Byron wouldn't take her babies and melt off into the night, only to turn up in some foreign country with byzantine custody laws, leaving her no hope of ever seeing her baby again. Would he?

No. *No.* Byron loved Percy and he would not treat her like his own mother had been treated—discarded and destroyed. They might not be able to live together, but he wanted what was best for Percy.

She'd fought too hard for her independence to crumple just because Byron didn't want her and her father lied. She was stronger than that, by God.

So she took a deep breath and stood straighter. True, she was holding on tight to the door, but it was the best she could do. "I could invite you in, but I won't. I don't know what game you're playing, but you're forgetting one simple thing. I know you too well to trust a single word that comes out of your mouth."

Her father's face hardened in rage, but she wasn't done with him. With each word she spoke, she pushed back against the terror this man had inspired in her for the past twenty-five years.

"If you ever come near me or my son again, I'll call the cops and file a restraining order against you," she promised. "If you're still on my property within five minutes, I'll make the call now. I left home for a reason, and nothing you can say or do will convince me that I have to come back for your 'protection.' I don't need it. I don't want it. The only person I need protection from is you." She tried to give him a dismissive look. "And I'll protect myself from you, thank you very much."

With that, she slammed the door in his face. Then she realized she was still holding the envelope. She threw the door back open and launched the envelope at his head before slamming the door shut again. Then she threw the bolt and sagged against the wood.

Except the sagging continued until she had to struggle to her feet and rush to the bathroom.

It was only after her system had cleared itself out and she'd brushed her teeth that she realized she didn't know if her father had been to see Byron or not.

Seventeen

The front door banged open so hard that Leona jumped and dropped her phone milliseconds after hitting Send to Byron.

The figure in the door shouted, "Leona?" at the same moment she heard the chime that Byron had picked out for her.

"Byron?" Yes, it looked like him, but at this point in her day, she wasn't sure she could trust her eyes. "Did you call my father?" she demanded angrily. "Did you tell him you were leaving me?"

Byron gaped at her. "God, no. If I never see him again, it'll be too soon." His brow furrowed. "I guess that answers the question of whether or not you've seen him. He must have come straight here." He looked like he wanted to hold her, but didn't. "Are you pregnant?"

Her eyes fluttered shut. "Yes."

"And you didn't tell me."

"I tried. Last night. And you cut me off." She walked to the kitchen island and grabbed the notebook. "So I was writing you a letter. When my father showed up—and cut me off," she said.

Byron grabbed the notebook and read the few lines she'd written down. "How do I know you didn't write this confession after he left? How do I know you didn't call him and tell him you were done with me? How do I know you're not still lying to me?"

Her mouth dropped open. "You don't, Byron. You can't

independently verify every single thing I do and say as being one hundred percent truthful at all times. You have to take it on faith when I tell you that I'm sorry for the mistakes I made in the past, that I was in the process of writing you a letter because every time we talk it turns into a fight, that I wanted you to know I was pregnant."

"So who told your father?"

She picked up her phone and dialed May—then she put it on speaker. "Hey, Leona. How's Percy?"

Leona took a deep breath and tried to project calm. "May, did you call our father?"

She could sense May's hesitancy. "Well…"

"Did you tell him I was pregnant?"

There was a long pause on May's end. Finally, she said, "The pregnancy test was right there in the trash." Her voice was accusatory, as if Leona had hidden it there just so May could find it.

The curse was right on Leona's lips. But this was still her little sister. So instead she said, "What did he give you?"

"I got an allowance." May sniffed again. "And a new car."

This time, Leona couldn't keep her anger in. "Damn it, May!"

"But Byron's going to leave you—you know he will!" May all but shouted. "He's going to abandon you again, and I can't stand to see you hurt like that—not a second time. We were happy, weren't we? We didn't need him. We could take care of the new baby like we did Percy! I thought it'd be nice to have some better things, not the junk we've had to make do with."

Byron looked at Leona in surprise, but he didn't say anything.

Leona closed her eyes and took another deep breath. "May, I am a grown woman. I know you meant well, but even if I'm going to screw up, I'll do it on my terms. I'll thank you from now on to stay out of my business."

May was crying now and it made a part of Leona hurt. She'd spent years trying to protect May from her father. She never would have guessed that May wouldn't return the favor.

"Are you mad?" May sniffed.

"You have *no* idea. I'm going to hang up now and talk with Byron. I'll call you when I'm ready to talk to you."

"But—"

Leona ended the call and stood there. "I have the pregnancy test in my room. I took it three days ago. I didn't tell you immediately because I knew you'd tell me I had to marry you and I wanted to figure out how to have that discussion. I tried last night but we both know how that went."

Byron was staring at her, openmouthed.

"So this is the deal. I'm pregnant. We already have a child together. But I won't marry you just to have you accuse me of lying to you every day. And I won't marry you and live with the fear that, as soon as you don't want me anymore, I'll be put out on the streets without a home, an income or my children. After you left and I got away from my family, I found out I could survive—even more than that, I could thrive. And I'm not going to give up that independence to exist at your whim *or* my father's."

He still hadn't come up with a response, so she went on. For once, no one was interrupting her. "I should have told you who I really was. I should have told you I was pregnant with Percy. I am sorry I didn't, but I didn't want my father to matter. *I* wanted to matter and for a long time, you made me feel like I did."

"You were the only thing in the world that mattered to me," he said in a quiet voice.

A thrill of something she only vaguely recognized as hope shot through her. She ignored it. This was not the time for hope. This was the time for the truth. "But you act as if I kept Percy a secret from you when that's not what happened. I had taken a pregnancy test that afternoon and gone to the restaurant. I was going to tell you that night, Byron, right after we got off work. And instead my father showed up—a maid had found the test and given it to my mom, who told my father. And then you were *gone*. I didn't hide Percy from you, Byron, I just never got the chance to tell you. So I'll say it again. I'm pregnant. You're the father. Now what?"

Byron looked down at the notebook he was still holding. "Is there anything else I need to know? Because if we are going to find a way to make this work, I need complete honesty from you."

She gave him a long look—so long that he lifted his gaze back to her. "I will not marry you for the children."

He nodded slowly. "And?"

Suddenly her heart was pounding faster. "And I love you. I've always loved you. I just didn't allow myself to love you when you were gone because what good would it have done me? And then you came back and I was afraid you'd become the Beaumont my father always warned me about, when all I wanted was Byron. But I will not allow you to use my feelings against me."

He took a step toward her. The air between them seemed to sharpen. "Is that why you've been fighting my apologies this week?"

"Yes. I know we can't go back to where we were before. But I just… I want something better for our family." Her eyes began to water but she blinked the tears away. "For *us*."

He took another step toward her, close enough that she could feel the warmth of his body. "Tell me what you want."

"You. I want you. I want to spend the rest of my days loving you and I want to know that you will always love me, too. I don't want to live under a cloud of suspicion or worry. And if you can't give me that, then it's better to know now. I'd rather be on my own again than live like my parents or yours."

"Is that the truth?"

"Yes, damn it." Her voice caught, but she ignored it.

Then he lifted his hand and cupped her cheek. "You want me to take it on faith that you'll be honest with me from here on out? I want the same thing from you. I will not abandon you, no matter what. I love you, too—I always have. Buying you this house—asking you to marry me—I'm just trying to show you that I won't leave you. God knows I tried and see where it got me? The moment I set foot back in Denver, I looked you up and hired you."

Her throat started to close up. "Can we do this? Can we actually make this work?"

He pulled her into him. "I won't give up on you, Leona. That was the mistake I made last time. I gave up on you—on us. I didn't fight for you. I was stupid and a coward, and I believed that rat of a man when he told me that I could never have you and I will forever regret that."

"Oh, Byron—" she started to say, but he shook his head.

"I should have waited for you. To hell with that— I should have come after you." He dropped his face and leaned his forehead against her hands. "I should have come for you because that's what a Beaumont does—we fight for what we want, to hell with what anyone else thinks. And I didn't. I hope… I hope you can forgive me for failing you."

The strain of the afternoon was too much for her. She couldn't stand in judgment of him—she wasn't doing all that great of a job at standing, period. Tears started to trickle down her face as her legs shook.

Byron sat on one of the island stools and pulled her onto his lap. He stroked her back.

"I didn't tell you I thought I was pregnant," she said, her voice trembling as the tears started to spill down her cheeks. "I was afraid—afraid that you'd find out who my father was and we'd lose everything we had. I should have called you the moment I found out—I should have told you the moment I suspected. But I was scared, too. And when he showed up—he made it seem like everything I'd ever been taught about the Beaumonts had come true."

"If I had asked you, a year ago..." He shifted, pulling his key ring out of his pocket. "If I had asked you to marry me before it all went to hell, would you have said yes? You never answered that question the other night."

She curled up into him, feeling warm and safe. "I would have. I would have said yes."

Byron hugged her fiercely. "I need you. I've always needed you. I thought— I was afraid you didn't need me."

She looked up at him, unable to stop the tears. "I need you, too. I want this to work so badly, Byron."

"I'm here for you now and I will always be here for you and Percy. No more running, no more hiding. Just you and me and our family." He unhooked the engagement ring from the key chain and held it up. "Leona, I have a very important question for you."

She grinned. "Not an order this time?"

"No. No more orders. Will you marry me? Not for Percy, not for the baby but because I love you and I want to spend the rest of my life by your side. Because it was always meant to be this way—you and me, together."

"Yes, Byron. Yes." Leona couldn't fight the tears— happy tears—as he slid the ring onto her finger.

"Oh, babe," he whispered against the spot right below her ear. "It's going to be different this time. I want to go to all your appointments and hear the heartbeat and *everything*. You and me, babe. You and me and our family."

And then Leona was laughing and crying all at the same time and Byron was kissing her and she was taking the ring from him and putting it on her finger.

"Marry me," Byron said, wiping away her happy tears with his thumb. "Not because you have to and not because it's the best way to protect Percy—marry me because you want to and I want you to."

"Oh, Byron," she said, throwing her arms around his neck and holding him tight. Finally, finally things were going how she'd always dreamed they would. She'd told her father off and defended herself and Byron was here and she'd forgiven him and he'd forgiven her and they were together. They'd always be together.

"Tell me what you want," he whispered against the sensitive skin of her neck. His voice had dropped an octave and he pressed her against his body—all of it. "Tell me you want me."

"You," she whispered back. "All I want is you."

"Then I'm yours. Forever yours."

And that was a promise she knew he'd keep.

* * * * *

FALLING FOR HER
FAKE FIANCÉ

BY
SARAH M. ANDERSON

To Jennifer Porter, who took me under her wing
before I was published and helped give me a
platform to talk about heroes in cowboy hats.
Thank you so much for supporting me! We'll
always have dessert at Junior's together!

One

"*Mis*-ter Logan," the old-fashioned intercom rasped on Ethan's desk.

He scowled at the thing and at the way his current secretary insisted on hissing his name. "Yes, Delores?" He'd never been in an office that required an intercom. It felt as if he'd walked into the 1970s.

Of course, that was probably how old the intercom was. After all, Ethan was sitting in the headquarters of the Beaumont Brewery. This room—complete with hand-carved everything—probably hadn't been redecorated since, well...

A very long time ago. The Beaumont Brewery was 160 years old, after all.

"*Mis*-ter Logan," Delores rasped again, her dislike for him palatable. "We're going to have to stop production on the Mountain Cold and Mountain Cold Light lines."

"What? Why?" Logan demanded. The last thing he could afford was another shutdown.

Ethan had been running this company for almost three months now. His firm, Corporate Restructuring Services, had beat out some heavy hitters for the right to handle the reorganization of the Beaumont Brewery, and Ethan had to make this count. If he—and, by extension, CRS—could turn this aging, antique company into a modern-day business, their reputation in the business world would be cemented.

Ethan had expected some resistance. It was only natural. He'd restructured thirteen companies before taking the helm of Beaumont Brewery. Each company had emerged from the reorganization process leaner, meaner and more competitive in a global economy. Everyone won when that happened.

Yes, thirteen success stories.

Yet nothing had prepared him for the Beaumont Brewery.

"There's a flu going around," Delores said. "Sixty-five workers are home sick, the poor dears."

A flu. Wasn't that just a laugh and a half? Last week, it'd been a cold that had knocked out forty-seven employees. And the week before, after a mass food poisoning, fifty-four people hadn't been able to make it in.

Ethan was no idiot. He'd cut the employees a little slack the first two times, trying to earn their trust. But now it was time to lay down the law.

"Fire every single person who called in sick today."

There was a satisfying pause on the other end of the intercom, and, for a moment, Ethan felt a surge of victory.

The victorious surge was short-lived, however.

"*Mis*-ter Logan," Delores began. "Regretfully, it seems that the HR personnel in charge of processing terminations are out sick today."

"Of course they are," he snapped. He fought the urge to throw the intercom across the room, but that was an impulsive, juvenile thing to do, and Ethan was not impulsive or juvenile. Not anymore.

So, as unsatisfying as it was, he merely shut off the intercom and glared at his office door.

He needed a better plan.

He always had a plan when he went into a business.

His method was proven. He could turn a flailing business around in as little as six months.

But this? The Beaumont freaking Brewery?

That was the problem, he decided. Everyone—the press, the public, their customers and especially the employees—still thought of this as the Beaumont Brewery. Sure, the business had been under Beaumont management for a good century and a half. That was the reason All-Bev, the conglomerate that had hired CRS to handle this reorganization, had chosen to keep the Beaumont name a part of the Brewery—the name-recognition value was through the roof.

But it wasn't the Beaumont family's brewery anymore. They had been forced out months ago. And the sooner the employees realized that, the better.

He looked around the office. It was beautiful, heavy with history and power.

He'd heard that the conference table had been custom-made. It was so big and heavy that it'd been built in the actual office—they might have to take a wall out to remove it. Tucked in the far corner by a large coffee table was a grouping of two leather club chairs and a matching leather love seat. The coffee table was supposedly made of one of the original wagon wheels that Phillipe Beaumont had used when he'd crossed the Great Plains with a team of Percheron draft horses back in the 1880s.

The only signs of the current decade were the flat-screen television that hung over the sitting area and the electronics on the desk, which had been made to match the conference table.

The entire room screamed Beaumont so loudly he was practically deafened by it.

He flipped on the hated intercom again. "Delores."

"Yes, *Mis—*"

He cut her off before she could mangle his name again.

"I want to redo the office. I want all this stuff gone. The curtains, the woodwork—and the conference table. All of it." Some of these pieces—hand carved and well cared for, like the bar—would probably fetch a pretty penny. "Sell it off."

There was another satisfying pause.

"Yes, sir." For a moment, he thought she sounded subdued—cowed. As if she couldn't believe he would really dismantle the heart of the Beaumont Brewery. But then she added, "I know just the appraiser to call," in a tone that sounded…smug?

He ignored her and went back to his computer. Two lines shut down was not acceptable. If either line didn't pull double shifts tomorrow, he wouldn't wait for HR to terminate employees. He'd do it himself.

After all, he was the boss here. What he said went.

And that included the furniture.

Frances Beaumont slammed her bedroom door behind her and flopped down on her bed. Another rejection—she couldn't fall much lower.

She was tired of this. She'd been forced to move back into the Beaumont mansion after her last project had failed so spectacularly that she'd had to give up her luxury condo in downtown Denver. She'd even been forced to sell most of her designer wardrobe.

The idea—digital art ownership and crowdsourcing art patronage online by having buyers buy stock in digital art—had been fundamentally sound. Art might be timeless, but art production and collection had to evolve. She'd sunk a considerable portion of her fortune into Art Digitale, as well as every single penny she'd gotten from the sale of the Beaumont Brewery.

What an epic, crushing mistake. After months of delays and false starts—and huge bills—Art Digitale had been live for three weeks before the funds ran out. Not a single transaction had taken place on the website. In her gilded life, she'd never experienced such complete failure. How could she? She was a Beaumont.

Her business failure was bad enough. But worse? She couldn't get a job. It was as if being a Beaumont suddenly counted for nothing. Her first employer, the owner of Galerie Solaria, hadn't exactly jumped at the chance to have Frances come back, even though Frances knew how to flatter the wealthy, art-focused patrons and massage the delicate egos of artists. She knew how to sell art—didn't that count for something?

Plus, she was a *Beaumont*. A few years ago, people would have jumped at the chance to be associated with one of the founding families of Denver. Frances had been an in-demand woman.

"Where did I go wrong?" she asked her ceiling.

Unsurprisingly, it didn't have an answer.

She'd just turned thirty. She was broke and had moved back in with her family—her brother Chadwick and his family, plus assorted Beaumonts from her father's other marriages.

She shuddered in horror.

When the family still owned the Brewery, the Beaumont name had meant something. *Frances* had meant something. But ever since that part of her life had been sold, she'd been…adrift.

If only there was some way to go back, to put the Brewery under the family's control again.

Yes, she thought bitterly, that was definitely an option. Her older brothers Chadwick and Matthew had walked away and started their own brewery, Percheron Drafts. Phillip, her favorite older brother, the one who had gotten her into parties and helped her build her reputation as the Cool Girl of Denver high society, had ensconced himself out on the Beaumont Farm and gotten sober. No more parties with him. And her twin brother, Byron, was starting a new restaurant.

Everyone else was moving forward, pairing off. And Frances was stuck back in her childhood room, alone.

Not that she believed a man would solve any of her problems. She'd grown up watching her father burn through marriage after unhappy marriage. No, she knew love didn't exist. Or if it did, it wasn't in the cards for her.

She was on her own here.

She opened up a message from her friend Becky and stared at the picture of a shuttered storefront. She and Becky had worked together at Galerie Solaria. Becky had no famous last name and no social connections, but she knew art and had a snarky sense of humor that cut through the bull. More to the point, Becky treated Frances like she was a real person, not just a special Beaumont snowflake. They had been friends ever since.

Becky had a proposition. She wanted to open a new gallery, one that would merge the new-media art forms with the standard classics that wealthy patrons preferred. It wasn't as avant-garde as Frances's digital art business had been, but it was a good bridge between the two worlds.

The only problem was Frances did not have the money to invest. She wished to God she did. She could co-own and comanage the gallery. It wouldn't bring in big bucks, but it could get her out of the mansion. It could get her back to being a somebody. And not just any somebody. She could go back to being Frances Beaumont—popular, respected, *envied*.

She dropped her phone onto the bed in defeat. *Right*. Another fortune was just going to fall into her lap and she'd be in demand. *Sure*. And she would also sprout wings.

True despair was sinking in when her phone rang. She

answered it without even looking at the screen. "Hello?" she said morosely.

"Frances? Frannie," the woman said. "I know you may not remember me—I'm Delores Hahn. I used to work in accounting at—"

The name rang a bell, an older woman who wore her hair in a tight bun. "Oh! Delores! Yes, you were at the Brewery. How are you?"

The only people besides her siblings who called her Frannie were the longtime employees of the Beaumont Brewery. They were her second family—or at least, they had been.

"We've been better," Delores said. "Listen, I have a proposal for you. I know you've got those fancy art degrees."

In the safety of her room, Frances blushed. After today's rejections, she didn't feel particularly fancy. "What kind of proposal?" Maybe her luck was about to change. Maybe this proposal would come with a paycheck.

"Well," Delores went on in a whisper, "the new CEO that AllBev brought in?"

Frances scowled. "What about him? Failing miserably, I hope."

"Sadly," Delores said in a not-sad-at-all voice, "there's been an epidemic of Brew Flu going around. We had to halt production on two lines today."

Frances couldn't hold back the laugh that burst forth from her. "Oh, that's fabulous."

"It was," Delores agreed. "But it made Logan—that's the new CEO—so mad that he decided to rip out your father's office."

Frances would have laughed again, except for one little detail. "He's going to destroy Daddy's office? He wouldn't dare!"

"He told me to sell it off. All of it—the table, the bar,

everything. I think he'd even perform an exorcism, if he thought it'd help," she added.

Her father's office. Technically, it had most recently been Chadwick's office. But Frances had never stopped thinking of her father and that office together. "So what's your proposal?"

"Well," Delores said, her voice dropping past whisper and straight into conspirator. "I thought you could come do the appraisals. Who knows—you might be able to line up buyers for some of it."

"And…" Frances swallowed. The following was a crass question, but desperate times and all that. "And would this Logan fellow pay for the appraisal? If I sold the furniture myself—" say, to a certain sentimental older brother who'd been the CEO for almost ten years "—would I get a commission?"

"I don't see why not."

Frances tried to see the downside of this situation, but nothing popped up. Delores was right—if anyone had the connections to sell off her family's furniture, it'd be Frances.

Plus, if she could get a foothold back in the Brewery, she might be able to help all those poor, flu-stricken workers. She wasn't so naive to think that she could get a conglomerate like AllBev to sell the company back to the family, but…

She might be able to make this Logan's life a little more difficult. She might be able to exact a little revenge. After all—the sale of the Brewery had been when her luck had turned sour. And if she could get paid to do all of that?

"Let's say Friday, shall we?" That was only two days away, but that would give her plenty of time to plan and execute her trap. "I'll bring the donuts."

Delores actually giggled. "I was hoping you'd say that."

Oh, yes. This was going to be great.

* * *

"*Mis*-ter Logan, the appraiser is here."

Ethan set down the head count rolls he'd been studying. Next week, he was reducing the workforce by 15 percent. People with one or more "illness absences" were going to be the first to find themselves out on the sidewalk with nothing more than a box of their possessions.

"Good. Send him in."

But no nerdy-looking art geek walked into the office. Ethan waited and then switched the intercom back on. Before he could ask Delores the question, though, he heard a lot of people talking and laughing?

It sounded as though someone was having a party in the reception area.

What the hell?

He strode across the room and threw open his office door. There was, point of fact, a party going on outside. Workers he'd only caught glimpses of before were all crowded around Delores's desk, donuts in their hands and sappy smiles on their faces.

"What's going on out here?" he thundered. "This is a business, people, not a——"

Then the crowd parted, and he saw her.

God, how had he missed her? A woman with a stunning mane of flame-red hair sat on the edge of Delores's desk. Her body was covered by an emerald-green gown that clung to every curve like a lover's hands. His fingers itched to trace the line of her bare shoulders.

She was not an employee. That much was clear.

She was, however, holding a box of donuts.

The good-natured hum he'd heard on the intercom died away. The smiles disappeared, and people edged away from him.

"What is this?" he demanded. The color drained out

of several employees' faces, but his tone didn't appear to have the slightest impact on the woman in the green gown.

His eyes were drawn to her back, to the way her ass looked sitting on the edge of the desk. Slowly—so slowly it almost hurt him—she turned and looked at him over her shoulder.

He might have intimidated the workers. He clearly had not intimidated her.

She batted her eyelashes as a cryptic smile danced across her deep red lips. "Why, it's Donut Friday."

Ethan glared at her. "What?"

She pivoted, bringing more of her profile into view. *Dear God, that dress—that body.* The strapless dress came to a deep V over her chest, doing everything in its power to highlight the pale, creamy skin of her décolletage.

He shouldn't stare. He *wasn't* staring. Really.

Her posture shifted. It was like watching a dancer arrange herself before launching into a series of gravity-defying pirouettes. "You must be new here," the woman said in a pitying tone. "It's Friday. That's the day I bring donuts."

Individually, he understood each word and every implication of her tone and movement. But together? "Donut Friday?" He'd been here for months, and this was the first time he'd heard anything about donuts.

"Yes," she said. She held out the box. "I bring everyone a donut. Would you like the last one? I'm afraid all I have left is a plain."

"And who are you, if I may ask?"

"Oh, you may." She lowered her chin and looked up at him through her lashes. She was simply the most beautiful woman he'd ever seen, which was more than enough to turn his head. But the fact that she was playing him for the fool—and they both knew it?

There were snickers from the far-too-large audience as

she held out her hand for him—not to shake, no. She held it out as though she expected him to kiss it, as if she were the queen or something.

"I'm Frances Beaumont. I'm here to appraise the antiques."

Two

Oh, this *was* fun.

"Donut?" she asked again, holding out the box. She kept as much innocence as she could physically manage on her face.

"You're the *appraiser*?"

She let the donut box hang in the space between them a few more moments before she slowly lowered the box back to her lap.

She'd been bringing donuts in on Fridays since—well, since as long as she could remember. It'd been her favorite part of the week, mostly because it was the only time she ever got to be with her father, just the two of them. For a few glorious hours every Friday morning, she was Daddy's Little Girl. No older brothers taking up all his time. No new wives or babies demanding his attention. Just Hardwick Beaumont and his little girl, Frannie.

And what was more, she got to visit all the grown-ups—including many of the same employees who were watching this exchange between her and Logan with rapt fascination—and hear how nice she was, how pretty she looked in that dress, what a sweetheart she was. The people who'd been working for the Brewery for the past thirty years had made her feel special and loved. They'd been her second family. Even after Hardwick had died and regular Donut

Fridays had faded away, she'd still taken the time to stop in at least once a month. Donuts—hand-delivered with a smile and a compliment—made the world a better place.

If she could repay her family's loyal employees by humiliating a tyrant of an outsider, then that was the very least she could do.

Logan's mouth opened and closed before he ordered, "Get back to work."

No one moved.

She turned back to the crowd to hide her victorious smile. They weren't listening to him. They were waiting on her.

"Well," she said graciously, unable to keep the wicked glint out of her eye. Just so long as Logan didn't see it. "It has been simply wonderful to see everyone again. I know I've missed you—we all have in the Beaumont family. I do hope that I can come back for another Donut Friday again soon?"

Behind her, Logan made a choking noise.

But in front of her, the employees nodded and grinned. A few of them winked in silent support.

"Have a wonderful day, everyone," she cooed as she waved.

The crowd began to break up. A few people dared to brave what was no doubt Logan's murderous glare to come close enough to murmur their thanks or ask that she pass along their greetings to Chadwick or Matthew. She smiled and beamed and patted shoulders and promised that she'd tell her brothers exactly what everyone had said, word for word.

The whole time she felt Logan's rage rolling off him in waves, buffeting against her back. He was no doubt trying to kill her with looks alone. It wouldn't work. She had the upper hand here, and they both knew it.

Finally, there was only one employee left. "Delores,"

Frances said in her nicest voice, "if Mr. Logan doesn't want his donut—" She pivoted and held the box out to him again.

Oh, yes—she had the advantage here. He could go right on trying to glare her to death, but it wouldn't change the fact that the entire administrative staff of the Brewery had ignored his direct order and listened to hers. That feeling of power—of importance—coursed through her body. God, it felt *good*.

"I do not," he snarled.

"Would you be a dear and take care of this for me?" Frances finished, handing the box to Delores.

"Of course, Ms. Frances." Delores gave Frances a look that was at least as good as—if not better than—an actual hug, then shuffled off in the direction of the break room, leaving Frances alone with one deeply pissed-off CEO. She crossed her legs at the ankle and leaned toward him, but she didn't say anything else. The ball was firmly in his court now. The only question was did he know how to play the game?

The moment stretched. Frances took advantage of the silence to appraise her prey. This Logan fellow was *quite* an attractive specimen. He was maybe only a few inches taller than Frances, but he had the kind of rock-solid build that suggested he'd once been a defensive linebacker—and an effective one at that. His suit—a very good suit, with conservative lines—had been tailored to accommodate his wide shoulders. Given the girth of his neck, she'd put money on his shirts being made-to-order. Bespoke shirts and suits were not cheap.

He had a square jaw—all the squarer right now, given how he was grinding his teeth—and light brown hair that was close cut. He was probably incredibly good-looking when he wasn't scowling.

He was attempting to regain his composure, she realized. Couldn't have that.

Back when she'd been a little girl, she'd sat on this very desk, kicking her little legs as she held the donut box for everyone. Back then, it'd been cute to hop down off the desk when all the donuts were gone and twirl in her pretty dress.

But what was cute at five didn't cut it at thirty. No hopping. Still, she had to get off this desk.

So she extended her left leg—which conveniently was the side where one of the few designer dresses she'd hung on to was slit up to her thigh—and slowly shifted her weight onto it.

Logan's gaze cut to her bare leg as the fabric fell away.

She leaned forward as she brought her other foot down. The slit in the dress closed back over her leg, but Logan's eyes went right where she expected them to—her generous cleavage.

In no great hurry, she stood, her shoulders back and her chin up. "Shall we?" she asked in a regal tone. "My cloak," she added, motioning with her chin toward where she'd removed the matching cape that went with this dress.

Without waiting for an answer from him, she strode into his office as if she owned it. Which she once had, sort of.

The room looked exactly as she remembered it. Frances sighed in relief—it was all still here. She used to color on the wagon wheel table while she waited for the rest of the workers to get in so she could hand out the donuts. She'd played dolls on the big conference table. And her father's desk...

The only time her daddy hugged her was in this room. Hardwick Beaumont had not been a hard-driven, ruthless executive in those small moments with her. He'd told her things he'd never told anyone else, like how his father, Frances's grandfather John, had let Hardwick pick out the color of the drapes and the rug. How John had let Hardwick try a new beer fresh off the line, and then made him tell the older man why it was good and what the brewers should do better.

"This office," her daddy used to say, "made me who I am." And then he'd give her a brief, rare hug and say, "And it'll make you who you are, too, my girl."

Ridiculous how the thought of a simple hug from her father could make her all misty-eyed.

She couldn't bear the thought of all this history—all *her* memories—being sold off to the highest bidder. Even if that would result in a tidy commission for her.

If she couldn't stop the sale, the best she could do was convince Chadwick to buy as much of his old office as possible. Her brother had fought to keep this company in the family. He'd understand that some things just couldn't be sold away.

But that wasn't plan A.

She tucked her tenderness away. In matters such as this one, tenderness was a liability, and God knew she couldn't afford any more of those.

So she stopped in the middle of the office and waited for Logan to catch up. She did not fold herself gracefully into one of the guest chairs in front of the desk, nor did she arrange herself seductively on the available love seat. She didn't even think of sprawling herself out on the conference table.

She stood in the middle of the room as though she was ruler of all she saw. And no one—not even a temporary CEO built like a linebacker—could convince her otherwise.

She was surprised when he did not slam the door shut. Instead, she heard the gentle whisper of it clicking closed. *Head up, shoulders back*, she reminded herself as she stood, waiting for him to make the next move. She would show him no mercy. She expected nothing but the same returned in kind.

She saw him move toward the conference table, where he draped her cape over the nearest chair. She felt his eyes on her. No doubt he was admiring her body even as he debated wringing her neck.

Men were so easy to confuse.

He was the kind of man, she decided, who would need to reassert his control over the situation. Now that the audience had dispersed, he would feel it a moral imperative to put her back in her place.

She could not let him get comfortable. It was just that simple.

Ah, she'd guessed right. He made a wide circle around her, not bothering to hide how he was checking out her best dress as he headed for the desk. Frances held her pose until he was almost seated. Then she reached into her small handbag—emerald-green silk, made to match the dress, of course—and pulled out a small mirror and lipstick. Ignoring Logan entirely, she fixed her lips, making sure to exaggerate her pouts.

Was she hearing things or had a nearly imperceptible groan come from the area behind the desk?

This was almost too easy, really.

She put the lipstick and mirror away and pulled out her phone. Logan opened his mouth to say something, but she interrupted him by taking a picture of the desk. And of him.

He snapped his mouth shut. "Frances *Beaumont*, huh?"

"The one and only," she purred, taking a close-up of the carved details on the corner of the desk. And if she had to bend over to do so—well, she couldn't help it if this dress was exceptionally low-cut.

"I suppose," Logan said in a strangled-sounding voice, "that there's no such thing as a coincidence?"

"I certainly don't believe in them." She shifted her angle and took another shot. "Do you?"

"Not anymore." Instead of sounding flummoxed or even angry, she detected a hint of humor in his voice. "I suppose you know your way around, then?"

"I do," she cheerfully agreed. Then she paused, as if she'd just remembered that she'd forgotten her manners. "I'm so sorry—I don't believe I caught your name?"

My, *that* was a look. But if he thought he could intimidate her, he had no idea who he was dealing with. "My apologies." He stood and held out his hand. "I'm Ethan Logan. I'm the CEO of the Beaumont Brewery."

She let his hand hang for a beat before she wrapped her fingers around his. He had hands that matched his shoulders—thick and strong. This Ethan Logan certainly didn't look a thing like the bean-counting lackey she'd pictured.

"Ethan," she said, dropping her gaze and looking up at him through her lashes.

His hand was warm as his fingers curled around her smaller hand. Strong, oh yes—he could easily break her hand. But he didn't. All the raw power he projected was clearly—and safely—locked down.

Instead, he turned her hand over and kissed the back of it. The very thing she'd implied he should do earlier, when they'd had an audience. It'd seemed like a safe move then, an action she knew he'd never take her up on.

But here? In the enclosed space of the office, with no one to witness his chivalrous gesture? She couldn't tell if the kiss was a threat or a seduction. Or both.

Then he raised his gaze and looked her in the eyes. Suddenly, the room was much warmer, the air much thinner. Frances had to use every ounce of her self-control not to take huge gulping breaths just to get some oxygen into her body. Oh, but he had nice eyes, warm and determined and completely focused on her.

She might have underestimated him.

Not that he needed to know that. She allowed herself an

innocent blush, which took some work. She hadn't been innocent for a long time. "A pleasure," she murmured, wondering how long he planned to kiss her hand.

"It's all mine," he assured her, straightening up and taking a step back. She noted with interest that he didn't sit back down. "So you're the appraiser Delores hired?"

"I hope you won't be too hard on her," she simpered, taking this moment to put another few steps between his body and hers.

"And why shouldn't I be? Are you even qualified to do this? Or did she just bring you in to needle me?"

He said it in far too casual a tone. *Damn.* His equilibrium was almost restored. She couldn't have that.

And what's more, she couldn't let him impinge on her ability to do this job.

Then she realized that his lips —which had, to this point, only been compressed into a thin line of anger or dropped open in shock—were curving into a far-too-cocky grin. He'd scored a hit on her, and he knew it.

She quickly schooled her face into the appropriate demureness, using the excuse of taking more pictures to do so.

"I am, in fact, highly qualified to appraise the contents of this office. I have a bachelor's degree in art history and a master's of fine art. I was the manager at Galerie Solaria for several years. I have extensive connections with the local arts scene."

She stated her qualifications in a light, matter-of-fact tone designed to put him at ease. Which, given the little donut stunt she'd pulled, would probably actually make him more nervous—if he had his wits about him. "And if anyone would know the true value of these objects," she added, straightening to give him her very best smile, "it'd be a Beaumont—don't you think? After all, this was ours for *so* long."

He didn't fall for the smile. Instead, he eyed her suspiciously, just as she'd suspected he would. She would have to reconsider her opinion of him. Now that the shock of her appearance was wearing off, he seemed more and more up to the task of playing this game.

Even though it shouldn't, the thought thrilled her. Ethan Logan would be a formidable opponent. This might even be fun. She could play the game with Ethan—a game she would win, without a doubt—and in the process, she could protect her family legacy and help out Delores and all the rest of the employees.

"How about you?" she asked in an offhand manner.

"What about me?" he asked.

"Are you qualified to run a company? This company?" She couldn't help it. The words came out a little sharper than she had wanted them to. But she followed up the questions with a fluttering of her eyelashes and another demure smile.

Not that they worked. "I am, in fact," he said in a mocking tone as he parroted her words, "highly qualified to run this company. I am a co-owner of my firm, Corporate Restructuring Services. I have restructured thirteen previous companies, raising stock prices and increasing productivity and efficiency. I have a bachelor's degree in economics and a master's of business administration, and I *will* turn this company around."

He said the last part with all the conviction of a man who truly believed himself to be on the right side of history.

"I'm quite sure you will." Of course she agreed with him. He was expecting her to argue. "Why, once the employees all get over that nasty flu that's been going around…" She lifted a shoulder, as if to say it was only a matter of time. "You'll have things completely under control within days." Then, just to pour a little lemon juice in the wound, she leaned forward. His gaze held—he didn't even glance at her cleavage. *Damn. Time to up the ante.*

She let her eyes drift over those massive shoulders and the broad chest. He was quite unlike the thin, pale men who populated the art world circles she moved within. She could still feel his lips on the back of her hand.

Oh, yes, she could play this game. For a short while, she could feel like Frances Beaumont again—powerful, beautiful, holding sway over everyone in her orbit. She could use Ethan Logan to get back what she'd lost in the past six months and—if she was very lucky—she might even be able to inflict some damage on AllBev through the Brewery. Corporate espionage and all that.

So she added in a confidential voice, "I have faith in your abilities."

"Do you?"

She looked him up and down again and smiled. A real smile this time, not one couched to elicit a specific response. "Oh, yes," she said, turning away from him. "I do."

Three

He needed her.

That crystal clear revelation was quickly followed by a second—and far more depressing one—Frances Beaumont would destroy him if he gave her half the chance.

As he watched Frances move around his office, taking pictures of the furniture and antiques and making completely harmless small talk about potential buyers, he knew he would have to risk the latter to get the former.

The way all those workers had been eating out of her hand—well, out of her donut box? The way not a single damn one of them had gotten back to work when he'd ordered them to—but they'd all jumped when Frances Beaumont had smiled at them?

It hurt to admit—even to himself—that the workers here would not listen to him.

But they would listen to her.

She was one of them—a Beaumont. They obviously adored her—even Delores, the old battle-ax, had bowed and scraped to this stunningly beautiful woman.

"If you wouldn't mind," she said in that delicate voice that he was completely convinced was a front. She kicked out of her shoes and lined one of the conference chairs up beneath a window. She held out her hand for him. "I'd like to get a better shot of the friezes over the windows."

"Of course," he said in his most diplomatic voice.

This woman—this stunning woman who's fingertips were light and warm against his hand as he helped her balance onto the chair, leaving her ass directly at eye level—had already ripped him to shreds several times over.

She was gorgeous. She was clearly intelligent. And she was obviously out to undermine him. That's what the donuts had been about. Announcing to the world in general and him in particular that this was still the Beaumont Brewery in every sense of the word.

"Thank you," she murmured, placing her hand on his shoulder to balance herself as she stepped down.

She didn't stick the landing, although he couldn't say if that was accidental or on purpose.

Before he could stop himself, his arm went around her waist to steady her.

Which was a mistake because electricity arced between them. She looked up at him through those lashes—he'd lost count of how many times she'd done that so far—but this time it hit him differently.

After almost a month of dealing with passive-aggressive employees terrified of being downsized he suddenly felt like a very different man altogether.

"Thank you," she said again, in a quiet whisper that somehow felt more honest, less calculated than almost every other word she'd uttered so far. Imperceptibly, she leaned into him. He could feel the heat of her breasts through his suit.

As soon as he was sure she wouldn't fall over, he stepped well clear of her. He needed her—but he could not need her like that. Not now, not ever. Because she *would* destroy him. He had no doubt about that. None.

Still…an idea was taking shape in his mind.

Maybe he'd been going about this all wrong. Instead of trying to strip the Beaumont out of the Beaumont Brewery, maybe what he needed to do was bring in a Beaumont. The moment the idea occurred to him, he latched on to it with both hands.

Yes. What he really needed was to have a Beaumont on board with the management changes he was implementing. If the workers realized their old bosses were signing off on the reorganization, there wouldn't be any more mass food poisonings or flu or whatever they'd planned for next week. Sure, there'd still be grumbling and personnel turnover, but if he had a Beaumont by his side...

"So!" Frances said brightly, just as she leaned over to adjust the strap on her shoe.

Ethan had to slam his eyes shut so he wouldn't be caught staring at her barely contained cleavage. If he was going to pull this off, he had to keep his wits about him and his pants zipped.

"How would you like to proceed? Ethan?" It was only when she said his name that he figured it was safe to look.

As safe as it got, anyway. More than any other woman he'd seen in person, Frances looked as if she'd walked right off a movie screen and into his office. Her hair fell in soft waves over her shoulders and her eyes were a light blue that took on a greenish tone that matched her dress. She was the stuff of fantasies, all luscious curves and soft skin.

"I want to hire you."

Direct was better. If he tried to dance around the subject, she'd spin him in circles.

It worked, too—at least for a second. Her eyes widened in surprise, but she quickly got herself back under control. She laughed lightly, like a chime tinkling in the wind. "Mr. Logan," she said, beaming a high-wattage smile at him. "You already have hired me. The furniture?" she reminded him, looking around the room. "My family's legacy?"

"That's not what I mean," he replied. "I want you to come work for me. Here. At the Brewery. As..." His mind spun for something that would be appropriate to a woman like her. "As executive vice president of human resources. In charge of employee relations." *There.* That sounded fancy without actually meaning anything.

A hint of confusion wrinkled her forehead. "You want me to be a...manager?" She said the word as if it left a bad taste in her mouth. "Out of the question." But she favored him with that smile he'd decided she wielded like other people might wield a knife in a street fight. "I'm so sorry, but I couldn't possibly work for the Beaumont Brewery if it wasn't owned by an actual Beaumont." With crisp efficiency, she snatched up her cape and elegantly swirled it around her shoulders, hiding her body from his eyes.

Not that he was looking at it. He felt the corners of his mouth curve up in a smile. He had her off balance for possibly the first time since she'd walked onto the Brewery property.

"I'll work up an appraisal sheet and a list of potential buyers for some of the more sentimental pieces," she announced, not even bothering to look over her shoulder as she strode toward the door.

Before he realized what he was doing, he ran after her. "Wait," he said, getting to the door just as she put her hand on the knob. He pushed the door shut.

And then realized he basically had her trapped between the door and his body.

She knew it, too. Moving with that dancer's grace, she pivoted and leaned back, her breasts thrust toward him and her smile coy. "Did you need something else?"

"Won't you at least consider it?"

"About the job offer?" She grinned. It was too victorious to be pretty. "I rather think not."

What else would she be thinking about? His blood began to pound in his veins. He couldn't admit defeat, couldn't admit that a beautiful woman had spun him around until he hadn't realized he'd lost until it was too late. He had to come up with something to at least make her keep her options open. He could not run this company without her.

"Have dinner with me, then."

If this request surprised her, it didn't show. Instead, she tilted her head to one side, sending waves of beautiful red hair cascading over her cloaked shoulders. Then she moved. A hand emerged from the folds of her cloak and she touched him. She touched the line of his jaw with the tips of her fingers and then slid them down to where his white shirt was visible beneath the V of his suit jacket.

Heat poured off her as she flattened her palm against him. He desperately wanted to close his eyes and focus on the way her touch made his body jump to full attention. He wanted to lower his head and taste her ruby-red lips. He wanted to pull her body into his and feel her skin against his.

He did none of those things.

Instead, he took it like a man. Or he tried to. But when she said, in that soft whisper of hers, "And why would I agree to *that*?" it nearly broke his resolve.

"I'd like the chance to change your mind. About the job offer." Which was not strictly true, not any longer. Not when her palm moved in the smallest of circles over his heart.

"Is that all?" she breathed. He could feel the heat from her hand burning his skin. "There's nothing else you want from me?"

"I just want what's best for the company." Damn it all; his voice had gotten deeper on him. But he couldn't help it, not with the way she was looking up at him. "Don't you?"

Something in her face changed. It wasn't resignation, not really—and it wasn't surrender.

It was engagement. It was a *yes*.

She lightly pushed on his chest. He straightened and

dropped his arm away from the door. "Dinner. For the company," she agreed. He couldn't interpret that statement, not when his ears were ringing with desire. "Where are you staying?"

"I have a suite at the Hotel Monaco."

"Shall we say seven o'clock tomorrow night? In the lobby?"

"It would be an honor."

She arched an eyebrow at him, and then, with a swirling turn, she was gone, striding into the reception area and pausing only to thank Delores again for all her help.

He had to find a way to get Frances on his side.

It had nothing to do with the way he could still feel her touch burned into his skin.

Four

In the end, it'd come down to one of two dresses. Frances only had four left after the liquidation of her closet anyway. The green one was clearly out—it would reek of desperation to wear the same dress twice, even if Ethan's eyes had bugged out of his head when he'd looked at her in it.

She also had her bridesmaid's dress from her brother Phillip's wedding, a sleek gray one with rhinestone accents. But that felt too formal for dinner, even if it did look good on her.

Which meant she had to choose between the red velvet and the little black dress for her negotiation masquerading as dinner with Ethan Logan.

The red dress would render him completely speechless; that she knew. She'd always had a fondness for it—it transformed her into a proper lady instead of what she often felt like, the black sheep of the family.

But there was nothing subtle about the red dress. And besides, if the evening went well, she might need a higher-powered dress for later.

The little black dress was really the only choice. It was a halter-top style and completely backless. The skirt twirled out, but there was no missing the cleavage. The dark color made it appear more subdued at first, which would work to her advantage. If she paired it with her cropped bolero jacket, she could project an air of seriousness, and then, when she needed to befuddle Ethan, she could slip off the jacket. *Perfect.*

She made it downtown almost twenty minutes late, which meant she was right on schedule. Ethan Logan could sit and cool his heels for a bit. The more she kept him off balance, the better her position would be.

Which did beg the question—what was her position? She'd only agreed to dinner because he'd said he wanted what was best for the company. And the way he'd said it...

Well, she also wanted what was best for the company. But for her, that word was a big umbrella, under which the employees were just as important as the bottom line.

And after all, if something continued to be named the Beaumont Brewery, shouldn't it still be connected to the Beaumonts?

So dinner was strictly about those two objectives. She would see what she could get Ethan to reveal about the long-term plan for the Brewery. And if there was something in those plans that could help her get her world back in order, so much the better.

Yes, that was it. Dinner had nothing to do with how she'd felt Ethan's chest muscles twitch under her touch, nothing to do with the simmering heat that had rolled off him. And it had even less to do with the way he'd looked down at her, like a man who'd been adrift at sea for too long and had finally spotted land.

She was Frances Beaumont. She could not be landed. For years, she'd had men look at her as if they were starving and she was a banquet. It was nothing new. Just a testament to her name and genetics. Ethan Logan would be no different. She would take what she needed from him—that feeling that she was still someone who mattered, someone who wielded power—and leave the rest.

Which did not explain why, for the first time in what felt

like years, Frances had butterflies in her stomach as she strode into the lobby of the Hotel Monaco. Was she nervous? It wasn't possible. She didn't get nervous, especially not about something like this. She'd spent her entire life navigating the shark-infested waters of wealthy and powerful men. Ethan was just another shark. And he wasn't even a great white. He was barely a dogfish.

"Good evening, Ms. Beaumont."

"Harold," she said to the doorman with a warm smile and a big tip.

"Ms. Beaumont! How wonderful to see you again!" At this rather loud pronouncement, several other guests in the immediate vicinity paused to gape at her.

Frances ignored the masses. "Thank you, Heidi," she said to the clerk at the front desk with another warm smile. The hotel had been catering to the Beaumont family for years, and Frances liked to keep the staff on her side.

"And what can we do for you tonight?" Heidi asked.

"I'm meeting someone for dinner." She scanned the crowd, but she didn't see Ethan. He wouldn't be easy to miss—a man as massively built as he was? All those muscles would stand out.

Then she saw him. And did a double take. Yes, those shoulders, that neck, were everything she remembered them being. The clothing, however? Unlike the conservative gray suit and dull tie he'd had on in the office, he was wearing a pair of artfully distressed jeans, a white button-up shirt without a tie and…a purple sports coat? A deep purple—plum, maybe. She would not have figured he was the kind of man who would stand outside a sartorial box with any great flair—or success.

When he saw her, he pushed himself off the column he was leaning against. "Frances, hello." Which was a perfectly normal thing to say. But he said it as if he couldn't quite believe his eyes—or his luck—as she strode toward him.

He should feel lucky. "Ethan." When he held out his hand, she took it and used it to pull herself up so she could kiss him on the cheek.

His free hand rested against her side, steadying her. "You look amazing," he murmured, his mouth close to her ear.

Warmth that bordered on heat started where his breath kissed her skin and flamed out over her body. That was what made her nervous. Not the man, not the musculature—not even his position as CEO of her family's company.

It was the way her body reacted to him. The way a touch, a look—a whispered word—could set her fluttering. *Ridiculous.* She was not flattered by his attentions. This was not a date. This was corporate espionage in a great dress. This was her using what few resources she had left at her disposal to get her life back on track. This was about her disarming Ethan Logan, not the other way around.

So she clamped down on the shiver that threatened to race across her skin as she lowered herself away from him. "That's a great color on you. Very…" She let the word hang in the air for a beat too long. "Bold," she finished. "Not just any man could pull off that look."

He raised his eyebrows. She realized he was trying not to laugh at her. "Says the woman who showed up in an emerald evening gown to hand out donuts. Have no fear, I'm comfortable in my masculinity. Shall we? I made reservations at the restaurant." He held out his arm for her.

"We shall." She lightly placed her hand in the crook of his elbow. She didn't need his help—she could walk in these shoes just fine—but this was part of setting him up. It had nothing to do with wanting another flash of heat from where their bodies met.

The restaurant was busy, as was to be expected on a Saturday night. When they entered, the diners paused. She and Ethan must have made quite a pair, her with her red hair and him in his purple jacket.

People were already forming opinions. That was something she could use to her advantage. She placed her free hand on top of Ethan's arm and leaned into him. Not much, but just enough to create the impression that this was a date.

The maître d' led them to a small table tucked in a dim corner. They ordered—she got the lobster, just to be obnoxious about it, and he got the steak, just to be predictable—and Ethan ordered a bottle of pinot grigio.

Then they were alone. "I'm glad you came out tonight."

She demurely placed her hands in her lap. "Did you think I would cancel?"

"I wouldn't have been surprised if you'd tried to string me along a little bit. Just to watch me twist." He said it in a jovial way but she didn't miss the edge to his voice.

So he wasn't totally befuddled. And he was more than sharp enough to know they were here for something much more than dinner.

That didn't mean she had to own up to it. "Whatever do you mean?"

His smile sharpened. The silence carried, and she was in serious danger of fidgeting nervously under his direct gaze.

She was saved by the sommelier, who arrived with the wine. Frances desperately wanted to take a long drink, but she could not let Ethan know he was unsettling her. So she slowly twirled the stem of her wineglass until he said, "I propose a toast."

"Do you now?"

"To a long and productive partnership." She did not drink. Instead, she leveled a cool gaze at him over the rim of her glass and waited for him to notice. Which, admittedly, did not take long. "Yes?"

"I'm not taking that job, you know. I have 'considered' it, and I can't imagine a more boring job in the history of employment," she told him.

She would not let the world know she was so desperate as to take a job in management at a company that used to belong to her family. She might be down on her luck, but she wasn't going to give up.

Then, and only then, did she allow herself to sip her wine. She had to be careful. She needed to keep her wits about her and not let the wine—and all those muscles— go to her head.

"I figured as much," he said with a low chuckle that Frances felt right in her chest. What was it with this man's voice?

"Then why would you toast to such a thing?" Maybe now was the time to take the jacket off? He seemed entirely too self-aware. She did not have the advantage here, not like she'd had in the office.

Oh, she did not like that smile on him. Well, she did— she might actually like it a great deal, if she wasn't the one in the crosshairs.

He leaned forward, his gaze so intense that she considered removing her jacket just to cool down. "I'm sure you know why I want you," he all but growled.

It *was* getting hotter in here. She tried to look innocent. It was the only look she could pull off with the level of blush she'd probably achieved by now. "My sparkling wit?"

There was a brief crack in his serious facade, as if her sparkling wit was the correct answer. "I consider that a fringe benefit," he admitted with a tilt of his head. "But let's not play dumb, you and I. It's far too beneath a woman with your considerable talents. And your talents…" She straightened her back and thrust her chest out in a desperate attempt to throw him off balance. It didn't work. His gaze never left her face. "Your talents are considerable. I'm not sure I've ever met a woman like you before."

"Are you hitting on me?"

The corner of his mouth quirked up, making him look like a predator. She might have to revise her earlier opinion of him. He was *not* a dogfish. More like…a tiger shark, sleek and fast. Able to take her down before she even realized she was in danger.

"Of course not."

"Then why do you want me?" Because honestly—for the first time in her adult life—she wasn't sure what the answer would be.

Men wanted her. They always had. The moment her boobs had put in an appearance, she'd learned about base male lust—how to provoke it, how to manage it, how to use it for her own ends. Men wanted her for a simple, carnal reason. And after watching stepmother after stepmother come and go out of her father's life, she had resolved never to be used. Not like that.

The upside was that she'd never had her heart broken. But the downside?

She'd never been in love. Self-preservation, however vital to survival, was a lonely way to live.

"It's simple, really." He leaned back, his posture at complete ease. "Obviously, everyone at the Brewery hates me. I can't blame them—no one likes change, especially when they have to change against their will." He grinned at her, a sly thing. "I should probably be surprised that Delores hasn't spiked my coffee with arsenic by now."

"Probably," she agreed. Where was he going with this?

"But you?" He reached over and picked up her hand, rubbing his thumb along the edges of her fingertips. Against her will, she shivered—and he felt it. That smile deepened—his voice deepened. Everything deepened. *Oh, hell.*

"I saw how the workers—especially the lifers—responded to you and your donut stunt," he went on, still stroking her hand. "There's nothing they wouldn't do for you, and probably wouldn't do for any Beaumont."

"If you think this is going to convince me to take that job, you're sorely mistaken," she replied. She wanted to jerk her hand out of his—she needed to break that skin-to-skin contact—but she didn't. If this was how the game was going to go, then she needed to be all in.

So instead she curled her fingers around his and made small circles on the base of his palm with her thumb. She was justly rewarded with a little shiver from him. *Okay, good. Great.* She wasn't entirely at his mercy here. She could still have an impact even without the element of surprise. "Especially if you're going to call them 'lifers.' That's insulting. You make them sound like prisoners."

He notched an eyebrow at her. "What would you call them?"

"Family." The simple reply—which was also the truth—was out before she could stop it.

She didn't know what she expected him to do with that announcement, but lifting her hand to his lips and pressing a kiss against her skin wasn't it. "And that," he whispered against her skin, "is exactly why I need you."

This time, she did pull her hand away. She dropped it into her lap and fixed him with her best polite glare, the one that could send valets and servers scurrying for cover. Just then, the waiter appeared with their food—and did, in fact, pause when Frances turned that glare in his direction. He set their plates down with a minimum of fanfare and all but sprinted away.

She didn't touch her food. "I'm hearing an awful lot about how much you need me. So let us, as you said, dispense with the games. I do not now, nor have I ever, formally worked for the Beaumont Brewery. I do not now, nor have I ever, had sex with a man who thought he was entitled to a piece of the Beaumont Brewery and, by extension, a piece of me. I will not take a desk job to help you win the approval of people you clearly dislike."

"They disliked me first," he put in as he cut his steak.

What she really wanted to do was throw her wine in his face. It'd feel so good to let loose and let him have it. Despite his claims that he recognized her intelligence, she had the distinct feeling that he was playing her, and she did not like it. "Regardless. What do you want, Mr. Logan? Because I'm reasonably certain that it's no longer just the dismantling and sale of my family's history."

He set his knife and fork aside and leaned his elbows on the table. "I need you to help me convince the workers that joining the current century is the only way the company will survive. I need you to help me show them that it doesn't have to be me against them or them against me—that we can work together to make the Brewery something more than it was."

She snorted. "I'll be sure to pass such touching sentiments along to my brother—the man you replaced."

"By all accounts, he was quite the businessman. I'm sure that he'd agree with me. After all, he made significant changes to the management structure himself after his father passed. But he was constrained by that sense of family you so aptly described. I am not."

"All the good it's doing you." She took another sip of wine, a slightly larger one than before.

"You see my problem. If the workers fight me on this, it won't be only a few people who lose their jobs—the entire company will shut down, and we will all suffer."

She tilted her head from side to side, considering. "Perhaps it should. The Beaumont Brewery without a Beaumont isn't the same thing, no matter what the marketing department says."

"Would you really give your blessing to job losses for hundreds of workers, just for the sake of a name?"

"It's *my* name," she shot at him.

But he was right. If the company went down in flames, it'd burn the people she cared for. Her brothers would be safe—they'd already ensconced themselves in the Percheron Drafts brewery. But Bob and Delores and all the rest? The ones who'd whispered to her how nervous they were about the way the wind was blowing? Who were afraid for their families? The ones who knew they were too old to start over, who were scared that they'd be forced into early retirement without the generous pension benefits the Beaumont Brewery had always offered its loyal employees?

"Which brings us back to the heart of the matter. I need you."

"No, you don't. You need my approval." Her lobster was no doubt getting cold, but she didn't have much of an appetite at the moment.

Something that might have been a smile played over his lips. For some reason, she took it as a compliment, as if he was acknowledging her intelligence for real this time, instead of paying lip service to it. "Why didn't you go into the family business? You'd have made a hell of a negotiator."

"I find business, in general, to be beneath me." She cast a cutting look at him. "Much like many of the people who willingly choose to engage in it."

He laughed then, a real thing that she wished grated on her ears and her nerves but didn't. It was a warm sound, full of humor and honesty. It made her want to smile. She didn't. "I'm not going to take the job."

"I wasn't going to offer it to you again. You're right— it is beneath you."

Here it came—the trap he was waiting to spring. He leaned forward, his gaze intent on hers and in the space of a second, before he spoke, she realized what he was about to say. All she could think was, *Oh, hell.*

"I don't want to hire you. I want to marry you."

Five

The weight of his statement hit Frances so hard Ethan was surprised she didn't crumple in the chair.

But of course she didn't. She was too refined, too schooled to let her shock show. Even so, her eyes widened and her mouth formed a perfect O, kissable in every regard.

"You want to…what?" Her voice cracked on the last word.

Turnabout is fair play, he decided as he let her comment hang in the air. She'd caught him completely off guard in the office yesterday and had clearly thought she could keep that shock and awe going. But tonight? The advantage was his.

"I want to marry you. More specifically, I want you to marry me," he explained. Saying the words out loud made his blood hum. When he'd come up with this plan, it had seemed like a bold-yet-risky business decision. He'd quickly realized that Frances Beaumont would absolutely not take a desk job, but the unavoidable fact was he needed her approval to validate his restructuring plans.

And what better way to show that the Beaumonts were on board with the restructuring than if he were legally wed to the favored daughter?

Yes, it had all seemed cut-and-dried when he'd formulated the plan last night. A sham marriage, designed to bolster his position within the company. He'd done a little digging into her past and discovered that she had tried to launch some sort of digital art gallery recently, but it'd gone under. So she might need funding. No problem.

But he'd failed to take into account the actual woman he'd just proposed to. The fire in her eyes more than matched the fire in her hair, and all of her lit a hell of a flame in him. He had to shift in his chair to avoid discomfort as he tried not to look at her lips.

"You want to get married?" She'd recovered some, the haughty tone of her voice overcoming her surprise. "How very flattering."

He shrugged. He'd planned for this reaction. Frankly, he'd expected nothing less, not from her.

He hadn't planned for the way her hand—her skin—had felt against his. But a plan was a plan, and he was in for far more than a penny. "Of course, I'm not about to profess my undying love for you. Admiration, yes." Her cheeks colored slightly. Nope, he hadn't planned for that, either.

Suddenly, his bold plan felt like the height of foolishness.

"My," she murmured. Her voice was soft, but he didn't miss the way it sliced through the air. "How I love to hear sweet nothings. They warm a girl's heart."

He grinned again. "I'm merely proposing an…arrangement, if you will. Open to negotiation. I already know a job in management is not for you." He sat back, trying to look casual. "I'm a man of considerable influence and power. Is there something you need that I can help you with?"

"Are you trying to *buy* me?" Her fingertips curled around the stem of her wineglass. He kept one hand on the napkin in his lap, just in case he found himself wearing the wine.

"As I said, this isn't a proposal based on love. It's based on need. You're already fully aware of how much I need you. I'm just trying to ascertain what you need to make this arrangement worth your time. Above and beyond making sure that your Brewery family is well taken care of, that is." He leaned forward again. He enjoyed negotiations like this—probing and prodding to find the other party's breaking point. And a little bit of guilt never hurt anything.

"What if I don't want to marry you? Surely you can't think you're the first man who's ever proposed to me out of the blue." The dismissal was slight, but it carried weight. She was doing her level best to toy with him.

And he'd be lying if he said he didn't enjoy it. "I have no doubt you've been fending off men for years. But this proposal isn't based on want." However, that didn't stop his gaze from briefly drifting down to her chest. She had *such* an amazing body.

Her lips tightened, and she fiddled with the button on her jacket. "Then what's it based on?"

"I'm proposing a short-term arrangement. A marriage of convenience. Love doesn't need to play a role."

"Love?" she asked, batting her eyelashes. "There's more to a marriage than that."

"Point. Lust also is not a part of my proposal. A one-year marriage. We don't have to live together. We don't have to sleep together. We need to occasionally be seen in public together. That's it."

She blinked at him. "You're serious, aren't you? What kind of marriage would *that* be?"

Now it was Ethan's turn to fidget with his wineglass. He didn't want to get into the particulars of his parents' marriage at the moment. "Suffice it to say, I've seen long-distance marriages work out quite well for all parties involved."

"How delightful," she responded, disbelief dripping off every word. "Are you gay?"

"What? No!" He jolted so hard that he almost knocked

his glass over. "I mean, not that there's anything wrong with that. But I'm not."

"Pity. I might consider a loveless, sexless marriage to a gay man. Sadly," she went on in a not-sad voice, "I don't trust you to hold up your sexless end of the bargain."

"I'm not saying we couldn't have sex." In fact, given the way she'd pressed her lips to his cheek earlier, the way she'd held his hand—he'd be perfectly fine with sex with her. "I'm merely saying it's not expected. It's not a deal breaker."

She regarded him with open curiosity. "So let me see if I understand this proposal, such as it is. You'd like me to marry you and lend the weight of the Beaumont name to your destruction of the Beaumont Brewery—"

"Reconstruction, not destruction," he interrupted.

She ignored him. "In a starter marriage that has a built-in sunset at one year, no other strings attached?"

"That sums it up."

"Give me one good reason why I shouldn't stab you in the hand with my knife."

He flinched. "Actually, I was waiting for you to give me a good reason." She looked at him flatly. "I read on-line that your digital art gallery recently failed." He said it gently. He could sympathize with a well-thought-out project going sideways—or backward.

She rested her hand on her knife. But she didn't say anything. Her eyes—beautiful light eyes that walked the line between blue and green—bore into him.

"If there was something that I—as an investor—could help you with," he went on, keeping his voice quiet, "well, that could be part of our negotiation. It'd be venture capital—*not* an attempt to buy you," he added. She took her hand off her knife and put it in her lap, which Ethan took as a sign that he'd hit the correct nerve. He went on, "I wouldn't—and couldn't—cut you a personal check. But as an angel investor, I'm sure we could come to terms you'd find satisfactory."

"Interesting use of the word *angel* there," she said. Her voice was quiet. None of the seduction or coquettishness that she'd wielded like a weapon remained.

Finally, he was talking to the real Frances Beaumont. No more artifice, no more layers. Just a beautiful, intelligent woman. A woman he'd just proposed to.

This was for the job, he reminded himself. He was only proposing because he needed to get control of the Beaumont Brewery, and Frances Beaumont was the shortest, straightest line between where he was today and where he needed to be. It had nothing to do with the actual woman.

"Do you do this often? Propose marriage to women connected with the businesses you're stripping?"

"No, actually. This would be a first for me."

She picked up her knife, and he unwittingly tensed. One corner of her perfect rosebud mouth quirked into a smile before she began to cut into her lobster tail. "Really? I suppose I should be flattered."

He began to eat his steak. It had cooled past the optimal temperature, but he figured that was the price one paid for negotiating before the main course arrived. "I'm never in one city for more than a year, usually only for a few months. I have, on occasion, made the acquaintance of a woman with whom I enjoy doing things such as this—dining out, seeing the sights."

"Having sex?" she asked bluntly.

She was trying to unnerve him again. It might be working. "Yes, when we're both so inclined. But those were short-term, no-commitment relationships, as agreed upon by both parties."

"Just a way to pass the time?"

"That might sound harsh, but yes. If you agree to the

arrangement, we could dine out like this, maybe attend the theater or whatever it is you do for fun here in Denver."

"This isn't exactly a one-horse town anymore, you know. We have theaters and gala benefits and art openings and a football team. Maybe you've heard of them?" Her gaze drifted down to his shoulders. "You might consider trying out for the front four."

Ethan straightened his shoulders. He wasn't a particularly vain man, but he kept himself in shape, and he'd be lying if he said he wasn't flattered that she'd noticed. "I'll keep it in mind."

They ate in silence. He decided it was her play. She hadn't stabbed him, and she hadn't thrown a drink in his face. He put the odds of getting her to go along with this plan at fifty-fifty.

And if she didn't… Well, he'd need a new plan.

Her lobster tail was maybe half-eaten when she set her cutlery aside. "I've never fielded a marriage proposal like yours before."

"How many have you fielded?"

She waved the question away. "I've lost count. A quickie wedding, a one-year marriage with no sex, an irreconcilable-differences, uncontested divorce—all in exchange for an investment into a property or project of my choice?"

"Basically." He'd never proposed before. He couldn't tell if her no-nonsense tone was a good sign or not. "We'd need a prenup."

"Obviously." She took a much longer pull on her wine. "I want five million."

"I'm sorry?"

"I have a friend who wants to launch a new art gallery, with me as the co-owner. She has a business plan worked up and a space selected. All we need is the capital." She pointed a long, red-tipped nail at him. "And you did offer to invest, did you not?"

She had him there. "I did. Do we have a deal?" He stuck out his hand and waited.

She must be out of her ever-loving mind.

As Frances regarded the hand Ethan had extended toward her, she was sure she had crossed some line from desperation into insanity to even consider his offer.

Would she really agree to marry the living embodiment of her family's downfall for what, essentially, was the promise of job security after he was gone? With five million—a too-large number she'd pulled out of thin air—she and Becky could open that gallery in grand style, complete with all the exhibitions and parties it took to wine and dine wealthy art patrons.

This time, it'd be different. It was Becky's business plan, after all. Not Frances's. But even that thought stung a bit. Becky's plan had a chance of working. Unlike all of Frances's grand plans.

She needed this. She needed something to go her way, something to work out right for once. With a five-million-dollar investment, she and Becky could get the gallery operational and Frances could move out of the Beaumont mansion. Even if she only lived in the apartment over the gallery, it'd still be hers. She could go back to being Frances Beaumont. She could feel like a grown-up in control of her own life.

All it'd take would be giving up that control for a year. Not just giving it up, but giving it to Ethan.

She felt as if she was on the verge of passing out, but she refused to betray a single sign of panic. She did not breathe in deep gulps. She did not drop her head in her hands. And she absolutely did not fiddle with anything.

She kept herself serene and calm and did all her panicking on the inside, where no one could see it.

"Well?" Ethan asked. But it wasn't a gruff demand for an answer. His tone was more cautious than that.

And then there was the man himself. This was all quite noble, this talk of no sex and no emotions. But that didn't change the fact of the matter—Ethan Logan was one hell of a package. He could make her shiver and shake with the kind of heat she hadn't felt in a very long time.

Not that it mattered, because it didn't.

"I don't believe in love," she announced, mostly to see what kind of reaction it'd get.

"You don't? That seems unusually cynical for a woman of your age and beauty."

She didn't try to hide her eye roll. "I only mention it because if you're thinking about pulling one of those 'I'll make her love me over time' stunts, it's best to nip it in the bud right now."

She'd seen what people did in the name of love. How they made grand promises they had every intention of keeping until the next pretty face came along. As much as she'd loved her father, she hadn't been blind to his wandering eye or his wandering hands. She'd seen exactly what had happened to her mother, Jeannie—all because she'd believed in the power of love to tame the untamable Hardwick Beaumont.

"I wouldn't dream of it." Ethan's hand still hung in the air between them.

"I won't love you," she promised him, putting her palm in his. "I'd recommend you not love me."

Something in his eyes tightened as his fingers closed around hers. "I hope admiration is still on the table?"

She let her gaze drift over his body again. It wasn't desire, not really. She was an art connoisseur, and she was merely admiring his form. And wondering how it'd function. "I suppose."

"When do you want to get married?"

She thought it over. *Married.* The word felt weird rattling around her head. She'd never wanted to be married, never wanted to be tied to someone who could hurt her.

Of course, her brother Phillip had recently had a fairytale wedding that had been everything she might have ever wanted, if she'd actually wanted it. Which she didn't.

No, a big public spectacle was not the way to go here. This was, by all public appearances, a whirlwind romance, starting yesterday when she'd sashayed into his office. "I think we should cultivate the impression that we are swept up in the throes of passion."

"Agreed."

"Let's get married in two weeks."

Just saying it out loud made her want to hyperventilate. What would her brothers say to this, her latest stunt in a long line of stunts? "Frannie," she could practically hear Chadwick intone in his too-serious voice. "I don't think…" And Matthew? He was the one who always wanted everyone to line up and smile for the cameras and look like a big happy family. What would he say when she up and got herself hitched?

Then there was Byron, her twin. She'd thought she'd known Byron better than any other person in the world, and vice versa. But in the matter of a few weeks, he'd gone from her brother to a married man with a son and another baby on the way. Well, if anyone would understand her sudden change in matrimonial status, it'd be Byron.

Everyone else—especially Chadwick and Matthew—would just have to deal. This was her life. She could damn well do what she pleased with it.

Even if that meant marrying Ethan Logan.

Six

Ethan didn't know if it was the wine or the woman, but throughout the rest of dinner, he felt light-headed.

He was going to get married. To Frances Beaumont. In two weeks.

Which was great. Everything was going according to plan. He would demonstrate to the world that the Beaumonts were behind the restructuring of the Beaumont Brewery. That would buy him plenty of goodwill at the Brewery.

Yup. It was a great plan. There was just one major catch.

Frances leaned toward him and shrugged her jacket off. The sight of her bare shoulders hammered a spike of desire up his gut. He wasn't used to this sort of craving. Even when he found a lady friend to keep him company during his brief stints in cities around the country, he didn't usually succumb to this much *lust*.

His previous relationships were founded on...well, on *not* lust. Companionship was a part of it, sure. The sex was a bonus, definitely. And the women he consorted with were certainly lovely.

But the way he reacted to Frances? That was something else. Something different.

Something that threatened to break free from him.

Which was ridiculous. He was the boss. He was in control of this—all of this. The situation, his desires—

Well, maybe not his desires, not when Frances leaned forward and looked up at him coyly through her lashes. It shouldn't work, but it did.

"Well, then. Shall we get started?"

"Started?" But the word died on his lips when she reached across the table and ran her fingertips over his chin.

"Started," she agreed. She held out her hand, and he took it. He had no choice. "I happen to know a thing or two about creating a public sensation. We're already off to a great start, what with the confrontation outside your office and now this very public dinner. Kiss my hand again."

He did as he was told, pressing her skin against his lips and getting a hint of expensive perfume and the underlying taste of Frances.

He looked up to find her beaming at him, the megawatt smile probably visible from out on the sidewalk. But it wasn't real. Even he could tell that.

"So, kissing hands is on the table?" He didn't move her hand far from his mouth. He didn't want to.

When had he lost his head this much? When had he been this swamped by raw, unadulterated want? He needed to get his head back out of his pants and focus. He had explicitly promised that he would not make sex a deal breaker. He needed to keep his word, or the deal would be done before it got started.

"Oh, yes," she purred. Then she flipped her hand over in his grip and traced his lower lip with her thumb. "I'd imagine that there are several things still on the table."

Such as? His blood was beating a new, merciless rhythm in his veins, driving that spike of desire higher and higher until he was in actual pain. His mind helpfully supplied several vivid images that involved him, Frances and a table.

He caught her thumb in his mouth and sucked on it, his tongue tracing the edge of her perfectly manicured nail. Her eyes widened with desire, her pupils dilating until he could barely see any of the blue-green color at all. He swore he could see her nipples tighten through the fabric of her dress. Oh, yeah—a table, a bed—any flat surface would do. It didn't even have to be flat. Good sex could be had standing up.

He let go of her thumb and kissed her hand again. "Do you want to get out of here?"

"I'd like that," she whispered back.

It took a few minutes to settle the bill, during which every single look she shot him only made his blood pound that much harder. When had he been this overcome with lust? When had a simple business arrangement become an epic struggle?

She stood, and he realized the dress was completely backless. The wide swath of smooth, creamy skin that was Frances's back lay bare before him. His fingers itched to trace the muscles, to watch her body twitch under his touch.

He didn't want her to put her jacket back on and cover up that beautiful skin. And, thankfully, she didn't. She waited for him to assist her with her chair and then said, "Will you carry my jacket for me?"

"Of course." He folded it over one arm and then offered his other to her.

She leaned into his touch, her gorgeous red curls brushing against his shoulder. "Did you ever play football?" she asked, running her hands up and down his forearms. "Or were you just born this way?"

There was something he was supposed to be remembering, something that was important about Frances. But he couldn't think about anything but the way she'd looked in that green dress yesterday and the way she looked right now. The way he felt when she touched him.

He flexed under her hands and was rewarded with a little gasp from her. "I played. I got a scholarship to play in college, but I blew out my knee."

They were walking down the long hallway that separated the restaurant from the hotel. Then it'd be a quick turn to the left and into the elevators. A man could get into a lot of trouble in an elevator.

But they didn't even make it to the elevator. The moment they got to the middle of the lobby, Frances reached across his chest and slid her hand under his coat. Just like it had in the office yesterday, her touch burned him.

"Oh, that sounds awful," she breathed, curling her fingers around his shirt and pulling him toward her.

The noise of the lobby faded away until there was only the touch of her hand and the beating of his heart.

He turned into her, lowering his head. "Terrible," he agreed, but he no longer knew what they were talking about. All he knew was that he was going to kiss her.

Their lips met. The kiss was tentative at first as he tested her and she tested him. But then her mouth opened for him, and his control—the control he'd maintained for years and years, the control that made him a savvy businessman with millions in the bank—shattered on him.

He tangled his hands into her hair and roughly pulled her up to his mouth so he could taste her better— taste all of her. Dimly, somewhere in the back of his mind where at least three brain cells were doing their best to think about something beyond Frances's touch, Frances's taste—dimly, he realized they were standing in the middle of a crowd, although he'd forgotten exactly where they were.

There was a wolf whistle. And a second one—this one accompanied by laughter.

Frances pulled away, her impressive chest heaving and her eyes glazed with lust. "Your suite," she whispered, and then her tongue darted out, tracing a path on her lips that he needed to follow.

"Yeah. Sure." She could have suggested jumping out of an airplane at thirty thousand feet and he would have done it. Just so long as she went down with him.

Somehow, despite the tangle of arms and jackets, they made it to the elevators and then onto one. Other people were waiting, but no one joined them on the otherwise-empty lift. "Sorry," Frances said to the waiting guests as she curled up against his chest. "We'll send it back down," she added as the doors closed and shut them away from the rest of the world.

Then they were alone. Ethan slid his hands down her bare back before he cupped her bottom. "Where were we?"

"Here," she murmured, pressing her lips against his neck, right above his collar. "And here." Her teeth scraped over his skin as she pressed the full length of her body against his. "And...here."

She didn't touch him through his pants, not with her hands—but with her body? She shifted against him, and the pressure drove those last three rational brain cells out of his mind. "God, yes," he groaned, fisting his hands into her curls and tilting her head back. "How could I forget?"

He didn't give her time to reply. He crushed his mouth against hers. There wasn't any more time for testing kisses—all that existed in the safe space of this little moving room was his need for her and, given the way she was kissing him back, her need for him.

He liked sex—he always had. He prided himself on being good at it. But had he ever been this excited? This consumed with need? He couldn't remember. He couldn't think, not with Frances moaning into his mouth and arching her back, pushing her breasts into his body.

He reached up and started to undo the tie at the back of her neck, but she grabbed his hand and held it at waist height. "We're almost there," she murmured in a coy tone. "Can you wait just a little longer?"

No. "Yes."

Love and sex and, yes, marriage—that was all about waiting. There'd never been any instant gratification in it for him. He'd waited until he'd been eighteen before losing his virginity because it was a test of sorts. Everyone else was going as fast as they could, but Ethan was different. Better. He could resist the fire. He would not get burned.

Frances shifted against him again, and he groaned in the most delicious agony that had ever consumed him. Her touch—even through his clothing— seared him. For the first time in his life, he wanted to dance with the flames.

One flame—one flame-haired woman—in particular. Oh, how they would dance.

The elevator dinged. "Is this us?" Frances asked in a shaky whisper.

"This way." He grabbed her hand and strode out of the elevator. It was perhaps not the most gentlemanly way of going about it— essentially dragging her in her impossible shoes along behind him—but he couldn't help himself. If she couldn't walk, he'd carry her.

His suite was at the end of a long, quiet hall. The only noise that punctuated the silence was the sound of his blood pounding in his temples, pushing him faster until he was all but running, pulling Frances in his wake. Each step was pain and pleasure wrapped in one, his erection straining to do anything but walk. Or run.

After what felt like an hour of never-ending journeying, he reached his door. Torturous seconds passed as he tried to get the key card to work. Then the door swung open and he was pulling her inside, slamming the door shut behind them and pinning her against it. Her hands curled into his shirt, holding him close.

He must have had one lone remaining brain cell functioning, because instead of ripping that dress off her body so he could feast himself upon it, he paused to say, "Tell me what you want."

Because whatever she wanted was what he wanted.

Or maybe she wasn't holding him close. The thought occurred to him belatedly, just about the time her mouth curved up into what was a decidedly nonseductive smile. She pushed on his chest, and he had no choice but to let her. "Anything I want?"

She'd pushed him away, but her voice was still colored with craving, with a need he could feel more than hear. Maybe she wanted him to tie her up. Maybe she wanted to tie him up instead. Whatever it was, he was game.

"Yeah." He tried to lean back down to kiss her again, but she was strong for a woman her size. She held him back.

"I wonder what's on TV?"

It took every ounce of her willpower to push Ethan back, to push herself away from the door, but she did it anyway. She forced herself to stroll casually over to the dresser that held the flat-screen television and grab the remote. Then, without daring to look at Ethan, she flopped down on the bed. It was only after she'd propped herself up on her elbows and turned on the television that she hazarded a look at him.

He was leaning against the door. His jacket was half off; his shirt was a rumpled mess. He looked as though she'd mauled him. She was a little hazy on the details, but, as best she could recall, she had.

She turned her attention back to the television, randomly clicking without actually seeing what was on-screen. She'd only meant to put on a little show for the crowd. If they were going to do this sham marriage thing in two weeks, they needed to start their scandalous activities right now. Kissing in a lobby, getting into the elevator together? She was unmistakable with her red hair. And Ethan—he wasn't that hard to look up. People would make the connection. And people, being reliable, would talk.

When she'd stroked his face at dinner, she'd seen the headlines in her mind. "Whirlwind Romance between Beaumont Heir and New Brewery CEO?" That was what Ethan wanted, wasn't it? The air of Beaumont approval. This was nothing but a PR ploy.

Except

Except for the way he'd kissed her. The way he'd kept kissing her.

At some point between when he'd sucked on her thumb and the kiss in the lobby—the first one, she mentally corrected—the game they'd been playing had changed.

It was all supposed to have been for show. But the way he had pinned her against the door in this very nice room? The way his deep voice had begged her to tell him what she wanted?

That hadn't felt like a game. That hadn't been for show.

The only thing that had kept her from spinning right over the edge was the knowledge that he didn't want her. Oh, he wanted her—naked, that was—but he didn't want *her*, Frances—complicated and crazy and more than a little lost. He'd only touched her because he wanted something, and she could not allow that to cloud her thinking.

"What—" He cleared his throat, but it didn't make his voice any stronger. "What are you doing?"

"Watching television." She kicked her heels up.

She cut another side glance at Ethan. He hadn't moved. "Why?"

It took everything Frances had to make herself sound glib and light. "What else are we going to do?"

His mouth dropped down to his chest. "I don't mean to sound crass, but...sex?"

Frances couldn't help it. Her gaze drifted down to the impressive bulge in his pants—the same bulge that had ground against her in the elevator.

Sex. The thought of undoing those pants and letting that bulge free sent an uncontrollable shiver down her back. She snapped her eyes back to the television screen. "Really," she said in a dismissive tone.

There was a moment where the only noise in the room was the sound of Ethan breathing heavily and some salesman on TV yelling about a cleaning cloth.

"Then what was that all about?" Ethan gruffly demanded.

"Creating an impression." She did not look at him.

"And who were we impressing in the elevator?"

She put on her most innocent look—which, granted, would have been a lot easier if her nipples weren't still chafing against the front of her dress. "Fine. A test, then."

Ethan was suddenly in front of the television, arms crossed as he glared down at her. "A *test*?"

"It has to be convincing, this relationship we're pretending to have," she explained, making a big show of looking around his body, rather than at the still-obvious bulge in his pants. "But part of the deal was that we don't have sex." She let that sink in before adding, "You're not going to back out of the deal, are you?"

Because that was a risk, and she knew it. There were many ways a deal could go south—especially when sex was on the line.

"You're testing *me*?" He took a step to the side, trying to block her view of the screen again.

"I won't marry just anyone, you know. I have standards."

She could feel the weight of his glare on her face, but

she refused to allow her skin to flush. She leaned the other way. Not that she had any idea of what she was watching. Her every sense was tuned into Ethan.

It'd be so easy to change her mind, to tell him that he'd passed his first test and that she had another test in mind—one that involved less clothing for everyone. She could find out what was behind that bulge and whether or not he knew how to use it.

She could have a few minutes where she wouldn't have to feel alone and adrift, where she could lose herself in Ethan. But that was all it would be. A few minutes.

And then the sex would be done, and she'd go back to being broke, unemployed Frances who was trading on her good looks even as they began to slip away. And Ethan? Well, he'd probably still marry her and fund her art gallery. But he'd know her in a way that felt too intimate, too personal.

Not that she was a shy, retiring virgin—she wasn't. But she had to keep her eye on the long game here, which was reestablishing herself and the Beaumont name and inflicting as much collateral damage on the new Brewery owners and operators as possible.

So this was her, inflicting a little collateral damage on Ethan—even if the dull throb that seemed to circle between her legs and up to her nipples felt like a punishment in its own right.

Okay, so it was a lot of collateral damage.

She realized she was holding her breath as she waited. Would he render their deal null and void? She didn't think so. She might not always be the best judge of men, but she was pretty sure Ethan wasn't going to claim sex behind tired old lines like "she led me on." There was something about him that was more honorable than that.

Funny. She hadn't thought of him as honorable before this moment.

But he was. He muttered something that sounded like a curse before he stalked out of her line of vision. She heard the bathroom door slam shut and exhaled.

The score was Frances: two and Ethan: one. She was winning.

She shifted on the bed. If only victory wasn't taking the shape of sexual frustration.

Frances had just stumbled on some sort of sporting event—basketball, maybe?—when Ethan threw the bathroom door open again. He stalked into the room in nothing but his trousers and a plain white T-shirt. He went over to the desk, set against the window, and opened his computer. "How long do you need to be here?" he asked in an almost-mean voice.

"That's open to discussion." She looked over at him. He was pointedly glaring at the computer screen. "I obviously didn't bring a change of clothing."

That got his attention. "You wouldn't stay the night, would you?"

Was she wrong, or was there a note of panic in his voice? She pushed herself into a sitting position, tucking her feet under her skirt. "Not yet, I don't think. But perhaps by next week, yes. For appearances."

He stared at her for another tight moment and then ground the heels of his palms into his eyes. "This seemed like *such* a good idea in my head," he groaned.

She almost felt bad for him. "We'll need to have dinner in public again tomorrow night. In fact, at least four or five nights a week for the next two weeks. Then I'll start sleeping over and—"

"Here?" He made a show of noticing there was only one bed and a pullout couch. "Shouldn't I come to your place?"

"Um, no." The very last thing she needed was to parade her fake intended husband through the Beaumont mansion. God only knew what Chadwick would do if he caught wind of this little scheme of hers. "No, we should stick to a more public setting. The hotel suits nicely."

"Well." He sagged back in his chair. "That's the evenings. And during the day?"

She considered. "I'll come to the office a couple of times a week. We'll say that we're discussing the sale of the antiques. On the days I don't stop by, you should have Delores order flowers for me."

At that, Ethan cocked an eyebrow. "Seriously?"

"I like flowers, and you want to look thoughtful and attentive, don't you?" she snapped. "Fake marriage or not, I expect to be courted."

"And what do I get out of this again?"

"A wife." A vein stood out on his forehead, and she swore she could see the pulse in his massive neck even at this distance. "And an art gallery." She smiled widely.

The look he shot her was hard enough that she shrank back.

"So," she said, unwilling to let the conversation drift back to sex just quite yet. "Tell me about this successful long-distance relationship that we're modeling our marriage upon."

"What?"

"You said at dinner that you've seen long-distance relationships work quite well. Personally, I've never seen any relationship work well, regardless of distance."

The silence between them grew. In the background, she heard the whistles and buzzers of the game on the TV.

"It's not important," he finally said. "So, fine. We won't exactly be long-distance for the next two weeks. Then we get married. Then what?"

"Oh, I imagine we'll have to keep up appearances for a month or so."

"A *month*?"

"Or so. Ethan," she said patiently. "Do you want this

to be convincing or not? If we stop being seen together the day after we tie the knot, no one will believe it wasn't a publicity stunt."

He jumped out of his chair and began to pace. "See— when I said long-distance, I didn't actually anticipate being in your company constantly."

"Is that a bad thing?" She batted her eyes when he shot her an incredulous look.

"Only if you keep kissing me like you did in the elevator."

"I can kiss you less, but we have to spend time together." She shifted so she was cross-legged on the bed. "Can you do that? At the very least, we have to be friends."

The look he gave her was many things—perhaps angry, horny—but "friendly" was not on the list.

"If you can't, we can still call it off. A night of wild indiscretion, we'll both 'no comment' to the press—it's not a big deal." She shrugged.

"It's a huge deal. If I roll into the Brewery after everyone thinks I had a one-night stand with you and then threw you to the curb, they'll hang me up by my toenails."

"I am rather well liked by the employees," she said, not a little smugly. "Which is why you thought up this plan in the first place, is it not?"

He looked to the ceiling and let out another muttered curse. "Such a good idea," he said again.

"Best laid plans of mice and men and all that," she agreed. "Well?"

He did a little more unproductive pacing, and she let him think. Honestly, she didn't know which way she wanted him to go.

There'd been the heat that had arced between them, heat that had melted her in places that hadn't been properly melted in a very long time. She'd kissed before, but Ethan's mouth against hers—his body against hers—

She needed the money. She needed the fresh start that an angel investor could provide. She needed to feel the power and prestige that went with the Beaumont name—or had, before Ethan had taken over. She needed her life back. And if she got to take the one man who embodied her fall from grace down a couple of pegs, all the better.

It was all at her fingertips. All she had to do was get married to a man she'd promised not to love. How hard could that be? She could probably even have sex with him—and it would be *so* good—without love ever entering into the equation.

"No more kissing in the elevator."

"Agreed." At least, that's what she said. She would be lying if she didn't admit she was enjoying the way she'd so clearly brought him to his knees with desire.

"What do people do in this town on a Sunday afternoon?"

That was a yes. She'd get her funding and make a few headlines and be back on top of the world for a while.

"I'll take it easy on you tomorrow—we need to give the gossip time to develop."

He shot her a look and, for the first time since dinner, smiled. It appeared to be a genuine smile even. It set off his strong chin and deep eyes nicely. Not that she wanted him to know that. "Should I be worried that you know this much about manipulating the press?"

She brushed that comment aside. "It comes with the territory of being a Beaumont. I'll leave after this game is over, and then I'll stop by the office on Monday. Deal?"

"Deal."

They didn't shake on it. Neither of them, it seemed, wanted to tempt fate by touching again.

Seven

"Becky? You're not going to believe this," Frances said as she stood in front of her closet, weighing the red evening gown versus something more…restrained. She hated being restrained, but on her current budget, it was a necessary concession.

"What? Something good?"

Frances grinned. Becky was easily excitable. Frances was pretty sure she could hear her friend bouncing up and down. "Something great. I found an investor."

There was some screaming. Frances held the phone as far away from her face as she could until the noise died down. She flicked through the hangers. She needed something sexy that didn't look as if she was trying too hard. The red gown would definitely be trying too hard for a Monday at the office. "Still with me?"

"Ohmygosh—this is so exciting! How much were they willing to invest?"

Frances braced herself for more screaming. "Up to five."

"Thousand?"

"Million." She immediately jerked the phone away from her head, but there was no sound. She cautiously put it back to her ear. "Becky?"

"I—it—what? I heard you wrong," she said with a nervous laugh. "I thought you said…"

"Million. Five million," Frances repeated, her fingers landing on her one good suit—the Escada. It was a conservative cut—at least by her standards—with a formfitting pencil skirt that went below her knee and a close-cropped jacket with only a little peplum at the waist.

It was the color, however—a warm hot pink—that made her impossible to miss.

Oh—this would be perfect. All business but still dramatic. She pulled it out.

"What—how? *How?*" Frances had never heard Becky this speechless before. "Your brothers?"

Frances laughed. "Oh no—you know Chadwick cut me off after the last debacle. This is a new investor."

There was a pause. "Is he cute?"

Frances scowled—not that Becky could see it, but she did anyway. She did not like being predictable. "No." And that wasn't a lie.

Ethan was *not* cute. He existed in the space between handsome and gorgeous. He wasn't pretty enough to be gorgeous—his features were too rough, too masculine. But handsome—that wasn't right, either. He exuded too much raw sexuality to be handsome.

"Well?" Becky demanded.

"He's…nice."

"Are you sleeping with him?"

"No, it's not like that. In fact, sex isn't even on the table." Her mind oh so helpfully provided a mental picture that completely contradicted that statement. She could see it now—Ethan bending her over a table, yanking her skirt up and her panties down and—

Becky interrupted that thought. "Frannie, I just don't want you to do something stupid."

"I won't," she promised. "But I have a meeting with

him tomorrow morning. How quickly can you revise the business plan to accommodate a five-million-dollar investment?"

"Uh... Let me call you back," Becky said.

"Thanks, Becks." Frances ended the call and fingered the fine wool of her suit. This wasn't stupid, really. This was...marriage with a purpose. And that purpose went far beyond funding an art gallery, although that was one part of it.

This was about putting the Beaumonts back in control of their own destiny. Okay, this was about putting one Beaumont—Frances—back in control of her destiny. But that still counted for a lot. She needed to get over this slump she was in. She needed her name to mean something again. She needed to feel as if she'd done something for the family honor instead of being a deadweight.

Marrying Ethan was the means to a bunch of different ends. That was all.

Those other men who'd proposed, they'd wanted what she represented, too—the Beaumont name, the Beaumont fortune—but they'd never wanted her. Not the real her. They had wanted the illusion of perfection she projected. They wanted her to look good on their arm.

What was different about Ethan? Well, he got points for being up front about his motivations. Nothing couched in sweet words about how special she was or anything. Just a straight-up negotiation. It was refreshing. Really. She didn't want anything sweet that was nothing but a lie. She didn't want him to try and make her love him.

She had not lied. She would not love him.

That was how it had to be.

"Delores," Frances said as she swept into the reception area. "Is Ethan—I mean, Mr. Logan—in?" She tried to blush at the calculated name screw-up, but she wasn't sure she could pull it off.

Delores shot her an unreadable glance over the edge of her glasses. "Had a good weekend, did we?"

Well. That was all the confirmation Frances needed that the stunt she'd pulled back in the hotel had done exactly as she'd intended. People had noticed, and those people were talking. Of course, there'd been some online chatter, but Delores wasn't the kind of woman who existed on social media. If she'd heard about the "date," then it was a safe bet the whole company knew all the gritty details.

"It was lovely." And that part was not calculated at all. Kissing Ethan had, in fact, been quite nice. "He's not all bad, I don't think."

Delores snorted. "Just bad enough?"

"Delores!" This time, her blush was more unplanned. Who knew the older lady had it in her?

"Yes, he's in." Delores's hand hovered near the intercom.

"Oh, don't—I want to surprise him," Frances said.

As she swept open the massive oak door, she heard Delores say, "Oh, we're all surprised," under her breath.

Ethan was sitting at her father's desk, his head bent over his computer. He was in his shirtsleeves, his tie loosened. When she flung the door open, his head popped up. But instead of looking surprised, he looked pleased to see her. "Ah, Frances," he said, rising to his feet.

None of the strain that she'd inflicted on him two days ago showed on his face now. He smiled warmly as he came around the desk to greet her. He did not, she noticed, touch her. Not even a handshake. "I was expecting you at some point today."

Despite the lack of physical contact, his eyes took in her hot-pink suit. She did a little twirl for him, as if she needed his approval when they both knew she didn't. Still, when he murmured, "I'm beginning to think the black dress is the most conservative look you have," she felt her cheeks warm.

For a second, she thought he was going to lean forward and kiss her on the cheek. He didn't. "You would not be wrong." She waltzed over to the leather love seats and spread herself out on one. "So? Heard any of the chatter?"

"I've been working. Is there chatter?"

Frances laughed. "You can be adorably naive. Of course there's chatter. Or did Delores not give you the same look she gave me?"

"Well..." He tugged at his shirt collar, as if it'd suddenly grown a half size too small. "She was almost polite to me this morning. But I didn't know if that was because of us or something else. Maybe she got lucky this weekend."

Unlike some of us. It was the unspoken phrase on the end of that statement that was as loud as if he'd pronounced the words.

She grinned and crossed her legs as best she could in a skirt that tight. "Regardless of Delores's private life, she's aware that we had an intimate dinner. And if Delores is aware of it, the rest of the company is, as well. There were several mentions on the various social media sites and even a teaser in the *Denver Post* online."

His eyes widened. "All of that from one dinner, huh? I am impressed."

She shrugged, as if this were all just another day at the office. Well, for her, it sort of was. "Now we're here."

He notched an eyebrow at her. "And we should be doing...what?"

She slipped the computer out of her bag. "You have a choice. We can discuss art or we can discuss art galleries. I've worked up a prospectus for potential investors."

Ethan let out a bark of laughter. "I've got to stop being surprised by you, don't I?"

"You really do," she agreed demurely. "In all honesty, I'm not that shocking. Not compared to some of my siblings."

"Tell me about them," he said, taking a perfectly safe seat to her right—not within touching distance. "Since we'll be in-laws and all that. Will I get to meet them?"

"It does seem unavoidable." She hadn't really considered the scene where the Beaumonts welcomed Ethan into the family fold with open arms. "I have nine half siblings from my father's four marriages. My older brothers are aware of other illegitimate siblings, but it's not unreasonable that there are more out there." She shrugged, as if that were normal.

Well, it was for her, anyway. Marriages, children, more children—and love had nothing to do with it.

Maybe there'd been a time, back when she was still a little girl who'd twirled in this office, when she'd been naive and innocent and had thought that her father loved her—and her brothers, their mother. That they were a family.

But then there'd been the day... She'd known her parents weren't happy. It was impossible to miss, what with all the screaming, fights, thrown dishes and slammed doors.

And it'd been Donut Friday and she'd been driven to the office with all those boxes and had bounced into the office to see her daddy and found him kissing someone who wasn't her mommy.

She'd stood there, afraid to yell, afraid to not yell—or cry or scream or do something that gave voice to the angry pain that started in her chest and threatened to leak out of her eyes. In the end, she'd done nothing, just like Owen, the driver who'd brought her and was carrying the donuts. Nothing to let her father know how much it hurt to see his betrayal. Nothing to let her mother know that Frances knew now what the fights were about.

But she knew. She couldn't un-know it, either. And

if she called her daddy on it—asked why he was kissing the secretary who'd always been so nice to Frances—she knew her father might put her aside like he'd put her mother aside.

So she said nothing. She showed nothing. She handed out donuts on that day with the biggest, best smile she could manage. Because that's what a Beaumont did. They went on, no matter what.

Just like now. So what if Ethan would eventually have to meet the family? So what if her siblings would react to this marriage with the same mix of shock and horror she'd felt when she'd walked in on her father that cold gray morning so long ago? She would go on—head up, shoulders back, a smile on her face. Her business failed? She couldn't get a job? She'd lost her condo? She'd been reduced to accepting the proposal of a man who only wanted her for her last name?

Didn't matter. Head up, shoulders back, a smile on her face. Just like right now. She called up the prospectus that Becky had put together yesterday in a flurry of excited phone calls and emails. Becky was the brains of the operation, after all—Frances was the one with the connections. And if she could deliver Ethan gift wrapped...

An image of him in nothing but a strategically placed bow popped before her. Christmas might be long gone, but there'd be something special about unwrapping *him* as a present.

She shook that image from her mind and handed the computer over to Ethan. "Our business plan."

He scrolled through it, but she got the distinct feeling he was barely looking at it. "Four wives?"

"Indeed. As you can see, my partner, Rebecca Rosenthal, has mocked up the design for the space as well as a cost-benefit analysis." She leaned over to click on the next tab. "Here's a sampling of the promotion we have planned."

"Ten siblings? Where do you fall in that?"

"I'm fifth." For some reason, she didn't want to talk about her family.

Detailing her father's affairs and indiscretions in this, his former office, felt wrong. This was where he'd been a good father to her. Even after she'd walked in on him cheating with his secretary, when she hadn't thrown a fit and hadn't tattled on him, he'd still doted on her when she was here. The next Donut Friday, she remembered, he'd had a pretty necklace waiting for her, and once again she'd been Daddy's girl for a few special minutes each week.

She didn't want to sully those memories. "Chadwick and Phillip with my father's first wife, Matthew and then Byron and me—we're twins—with his second wife." She hated referring to her mother by that number, as if that's all Jeannie had contributed. Wife number two, children three, four and five.

"You have a twin?" Ethan cut in.

"Yes." She gave him humorous look. "He's very protective of me." She did not mention that Byron was busy with his new wife and son. Better to let him worry about how her four older brothers would deal with him if he crossed a line.

Ethan's eyebrows jumped up. "And there were five more?"

"Yup. Lucy and Harry with my father's third wife. Johnny, Toni and Mark with his fourth. The younger ones are in their early twenties, for the most part. Toni and Mark are still in college and, along with Johnny, they all still live at the Beaumont mansion with Chadwick and his family." She rattled off her younger siblings' names as if they were items to be checked off a list.

"That must have been…interesting, growing up in that household."

"You have no idea." She made light of it, but *interesting* didn't begin to cover it.

She and Byron had been in an odd position in the household, straddling the line between the first generation of Hardwick Beaumont's sons and the last. Being five years older than she and Byron, Matthew was Chadwick and Phillip's contemporary. And since Matthew was their full brother, Byron and Frances had grown closer to the two older Beaumont brothers.

But then, her first stepmother—May, the not-evil one—had harbored delusional fantasies about how Frances and May's daughter, Lucy, would be the very best of friends, a period of time that painfully involved matching outfits for ten-year-old Frances and three-year-old Lucy. Which had done the exact opposite of what May intended—Lucy couldn't stand the sight of Frances. The feeling was mutual.

And the youngest ones—well, they'd been practically babies when Frances was a teenager. She barely knew them.

They were all Beaumonts, and, by default, that meant they were all family.

"What about you? Any strings of siblings floating around?"

Ethan shook his head. "One younger brother. No stepparents. It was a pretty normal life." Something in the way he said it didn't ring true, though.

No stepparents? What an odd way to phrase it. "Are you close? With your family, I mean." He didn't answer right away, so she added, "Since they'll be my in-laws, too."

"We keep in touch. I imagine the worst-case scenario is that my mother shows up to visit."

We keep in touch. What was it he'd said, about long-distance relationships working?

It was his turn to change the subject before she could

drill for more information. "You weren't kidding about an art gallery, were you?"

"I am *highly* qualified," she repeated. This time, her smile was more genuine. "We envision a grand space with enough room to highlight sculpture and nontraditional media, as well as hosting parties. As you can see, a five-million-dollar investment will practically guarantee success. I think that, as a grand opening, it would be ideal to host a showing of the antiques in this room. I don't want to auction off these pieces. Too impersonal."

He ignored the last part and focused instead on the one part Frances would have preferred to gloss over. "Practically?" He glanced at her. "What kind of track record do you have with these types of ventures?"

Frances cleared her throat as she uncrossed and re-crossed her legs before leaning toward Ethan. Her distraction didn't work this time. At least, not as well. His gaze only lingered on her legs for a few seconds. "This is a more conservative investment than my last ventures," she said smoothly. "Plus, Rebecca is going to be handling more of the business side of the gallery—that's her strong suit."

"You're saying you won't be in charge? That doesn't seem like you."

"Any good businesswoman knows her limitations and how to compensate for them."

His lips quirked up into a smile. "Indeed."

There was a knock at the door. "Come in," Ethan said. Frances didn't change her position. She wasn't exactly sitting in Ethan's lap, but her posture indicated that they were engaged in a personal discussion.

The door opened and what looked like two-dozen red roses walked into the room. "The flowers you ordered, Mr. Logan." Delores's voice came from behind the blooms. "Where should I put them?"

"On the table here." He motioned toward the coffee

table, but Delores couldn't see through that many blooms, so she put them on the conference table instead.

"That's a lot of roses," Frances said in shock.

Delores fished the card out of the arrangement and carried it over to her. "For you, dear," she said with a knowing smile.

"That'll be all, Delores. Thank you," Ethan said. But he was looking at Frances as he said it.

Delores smirked and was gone. Ethan stood and carried the roses over to the coffee table while Frances read the note.

Fran—here's to more beautiful evenings with a beautiful woman—E.

It hadn't been in an envelope. Delores had read it, no doubt. It was thoughtful and sweet, and Frances hadn't expected it at all.

With a sinking feeling in her stomach, Frances realized she might have underestimated Ethan.

"Well?" Ethan said. He sounded pleased with himself.

"Don't call me Fran," she snapped. Or she tried to. It came out more as a breathless whisper.

"What should I call you? It seems like a pet name would be the thing. Snoogums?"

She shot him a look. "I thought I said you should send me flowers when I didn't come to the office. Not when I was already here."

"I always send flowers after a great first date with a beautiful woman," he replied. He sounded sincere about it, which did not entirely jibe with the way he'd acted after she'd left him hanging.

In all honesty, it did sound sweet, as if the time they'd spent together had been a real date. But did that matter?

So what if this was a thoughtful gesture? So what if it

meant he'd been paying attention to her when she'd said she liked flowers and she expected to be courted? So what if the roses were gorgeous? It didn't change the fact that, at its core, this was still a business transaction. "It wasn't a great date. You didn't even get lucky."

He didn't look offended at this statement. "I'm going to marry you. Isn't that lucky enough?"

"Save it for when we're in public." But as she said it, she buried her nose in the roses. The heady fragrance was her favorite.

It'd been a while since anyone had sent her flowers. There was a small part of her that was more than a little flattered. It was a grand gesture—or it would have been, if it'd been sincere.

Honest? Yes. Ethan was being honest with her. He'd been totally up front about the reasons behind his interest in her.

But his attention wasn't sincere. These were, if possible, the most insincere roses ever. Just all part of the game— and she had to admit, he was playing his part well.

The thought made her sadder than she'd thought it might. Which was ridiculous. Sincerity was just another form of weakness that people could use to exploit you. Her mother had sincerely loved her father, and see where that had gotten her? Nowhere good.

The corners of Ethan's eyes crinkled, as if her less-than-gracious response amused him. "Fine. Speaking of, when would you like to be seen together in public again?"

"Tomorrow night. Mondays are not the most social day of the week. I think the roses today will accomplish everything we want them to."

"Dinner? Or did you have something else in mind?"

Did he sound hopeful? "Dinner is good for now. I'm keeping my eyes open for an appropriate activity this weekend."

He nodded, as if she'd announced that the sales projections for the quarter were on target. But then he stood and handed her computer back to her. As he did so, he leaned down and whispered, "I'm glad you liked the roses," in her ear. And, damn it all, heat flushed her body.

She tilted her head up to him. "They're beautiful," she murmured. There was no audience for this, no crowd to guess and gossip. Here, in the safety of this office, there was only him and her and dozens of honest roses.

He was close enough to kiss—more than close enough. She could see the golden tint to his brown eyes that made them lighter, warmer. He had a faint scar on the edge of his nose and another one on his chin. Football injuries or brawls? He had the body of a brawler. She'd felt that for herself the other night.

Ethan Logan was a big, strong man with big, strong muscles. And he'd sent her flowers.

She could kiss him. Not for show but for herself. She was going to marry him, after all. Shouldn't she get something out of it? Something beyond an art gallery and a restored sense of family pride?

His fingers slid under her chin, lifting her face to his. His breath was warm on her cheeks. Many things were warm at this point.

Not for the Beaumonts. Not for the gallery. Just for her. Ethan was just for *her*.

They held that pose as Frances danced right up to the line of kissing Ethan because she wanted to. But she didn't cross it. And after a moment, he relinquished his hold on her. But the warmth in his eyes didn't dim. He didn't act as if she'd rejected him.

Instead, he said, "You're welcome."

And that?

That was sincere.

Oh, hell.

Eight

First thing Tuesday morning, Ethan had Delores order lilies and send them to Frances. Roses every day felt too clichéd and he'd always liked lilies, anyway.

"Any message?" the old battle-ax asked. She sounded smug.

Ethan considered. The message, he knew, was as much for Delores's loose lips as it was for Frances. And no matter what Frances said, they needed pet names for each other. "Red—until tonight. E."

Delores snorted. "Will do, boss. By the way…"

Ethan paused, his hand on the intercom switch. *Boss?* That was the most receptionist-like thing Delores had said to him yet. "Yes?"

"The latest attendance reports are in. We're operating at full capacity today."

A sense of victory flowed through him. After four days, the implied Beaumont Seal of Approval was already working its magic. "I'm glad to hear it."

He switched off the intercom and stared at it for a moment. But instead of thinking about his next restructuring move, his thoughts drifted back to Frances.

She was going to kill him for the Red bit; he was reasonably confident about that. But there'd been that moment yesterday where he'd thought all her pretense had fallen away. She'd been well and truly stunned that he'd had flowers delivered for her. And in that moment, she'd seemed…vulnerable. All of her cynical world-weariness had fallen away, and she'd been a beautiful woman who'd appreciated a small gesture he'd made for her.

Marriage notwithstanding, she wasn't looking for anything long term. Neither was he. But that didn't mean the short term couldn't mean *something*, did it? He didn't need the fire to burn for long. He just needed it to burn bright.

He flipped the intercom back on. "Delores? Did you place that order yet?"

He heard her murmur something that sounded like, "One moment," before she said more clearly, "in process. Why?"

"I want to change the message. Red—" Then he faltered. "Looking forward to tonight. Yours, E." Which was not exactly a big change and he felt a little foolish for making it. He switched off the intercom again.

His phone rang. It was his partner at CRS, Finn Jackson. Finn was the one who pitched CRS to conglomerates. He was a hell of a salesman. "What's up?"

"Just wanted to let you know—there's activity," Finn began without any further introduction. "A private holding company is making noise about AllBev's handling of the Beaumont Brewery purchase."

Ethan frowned. "Link?"

"On its way." Seconds later, the email with the link popped up. Ethan scanned the article. Thankfully, it wasn't an attack on CRS's handling of the transition. However, this private holdings company, ZOLA, had written a letter stating that the Brewery was a poor strategic purchase for AllBev and they should dump the company—preferably on the cheap, no doubt.

"What is this?" he asked Finn. "A takeover bid? Is it the Beaumonts?"

"I don't think so," Finn replied, but he didn't sound convinced. "It's owned by someone named Zeb Richards—ring any bells for you?"

"None. How does this impact us?"

"This mostly appears to be an activist shareholder making noise. I'll keep tabs on AllBev's reaction, but I don't think this impacts you at the moment. I just wanted to keep you aware of the situation." Finn cleared his throat, which was his great tell. "You could ask your father if he knows anything."

Ethan didn't say a damned thing. His father? *Hell no*. He would never show the slightest sign of weakness to his old man because, unlike the Beaumonts, family meant nothing to Troy Logan. It never had, it never would.

"Or," Finn finally said, dragging out the word, "you could maybe see if anyone on the ground knows anything about this Zeb character?"

Frances. "Yeah, I can ask around. If you hear anything else, let me know. I'd prefer for the company not to be resold until we've fulfilled our contract. It'd look like a failure on the behalf of CRS—that we couldn't turn the company around fast enough."

"Agreed." With that, Finn hung up.

Ethan stared at his computer without seeing the files. He was just starting to get a grip on this company, thanks to Frances.

This ZOLA, whatever the hell it was, *felt* like it had something to do with the Beaumonts. Who else cared about this beer company? Ethan did a quick search. Privately held firm located in New York, a list of their successful investments—but not much else. Not even a picture of Zeb Richards. Something about it was off. This could easily be a shell corporation set up with the express purpose of wrestling the Brewery away from AllBev and back into Beaumont hands.

Luckily, Ethan happened to have excellent connections here on the ground. He'd have to tread carefully, though.

He needed Frances Beaumont. The production lines at full capacity today? That wasn't his keen management skills in action, as painful as it was to admit. That was all Frances.

But on the other hand…her sudden appearance happening so closely to this ZOLA business? It couldn't be a coincidence, could it?

Maybe it was; maybe it wasn't. One thing was for sure. He was going to find out *before* he married her and *before* he cut her a huge investment check.

He sent a follow-up message to his lawyers about protecting his assets and then glanced over Frances's art gallery plans again. He knew nothing about art, which was surprising, considering his mother was the living embodiment of "artsy-fartsy." So as an art space, it didn't mean much to him. But as a business investment?

It wasn't that he couldn't spot her the five million. He had that and much more in the bank—and that didn't count his golden-parachute bonuses and stock options. Restructuring corporations was a job that paid extremely well. It just felt…

Too familiar. Like he was hell-bent on replicating his parents' unorthodox marriage. And that wasn't what he wanted.

He pushed the thoughts of his all-business father and flighty mother out of his brain. He had a company to run, a private equity firm to investigate and a woman to woo, if people still did that. And above all that, tonight he had a date.

This really wasn't that different from what he normally did, Ethan told himself as he waited at the bar of some hip restaurant. He rolled into a new town, met a woman and did the wining-and-dining thing. He saw the sights, had a little fun and then, when it was time, he moved on. This was standard stuff for him.

Which did not explain why he was sipping his gin and tonic with a little more enthusiasm than the drink required. He was just…bracing himself for another evening of sexual frustration, that was all. Because he knew that, no matter what she was wearing tonight, he wouldn't be able to take his eyes off Frances.

Maybe it wouldn't be so bad if she were just another pretty face. But she wasn't. He'd have to sit there and look at her and then also be verbally pummeled by her sharp wit as she ran circles around him. She challenged him and pushed him to his very limits of self-control, and that was something he could honestly say didn't happen much. Oh, the women he'd seen in the past were all perfectly intelligent ladies, but they didn't see their role of temporary companion as one that included the kind of conversation that bordered on warfare.

But Frances? She was armed like a Sherman tank, and she had excellent aim. She knew how to take him out with a few well-chosen words and a tilt of her head. He was practically defenseless against her.

His only consolation—aside from her company—was that he'd managed to slip past her armor a few times.

Then Frances was there, framed by the doorway. She had on a thick white coat with a fur collar that was belted tightly at the waist and a pair of calf-high boots in supple brown leather. Her hair was swept into an elegant updo and—Ethan blinked. Did she have flowers in her hair? Lilies?

Perhaps the rest of the restaurant was pondering the same question because he would have sworn the whole place paused to note her arrival.

She spotted him and favored him with a small personal

smile. Then she undid the belt of her coat and let it fall off her shoulders.

This wasn't normal, the way he reacted to what had to be the calculated revelation of her body. Hell, it wasn't even that much of a reveal—she had on a slim brown skirt and a cream-colored sweater. The sweater had a sweetheart neckline and long sleeves. Nothing overtly sexual about her appearance tonight.

She was just a gorgeous woman. And she was headed right for him. The restaurant was so quiet he could hear the click of her heels on the parquet flooring as she crossed to the bar.

He couldn't take his eyes off her.

What if things were different? What if they'd met on different terms—him not trying to reconstruct her family's former company, her not desperate for an angel investor? Would he have pursued her? Well, that was a stupid question—of course he would have. She was not just a feast for the eyes. She was quite possibly the smartest woman he'd ever gone head-to-head with. He couldn't believe it, but he was actually looking forward to being demolished by her again tonight. Blue balls be damned.

He rose and greeted her. "Frances."

She leaned up on her tiptoes and kissed his cheek. "What," she murmured against his skin. "Not Red?"

He turned his head slightly to respond but just kissed her instead. He kissed her like he'd wanted to kiss her in his office the other day. The taste of her lips burned his mouth like those cinnamon candies his mother preferred—hot but sweet. And good. *So* good. He couldn't get enough of her.

And that was a problem. It was quickly becoming *the* problem. He was having trouble going a day or two without touching her. How was he supposed to make it a year in a sexless marriage?

She pulled away, and he let her. "Still trying to find the right name for you," he replied, hoping that how much she affected him didn't show.

"Keep trying." She cocked her head to one side. "Shall we?"

Ethan signaled for the hostess, who led them back to their private table. "How was your day, darling?" Frances asked in an offhand way as she accepted the menu.

The casual nature of the question—or, more specifically, the lack of sexual innuendo—caught him off guard. "Fine, actually. The production lines were producing today." She looked at him over the edge of her menu, one eyebrow raised. "And, yes," he said, answering the unspoken question. "I give you all the credit for that."

He wanted to ask about ZOLA and Zeb Richards, but he didn't. Maybe after they'd eaten—and shared a bottle of wine. "How about you?"

They were interrupted by the waitress, so it wasn't until after they'd placed their orders that she answered. "Good. We met with the Realtors about the space. Becky's very excited about owning the space instead of renting."

Ah, yes. The money he owed her. "Have you been monitoring the chatter, as you put it?"

At that, she leaned forward, a winning smile on her face. Ethan didn't like it. It wasn't real or true. It was a piece of armor, a shield in this game they were playing. She wasn't smiling for him. She was smiling for everyone else. "So far, so good," she purred, even though there was no one else who could have heard her. "I think this weekend, we should attend a Nuggets game."

He dimly remembered her watching a basketball game on Saturday when she'd been pointedly not sleeping with him. "Big fan?"

"Not really," she replied with a casual shrug. "But sports

fans drink a lot of beer. It'd signal our involvement to a different crowd and boost the chatter significantly."

All of that sounded fine in a cold, calculated kind of way. He found he didn't much care for the cold right now. He craved her heat.

It was his turn to lean forward. "And after that? I seem to recall you saying something about how you were going to start sleeping over this weekend. Of course, you're always welcome to do so sooner."

That shield of a smile fell away, and he knew he'd slipped past her defenses again. But the moment was short. She tilted her head to one side and gave him an appraising look. "Trying to change the terms of our deal again? For shame, Ethan."

"Are you coming back to the room with me tonight?"

"Of course." Her voice didn't change, but he thought he saw her cheeks pink up ever so slightly.

"Are you going to kiss me in the lobby again?"

Yes, she was definitely blushing. But it was her only tell. "I suppose you could always kiss me first. Just for a little variety."

Oh, he'd love to show her some variety. "And the elevator?"

"You *are* trying to change the terms," she murmured as she dropped her gaze. "We discussed that—at your request. There's no kissing in elevators."

He didn't respond. At the time, it'd seemed like the shortest path to self-preservation. But now? Now he wanted to push the envelope. He wanted to see if he could get to her like she was getting to him. "I like what you've done with the lily," he said, nodding toward where she'd worked the bloom into her hair. Because thus far, the flowers were by far the best way to get to her.

There was always a chance that she wasn't all that attracted to him—that the heat he felt when he was around her was a one-way street.

Damn, that was a depressing thought.

"They were beautiful," she said. And it could have easily been another too-smooth line.

But it wasn't.

"Not as beautiful as you are."

Before she could respond to that their food arrived. They ate and drank and made polite small talk disguised as sensual flirting.

"After the game, we'll have to deal with my family," she warned him over the lip of her second glass of wine after she'd pushed her plate away. "I'm actually surprised that my brother Matthew hasn't called to lecture me about the Beaumont family name."

Ethan was wrapped in the warm buzz of his alcohol. "Oh? That a problem?"

Frances waved her hand. "He's the micromanager of our public image. Was VP of marketing before you showed up. He did a great job, too."

She didn't say it as if she was intentionally trying to score a hit, but he felt a little wounded anyway. "I didn't fire him. He was gone before I got there."

"Oh, I know." She took another drink. "He left with Chadwick."

Ethan was pondering this information when someone said, "Frannie?"

At the name, Frances's eyes widened, and she sat bolt upright. She looked over Ethan's shoulder and said, "Phillip?"

Phillip? Oh, right. He remembered now. Phillip was one of her half brothers.

Oh, hell. Ethan was one sheet to the wind and about to meet a Beaumont.

Frances stood as a strikingly blond man came around

the table. He was holding the hand of a tall, athletic woman wearing blue jeans. "Phillip! Jo! I didn't expect to see you guys here."

Phillip kissed his sister on the cheek. "We decided it was time for our once-a-month dinner date." As the woman named Jo hugged Frances, Phillip turned a gaze that was surprisingly friendly toward Ethan. "I'm Phillip Beaumont. And you are?" He stuck out his hand.

Ethan glanced at Frances, only to find that both she and Jo were watching this interaction with curiosity. "I'm Ethan Logan," Ethan said, giving Phillip's hand a firm shake.

He tried to pull his hand back, but it didn't go anywhere. "Ah," Phillip said. His smile grew—at the same time he clamped down on Ethan's hand. "You're running the Brewery these days."

The strength with which Phillip had a hold on him was more than Ethan would have given him credit for. Ethan would have anticipated her brother to be someone pampered and posh and not particularly physically intimidating. But Phillip's grip spoke of a man who worked with his hands for a living—and wasn't afraid to use them for other purposes.

"Phillip manages the Beaumont Farm," Frances said, her voice slightly louder than necessary. Ah, that explained it. "He raises the Percherons. And this is Jo, his wife. She trains horses."

It was only then that Phillip let go of Ethan so Ethan could give Jo's hand a quick shake. "A pleasure, Ms. Beaumont."

To his surprise, Jo said, "Is it?" with the kind of smile that made no pretense of being polite. But she linked arms with Phillip and physically pulled him a step away.

"Would you like to join us?" Ethan offered, because it seemed like the sociable thing to do and also because he absolutely did not want Phillip Beaumont to catch a hint of fear. Ethan would act as though having his hot date with Frances suddenly crashed by an obviously overprotective older brother was the highlight of his night if it killed him.

And given the look on Phillip's face, it just might.

"No," Jo said. "That's all right. You both look like you're finishing up, anyway."

Phillip said, "Frannie, can I talk with you—in private?"

That was a dismissal if Ethan had ever heard one. "I'll be right back," he genially offered. This called for a tactical retreat to the men's room. "If you'll excuse me," he added to Frances.

"Of course," she murmured, nodding her head in appreciation.

As Ethan walked away, he heard nothing but chilly silence.

"What are you doing?" Phillip didn't so much say the words as hiss them. His fun-times smile never wavered, though.

In that moment Phillip sounded more like stuck-up Matthew than her formerly wild older brother. "I'm on a date. Same as you."

Beside her, Jo snorted. But she didn't say anything. She just watched. Sometimes—and not that Frances would ever tell her sister-in-law this—Jo kind of freaked her out. She was so quiet, so watchful. Not at all the kind of woman Frances had envisioned with Phillip.

Which was not a complaint. Phillip was sober now and, with Jo beside him, almost a new man.

A new man who'd tasked himself with making sure Frances toed the family line. *Ugh*.

"With the man who's running the Brewery? Are you drunk?"

"That is *such* a laugh riot, coming from you," she stiffly

replied. She felt Jo tense beside her. "Sorry." But she said it to Jo. Not to Phillip. "But no, thanks for asking, I'm not drunk. I'm not insane, and, just to head you off at the pass, I'm not stupid. I know exactly who he is, and I know exactly what I'm doing."

Phillip glared at her. "Which is *what*, exactly?"

"None of your business." She made damn sure to say it with her very best smile.

Phillip was not swayed. "Frannie, I don't know what you think you're doing here—either you're completely clueless and setting yourself up for yet another failure or—"

"And thank you for that overwhelming vote of confidence," she hissed at him, her best smile cracking unnaturally. "I liked you better when you were drunk. At least then you didn't assume I was an idiot like everyone else does."

"Or," Phillip went on, refusing to be sidetracked by her attack, "you think you're going to accomplish something at the Brewery." He paused, and when Frances didn't respond immediately to that spot-on accusation, his eyes widened. "What on earth do you think you're doing?"

"I don't see what it matters to you. You don't drink beer. You don't work at any brewery, old or new. You've got the farm, and you've got Jo. You don't need anything." He had his happy life now. He couldn't begrudge her this.

Phillip did grab her then, wrapping his hand around her upper arm. "Frannie—corporate espionage?"

"I'm just trying to restore the Beaumont name. You may not remember it, but our name used to mean something. And we lost that."

Unexpectedly, Phillip's face softened. "We didn't lose anything. We're still Beaumonts. You can't go back—why would you even want to? Things are better now."

If that wasn't the most condescending thing Phillip had

ever said to her, she didn't know what was. "Better for who? Not for me."

He was undaunted, damn him. "We've moved on—we *all* have. Chadwick and Matthew have their new business. Byron's back and happy. Even the younger kids are doing okay. None of us want the Brewery back, honey. If that's what you're trying to do here…"

A rush of emotions Frances couldn't name threatened to swamp her. It was what she wanted, but it wasn't. This was about *her*. She wanted Frances Beaumont back.

She turned to Jo, who'd been watching the entire exchange with unblinking eyes. "I'm sorry if this interrupted your night out. Ethan and I were almost done anyway."

"It's not a problem," Jo said. Frances couldn't tell if Jo was saying it to her husband or to Frances. Jo then slid her arm through Phillip's. "Let it be, babe."

Phillip gave his wife an apologetic look. "My apologies. I'm just surprised. I'd have thought…"

She knew what Phillip would have thought—and she knew what Chadwick and Matthew and even Byron would all be thinking, just as fast as Phillip could text them. Another Frances misadventure. "Trust me, okay?"

Phillip's gaze cut back over her shoulder. Even without looking, Frances could tell Ethan had returned. She could *feel* his presence. Warm prickles raised the hairs on the back of her neck as he approached.

Then his arm slid around her waist in an act that could only be described as possessive. Phillip didn't miss it, curse his clean-and-sober eyes. "Well. Logan, a pleasure to meet you. Frances…"

She could hear the unspoken *be careful* in his tone. She gave Jo another quick hug and Phillip a kiss on the cheek. Ethan's hand stayed on her lower back. "I'll come out soon," she promised, as if that was what their little chat had been about.

Phillip smirked at the dodge. But he didn't say anything else. He and Jo moved off to their own table.

"Everything okay?" Ethan said. His arm was firmly back around her waist and she wanted nothing more than to lean into him.

"Oh, sure." It wasn't a lie, but it wasn't the whole truth. For someone who'd been playing a game calculated on public recognition, Frances suddenly felt overexposed.

Ethan's fingertips tightened against her side, pulling her closer against his chest. "Do you want to go?"

"Yes."

Ethan let go of her long enough to fish several hundred-dollar bills out of his wallet, and then they were walking toward the front. He held her coat for her before he slid his own back on. Frances could feel the weight of Phillip's gaze from all the way across the room.

Why did she feel so…weird? It wasn't what Phillip thought. She wasn't being naive about this. She wasn't betraying the family name—she was rescuing it, damn it. She was keeping her friends—and family—close and her enemies closer, by God. That's all this was. There was nothing else to it.

Except…except for the way Ethan wrapped his strong arm around her and hugged her close as they walked out of the restaurant and into the bitterly cold night air. As they walked from the not-crowded sidewalk to the nearly empty parking lot, where he had parked a sleek Jaguar, he held her tighter still. He opened her door for her and then started the car.

But he didn't press. He didn't have to. All he did was reach over and take her hand in his.

When they arrived at the hotel, Ethan gave the keys to the valet, who greeted them both by name. They walked into the lobby, and this time, she did rest her head on his shoulder.

She shouldn't feel weird, now that someone in the family was aware of her...independent interests. Especially since it was Phillip, the former playboy of the family. She didn't need their approval, and she didn't want it.

But...she felt suddenly adrift. And what made it worse? Ethan could tell.

They didn't stop in the middle of the lobby and engage in heavy petting as planned. Instead, he walked her over to the elevator. While they waited, he lifted her chin with one gloved hand and kissed her.

Damn him, she thought even as she sighed into his arms. Damn Ethan all to hell for being exactly who he was—strong and tough and good at the game, but also honest and sincere and thoughtful.

She did not believe in love. She struggled with believing in *like.* Infatuation, yes—she knew that existed. And lust. Those entanglements that burned hot and fast and then fizzled out.

So no, this was not love. Not now, not ever. This was merely...fondness. She could be fond of Ethan, and he could return the sentiment. Perhaps they could even be friends. Wouldn't that be novel, being friends with her soon-to-be-ex husband?

The elevator doors pinged open, and he broke the kiss. "Shall we go up?" he whispered, his gaze never leaving hers as his fingers stroked her cheek. Why did he have to be like this? Why did he have to make her think he could care for her?

Why did he make her want to care for him?

"Yes," she said, her voice shaky. "Yes, let's."

They stepped onto the elevator.

The doors closed behind them.

Nine

Before she could sag back against the wall of the elevator, Ethan had folded her into his arms in what could only be described as a hug.

She sank into his broad and warm and firm chest. When was the last time she'd been hugged? Not counting when she went to visit her mother. Men wanted many things from her—sex, notoriety, sex, a crack at the Beaumont fortune and, finally, sex. But never something as simple as a hug, especially one seemingly without conditions or expectations.

"I'm fine," she tried to say, but her words were muffled by all his muscles.

His chest moved, as if he'd chuckled. "I'm sure you are. You are, without a doubt, the toughest woman I know."

Against her wishes, she relaxed into his embrace as they rode up and up and up. "You're just saying that."

"No, I'm not." He loosened his hold on her enough to look her in the eyes. "I'm serious. You've got some of the toughest, most effective armor I've ever seen a woman wear, and you hardly ever expose a chink."

Something stung at her eyes. She ignored it. "Save it for when we have an audience, Ethan."

Something hard flashed over his eyes. "I'm not saying this for the general public, Frances. I'm saying it because it's the truth." He traced his fingertips—still gloved—down the side of her face. "This isn't part of the game."

Her breath caught in her throat.

"But every so often," he went on, as if stunning her speechless was just par for the course, "something slips past that armor." She was not going to lean into his touch. Any more than she already had, that was. "It's subtle, but I can tell. You weren't ready for your brother just then. God knows I wasn't, either." His lips—lips she'd kissed—quirked into a smile. "I'd have loved to see what you'd done with him if you'd been primed for the battle."

"It's different when it's family," she managed to get out in a breathy whisper. "You have to love them even when they think you're making a huge fool of yourself."

She felt his body tense against hers. "Is that what he told you?"

"No, no—Phillip has far more tact than that," she told him. "But I don't think he approves."

The elevator slowed, and then the doors opened on Ethan's floor. Ethan didn't make a move to exit. "Does that bother you?"

She sighed. "Come on." It took more effort than she might have guessed to pull herself out of his arms, but when she held out her hand, he took it. They walked down the long hall like that, hand in hand. She waited while he got the door unlocked, and then they stepped inside.

This time, though, she didn't make a move for the remote. She just stood in the middle of his suite—the suite that she would be spending more and more time in. Spending the night in—until they got married. Then what? They'd have to get an apartment, wouldn't they? She couldn't live in a hotel suite. Not for a year. And she couldn't see moving Ethan into the Beaumont mansion with her. Just trying to picture that made her shudder in horror.

Good God, she was going to marry this man. In…a week and a half.

Ethan stepped up behind her and slid his hands around her waist. He'd shucked his gloves and coat, she saw as his fingers undid the belt at her waist. Then he removed her coat for her.

This wasn't an act. Or was it? He could still be working an angle, one in which his interests would best be served by making her think he was really a decent man, a good human being. It was possible. He could be looking to pump more information out of her. Looking to take another big chunk of power or money away from the Beaumonts. He could be building her up to drop her like a rock and put her in her place—especially after the stunt she'd pulled with Donut Friday.

Then his arms were around her again, pulling her back into him. "Does it bother you?" he asked again. "That they won't approve of this. Of us."

"They rarely approve of anything I do—but don't worry," she hurried to add, trying to speak over the catch in her voice. "The feeling is often mutual. Disapproval is the glue that holds the Beaumonts together." She tried to say it as if it were just a comical fact of nature—because it was.

But she felt so odd, so not normal, that it didn't come out that way.

"Is he your favorite brother? Other than your twin, I mean."

"Yes. Phillip threw the best parties and snuck me beers and…we were friends, I guess. We could do anything together, and he never judged me. But he's been sober for a while now. His wife helps."

"So he's not the same brother you knew." Ethan pulled the lily out of her hair and set it on the side table. Half of her hair fell out of the twist, and he used his fingers to unravel the rest.

"No, I guess not. But then, nothing stays the same. The only thing that never changes is change itself, right?"

She knew that better than anyone. Wasn't that how she'd been raised? There were no constants, no guarantees. Only the family name would endure.

Right up until it, too, had stopped meaning what it always had.

Unexpectedly, Ethan pressed his lips against her neck. "Take off your shoes," he ordered against her skin.

She did as he said, although she didn't know why. The old Frances wouldn't have followed an order from an admirer.

Maybe, an insidious little voice in the back of her head whispered, *maybe you aren't the same old Frances anymore*. And this quest, or whatever she wanted to call it, to undermine Ethan and strike a blow against the new owners of her family's brewery—all of that was to make her feel like the old Frances again. Even the art gallery was a step back to a place where she'd been more secure.

What if she couldn't go back there? What if she would never again be the redheaded golden girl of Denver? Of the Brewery? Of her family?

Ethan relinquished his hold on her long enough to peel back the comforter from the bed. Then he guided her down. "Scoot," he told her, climbing in after her.

She would have never done so, not back when she was at the top of her form. She would have demanded high seduction or nothing at all. Champagne. Wild promises. Diamonds and gems. Not this *fondness*, for God's sake.

He pulled the covers over them and wrapped his arm around her shoulder. She curled into his side, feeling warmer and safer by the moment. For some reason, it was what she needed. To feel safe from the winds of change that had blown away her prospects and her personal fortune. In Ethan's arms, she could almost pretend none of it had happened. She could almost pretend this was normal.

"What about you?" she asked, pressing her hand against his chest.

He covered her hand with his. Warm. Safe. "What about me?"

"You must be used to change. A new company and a new hotel in a new city every other month?" She curled her fingers into the crisp cotton of his shirt. "I guess change doesn't bother you at all."

"It doesn't feel like that," he said. "It's the same thing every time, with slightly different scenery. Hotel rooms all blend together, executive offices all look the same…"

"Even the women?"

The pause was long. "Yes, I guess you could say that. Even the women were all very similar. Beautiful, good conversationalists, cultured." He began to stroke her hair. "Until this time."

"This time?" Something sparked in her chest, something that didn't feel cynical or calculated. She didn't recognize what it was.

"The hotel is basically the same. But the company? I usually spend three to six months restructuring. I've already been here for three months and I've barely made any headway. The executive office—hell, the whole Brewery—is unlike any place I've ever worked before. It's not a sterile office building that's got the same carpeting and the same crappy furniture as every other office. It's like it's this…*thing* that lives and breathes on its own. It's not just real estate. It's alive."

"It's always been that way," she agreed, but she wasn't thinking about the Brewery or the antique furniture or the people who'd made it a second home to her.

She was thinking about the man next to her, the one

who'd just told her that women were as interchangeable as hotel rooms. Which was a cold, soulless thing to admit and also totally didn't match up with the way he was holding her.

"And?"

"And…" His voice trailed off as he wrapped his fingers more tightly around hers.

She swallowed. "The woman?"

For some reason, she needed to know that she wasn't like all the rest.

Please, she thought, *please say something I can believe. Something real and honest and sincere, even if it kills me.*

"The woman," he said, lifting her hand away from his chest and pressing a kiss to her palm, "the woman is unlike any other. Beautiful, a great conversationalist, highly cultured—but there's something else about her. Something that runs deeper."

Frances realized she was holding her breath, so she made herself breathe normally. Or as close to normal as she could get, what with her heart pounding as fast as it was. "You make her sound like a river."

"Then I'm not doing a very good job," he said with a chuckle. "I'm not used to whispering sweet nothings."

"They're not nothing." Her voice felt as if it were coming from somewhere far away.

His hand trailed down from her hair to her back, where he rubbed her in long, even strokes. "Neither are you."

She wasn't, was she? She was still Frances. Hell, in a few weeks, she wouldn't even be a Beaumont anymore. She'd be a Logan. And then after that… Well, nothing stayed the same, after all.

"We can call it off," he said, as if he'd been reading her mind.

She pushed herself up and stared down at him. *"What?"* Was he serious?

Or was this the real, honest, true thing she'd asked for? Because if this was it, she took it back.

"Nothing official has changed hands. No legal commitments have been made." She saw him swallow. He stared up at her with such seriousness that she almost panicked because the look on his face went so far beyond fond that she didn't know what to do. "If you want."

She sat all the way up, pushing herself out of what had been the safe shelter of his arms. She sat back on her heels, only vaguely aware that her skirt had twisted itself around her waist. "No. No! We can't end this!"

"Why not? Relationships end all the time. We had a couple of red-hot dates and it went nowhere." He tilted his head to the side. "We just walk away. No harm, no foul."

"*Just* walk away? We can't. *I* can't." Because that was the heart of the matter, wasn't it? She couldn't back out of this deal now. This was her ticket back to her old life, or some reasonable facsimile thereof. With Ethan's angel investment, she could get the gallery off the ground, she could get a new apartment and move out of the Beaumont mansion. She could go back to being Frances Beaumont.

He sat up, which brought their bodies into close proximity again. She didn't like being this aware of him. She didn't like the fact that she wanted to know what he'd look like without the shirt. She didn't want to like him. Not even a little.

He reached over and stroked her hair tenderly. She didn't want tenderness, damn it. She didn't want feelings. She wanted cutting commentary and wars of words and… She wanted to hate him. He was the embodiment of her family's failures. He was dismantling her second home piece by piece. He was using her for her familial connections.

And he was making it damned near impossible to hate him. Stupid tender fondness.

It only got worse when he said, "I'd like to keep seeing

you," as if he thought that would make it better when it only made everything worse. "I don't think it's an exaggeration to say that I haven't stopped thinking about you since the moment you offered me a donut. But we don't have to do this rush to the altar. We don't have to get married. Not if you'd like to change the deal. Since," he added with a wry smile, "things do change."

"But you need me," she protested, trying vainly to find some solution that would not lead to where she'd started—alone, living at the family home, broke, with no prospects. "You need *me* to make the workers like you."

His lips quirked up into a tender smile, and then he was closing the distance between them. "I need more than just that."

He was going to kiss her. He was being sweet and thoughtful and kind and he was going to kiss her and it was wrong. It was all wrong.

"Ethan," she said in warning, putting her hand on his chest and pushing lightly. "Don't do this."

He let her hold him back, but he didn't let go of her hair. He didn't let go of *her*. "Do what?"

"This—*madness*. Don't start to like me. I won't like you back." His eyes widened in shock. She dug deeper. "I won't love you."

Ever so slightly, his fingers loosened their hold on her hair. "You already said that."

"I meant it. Love is for fools, and I refuse to be one. Don't lower my opinion of you by being one, too." The words felt sharp on her tongue, as if she were chewing on glass.

Cruel to be kind, she told herself. If he got infatuated with her—if real emotions came into play—well, this whole thing would fall apart. This was not a relationship, not a real one. This was a business deal. They couldn't afford to forget that.

Well, she couldn't, anyway.

If she'd expected him to pull away, to be pissed at her blanket rejection, she was sorely disappointed. He did, in fact, lean back. And he did let his fingers fall away from her hair.

But he sat there, propped up on hotel pillows that were just like any other hotel pillows, and he smiled at her. A real smile, damn him. Honest and true.

"If you want out, that's fine," she pressed on. She would not be distracted by real emotions. "But don't take pity on me and don't like me, for God's sake. We had a deal. Don't patronize me by deciding what's best for me. If I want out of the deal, I'll tell you. In the meantime, I'll hold up my end of the bargain and you'll hold up yours—unless you've changed your mind?"

"I haven't," he said after a brief pause. His mouth was still slightly curved into a smile.

She wanted to wipe that smile off his face, but she couldn't think of a way to do it without kicking and screaming. So all she said was, "Fine."

They sat there for a few moments. Ethan continued to stare at her, as if he were trying to see into her. "Yes?" she demanded as she felt her face flush under his close scrutiny.

"The woman," he murmured in what sounded a hell of a lot like approval, "is a force unto herself."

Oh, she definitely took it back. She didn't want real or honest out of him. No tenderness and, for the love of everything holy, not a single hint of fondness.

She would not *like* him. She simply would not.

She had to nip this in the bud *fast*.

"Ethan," she said, baring her teeth in some approximation of a smile, "save it for when we're in public."

Ten

The next day, Ethan had Delores send a bird of paradise floral arrangement with a note that just read, "Yours, E." Then he sent Frances a text message telling her how much he was looking forward to seeing her again that night.

He wasn't surprised when she didn't respond. Not after the way she'd stalked out of his hotel room last night.

As hard as it was, he tried to put the events of the previous evening aside. He had work to do. The production lines were up to full speed. He checked in with his department heads and was stunned by the complete lack of pushback he got when he asked about head count and department budgets. A week ago, people would have been staring at the table or out the window and saying that the employees who had those numbers were out with the flu or on vacation or whatever lame excuse they assumed wouldn't be too transparent.

But now? After less than a week of having Frances Beaumont in his life, people were making eye contact and saying, "I've got those numbers," and smiling at him. Actually smiling! Even when a turnaround was going well, there weren't a lot of smiles in the process.

Then there was what happened at the end of the last meeting of the day. He'd been discussing the marketing budget in his office with the department managers. The men and women seated around the Beaumont conference table looked comfortable, as though they belonged there. For the briefest moment, Ethan was jealous of them. He didn't belong there, and they all knew it.

It was 4:45 and the marketing people were obviously ready to go home. Ethan wrapped things up, got the promises that he'd have the information he'd requested on his desk first thing in the morning and dismissed everyone.

"So, Mr. Logan," an older man said with a smile. Ethan thought his name was Bob. Larsen, maybe? "Are you going to get a donut on Friday?"

The room came to a brief pause, everyone listening for the answer. For what was quite possibly the first time, he grasped what Frances kept talking about when she said he should save it for the public.

Still, he had to say something. People were waiting for a reaction. More than that, they were waiting for the reaction that told them their trust in Ethan's decisions wasn't about to be misplaced. They were waiting for him to admit he was one of them.

"I hope she saves me a chocolate éclair this time," he said in a conspiratorial whisper. He didn't specify who "she" was. He didn't have to.

This comment was met with an approving noise between a chuckle and a hum. *Whew*, Ethan thought as people cleared out. At least he hadn't stuck his foot in it. Not like he had with Frances last night.

She'd been right. He *did* need her. If they walked away right now, whatever new, tenuous grip he had on this company would float away as soon as the last donut had been consumed. He'd gotten more accomplished in the past week than he had in three months, and, as much as it pained him to admit it, it had nothing to do with his keen managerial handling.

So why had he offered to let her out of their deal?

He didn't know the answer to that, except there'd been a chink in her armor and instead of looking like a worthy opponent, Frances had seemed delicate and vulnerable. There'd been this pull—a pull he wasn't sure he'd ever felt before—to take care of her. Which was patently ridiculous. She could take care of herself. Even if she hadn't seen fit to remind him of that fact, he knew it to be true.

But the look on her face after they'd left her brother behind…

Ethan hadn't lied. There were similarities between Frances and all his previous lady friends. Cultured, refined—the sort of woman who enjoyed a good meal and a little evening entertainment, both the kind that happened at the theater and in the hotel room.

So what was it about her that was so damn different?

It wasn't her name. Sure, her name was the starting point of this entire relationship, but Ethan was no sycophant. The Beaumont name was only valuable to him as long as it let him do his job at the Brewery. He had no desire to get in with the family, and Ethan had his own damn fortune, thank you very much.

Was it the fact that, for the first time in his life, he was operating with marriage in mind? Was that alone enough to merit this deeper…engagement, so to speak? He would be tied to Frances for the next calendar year. Maybe it was only natural to want to take care of the woman who would be his wife.

Not that he knew what that looked like. His father had certainly never taken care of his mother, aside from providing the funds for her to do whatever she liked. Troy Logan's involvement with the mother of his two sons was strictly limited to paying the bills. Maybe that was why his mother never stayed home for longer than a few months at a time. Troy Logan wasn't capable of deeper feeling, so

Wanda had sought out that emotional connection somewhere else. Anywhere else, really.

Ethan went to the private bathroom and splashed cold water on his face. This wasn't supposed to be complicated, not like his parents' relationship. This was cut-and-dried. No messy emotions. Just playing a game with one hell of an opponent who made him want to do things that were completely out of character. No problem.

He checked his jaw in the mirror—maybe he wouldn't shave before dinner tonight. As he was debating the merits of facial hair, he heard his office door shut with a decent amount of force.

"Frances?" he called out. "Is that you?"

There was no response.

He unrolled his sleeves and slid his jacket back on. The only other person who walked into his office without being announced by Delores was Delores herself. Even if it was near quitting time, he still needed to maintain his professional image.

But as he walked back into his office, he knew it wasn't Delores. Instead, a tall, commanding man sat in one of the two chairs in front of the desk.

The man looked like Phillip Beaumont—until he gave Ethan such an imperious glare that Ethan realized it wasn't the same Beaumont.

He recognized that look. He'd seen it on the covers of business magazines and in the *Wall Street Journal*. None other than Chadwick Beaumont, the former CEO of the Beaumont Brewery, was sitting in Ethan's office. The man every single employee in this company wanted back.

Ethan went on high alert. Beaumont had, until this very moment, been more of a ghost that Ethan had to work around than an actual living man to be dealt with. Yet here he was, months after Ethan had taken over. This couldn't be a coincidence, not after the interaction with Phillip last night.

"I had heard," Beaumont began with no other introduction, "that you were going to tear this office out."

"It's my prerogative," Ethan replied, keeping his voice level. He had to give Beaumont credit—at least he hadn't said *my office.* "As I am the current CEO."

Beaumont tilted his head in acknowledgment.

"To what do I owe the honor?" Ethan asked, as if this were a social call when it was clearly anything but. He took his seat behind his desk, leaving both hands on the desktop, as if all his cards were on the table.

Beaumont did not answer immediately. He crossed his leg and adjusted the cuff of his pants. Which was to be expected, Ethan figured. Beaumont was a notoriously tough negotiator, much like his father had been.

Well, two could play at this game. Troy Logan had earned his reputation as a corporate raider during the 1980s the hard way. His name alone could make high-powered bankers turn tail and run. Ethan had learned at the feet of the master. If Beaumont thought he could gain something with this confrontation, he was going to be sorely disappointed.

While Beaumont tried to wait Ethan out, Ethan studied him.

Chadwick Beaumont—the scion of the Beaumont family—was taller and blonder than Frances or even his brother Phillip. His hair held just a shine of redness, whereas Frances's was all flame. There was enough similarity that, even if Ethan hadn't met Phillip the night before, he would have recognized the Beaumont features—the chin, the nose, the ability to command a room just by existing in it.

How had the company been sold away from this man? Ethan tried to recall. An activist shareholder had precipitated the sale. Beaumont had fought against it tooth and nail, but once the sale had been finalized, he'd packed up and moved on.

So, yeah—this wasn't about the company. This was about Frances.

Which Beaumont proved when he tried out something that was probably supposed to be a smile but didn't even come close. "You're making me look bad. Flowers every day? My wife is beginning to complain."

Ethan didn't smile back. "My apologies for that." He was not sorry. "That's not my intention."

One eyebrow lifted. "What are your intentions?"

Damn, Ethan had walked right into that one. "I'm sorry—is that any of your business?"

"I'm making it my business." The statement was made in a casual enough tone, but there was no missing the implicit threat. Beaumont tried to stare him down for a moment, but Ethan didn't buckle.

"Good luck with that."

Beaumont's eyes hardened. "I don't know what your game is, Logan, but you really don't know what you're getting into with her."

That might be a true enough observation, but Ethan wasn't about to concede an inch. "As far as I can tell, I'm getting into a relationship with a grown woman. Still don't see how that's any of your concern."

Beaumont shook his head slowly, as if Ethan had blundered into admitting he was an idiot. "Either she's using you or you're using her. It won't end well."

"Again, not your concern."

"It is my concern because this will be just another one of Frances's messes that I have to clean up after."

Ethan bristled. "You talk as if she's a wayward child."

Beaumont's glare bore into him. "You don't know her like I do. She's lost more fortunes than I can count. Keeping her out of the public eye is a challenge during the best of times. And you," he said, pointing his chin at Ethan, "are pushing her back into the public eye."

Ethan stared at Beaumont. Was he serious? But Chadwick Beaumont did not look like the kind of man who made a joke. Ever.

What had Frances said last night? "Don't patronize me by deciding what's best for me." Suddenly, that statement made sense. "Does she know you're here?"

"Of course not," Beaumont replied.

"Of course not," Ethan repeated. "Instead, you took it upon yourself to decide what was best not only for her but for me, as well." He gave his best condescending smile, which took effort. He did not feel like smiling. "You'll have to excuse me, but I'm trying to figure out what gives you the right to be such a patronizing asshole to a pair of consenting adults. Any thoughts on that?"

Beaumont gave him an even look.

"I suppose," Ethan went on, "that the only surprising thing is that you came alone to intimidate me, instead of with a herd of Beaumont brothers."

"We don't tend to travel in a pack," Beaumont said coolly.

"And I'm equally sure you didn't think you'd need any help in the intimidation department."

Beaumont's eyes crinkled a little at the corners, as if he might have actually found that observation amusing. "How's the Brewery doing?"

Ethan blinked at the subject change, but only once. "We're getting there. You cultivated an incredibly loyal staff. The ones that didn't follow you to your new company were not happy about the changes."

Beaumont tilted his head at the compliment. "I imagine not. When I took over after my father's death, there was a period of about a year where we verged on total collapse. Employee loyalty can be a double-edged sword."

Ethan didn't bother to hide his surprise. *"Really."*

Beaumont nodded. "The club of Beaumont Brewery CEOs is even more exclusive than the Presidents' Club. There are only two of us alive in the world. You're only the fifth person to helm this company." He stared down at Ethan, but the intimidation wasn't as overbearing. "It's not a position to be taken lightly."

Honest to God, Ethan had never thought about it in those terms. The companies he usually restructured had often gone through a new CEO every two or three years as part of their downhill spiral. He'd never been anything special, in terms of management. He'd waltzed in, righted the sinking ship and moved on—just another CEO in a long line of them. There'd been nothing for the other employees to be loyal to except a paycheck and benefits.

Beaumont was right. Frances was right. Everything about this place, these people—this was different.

"If you need any help with the company…"

Ethan frowned. Accepting help was not something he did, especially not when it came to his job.

Except for Frances, a silky voice in the back of his head whispered. It sounded just like her.

"Actually, I do have a question. Have you ever heard of ZOLA?"

"ZOLA?" Beaumont mouthed the word like it was foreign. "What's that?"

"A private holdings company. They're making noise about the Brewery. I think they're trying to undermine—well, I'm not sure who they're trying to undermine. Not you, obviously, since you're no longer the boss around here. But it could be my company, or it could be AllBev." He fought the urge to get up and pace. "Unless, of course, ZOLA is representing your interests."

"I have no interest in reclaiming the Brewery. I've

moved on." His gaze was level, and his hands and feet were calm. Beaumont was telling the truth, damn it.

"And the rest of your family?"

"I don't speak for the entire Beaumont family."

"I'll be sure and pass that information along to Frances."

Beaumont's eyes widened briefly in surprise at this barb. "Phillip has no interest in beer. Matthew is one of my executives. Byron has his own restaurant in our new brewery. The younger Beaumonts never had anything to do with the Brewery in the first place. And you seem to be in a position to form your own opinion of Frances's motivations."

Point. Ethan was quite proud that his ears didn't burn under that one. "I appreciate your input."

Beaumont stood and held out his hand. Ethan rose to shake it. "Good to meet you, Logan. Stop by the mansion sometime."

"Likewise. Anytime." He was pretty sure they were both lying through their teeth.

Beaumont didn't let go of his hand, though. If anything, his grip tightened down. "But be careful with Frances. She is not a woman to be trifled with."

Ethan cracked a real smile. As if anyone could trifle with Frances Beaumont and hope to escape with their dignity—or other parts—intact.

Still, this level of meddling was something new to Ethan. No wonder seeing her other brother last night had shaken her so badly. Ethan hadn't really anticipated this much peer pressure. He increased his grip right back. "I think she can take care of herself, don't you?"

He waited for Beaumont to make another thinly veiled threat, but he didn't. Instead, he dropped Ethan's hand and turned toward the door.

Ethan watched him go. If Beaumont had shown up here,

had anyone been designated to give Frances a talking-to? Hopefully she'd had her armor on.

Then Beaumont paused at the door. He turned back, his gaze sweeping the entirety of the room. Instead of another pronouncement about how they were members of the world's smallest club, he only gave Ethan a little grin that was somehow tinged with sadness before he turned and was gone.

Ethan got the feeling that Beaumont wouldn't come back to the Brewery again.

Ethan collapsed back into his chair. What the everloving hell was that all about, anyway? He still wasn't going to rule out Beaumont—any Beaumont—of having direct involvement with ZOLA. Including Frances. There were no such things as coincidences—she'd said so herself. Frances had waltzed into his life just as ZOLA had started making noise. There had to be a connection—didn't there? But if that connection didn't run through her brothers, what was it?

Frances. His thoughts always came back to her. He couldn't wait to see her at dinner tonight, but he got the feeling that she might need something a little more than a floral arrangement, if she'd gotten half the pushback Ethan had today.

He checked his watch. He had time to make a little side trip, if he didn't shave.

Hopefully Frances liked stubble.

Eleven

Frances was unsurprised to find Byron waiting for her when she got back to the mansion after a long day of going over real estate contracts.

"Phillip called you, didn't he?" she began, pushing past her twin brother on her way up to her room. She had a date tonight, and she was already on edge. This would be a great night to put on the red dress. That'd drive any thoughts of affection right out of Ethan's mind. He'd be nothing but a walking, talking vessel of lust, and that was something she knew how to deal with.

No more tenderness. End of discussion.

"He might have," Byron admitted as he followed her into her room.

She was about to tear Byron a new one when she saw the huge floral arrangement on her nightstand table. "Oh!"

The card read, "Yours, E." Of course it did.

Those two little words—a mere six letters—made her smile. Which was just another sign that she needed a shower and a stiff drink. Ethan was not hers any more than she was his. She would not like him.

It would be easier to hold that line if he could just stop being so damn perfect.

"George said you've gotten flowers every day this week."

Frances rolled her eyes. George was the chef at the mansion and far too close with Byron. "So?" she said, pointedly ignoring the massive arrangement of blooms. "It's not like I haven't gotten flowers before."

"From the guy running the Brewery?"

She leveled a tired look at Byron. It was not a stretch to pull it off. "Why are you here? Aren't you running a restaurant or something? It's almost dinnertime, you know."

Byron flopped down on her bed. "We haven't officially opened yet. If you're going to flounce all around town with this new guy, you could at least plan on stopping by next week when we open. We could use the boost."

Frances stalked to her closet and began wrenching the hangers from side to side. "Excuse me? I do not *flounce*, thank you very much."

"Look," Byron said, staring at her. "Phillip seemed to think you were making a fool of yourself. I'm sure Chadwick has been updated. But whatever's going on, you're more than capable of dealing with it. If you're seeing this guy because you like him, then I want to meet him. And if you're seeing him for some other reason…"

The jerk had the nerve to crack his knuckles.

"Oh, for God's sake, Byron," she huffed at him. "Ethan could break you in half. No offense."

"None taken," Byron said without a trace of insult in his voice. "All I'm saying is that Phillip asked me to talk to you, and I've done that. Consider yourself talked to."

She pulled out the red dress and hung it on the closet door. "Seriously?"

Byron looked at the dress and then whistled. "Damn, Frannie. You either really like him or…"

This was part of the game, wasn't it? Convincing other people that she did like Ethan a great deal. Even if those people were Byron. She wasn't admitting to anything, not really. Not as long as she knew the truth deep down inside.

"I do, actually." It was supposed to come out strong and powerful because she was a woman in control of the situation.

It didn't. And Byron heard the difference. He wrinkled his forehead at her.

She was suddenly talking far more than was prudent. But this was Byron, damn it. She'd been sharing with him since their time in the womb, for crying out loud. "I mean, I do like him. There's something about him that's not your typical multimillionaire CEO. But I don't like *like* him, you know?" Which did not feel like the most honest thing to say. Because she might like him, even if it were a really bad idea.

Wasn't that what had almost happened last night? She'd let her guard down, and Ethan had been right there, strong and kind and thoughtful and she almost liked him.

Byron considered her juvenile argument. "So if you don't like *like* him, you're busting out the red dress because..."

Her mouth opened, and she almost admitted to the whole plan—the sham wedding, the angel investment, how she'd originally agreed to the whole crazy plan so she could inflict a little collateral damage on the current owners of the Brewery. For the family honor. If anyone would understand, it'd be Byron. She could always trust her brother and, no matter how crazy the situation was, he'd always stand behind her. *Always.*

But...

She couldn't do it. She couldn't admit she was breaking out the red dress because this was all a game, with high-dollar, high-power stakes, and she needed to level the playing field after the disaster that had been last night.

Her gaze fell on the bird of paradise arrangement. It was beautiful and had no doubt cost Ethan a fortune. She couldn't admit to anyone that she might not be winning the game. Not to Byron. Not to herself.

She decided it was time for a subject change. "How's the family?" Byron had recently married Leona Harper, an old girlfriend who was, awkwardly, the daughter of the Beaumonts' nemesis. Leona and Byron had a baby boy and another baby on the way. "Any other news from Leon Harper?"

"No," Byron said. "I don't know what we're paying the family lawyers these days, but it's worth it. Not a peep." He dug out his phone and called up a picture. "Guess what?"

Frances squinted at the ultrasound. "It's a…baby? I already knew Leona was pregnant, you goof."

"Ah, but did you know this? It's a girl," he said, his voice brimming with love. It almost hurt Frances to hear it—and to know that was not what she had with Ethan. "We're going to name her Jeannie."

"After Mom?" Frances didn't have a lot of memories of her mother and father together—at least, not a lot of memories that didn't involve screaming or crying. But Mom had made a nice, quiet life for herself after Hardwick.

There had been times when Frances had been growing up in this mansion that she'd wanted nothing more than to move in with Mom and live a quiet life, too. Frances bore the brunt of the new wives' dislike. By then, her older brothers had been off at college or, in Byron's case, off in the kitchen. Frances was the one who'd been expected to make nice with the new wives and the new kids—and Frances was the one who was supposed to grin and bear it when those new wives felt the need to prove that Hardwick loved them more than he'd loved anyone else. Even his own daughter.

Love had always been a competition. Never anything more.

Until now, damn it. Chadwick had married his assistant,

and no matter which way Frances looked at it, the two of them seemed to be wildly in love. And Phillip—her former partner in partying—had settled down with Jo. He had never been the kind of man to stick to one woman, and yet he was devoted to Jo. Matthew had decamped to California to be with his new wife. And now this—Byron and his happy, perfect little family.

Were you winning the game if you were the only one still playing it?

Byron nodded. "Mom's going to move in with us."

Frances looked at him in surprise. "Really?"

"Dad was such a mess, and God knows Leona's parents are, too. But Mom can be a part of the family again. And we've got plenty of room," he added, as if that were the deciding factor. "A complete mother-in-law apartment. Percy adores her, and I think Leona is thrilled to have Mom around. She never had much of a relationship with her own mother, you know."

Frances, as jaded as she was, felt tears prick at her eyes. The one thing their mother had never gotten over was losing her sense of family when Hardwick Beaumont had steamrolled her in court. When she'd lost her game, she'd lost *everything*.

That wasn't going to be how Frances wound up. "Oh, Byron—Mom's going to be *so* happy."

"So," Byron said, standing and taking his phone back. "I know you. And I know that you are occasionally prone to rash decisions."

She narrowed her eyes at him. "Is this the part where I get to tell you to go to hell, so soon after that touching moment?"

But Byron held up his hands in surrender. "All I'm saying is, if you do something that some people *might* consider rash, just call Mom first, okay? She was there when

Matthew got married and when I got married. And I get dibs on walking you down the aisle."

Frances stared at him. *"What?"* Where had he gotten *that*? The impending wedding was something that she and Ethan had only discussed behind closed doors. No one else was supposed to have a clue.

No one but Byron, curse him. She'd never been able to hide anything from him for long, anyway, and he knew it. He gave her a wry smile and said, "You heard me. And come to the restaurant next week, okay? I'll save you the best table." He kissed her on the cheek and gave her shoulders a quick hug. "I've got to go. Take care, Frannie."

She stood there for several moments after Byron left. *Rash?* This wasn't rash. This was a carefully thought-out plan. A plan that did not necessarily include her mother watching her get married to Ethan Logan or having Byron—or any other brother—walk her down the aisle.

She didn't want her mother to think she'd found a happily-ever-after. Maybe she should call Mom and warn her that this whole thing wasn't real and it wouldn't last.

Frances found herself sitting on her bed, staring at the flowers. She was running out of room in here—the roses were on the dresser, the lilies on the desk. He didn't have to spend this much on flowers for her.

She plucked the card out and read it again. It didn't take long to process the two words. *Yours, E.*

She grinned as her fingertip traced the *E*. No, he was not particularly good at whispering—or writing—sweet nothings.

But he was hers, at least for the foreseeable future.

She needed to call her mom. And she would. Soon.

Right now, however, she had to get ready for a date.

Ethan knew the moment Frances walked into the restaurant. Not because he saw her do it, but because the entire place—including the busboy passing by and the bartender pouring a glass of wine—came to a screeching halt. There wasn't a sound, not even a fork scraping on a plate.

He knew before he even turned around that he wasn't going to make it. He wasn't going to be able to wall himself off from whatever fresh hell Frances had planned for him tonight. And what only made it worse? He didn't want to. God help him, he didn't want to.

While he finished his whiskey he took a moment to remind himself that part of the deal was that sex was not part of the deal. It didn't matter if she were standing there completely nude—he would give her his present and take her up to his hotel room and lock himself in the bathroom if he had to. He'd control himself. He'd never succumbed to wild passion before. Now was not the time to start.

After a long, frozen moment, everyone moved again. Ethan took a deep breath and turned around.

Oh, Jesus. She was wearing a strapless fire-engine-red dress that hugged every curve. And as good as she looked, all he wanted to do was strip that dress off her and see the real her, without armor—or anything else —on.

Even across the dim restaurant, he saw her smile when their eyes met. She did not like him, he reminded himself. That smile was for public consumption, not for him. But damned if it didn't make him smile back at her.

He got off his stool and went to meet her. He knew he needed to say things—for the diners who were all not so subtly listening in. He needed to compliment Frances's dress and tell her how glad he was to see her.

He couldn't get his stupid mouth to work. Even as part of his brain knew that was the whole point of that dress, he couldn't fight it.

He couldn't fight her.

So instead of words, he did the next best thing—he pulled her into his arms and kissed her like he'd been thinking of doing all damn day long. And it wasn't for the viewing public, either.

It was for her. All for her.

Somehow, he managed to pull away before he slid his hands down her back and cupped her bottom in the middle of the restaurant. "I missed you today," he whispered as he touched his forehead to hers.

"Did you?"

Maybe it was supposed to sound dismissive, but that's not how it hit his ears. Instead, she sounded as if she couldn't quite believe he was being sincere—but she wanted him to be.

"I did. Our table's ready." He took her hand in his and led her to the waiting table. After they were seated, he asked, "Anything interesting happen today?"

She arched an eyebrow at him. "Yes, actually. My twin, Byron, came to see me."

"Oh?" Had it been the same kind of visit he'd gotten from Chadwick?

Frances was watching him closely. "His new restaurant opens next week. He'd appreciate it if we could put in an appearance. Apparently, we're great publicity right now."

"Which was the plan," he said, more to remind himself than her. Because he had to stick to that plan, come hell or high water.

She leaned forward on her elbows, her generous cleavage on full display. He felt his pulse pick up a notch. "Indeed. You? Anything interesting today?"

"A few things," he tried to say casually. "Everyone at the Brewery is waiting to see if you bring me my very own donut this Friday."

A dazzling—and, he hoped, genuine—smile lit up her face. "Oh, really? I guess I should plan on coming, then?" Her tone was light and teasing.

This was what he'd missed today. She could talk circles

around him, and all he could do was keep up. He reached over and cupped her cheek in his hand, his thumb stroking her skin.

She leaned into his touch—a small movement that no one else could see. It was just for him, the way she let him carry a little of her weight. Just for him, the way her eyelashes fluttered. "I requested a chocolate éclair."

"Maybe I'll bring you a whole box, just to see what they say."

She would not like him. He should not like her.

But he did, damn it all. He liked her a great deal.

He didn't want to tell her the other interesting thing. He didn't want to watch her armor snap back into place at the mention of one of her brothers. Hell, for that matter, he didn't really want to be sitting in this very nice restaurant. He wanted to be someplace quiet, where they could be alone. Where her body could curl up against his and he could stroke her hair and they could talk about their days and kiss and laugh without giving a flying rat's ass what anyone else saw, much less thought.

"Chadwick came by the office today."

It was a hard thing to watch, her reaction. She sat up, pulling away from his touch. Her shoulders straightened and her eyes took on a hard look. "Did he now?"

Ethan let his hand fall away. "He did."

She considered this new development for a moment. "I suppose Phillip talked to him?"

"I got that feeling. He also said I'm making him look bad, with all the flowers."

Frances waved this excuse away as if it were nothing more than a gnat. "He can afford to buy Serena flowers—and does, frequently." Her eyes closed and, elbows back on the table, she clasped her hands in front of her. She looked as though she was concentrating very hard—or praying. "Do I even want to know what he said?"

"The usual older-brother stuff. What are my intentions, I'd better not break his little sister's heart—that sort of thing." He shrugged, as if it'd been just another day at the office.

She opened her eyes and stared at him over the tops of her hands. "What did you say? Please tell me you didn't kowtow to him. It's not good for his already-massive ego."

Ethan leaned back. "I merely informed him that what happens between two consenting adults is none of his business and for him to presume he knows best for either of us was patronizing at best. A fact I have recently been reminded of myself."

Frances's mouth opened, but then what he said registered and she closed it again. A wry smile curved her lips. He wanted to kiss that smile, those lips—but there was a table in the way. "You didn't."

"I did. I don't recall any kowtowing."

She laughed at that, which made him feel good. It wasn't as if he'd fought to the death for her honor or anything, but he'd still protected her from a repeat of what had happened last night.

She shifted and the toes of her foot came into contact with his shin. Slowly, she stroked up and down. His pulse kicked it up another notch—then two.

"I got you something," he said suddenly. He had decided it would be better to wait to give her the jewelry until after dinner, but the way she was looking at him? The way she was touching him? He'd changed his mind.

"The flowers were beautiful," she murmured. Her foot moved up and then down again, stroking his desire higher.

The room was too warm. Too hot. He was going to fall into the flames and get burned, and he couldn't think of a better way to go.

He reached into his pocket and pulled out the long, thin

velvet box. "I picked it out," he told her, holding it out to her. "I thought it suited you."

Her foot paused against his leg, and he took advantage of the break to adjust his pants. Sitting had suddenly become uncomfortable.

Her eyes were wide as she stared at the box. "What did you do?"

"I bought my future wife a gift," he said simply. The words felt right on his tongue, like they belonged there. *Wife*. "Open it."

She hesitated, as if the box might bite her. So he opened it for her.

The diamond necklace caught the light and glittered. He'd chosen the drop pendant, a square-cut diamond that hung off the end of a chain of three smaller diamonds, all set in platinum. Tiffany's had some larger solitaires, but this one seemed to fit Frances better.

"Oh, Ethan," she gasped as he held the box out toward her. "I didn't expect this."

"I like to keep you guessing," he told her. He set the box down and pulled the platinum chain out of its moorings. "Here," he said, his voice deeper than he remembered it being. "Allow me."

He stood and moved behind her, draping the necklace in front of her. She swept her mane of hair away from her neck, exposing the smooth skin. Ethan froze. He wanted nothing more than to lean down and taste her, to run his lips over the delicate curve where her neck met her shoulders—to see how she would react if he trailed kisses lower, pulling the dress down farther until...

She tilted her head down, pulling him back to the reality of standing in a crowded restaurant, holding nine thousand dollars' worth of diamonds. As he tried to fasten the clasp, his hands began to shake with need—the need to hold her, the need to stroke her bare shoulders. The need to make her *his*.

He'd had other lady friends, bought them nice gifts—usually when it was time for him to move on—but he had never felt this much need before. He didn't know what it was—only that it was because of her.

He willed his hands—and other body parts—to stand down. This was just a temporary madness; that was all. A beautiful woman in a gorgeous dress designed to inspire lust—nothing more, really.

Except it wasn't. No matter what he told himself, he knew he wasn't being honest—not with himself, not with her.

Honesty was not supposed to figure into this, after all. The whole premise of their relationship was based on a stack of lies that only got taller with each passing day and each passing floral arrangement. No, it was not supposed to be honest, their relationship. It was, however, supposed to be simple. She needed the money. He needed the Beaumont seal of approval. Everyone came out a winner.

That was possibly the biggest lie of all. Nothing about Frances Beaumont had been simple since the moment he'd laid eyes on her.

Finally, he got the clasp hooked. He managed to restrain himself enough that he did not press a kiss to her neck, did not wind her long hair into his hands.

But he was not exactly restrained. His fingertips drifted over the skin she'd exposed when she'd moved her hair and then down her bare shoulders with the lightest of touches. It shouldn't have been overtly sexual, shouldn't have been all that erotic—but unfamiliar need hammered through his gut.

It only got worse when she let go of her hair and that mass of fire-red silk brushed over the backs of his hands. Without meaning to—without meaning any of this—he dug his fingers into her skin, pulling her against him. She was soft and warm, and she leaned back and looked up at him.

Their gazes met. He supposed that, with another woman, he'd be staring down her front, looking at how his diamonds were nestled between her breasts, so large and firm and on such display at this angle.

But he was only dimly aware of her cleavage because Frances was staring up at him, her lips parted ever so slightly. Color had risen in her cheeks, and her eyes were wide. One of her hands reached up and found his. It was only when she pressed his hand flat against her skin that he realized his palms were moving along her skin, moving to feel everything about her—to learn everything about her.

He stroked his other thumb over her cheek. She gasped, a small movement that he felt more than saw. His body responded to her involuntary reaction with its own. Blood pounded in his ears as it raced from his brain to his erection as fast as it could. And, given how she was leaning against it, she knew it, too.

This was the moment, he thought dimly—as much as he could think, anyway. She could say something cutting and put him in his place, and he'd have to sit down and eat dinner with blue balls and not touch her like he meant it.

"Ethan," she whispered as she stared up at him. Her eyes seemed darker now, the pupils widening until the blue-green had almost disappeared.

Yes, he wanted to shout, to groan—yes, yes. He wanted to hear his name on her lips, over and over, in the most intimate of whispers and the loudest of passionate shouts. He wanted to push her to the point where all she could do, say—think—was his name. Was him.

His hand slipped lower, stroking the exposed skin of her throat. Lower still, tracing the outline of the necklace he'd bought for her.

Her grip on his hand tightened as his fingers traced the pendant. She didn't tell him to stop, though. She didn't lean away, didn't give a single signal that he should stop touching her. His hand started to move even lower, stroking down into the body of her dress and—

"Are we ready to order?" a too-bright, too-loud voice suddenly demanded.

Frances and Ethan both jumped. Suddenly he was aware that they were still in public, that at least half the restaurant was still watching them—that he'd been on the verge of sheer insanity in the full view of anyone with a cell phone. What the hell was wrong with him?

He tried to step away from her, to put at least a respectable three inches between their bodies—but Frances didn't let go of his hand.

Instead—incredibly—she stood and said, "Actually, I'm not hungry. Thanks, though." Then she turned to give him a look over her shoulder. "Shall we?"

"We shall," was the most intelligent thing he was capable of coming up with. The waiter smirked at them both as Ethan fished a fifty out of his wallet to cover his bar tab.

Every eye was on them as they swept up to the front together. Ethan took Frances's coat from the coat check girl and held it as Frances slipped her bare arms into it. They didn't speak as they braved the cold wind and waited for the valet to bring his car around. But Ethan put his arm around her shoulders and pulled her close. She leaned her head against his chest. Was he imagining things, or was she breathing hard—or at least, harder than normal? He wasn't sure. Maybe that was his chest, rising and falling faster than he normally breathed.

He didn't feel normal. Sex was always fun, always enjoyable—but something he could take or leave. He liked the release of it, and, yeah, sometimes he needed that release more than other times. But that's all it was. A pressure valve that sometimes needed to be depressurized a bit.

It wasn't this pain that made thinking rationally impossible—a pain that could only be erased by burying himself in her body over and over again until he was finally sated.

This wasn't about a simple release. He could achieve that with anyone. Hell, he didn't even need another person.

But this? Right now? This was about Frances and this unknown need she inspired in him. And the more he tried to name that need, the more muddled his head became. He wanted to show her what he could do for her, how he could take care of her, protect her and honor her. That they could be good together. For each other.

Finally, the car arrived. Ethan held her door for her and then got behind the wheel. He gunned it harder than he needed to, but he didn't want to waste another minute, another second, without Frances in his arms.

They weren't far from the hotel. He wouldn't have even bothered with the car if it'd been twenty degrees warmer. The drive would take five minutes, tops.

Or it would have—until Frances leaned over and placed her hand on his throbbing erection. Even through the layers of his boxers and wool trousers, her touch burned hot as she tested his length. Ethan couldn't do anything but grip the steering wheel as she made her preliminary exploration of his arousal.

It was when she squeezed him, shooting the pain that veered into pleasure through his whole body, that he forced out the words. "This isn't a game, Frances."

"No, it's not," she agreed, her voice breathy as her fingers stroked him. His body burned for her. If she stopped, he didn't know if he could take it. "Not anymore."

"Are you coming up to my room?" It came out far gruffer than he'd intended—not a request but not quite a demand.

"I don't think the hotel staff would appreciate it if we had sex in the lobby." She didn't let go of him when she said it. If anything, her hand was tighter around him.

"Is that what you really want? Sex, I mean. Not the lobby part." Because he was honor-bound to ask and more than honor-bound to accept her answer as the final word on the matter. Even if it killed him. "Because it wasn't part of the original deal."

That pushed her away from him. Her hot hand was gone, and he was left aching without her touch. "Ethan," she said in the most severe voice he'd heard her use all night long. "I don't want to talk about the damned deal. I don't want to think about it."

"Then what do you want?" he asked as they pulled up in front of the hotel.

She didn't answer. Instead, she got out, and he had no choice but to follow her, handing his keys to the valet. They walked into the hotel without touching, waited for the elevator without speaking. Ethan was thankful his coat was long enough to hide his erection.

They walked into the elevator together. Ethan waited until the doors were closed before he moved on her. "Tell me what you want, Frances," he said, pinning her against the back of the elevator. Her body was warm against his as she looked up at him through her lashes and he saw her. Not her armor, not her carefully constructed front— he saw *her*. "To hell with the deal. Tell me what you want right now. Is it sex? Is it *me*?"

"I shouldn't want you," she said, her voice soft, almost uncertain. She took his face in her hands, their mouths a whisper away. "I shouldn't."

"I shouldn't want you, either," he told her, an unfamiliar flash of anger pushing the words out of his mouth. "You drive me mad, Frances. Absolutely freaking mad. You undermine me at the Brewery and work me into a lather, and you turn my head around so fast that I get dizzy every time I see you. And, damn it all, you do it with that smile that lets me know it's easy for you. That *I'm* easy for you." He touched his thumb to her lips. She tried to kiss his thumb, and when he pulled it away, she tried to kiss him, pulling his head down to hers.

He didn't let her. He peeled her hands off his face and pinned them against the elevator walls. For some reason, he had to tell her this now before they went any further. "You *complicate* things. God help me—you make everything harder than it has to be, and I don't want you any other way."

Her eyes were wide, although he didn't know if that was because he was holding her captive or what he'd said. "You…don't?"

"No, I don't. I want you complicated and messy." He leaned against her, so she could feel exactly how much he wanted her. "I want you taunting and teasing me, and I want you with your armor up because you're the toughest woman I know. And I want you with your armor off entirely because—" Abruptly, the flash of anger that gave him all of those words was gone, and he realized that instead of telling a beautiful woman how wonderful she was, he was pretty sure he'd been telling her that she irritated him. "Because that's how I want you," he finished, unsure of himself.

Her lips parted and her mouth opened—right as the elevator did the same. They were on Ethan's floor. He held her like that for just a second longer, then released his hold in time to keep the doors from closing on them.

He held out his hand for her.

And he waited.

Twelve

"You *want* me complicated?" Frances stood there, staring at Ethan as if he'd casually announced he wore a cape in his off time while fighting crime.

No one had wanted her messy and complicated before. They wanted her simply, as an object of lust or as a step up the social ladder. It was when things got messy or complicated or—God help her—both that men disappeared from her life. When Frances dared to let her real self show through—that was when the trouble began. She was too dramatic, too high-maintenance, her tastes and ambitions too expensive. Her family life was far too complex—that was always rich, coming from the ones who wanted an association with the prestige of the Beaumont name but none of the actual work that went into maintaining it.

She'd heard it all before. *So* many times before.

The elevator beeped in warning. Ethan said, "I do," and grabbed her, hauling her past the closing doors.

She didn't know what to say to that, which was a rarity in itself. They stood in the middle of the hallway for a moment, Ethan holding on to her hand tightly. "Do you?" he asked in a gentle voice. "Want me, that is."

She felt the cool weight of the diamonds he'd laid against her skin. How many thousands of dollars had he spent on them? On her? It was not supposed to be complicated. If they had sex, then it was supposed to be this simple quid pro quo. This was the way of her world—it always had been. The man buys an expensive, extravagant gift and the woman takes her clothes off. It was not messy.

Except it was.

"You're ruining the last of my family's legacy and business," she told him. "You're everything that went wrong. When we lost the Brewery, I lost a part of my identity and I should hate you for being party to that. God, how I wanted to hate you."

Oh, Lord—were her eyes watering? No. Absolutely not. There was no crying in baseball or in affairs of the heart. At least, not in her affairs of the heart, mostly because her affairs never actually involved her heart.

She kept that locked away from everyone, and no one had ever realized it—until Ethan Logan had shown up and seen the truth of the matter. Until he'd seen the truth of her.

"You can still hate me in the morning," he told her. "I don't expect anything less from you."

"But what about tonight?" Because it was all very well and good to say that he liked her messy, but that didn't mean she wasn't still a mess. And that wore on a man after a while.

He stepped into her. His body was strong and warm, and she knew if she gave first and leaned against him, breathed in his woodsy scent, that she would be lost to him.

She'd already lost so much. Could she afford to lose anything else?

He stroked his fingers down her face, then slid them back through her hair, pulling her up to him. "Let me love you tonight, Frances. Just you and me. Nothing else."

It was real and honest and sincere, damn him to hell. It was true because he was true. None of those little lies and half glosses of compliments that hid the facts better than they illuminated them. And for a man who did not

grasp the finer points of sweet nothings, it was the sweet-
est damn something she'd ever heard.

A door behind them opened. She didn't know if it was
the elevator or another guest and she didn't much care.
She took off down the hall toward Ethan's room without
letting go of his hand.

He got the door open and pulled her inside. "I won't
like you in the morning," she told him, her voice shaking
as he undid the belt at her waist and pushed the coat from
her shoulders.

"But you like me now," he replied, shucking his own
coat in the process. "Don't you?"

She did. Oh, this was a heartache waiting to happen,
this thing between her and Ethan.

"I don't want to talk anymore," she said in as commanding a voice as she could muster. More than that, she didn't
want to think anymore. She only wanted to feel, to get lost
in the sweet freedom of surrendering to her baser lust.

She grabbed him by the suit jacket and jerked it down
his arms, trying to get him as naked as possible as fast as
possible. He let her, but he said, "Don't you dare hide behind that wall, Frances."

"I'm not hiding," she informed him, grabbing his belt
and undoing it. "I'm getting you naked. That's generally
how sex works best."

The next thing she knew, they were right back to where
they'd been in the elevator, with the full weight of his
body pinning her against the door, her wrists in his hands.
"Don't," he growled at her. "I don't want to sleep with your
armor. I want to sleep with you, damn it. I *like* you. Just
the way you are. So don't try to be some flippant, distant
princess who's above this. Above us."

Her breath caught in her throat. "You don't know what
you're asking of me." It didn't come out confident or cocky
or even flippant.

"Maybe I do." He kissed her then, with enough force to knock her head back. "Sorry," he murmured against her lips.

"It's okay," she replied because if they were getting to the sex part, they'd stop talking and she could just feel. Even the small pain in the back of her head was okay because she didn't have to talk about it, about what it really meant. "Just keep kissing me hard."

"Is that how you want it?"

She tested her wrists against his grip. There was a little give, but not much. "Yes," she said, knowing full well that he was a man who knew exactly what that meant. "That's how I want *you*." Hard and fast with no room to stop and think. None.

A deep sound came out of his chest, a growl that she felt in her bones. His hips shifted and his erection ground against her. Yes, she wanted to feel all of that.

But then he said, "Tell me if something doesn't work," and she heard his control starting to fray. "Promise me that, babe."

She blinked up at him through a haze of desire. Had anyone ever said that to her before? "Of course," she said, trying to make it sound as though all of her previous lovers had put her orgasms first—had put her first.

He raised an eyebrow at her. He didn't even have to say it—she could still hear him telling her not to pretend.

Then he moved. "Whatever else," he said as he slid her hands up over her head and put both her wrists under one of his massive hands, "I expect complete and total honesty in bed."

"We aren't currently in bed," she reminded him. She tested her wrists again, but he wasn't playing around. He had her pinned.

It wasn't that she wasn't turned on—she was. But a new kind of excitement started to build underneath the standard sexual arousal that she normally felt. Ethan had her pinned. He had a free hand. He could do anything that he wanted to her.

And he'd stop the moment she told him to.

For once in her life, she wouldn't have to think about anything except what he was going to do next.

"Turn around," he ordered as he lifted her wrists away from the door just enough that she could spin in place. Then he swept her hair away from her neck and—and—oh, God. He didn't just kiss her there, he scraped his teeth over her exposed skin, raw and hungry.

Frances sucked in air at the unexpected sensation. "Good?" he asked.

"Yeah."

"Good," he said, biting a little harder this time, then kissing the sore spot.

Frances shifted, the weight between her legs growing hotter and heavier as he worked over her skin. Then he was pulling the zipper down on her dress, and the whole thing fell to her feet, leaving her in nothing but a white lace pair of panties that left very little to the imagination.

"Oh, babe," Ethan said in undisguised appreciation. She started to turn so she could see his face when he said it, but he gave her bottom a light smack and then used his body to keep hers flat against the door. "No, don't look," he ordered. "Just feel."

"Yeah," she moaned, her skin slightly stinging from where he'd smacked her. "I want to feel you."

His hand popped against her bare bottom again—not hard. He wasn't hurting her. But the unexpected contact made her body involuntarily tighten, and the anticipation of the next touch drove everything else from her mind.

Ethan's free hand circled her waist, pushing her just far enough away from the door that he could cup one of her breasts, teasing the nipple until it was hard with desire.

Then he tugged at it with more force. "Yeah?" he asked, his breath hot against her neck. He shoved one of his knees between her legs and she sagged onto it, grinding her hips, trying to take the pressure off the one spot in her body that made standing hard.

"Yeah," she moaned, her body moving without her permission, trying to find release, that moment where there was a climax that only Ethan could bring her to.

"You want more?" he demanded, tugging at her nipple again.

"Ethan, please," she panted, for no matter how she shifted her hips, the only pressure she felt did not push her over the edge.

He pulled away from her. "Don't move," he said. Then her wrists were free and his knee was gone and she felt cold, pressed up against this impersonal hotel door. Behind her, she heard the sound of plastic tearing. The condom. *Good.*

Then Ethan put his hand on the back of her neck and pulled her away from the door. "Hard?" he asked again, as if he wanted to make absolutely sure.

"Hard," she all but begged. "Hard and fast and—"

He led her to the bed, but instead of laying her out on it, he bent her over the edge. Her panties were pulled down, and she was exposed before him.

Her body quivered with need and anticipation and excitement because this was not gentle and sweet, not when he grabbed her by the hips and lifted her bottom against his rock-hard erection. His fingers dug into her flesh in a hungry way.

"Ethan," she moaned as he smacked her bottom again, just hard enough that her muscles tightened and she almost came right then. She fisted the bedclothes in her hands and tensed, hoping and praying for the next touch. "Hard and fast and now. Now, Ethan, or I won't like you in the morning, I swear to God, I'll hate you. *Now*, Ethan, *now*."

Then he was against her, and, with a moan of pure masculine satisfaction, he was in her, thrusting hard. Frances gasped at the suddenness of him—oh, he was huge—but her body took him in as he pounded her with all the aggression she needed so badly.

She hit her peak, moaning into the sheets as the wave cascaded over her. *Thank heavens*, she thought, going soft after it'd passed. She'd wanted to come so badly and—and—

And Ethan didn't stop. He didn't sputter to a finish. Instead, he paused long enough to reach forward and tangle his hands in her hair and pull so that her head came off the bed. "Are you nice and warmed up now?" he demanded, and a shiver ran through her body. He felt it, too—she could tell by the way he twined her hair around his fingers. "That's it, babe. Ready?"

He wasn't done. Oh, he wasn't done with her. He was going to make her come again, so fast and so hard that when he began to thrust again, all she could do was take him in. He kept one hand tangled in her hair, lifting her head up and back so that she arched away from him and her bottom lifted up to his greedy demands.

All she could do was moan—she wanted to cry out, but the angle of her neck made that too hard. Everything about her tightened as Ethan gave her exactly what she wanted—him, hard and fast.

This time, when he brought his hand against her ass in time with his thrusting, she came equally as hard. She couldn't help it. Her body acted without her input at all. All she was, all she could feel, was what Ethan did to her. The climax was unlike anything she'd ever felt before, so intense she forgot to breathe even.

Ethan held her there as waves of pleasure washed her

clean of everything but satisfaction. When she sagged against the bed, spent and panting, he let go of her hair, dug his fingertips back into her hips and pumped into her three more times before groaning and falling forward onto her.

They lay there for a moment, his body pressing hers against the mattress while she tried to remember how to breathe like a normal human. She didn't feel normal anymore; that was for sure.

She didn't know how she felt. Good—oh, yes. She felt wonderful. Her body was limp and her skin tingled and everything was amazing.

But when Ethan rolled off her and then leaned down and pressed a kiss between her shoulder blades—she felt decidedly not normal. She didn't turn her head to look at him. She didn't know what to say. Her! Frances Beaumont! Speechless! That was hard enough to accomplish by itself—but to have had sex so intense and so satisfying that she had not a single snappy observation or cutting comeback?

Not that he was waiting for her to say something. He kissed her on the shoulder and said, "I'll be right back," before he hefted himself off the bed. She heard the bathroom door click shut, and then she was alone in the hotel room with only her feelings.

Now what was she going to do?

Thirteen

Ethan splashed cold water on his face, trying to get his head to clear. He felt like a jackass. That wasn't how he normally took a woman to bed. Not even close. He usually took his time, making sure the foreplay left everyone satisfied before the actual sex.

But pinning Frances against the door and then bending her over the edge of the bed? Pawing at her as if he were little more than a lust-crazed animal? That hadn't been tender and sweet.

He didn't want to be responsible for his actions. He'd smacked her bottom—more than once! That wasn't like him. He wanted that to be her fault—she'd worn the red dress, she'd been this *siren* that pushed him past sanity, past responsibility.

But that was crap, and he knew it. All she'd said was that she wanted it hard and fast. He could have still been a gentleman about it. Instead, he'd gotten rough. He'd never done that before. He didn't know…

Well, he just didn't know.

And he wasn't going to find out hiding in the bathroom.

He'd apologize; that was all there was to it. He'd gotten carried away. It wouldn't happen again.

He finished up and headed out. He hadn't even gotten undressed. He'd stripped her down, but aside from shoving his pants out of the way, he was still dressed. Yes, that was quite possibly the best sex of his life, but still. He couldn't shake the feeling that he'd gone too far.

That feeling got even stronger when he saw her. Frances had curled up on her side. She looked impossibly small against the expanse of white sheets. She watched him, her eyes wide. Was she upset? *Hell.*

Then her nose wrinkled, and he was pretty sure she smiled. "You're not naked," she said. Her voice was raw, as if she'd been shouting into the wind for hours.

"Is that a problem?" He tried to keep it casual sounding. He wasn't sure he made it.

She uncurled from the bed like a flower opening for him. "I wanted to see you. And I didn't get to."

"My apologies for the disappointment." He started to jerk open the buttons on his shirt, but she stood and closed the distance between them. His hands fell around her waist, still warm from the sex. He wanted to fold her into his arms and hold her for as long as he could.

Where was all this ridiculous sentiment coming from? He wasn't a sentimental guy.

"Let me," she said. He saw that her hands were trembling. "And it wasn't disappointing. It was wonderful. Except that I couldn't see you."

Ethan blinked twice, trying to process that. "I didn't go too far?"

"No," she said, giving him a nervous smile. "I—" She paused and took a deep breath. "Honestly?"

"Even though we're still not in bed," he said with a grin, tilting her chin up so he could look her in the eyes.

She held his gaze for a moment before forcibly turning her attention back to his buttons. "Thank you," she said quietly.

That was not quite what he'd been expecting. "For what? I think I got just as much out of that as you did."

She undid the last button and pushed the shirt off him. Then his T-shirt followed. Finally she shoved his pants down, and Ethan kicked out of them.

"Oh, my," she whispered, skimming her fingers over his chest and ruffling his hair.

He fought the urge to flex. The urge won. She giggled as his muscles moved under her hands. "Ethan!"

"Sorry," he said, walking her back toward the bed. "I can't seem to help myself around you."

This time, they actually got under the covers. Ethan pulled her on top of him. He didn't mean it in an explicitly sexual way, but her body covering his? Okay, it was more than a little sexual. "Why did you thank me?"

She laid out on him, her head tucked against his chest. "You really want me messy and complicated?"

"Seems to be working so far."

She sighed, tracing small circles against his skin. "No one's ever wanted me. Not the real me. Not like this."

"I find that hard to believe. You are a hell of a woman."

"They don't want me," she insisted. "They want the fantasy of me. Beautiful and sexy and rich and famous. They want the mystique of the Beaumont name. That's what I am to people." When he didn't have a response to that, she propped herself up on one elbow and stared down at him. "That's what I was to you, wasn't I?"

There was no point in playing games about it. "You were. But you're not anymore."

Her smile was tinged with sadness. "I'm not used to being honest, I guess."

He cupped her face in his hands and kissed her. He didn't intend for it to be a distraction, but she must have taken it that way because she pulled back. "Why did you agree to a sham marriage? And don't give me that line about the workers loving me."

"Even though they do," he put in.

"Most men do not agree to sham marriages as business deals," she went on as if he hadn't interrupted her. "I seem to recall you making quite a point of saying love wasn't a part of marriage when we came to terms. So spill it."

She had him trapped. Sure, he could throw her off him, but then she shifted and straddled him, and his body stirred at the thought of her bare legs wrapped around his waist, her body so close to his.

So, with mock exasperation, he flopped back against the bed. "My parents have an...unusual relationship," he said.

She leaned down on him, her arms crossed over her chest, her chin on her arms. "I don't want you to take this the wrong way, but so? I mean, my mom was second out of four wives for my dad. I wouldn't know a usual relationship if it bit me. Present company included."

He wrapped his arms around her body, enjoying the warmth she shared with him. No, this wasn't usual, not even close. But he was enjoying it anyway. "Have you ever heard of Troy Logan?"

"No. Brother or father?"

He wasn't surprised. Her brother Chadwick would probably recognize the name, but that wasn't Frances's world. "Father. Notorious on Wall Street for buying companies and dismantling them at a profit."

She tilted her head from side to side. "I take it the apple did not fall terribly far from the tree?"

"I don't take companies apart. I restructure them." She gave him an arch look, and he gave in. "But, yes, you're correct. We're in nearly the same line of work."

"And..." she said. "Your mother?"

"Wanda Kensington." He braced for the reaction.

He didn't have to wait long. She gasped, which made him wince. "What? You don't mean—*the* Wanda Kensington? The artist?"

"I can't tell you how rare it is that someone knows my

mother's name but not my father's," he said, stroking her hair away from her face.

"Don't change the subject," she snapped, sitting all the way up. Which left her bare breasts directly in Ethan's line of sight. The diamonds he'd bought for her glittered between those perfect breasts. "Your mother is—but Wanda's known for her art installations! Massive performance pieces that take like a year to assemble! I don't ever remember reading anything about her having a family."

"She wasn't around much. I don't know why they got married, and I don't know why they stayed married. I'm not even sure they like each other. They never made sense," he admitted. "She'd be gone for months, a year—we had nannies that my father was undoubtedly sleeping with—and then she'd walk back in like no time at all had passed and pretend to be this hands-on mother who cared."

He was surprised to hear the bitterness in his voice. He'd long ago made peace with his mother. Or so he'd thought. "And she'd try, I think. She'd stick it out for a few weeks—once she was home for almost three months. She made it to Christmas, and then she was gone again. We never knew, my brother and I. Never had a clue when she'd show up or when she'd disappear again."

"So you were—what? Another piece of performance art? The artist as a mother?"

"I suppose." Not that he'd ever thought about it in those terms. "It wasn't bad. Dad wasn't jealous of her. She wasn't jealous of him. It wasn't like there was drama. It was just… a marriage on paper."

"It was a sham," Frances corrected.

He skimmed his hands up and down her thighs, shifting her weight against him. His erection was more than interested in the shifting. "Didn't seem like it'd be hard to replicate," he agreed.

But that was before—before he'd seen past Frances's

armor, before he'd stupidly begun to like the real woman underneath.

She rocked her hips, and his body responded. He stroked her nipples—this time, without the roughness—and Frances moaned appreciatively. He shouldn't want her this much, shouldn't *like* her this much. Passion wasn't supposed to figure into his plans. It never had before.

He lifted her off long enough to roll on another condom, and then she settled her weight back onto him, taking him in with a sigh of pure pleasure. *This* was honesty. This was something real between them because she meant something more to him than just her last name.

She rode him slowly, taking her time, letting him play with her breasts and her nipples until she was panting and he was driving into her. He leaned forward enough to catch one of her breasts in his mouth and sucked her nipple hard between his teeth.

She might not like him in the morning, and she'd be well within her rights.

But he was going to like her. Hell, he already did. It was going to be a huge problem.

As she shuddered down on him, urging him to suck her nipples harder as she came apart, he didn't care. Complicated and messy and his.

She was his.

After she'd collapsed onto him and he'd taken care of the condom, they lay in each other's arms. He had things he wanted to say to her, except he didn't know what those things were, which wasn't like him. He was a decisive man. The buck stopped with him.

"Are we still going to get married next week?" she asked in a drowsy voice.

"If you want," he said, feeling even as he said it that it was not the best response. He tried again. "I thought we weren't going to talk about the deal tonight."

"We aren't," she agreed and then immediately qualified that statement. "It's just that…this changes things."

"Does it?" He leaned over and turned out the light and then pulled the covers up over them both. When was the last time he'd had a woman spend the night in his arms? He couldn't think of when. His previous relationships were not spend-the-night relationships.

He tucked his arm around her body and held her close. Something cold and metallic poked at his side—the necklace. It was all she had on.

"We were supposed to barely live together," she reminded him. "We weren't supposed to sleep together. We weren't…"

He yawned and shrugged. "So we'll be slightly more married than we planned on. The marital bed and all that."

"And you're okay with that?"

"I'm okay with you." He kissed the top of her head. "I guess… Well, when we made the deal, I didn't think I'd enjoy spending time with you."

"You mean sex. You didn't think you'd enjoy sleeping with me." She sounded hurt about that, although he couldn't tell if she was playing or actually pouting.

"No, I don't," he clarified. "I mean, I didn't think I'd want to spend time with you. I didn't think I'd like you this much."

The moment the words left his mouth, he knew that he'd said too much. Damn it, they were supposed to roll over and go to sleep and not have deep, meaningful conversations until he'd recovered from the sex and had some more.

Instead, Frances tensed and then sat up, pulling away from him. "Ethan," she said, her voice a warning. "I told you not to like me."

"You make it sound like I have a choice about it," he said.

"You do."

"No, I don't. I can't help it." She didn't reply, didn't curl back into his arms. "We don't have to rush to get married. I'm willing to wait for you."

"Jesus," she said. The bed shifted, and then she was out of it, fumbling around the room in the dark. "Jesus, you sound like you *want* to marry me."

He turned on the light. "What's wrong?"

She threw his words back at him. "What's wrong?" She grabbed her dress and started to shimmy into it. Any other time, watching Frances Beaumont get dressed would be the highlight of his day. But not now, not when she was angrily trying to jerk up the zipper.

"Frances," he said, getting out of bed. "Where are you going?"

"This was a mistake," was the short reply.

He could see her zipping into her armor as fast as the dress—if not faster. "No, it wasn't," he said defensively, trying to catch her in his arms. "This was good. Great. This was us together. This is what we could be."

"Honestly, Ethan? There is no us. Not now, not ever. My God," she said, pushing him away and snagging her coat. "I thought you were smarter than this. Good sex and you're suddenly in love—in like?" she quickly corrected. "Unacceptable."

"Like hell it is," he roared at her.

"This is causal at best, Ethan. *Casual.* Casual sex, casual marriage." She flung her coat over her barely zipped dress and hastily knotted the belt. "I warned you, but you didn't listen, did you?"

"Would you calm the hell down and tell me what's wrong?" he demanded. "I did listen. I listened when you told me you expected to be courted with flowers and gifts and thoughtfulness."

"I did not—"

But he cut her off. "I listened when you told me about

your plans for a gallery. I listened when your family caught you off guard."

"I do not like you." She bit the words off as if she were killing them, one syllable at a time.

"I don't believe you. Not anymore. I've seen the real you, damn it all."

She drew herself up to her full height, a look on her face like a reigning monarch about to deliver a death sentence. "Have you?" she said. "I thought you were better at the game than this, Ethan. How disappointing that you're like all the rest."

And then she was gone. The door to the room swung open and slammed shut behind her, leaving Ethan wondering what the holy hell had just happened.

Fourteen

When had Frances lost control? That was the question she kept asking herself on the insanely long elevator ride down to the hotel lobby. She asked it as the valet secured a cab for her, and she asked it again on the long ride out to the mansion.

Because she had. She'd lost all sorts of control.

She slipped into the mansion. The place was dark and quiet—but then, it was late. Past midnight. The staff had left hours ago. Chadwick and Serena and their little girl were no doubt asleep, as were Frances's younger siblings.

She felt very much alone.

She took off her shoes and tiptoed up to her room. She jerked her zipper down so hard she heard tearing, which was a crying shame because this dress was her best one. But she couldn't quite care.

Frances dug out her ugly flannel pajamas, bright turquoise plaid and baggy shapelessness. They were warm and soft and comforting, and far removed from the nothing she'd almost fallen asleep wearing when she'd been in bed with Ethan.

God, what a mess. And, yes, she was aware that she was probably making it messier than it had to be, just by virtue of being herself.

But was he serious? Sure, she could have believed it if

he'd said he loved being with her and she was special and wonderful before the sex. It was expected, those words of seduction. Except he hadn't said them then. He'd said things that should have been insults—that she made his life harder than he wanted her to, that she drove him mad, that she was a complicated hot mess.

Those were not the words of a man trying to get laid.

Those were the words of an honest man.

And then after? To lay there in his arms and feel as if she'd exposed so much more than her body to him and to have him tell her that he enjoyed being with her, that he liked her, that—

That he'd happily push back their agreed-on marriage because she was worth waiting for?

It was all supposed to be a game. A game she'd played before and a game she'd play again. Yes, this was the long game—a wedding, a yearlong marriage—but that didn't change the rules.

Did it?

She climbed under her own covers in her own bed, a bed that was just as large as Ethan's. It felt empty compared with what she'd left behind.

Ethan wasn't following the rules. He was changing them. She'd warned him against doing so, but he was doing so anyway. And it was all too much for Frances. Too much honesty, too much realness. Too much intimacy.

Men had proposed before. Professed their undying love and admiration for her. But no one had ever meant it. No one ever did, not in her world. Love was a bargaining chip, nothing more. Sex was calling a bluff. All a game. Just a game. If you played it right, you got diamonds and houses and money. And if you lost…you got nothing.

Nothing.

She curled up into a tight ball, just like she'd always done back when she was little and her parents were fighting. On bad nights, she'd sneak into Byron's room and curl up in his bed. He took the top half and she took the bottom, their backs touching. That's how they'd come into this world. It felt safer that way.

Once, Mom had loved Dad. And Dad must have had feelings for Mom, right? That's why he'd married her and made their illegitimate child, Matthew, legitimate.

But they couldn't live together. They couldn't share a roof. They'd have been better off like Ethan's folks, going their separate ways 85 percent of the time and only coming together when the stars aligned just so. And in the end, her father had won and her mother had lost, and that had been the game.

She almost got up and got her phone to call Byron. To tell him she might have been rash and that she needed to come hang out for a couple of days until things cooled off. Mom was out there, anyway.

It was late. Byron was probably still asleep.

And then there was Friday. Donut Friday.

She had to face Ethan again. With an audience. Just like they'd planned it.

She had nothing to wear.

Delores walked in with a stack of interoffice envelopes. Ethan glared at her, trying to get his heart to calm down.

He hadn't heard from Frances since she'd stormed out of his room two nights ago, and it was making him jumpy. He did not like being jumpy.

"Any donuts yet?" he made himself say casually.

"Haven't seen her yet, but I can check with Larry to find out if she's on the premises," Delores said in a genial manner. She handed him a rather thick envelope. It had no return address. It just said, "E. Logan."

"What's this?"

"I'm sure I don't know." When Ethan glared at her, she said, "I'll go check on those donuts."

The old battle-ax, he thought menacingly as he undid the clasp and slid out a half-inch-thick manila folder.

"Potentially of our mutual interest—C. Beaumont," proclaimed a small, otherwise benign yellow sticky note on the front of the folder.

The only feeling that Ethan did not enjoy more than jumpiness was uncertainty. And that's what the manila folder suddenly represented. What on earth would Chadwick Beaumont consider of mutual interest? The only thing that came to mind was Frances.

And what of Frances could merit a folder this thick?

The possibilities—everything from blackmail to depravities—ran together in his mind. He shoved them aside and opened the file.

And found himself staring at a dossier for one Zeb Richards, owner of ZOLA.

Ethan blinked in astonishment as he scanned the information. Zeb Richards, born in Denver in 1973, graduated from Morehouse College with a bachelor of arts degree and from the University of Georgia with a master's in business administration. Currently resided in New York. There was a small color photo of the man, the first that Ethan had seen.

Wait—had he met Zeb Richards before? There was something about the set of the man's jaw that looked familiar. He had dark hair that was cropped incredibly close to his head, the way many black men wore it.

But Ethan would remember meeting someone named Zeb, wouldn't he?

Then he flipped the page and found another document—a photocopy of a birth certificate. Well, he had to hand it to Chadwick—he was nothing if not thorough. The certificate confirmed that Zebadiah Richards was born in Denver in 1973. His mother was Emily Richards and his father was...

Oh, hell.

Under "Father" was the unmistakable name of one Hardwick James Beaumont.

Ethan flipped back to the photo. Yes, that jaw—that was like Chadwick's jaw, like Phillip's. Those two men had been unmistakably brothers—full brothers. The resemblance had been obvious. And they'd looked a fair deal like Frances. The jaw was softer on her, more feminine—more beautiful.

But if Zeb's mother had been African-American... That would account for everything else.

Oh, hell.

Suddenly, it all made sense. This agitation on behalf of ZOLA to sell the Beaumont Brewery? It wasn't a rival firm looking to discredit Ethan's company, and it wasn't an activist shareholder looking to peel the Beaumont Brewery off so it could pick it up for pennies on the dollar and sell it off, like Ethan's father did.

This was personal.

And it had nothing to do with Ethan.

Except he was, as of about two nights ago, sleeping with a Beaumont. He was probably still informally engaged to be married to said Beaumont, although he wouldn't be sure of that until the donut situation was confirmed. And, perhaps most important of all, he was currently running the Beaumont Brewery.

"Delores," he said into the intercom. "Was this envelope hand-delivered to you?"

"It was on my desk this morning, Mr. Logan."

"I need to speak to Chadwick Beaumont. Can you get me his number?"

"Of course." Ethan started to turn the intercom off, but then she added, "Oh, Ms. Beaumont is on the premises."

"Thank you," he said. He flipped the intercom off and stuffed the folder back into the envelope. It was no joke to say he was out of his league here. A bastard son coming back to wreak havoc on his half siblings? Yeah, Ethan was *way* out of his league.

Chadwick must have a sense of humor, what with that note about Zeb Richards being "potentially" a mutual interest.

But Frances—she didn't know anything about her siblings from unmarried mothers, did she? No, Ethan was certain he remembered her saying she didn't know any of them. Just that there were some.

So Zeb Richards was not, at this exact moment, something she needed to know about.

Unless...

He thought back to the way she'd stood before him last night, all of her armor fully in place while he'd been naked in every sense of the word. And she'd said—*No, be honest*, he told himself—*sneered* that she'd thought he'd be better at the game.

Was Zeb Richards part of the game?

Just because Frances said she didn't know any of the illegitimate Beaumonts didn't mean she'd been truthful about it.

She'd asked Ethan why he wanted to marry her. Had he asked why she'd agreed to marry him? Beyond the money for her art gallery?

What else was she getting out of their deal?

Why had she shown up with donuts last week?

The answer was right in front of him, a manila folder in an envelope.

Revenge.

Hadn't she told him that she'd lost part of herself when the family lost the Brewery? And hadn't she said she should hate him for his part in that loss?

What had seemed like a distant coincidence—Frances disrupting his personal life at nearly the exact same time some random investor was trying to disrupt his business—now seemed less like a coincidence and more like directly correlated events.

What if she not only knew Zeb Richards was her half brother— what if she was helping him? Getting insider information? Not from Ethan, necessarily—but from all the people here who loved and trusted her because she was their Frannie?

Did Chadwick know? Or did he suspect? Was that why he'd sent the file?

Ethan had assumed it'd been the encounter with Phillip Beaumont that had prompted Chadwick's appearance at the Brewery the other day. But what if there'd been something else? What if one of Chadwick's loyal employees had tipped him off that Frances was asking around, digging up dirt?

And if that was possible, who's side was Chadwick on? Ethan's? Frances's? Zeb Richards's?

Ethan's head began to ache. This, he realized with a half laugh, was what he was trying to marry into—a family so sprawling, so screwed up that they didn't even have a solid head count on all their relatives.

"She's here," Delores's voice interrupted his train of thought.

Ethan stood and straightened his tie. He didn't know why. He pushed the thought of bastards with an ax to grind out of his head. He had to focus on what was important here—Frances. The woman he'd taken to his bed last night and then promptly chased right out of it, all because he was stupid enough to develop feelings for her.

The woman who might be setting him up to fail because it was a game. Nothing but a game.

He had no idea which version of Frances Beaumont was on the other side of that door.

He wanted to be wrong. He wanted it to be one giant coincidence. He did not want to know that he'd misjudged her so badly, that he'd been played for such a fool.

Because if he had, he didn't know where he would go from here. He was still the CEO of this company. He still had a deal to marry her and invest in her gallery. He had his own company to protect. As soon as the Brewery was successfully restructured, he'd pull up stakes and move on to the next business that needed to be run with an iron fist and an eye to the bottom line. They'd divorce casually and go on with their lives.

And once he was gone, he'd never have to think about anything Beaumont ever again.

He opened his door. Frances was standing there in jeans and boots. She wore a thick, fuzzy cable-knit sweater, and her hair was pulled back into a modest bun. Not a sky-high heel or low-cut silk blouse in sight. She looked...plain, almost, which was something because if there was one thing Frances Beaumont wasn't, it was plain.

And despite the fact that his head felt as if an anvil had just been dropped on it, despite the fact that he was in over his head—despite the fact that, no, he was most likely not as good at the game as he'd thought he was and, no, she did not like him—he was glad to see her. He absolutely shouldn't be, but he was.

It only got worse when she lifted her head. There was no crowd today, no group of eager employees around to stroke her ego or destroy his. Just her and Delores and a box.

"Frances."

"Chocolate éclair?" she asked simply.

Even her makeup was simple today. She looked almost innocent, as if she was still trying to understand what had happened between them last night, just like he was.

But was that the truth of the matter? Or was this part of the game?

"I saved you two," she told him, holding the box out.

"Come in," he said, holding his door open for her. "Delores, hold my calls."

"Even—" she started to say.

"I'll call him back." Yes, he needed to talk to Chadwick, but he needed to talk to Frances more. He wasn't sleeping with Chadwick. Frances came first.

Frances paused, a look on her face that yesterday Ethan would have assumed to be confusion. Today? He couldn't be sure.

She walked past him, her head held high and her bearing regal. Ethan wanted to smile at her. Evening gowns or blue jeans, she could pull off imperial like nobody's business.

But he didn't smile. She did not like him. And liking her? Wanting to take care of her, to spend time with her? That had been a massive error on his part.

So the moment the door shut, he resolved that he would not care about her. He would not pull her into his arms and hold her tight and try to find the right sweet nothings to whisper in her ear to wipe that shell-shocked look off her face.

He would not comfort her. He couldn't afford to.

She carried the donut box over to the wagon-wheel coffee table and set it down. Then she sat on the love seat, tucking her feet up under her legs. "Hi," she said in what seemed like a small voice.

He didn't like it, that small voice, because it pulled at him, and he couldn't afford to let her play his emotions like that. "How are you today?" he asked politely. He went back to his desk and sat. It seemed like the safest place to be, with a good fifteen feet and a bunch of historic furniture between them.

She watched him with those big eyes of hers. "I brought you donuts," she said.

"Thank you." He realized his fingers were tapping on the envelope Chadwick had sent. He made them be still.

She said, "Oh. Okay," in such a disappointed voice that it almost broke him because he didn't want to disappoint her, damn it, and he was anyway.

But then, what was he supposed to do? He'd given her everything he had last night, and look how that had turned out. She'd cut him to shreds. She'd been disappointed that he'd liked her.

So she wasn't allowed to be disappointed that he was keeping his distance right now. End of discussion.

He stared at the envelope again. He had to know—how deep was she in this? "So," he said. "How are the plans for the art gallery going?"

"Fine. Are we…"

"Yes?"

She cleared her throat and stuck out her chin, as if she was trying to look tough and failing, miserably. "Are we still on? The deal, that is."

"Of course. Why would you think it's off?"

She took a deep breath. "I—well, I said some not-nice things last night. You've been nothing but wonderful and I… I was not gracious about it. About you."

Was she apologizing? For hurting his feelings? Not that he'd admit to having his feelings hurt.

Was it possible that, somewhere under the artifice, she actually cared for him, too?

No, probably not. This was just another test, another move. Ethan made a big show of shrugging. "At no point did I assume that this relationship—or whatever you want to call it—is based on 'niceness.'" She visibly winced. "You were right. Affection is irrelevant." This time, he did not offer to let her out of the deal or postpone the farce that would be their wedding. "And a deal's a deal, after all."

A shadow crossed her face, but only briefly. "Of course," she agreed. She wrapped her arms around her waist. She looked as though she was trying to hold herself together. "So we'll need to get engaged soon?"

"Tonight, if that's all right with you. I've made reservations for us as we continue our tour of the finer restaurants in Denver." He let his gaze flick over her outfit in what he hoped was judgment.

"Sounds good." That's what she said. But the way she said it? Anything but good.

"I did have a question," he said. "You asked me last night why I'd agreed to get married to you. To a stranger."

"Because it seems normal enough," she replied. He refused to be even the slightest bit pleased that she recalled their conversation about his parents. "And the workers love me."

He tilted his head in appreciation. "But when we were naked and sharing, I failed to ask what you were getting out of this deal. Why *you* would agree to marry a total stranger."

She paled, which made her red hair stand out that much more. "The gallery," she said in a shaky voice. "It's going to be my job, my space. Art is what I'm good at. I need the gallery."

"Oh, I'm quite sure," he agreed, swiveling his chair so he was facing her fully. His hand was tapping the envelope again. Damn that envelope. Damn Zebadiah Richards. Hell, while he was at it, damn Chadwick Beaumont, too. "But that's not all, is it?"

Slowly, her head moved from side to side, a no that she was apparently unaware she was saying. "Of course that's all. A simple deal."

"With the man who represented the loss of your family business and your family identity."

"Well, yes. That's why I need the gallery. I need a fresh start."

He leveled his stoniest glare at her, the one that produced results in business negotiations. The very look that usually had employees falling all over themselves to do what he wanted, the way he wanted it.

To her credit, she did not buckle. He would have been disappointed if she had, frankly. He watched her armor snap into place. But it didn't stop the rest of the color from draining out of her face.

He had her, and they both knew it.

"You wanted revenge."

The statement hung in the air. Frances's gaze darted from side to side as if she was looking for an escape route. When she didn't find what she wanted, she sat up straighter.

Good, Ethan thought. She was going to brazen this out. For some reason, he wanted it that way, wanted her to go down fighting. He didn't want her meek and apologetic and fragile, damn it. He wanted her biting and cutting, a warrior princess with words as weapons.

He wanted her messy and complicated, and, damn it all, he was going to get her that way. Even if it killed him.

"I don't know what you're talking about." As she said it, she uncurled on the couch. Her legs swung down and stretched out before her, long and lean, the very legs that had been wrapped around him. At the same time, she stretched up, thrusting out her breasts.

This time, he did smile. She was going to give him hell. *This* was the woman who'd walked into his office a week ago, using her body as a weapon of mass distraction.

This was the woman he could love.

He pushed that thought aside.

"How did you plan to do it?" he asked. "Did you plan on pumping me for information, or just gather some from the staff while you plied them with donuts?"

One eyebrow arched up. "*Plied?* Really, Ethan." She shifted forward, which would have worked much better to distract him if she'd been in a low-cut top instead of a sweater. "You make it sound like I was spiking the pastries with truth-telling serum."

He caught the glint of a necklace—his necklace, the one he'd given her last night. She was wearing it. For some reason, that distracted him far more than the seductive pose did.

"What I want to know," he said in a calm voice, "is if Richards contacted you first, or if you contacted him."

Her mouth had already opened to reply, but the mention of Richards's name pulled her up short. She blinked at him, her confusion obvious. Too obvious. "Who?"

"Don't play cute with me, Frances. You said so yourself, didn't you? This is all part of the game. I just didn't realize how far it went until this morning."

Her brow wrinkled. "I don't—who is Richards?"

"This innocent thing isn't working," he snapped.

Abruptly, she stood. "I don't know who Richards is. I didn't ply anyone with donuts to tell me anything they weren't willing to tell me anyway—which, for the most part, was how you were a jerk who didn't know the first thing about running the Brewery. So you can accuse me of plotting some unspecified revenge with some unspecified man named Richards, if that makes you feel better about not being able to do your own job without me smiling like an idiot by your side. But in the meantime, go to hell." She swept out of the room with all the cold grace he could have expected. She didn't even slam the door on the way out, probably because that would have been beneath her.

"Dinner tonight," he called after her, just so he could get in the last word.

"Ha!" he heard her say as she walked away from him.

Damn, that last bit had been more than loud enough that Delores would have heard. And Ethan knew that whatever Delores heard, the rest of the company heard.

The thing was, he was still no closer to an answer about Frances's level of involvement with ZOLA and Zeb Richards than he'd been before she'd shown up. He'd thought he'd learned how to read her, but last night, she'd made him question his emotional investment in her.

He had no idea how to trust anything she said or how to decide if she was telling the truth.

A phone rang. It sounded as if it came from a long way away. Delores stuck her head through the door. "I know you said to hold your calls," she said in a cautious voice, "but Chadwick's on the phone."

"I'll take it," he said because to pretend he was otherwise involved would look ridiculous.

He was going to get engaged tonight. Frances was supposed to start sleeping over. He was going to get married to her next weekend so he could maintain control over his company.

Because that was the deal.

He picked up his phone. "Who the hell is Zeb Richards?"

Fifteen

Frances found herself at the gallery—actually, at what would become the gallery. It wasn't a gallery yet. It was just an empty industrial space.

Becky was there with some contractors, discussing lighting options. "Oh, Frances—there you are," she said in a happy voice. But then she paused. "Are you okay?"

"Fine," Frances assured her. "Why would anything be wrong? Excuse me." She dodged contractors and headed back to the office. This room, at least, was suitable to hide in. It had walls, a door—and a lock.

Why would anything be wrong? She'd only screwed up. That wasn't unusual. That was practically par for the course. Ethan had been   well, he'd been wonderful. She'd spent a week with him. She'd let her guard down around him. She'd even slept with him—and he was amazing.

So of course she'd gone and opened her big mouth and insulted him, and now he was colder than a three-day-old fish.

She sat down at what would be her desk when she got moved in and stared at the bare wooden top. He'd said he liked her messy and complicated. And for a moment, she'd almost believed him.

But he hadn't meant it. Oh, he thought he had, of that she had no doubt. He'd thought he liked her all not simple.

He'd no doubt imagined he'd mastered the complexities of her extended family, besting her brothers in a show of sheer skill and Logan-based manliness.

The fool, she thought sadly. He'd gone and convinced himself that he could handle her. And he couldn't. Maybe no one could.

Then there'd been the conversation today. What the ever-loving hell had that been about? Revenge? Well, yeah—revenge had been part of it. She hadn't lied, had she? She'd told him that she'd lost part of herself when the Brewery had been sold. She just hadn't expected him to throw that back in her face.

And who the hell was this Richards she was supposed to be conspiring with?

Still, a deal was a deal. And as Ethan had made it quite clear that morning, it was nothing but a deal. She supposed she'd earned that.

It was better this way, she decided. She couldn't handle Ethan when he was being tender and sweet and saying absolutely ridiculous things like how he'd happily put the wedding off because she was worth the wait.

The sooner he figured out she wasn't worth nearly that much, the better.

The doorknob turned, but the lock held. This was followed by a soft knock. "Frances?" Becky said. "Can I come in?"

Against her better judgment, Frances got up and unlocked the door for her friend. A deal was a deal, after all—especially since Frances wasn't the only one who needed this gallery. Becky was depending on it just as much as Frances was. "Yes?"

Becky pushed her way into the office and shut the door behind her. "What's wrong?"

"Nothing," Frances lied. Too late, she remembered she

should try to look as if that statement were accurate. She attempted a lighthearted smile.

Becky's eyes widened in horror at this expression. "Ohmygosh—what happened?"

Maybe she wouldn't try to smile right now. It felt wrong, anyway. "Just a…disagreement. This doesn't change the deal. It's fine," Frances said with more force. "I just thought—well, I thought he was different. And I think he's really much the same."

That was the problem, wasn't it? For a short while, she'd believed Ethan might actually be interested in her, not her famous name or famous family.

Why hadn't she just taken him at his word? Why had she pushed and pushed and pushed, for God's sake, until whatever honest fondness he felt for her had been pushed aside under the glaring imperfection that was Frances Beaumont? Why couldn't she have just let good enough alone and accepted his flowers and his diamonds and his offers of affection and companionship?

Why did she have to ruin everything?

She'd warned him. She'd told him not to like her. She just hadn't realized that she'd do everything in her power to make sure he didn't.

She'd screwed up *so* much. She'd lost a fortune three separate times. Every endeavor she'd ever attempted outside of stringing a man along had failed miserably. She'd never had a relationship that could come close to breaking her heart because there was nothing to break.

So this relationship had been doomed from the get-go. Nothing lost, nothing gained. She was not going to let this gallery fail. She needed the steady job and the sense of purpose far more than she needed Ethan to look her in the eye and tell her that he wanted her just as complicated as she was.

Unexpectedly, Becky pulled her into a tight hug. "I'm so sorry, honey," she whispered into Frances's ear.

"Jeez, Becks—it was just a disappointing date. Not the end of the world." And the more Frances told herself that, the truer it'd become. "Now go," she said, doing her best to sound as if it was just another Friday at the office. "Contractors don't stand around for free."

She had to make this gallery work. She had to…

She had to do something to not think about Ethan.

That was going to be rather difficult when they had dinner tonight.

She wore the green dress. She felt more powerful in the green dress than she did in the bridesmaid's dress. And she'd only worn the green dress to the office, not out to dinner, so it wasn't like wearing the same outfit two days in a row.

The only person who would recognize the dress was Ethan, and, well, there was nothing to be done about that.

Frances twisted her hair up. The only jewelry she wore was the necklace. The one he'd gotten for her. It felt odd to wear it, to know he'd picked it out on his own and that, for at least a little while, she'd been swayed by something so cliché as diamonds.

But it was a beautiful piece, and it went with the dress. And, after all, she was getting engaged tonight so it only seemed right to wear the diamonds from her fiancé.

She swept into the restaurant, head up and smile firmly in place. She'd given herself a little pep talk about how this wasn't about Ethan; this was about her and she had to get what she needed out of it. And if that occasionally included mind-blowing sex, then so be it. She needed to get laid every so often. Ethan was more than up to the task. Casual sex in a casual marriage. No big whoop.

Ethan was waiting for her at the bar again. "Frances,"

he said, pulling her into a tight embrace and brushing his lips over her cheek. She didn't miss the way he avoided her lips. "Shall we?"

"Of course." She was ready for him tonight. He was not going to get to her.

"You're looking better," he said as he held her chair for her.

"Oh? Was I not up to your usual high standards this morning?"

Ethan's mouth quirked into a wry smile. "You seem better, too."

She waved away his backhanded compliment. "So," she said, not even bothering to look at the menu, "tell me about this mysterious Richards person. If I'm going to be accused of industrial espionage, I should at least get some of the details."

His smile froze and then fell right off his face. It made Frances feel good, the rush of power that went with catching him off guard.

So she'd had a rough night and a tough morning. She was not going down with a whimper. And if he thought he could steamroll her, well, he'd learn soon enough.

"Actually," he said, dropping his gaze to his menu, "I did want to talk to you about that. I owe you an apology."

He owed her an apology? This morning he'd accused her of betrayal. This evening—apologies?

No. She did not want to slide back into that space where he professed to care about her feelings because that was where she got into trouble. She pointedly stared at her menu.

"Do you know who Zeb Richards is?"

"No. I assume he is the Richards in question, however." She still didn't look at Ethan. She realized she was fiddling with the diamonds at her neck, but she couldn't quite help herself.

"He is." Out of the corner of her eye, she saw Ethan lay down his menu. "I don't feel it's my place to tell you this, but I don't want to come off as patronizing, so—"

"A tad late for that," she murmured in as disinterested a voice as possible.

"A company called ZOLA is trying to make my life harder. They're making noises that my company is failing at restructuring and that AllBev should sell off the Brewery. One presumes that they'll either buy it on the cheap or buy it for scrap. A company like the Brewery is worth almost as much for its parts as it is for its value."

"Indeed," she said. She managed to nail "faux sympathetic," if she did say so herself. "And this concerns me how?"

"ZOLA is run by Zeb Richards."

This time, she did put down her menu. "And…? Out with it, Ethan."

For the first time, Ethan looked unsure of himself. "Zeb Richards is your half brother."

She blinked a few times. "I have many half brothers. However, I don't particularly remember one of them being named Zeb."

"When I found out this morning that he was related to you, I assumed you were working with him."

She stared at him. "How do you know about any supposed half brothers of mine?"

"Chadwick," he added with an apologetic smile.

"I should have known," she murmured.

"I asked him if he knew about ZOLA, and he gave me a file on Richards. Including proof that you and Zeb are related."

"How very nice of him to tell *you* and not *me*." Oh, she was damnably tired of Chadwick meddling in her affairs.

"Hence why I'm trying not to be patronizing." Ethan

fiddled with his silverware. "I did not have all the facts this morning when you got to the office and I made a series of assumptions that were unfair to you."

She looked at him flatly. "Is that so? And what, pray tell, was this additional information that has apparently exonerated me so completely?"

He dropped his gaze and she knew. "Chadwick again?"

"Correct. He believes that you have never had contact with your other half brothers. So, I'm sorry about my actions this morning. I was concerned that you were working with Richards to undermine the Brewery and I know now that simply isn't the case."

This admission was probably supposed to make her feel better. It did not. "*That's* what you were concerned with? *That's* what this morning was about?"

And not her? Not the way she'd insulted him last night, the way she'd stormed out of the hotel room without even pausing long enough to get her dress zipped properly?

He'd been worried about the company. His job.

Not her.

It shouldn't hurt. After all, this entire relationship was built on the premise that he was doing it for the company. For the Brewery and for his private firm.

No, it shouldn't have hurt at all.

Funny how it did.

"I could see how you were trying to get your family identity back. It wasn't a difficult mental leap to make, you understand. But I apologize."

She stared at him. She'd wanted to get revenge. She'd wanted to bring him down several pegs and put him in his place. But she hadn't conspired with some half brother she didn't even know existed to take down the whole company.

She didn't want to take down the company. The people

who worked there were her friends, her second family. Destroying the company would be destroying them.

It'd mean destroying Ethan, too.

"You're serious. You're really apologizing?"

He nodded, the look in his eyes deepening as he leaned forward. "I should have had more faith in you. It's a mistake I won't make again."

As an apology went, it wasn't bad. Actually, it was pretty damned good. There was only one problem with it.

"So that's it? The moment things actually get messy, you assume I'm trying to ruin you. But now that my brother has confirmed that I've never even heard of Zeb Richards or whatever his name is, you're suddenly all back to 'I like you complicated, Frances'?" She scoffed and slouched away from the table.

It must have come out louder than she realized because his eyes hardened. "We are in public."

"So we are. Your point?"

A muscle in his jaw tensed. "This is the night when I ask you to marry me," he said in a low growl that, despite the war of words they were engaged in, sent a shiver down her spine because it was the exact same voice he'd used when he'd bent her over the bed and made her come. Twice.

"Is it?" she growled back. "Do you always ask women to marry you when you're losing an argument?"

He stared hard at her for a second and then, unbelievably, his lips curved into an almost smile, as if he enjoyed this. "No. But I'll make an exception for you."

"Don't," she said, suddenly afraid of this. Of him. Of what he could do to her if she let him.

"This was the deal."

"Don't," she whispered, terrified.

He pushed back from his chair in full view of everyone in the restaurant. He dropped to one knee, just like in the movies, and pulled a robin's-egg-blue box out of his pocket. "Frances," he said in a stage voice loud enough to carry across the whole space. "I know we haven't known each other very long, but I can't imagine life without you. Will you do me the honor of marrying me?"

It sounded rehearsed. It wasn't the fumbling failure at sweet nothings she'd come to expect from him. It was for show. All for show.

Just like they'd planned.

This was where the small part of her brain that wasn't freaking out—and it was a very small part—was supposed to say yes. Where she was publically supposed to declare her love for him, and they were supposed to ride off into the sunset—or, at the very least, his hotel room—and consummate their relationship. Again.

He was handsome and good in bed and a worthy opponent and rich—couldn't forget that. And he liked her most of the time. He liked her too much.

She was supposed to say yes. For the gallery. For Becky. For the Brewery, for all the workers.

She was supposed to say yes so she could make Frances Beaumont important again, so that the Beaumont name would mean what she wanted it to mean—fame and accolades and people wanting to be her friend.

She was supposed to say yes for *her*. This was what she wanted.

Wasn't it?

Ethan's face froze. "Well?" he demanded in a quiet voice. "Frances."

Say yes, her brain urged. *Say yes right now.*

"I…" She was horrified to hear her voice come out as a whisper. "I can't."

His eyes widened in horror or confusion or some unholy mix of the two, she didn't know. She didn't wait around to find out. She bolted out of the restaurant as fast as she could in her heels. She didn't even wait to get her coat.

She ran. It was an act of cowardice. An act of surrender.

She'd ceded the game.

She'd lost everything.

Sixteen

"Frances?"

What the hell just happened? One second, he was following the script because, yes, he damn well had planned out the proposal. It was for public consumption.

The next second, she was gone, cutting an emerald-green swath through the suddenly silent restaurant.

"Frances, wait!" he called out, painfully aware that this was not part of the plan. He lunged to his feet and took off after her. She couldn't just leave—not like that. This wasn't how it was supposed to go.

Okay, today had not been his best work. He'd acted without all the available facts this morning and clearly, that had been a bad move. There were no such things as coincidences—except, it seemed, for right now.

Yes, he should have given her the benefit of the doubt and yes, he probably should have groveled a little more. The relief Ethan had felt when Chadwick had told him the only Beaumonts who knew of Zeb's identity were him and Matthew had been no small thing. Frances hadn't been plotting to overthrow the company. In fact, she'd been apologizing to Ethan. They could reset at dinner and continue on as they had been.

But he hadn't expected her to run away from him—es-

pecially not after the way she'd dressed him down after
they'd had sex.

If she didn't want to get married, he thought as he gave
chase, why the hell hadn't she just said so? He'd given her
an out—several outs. And she'd refused his concessions
at every turn, only to leave him hanging with a diamond
engagement ring in his hand.

This wasn't right, damn it.

He caught up with her trying to hail a cab. He could see
her shivering in the cold wind. "For God's sake, Frances,"
he said, shucking his suit jacket and slinging it around her
shoulders. "You'll catch your death."

"Ethan," she said in the most plaintive voice he'd ever
heard.

"What are you doing?" he demanded. "This was the
deal."

"I know, I know…" She didn't elucidate on that knowledge, however.

"Frances." He took her by the arm and pulled her a step
back from the curb. "We agreed—we agreed this *morning*—that I was going to ask you to marry me and you
were going to say yes." When she didn't look at him, he
dropped her arm and cupped her face in his hands. "Babe,
talk to me."

"Don't *babe* me, Ethan."

"Then talk, damn it. What the hell happened?"

"I—I can't. I thought I could, but I can't. Don't you
see?" He shook his head. "I thought—I thought I didn't
need love. That I could do this and it'd be no different than
watching my parents fight, no different than all the other
men who wanted to get close to the Beaumont name and
money. You weren't supposed to be *different*, Ethan. You
were supposed to be the *same*."

Then, as he watched in horror, a tear slipped past her
blinking eyelid and began to trickle down her cheek.

"I wasn't supposed to like you. And you, you big idiot, you weren't supposed to like me," she said, her voice quiet and shaky as more tears followed the first.

He tried to wipe the tears away with his thumb, but they were replaced too quickly. "I don't understand how liking each other makes marrying each other a bad thing," he said.

"You're here for your company. You're not here for me," she said, cutting him off before he could protest.

An unfamiliar feeling began to push past the confusion and the frustration—a feeling that he hadn't often allowed himself to feel.

Panic.

And he wasn't sure why. It could be that, if the workers at the Brewery got it in their collective heads that he'd broken their Frannie's heart, they might draw and quarter him. He could be panicking that his foolproof method of regaining control over his business felt suddenly very foolish.

But that wasn't it. That wasn't it at all.

"See?" She sniffed. She was openly crying at this point. It was horrifying because as much as she might have berated him for being lousy at the game when he dared admit that he might have feelings for her, he knew this was not a play on her part. "How long will it last?"

His mouth opened. *A year*, he almost said, because that was the deal.

"I could love you," he told her and it was God's honest truth. "If you'll let me."

Her eyes closed, and she turned her head away. "Ethan…" she whispered, so softly he almost didn't hear it over the sound of a cab pulling up next to them. "I could love you, too." For a moment, he thought she was agreeing; she was seeing the light, and they'd get in the cab and carry on as planned.

But then she added, "I won't settle for *could*. Not anymore. I can't believe I'm saying this, but I want to be in love with the man I marry. And I want him to be in love with me, too. I want to believe I'm worth that—worth something more than a business deal. Worth more than some company."

"You are," he said, but it didn't sound convincing, not even to his own ears. "You *are*, Frances."

She gave him a sad smile full of heartache. "I want to believe that, Ethan. But I'm not a prize to be won in the game. Not anymore."

She slipped his jacket off her slim shoulders and held it out to him.

He didn't want to take it. He didn't want her to go. "Keep it. I don't want you to freeze."

She shook her head no, and the cabbie honked and shouted, "Lady, you need a ride or not?" so Frances ducked into the cab.

He stood there, freezing his ass off as he watched the cab's taillights disappear down the street.

When he'd talked to Chadwick Beaumont on the phone today, he'd barely been able to wait for Chadwick to get done explaining who the hell Zeb Richards was before asking, "Does Frances know about this?" because he'd been desperate to know if she was leading him on or if those moments he'd thought where honesty were real.

"Unless she's hired her own private investigators, the only people who know about my father's illegitimate children are me and Matthew. My mother was the one who originally tracked down the oldest three. She'd long suspected my father was cheating on her," he had added. "There are others."

"And you don't think Frances would have hired her own PI?"

"Problem?" Chadwick had said in such a genial way that

Ethan had almost confided in him that he might have just accused Chadwick's younger sister of industrial espionage.

"No," Ethan had said because, at the time, it hadn't been a problem. A little lover's quarrel, nothing that a thirty-thousand-dollar diamond ring couldn't fix. "Just trying to understand the Beaumont family tree."

"Good luck with that," was all Chadwick had said.

Ethan had thanked him for the information and promised to pass along anything new he learned. Then he'd eaten his donuts and thought about how he'd make it up to Frances.

She'd promised not to love him—not to even like him. She'd told him to do the same. He should have listened to her, but he hadn't lied. When it came to her, he couldn't quite help himself. Everything about her had been an impulse. Even his original proposal had been half impulse, driven by some basic desire to outwit Frances Beaumont.

Their entire relationship had been based on a game of one-upmanship. In that regard, she'd gotten the final word. She'd said no.

Well, hell. Now what? He'd publically proposed, been publically rejected and his whole plan had fallen apart on him. And the worst thing was that he wasn't sure *why*. Was it because he hadn't trusted her this morning when she'd said she didn't know anything about Richards?

Or was it because, despite it all, he did like her? He liked her a great deal. More than was wise, that much was sure.

This morning she'd shown up at his office with the donuts he'd requested. She hadn't had on a stitch of her armor—no designer clothes, no impenetrable attitude. She'd been a woman who'd sat down, admitted fault and apologized for her actions.

She'd been trying to show him that she liked him. Enough to be honest with him.

He'd thrown that trust back in her face. And then cavalierly assumed that a big rock was going to make it up to her.

Idiot. She wanted to know she was worth it—and she hadn't meant worth diamonds and roses.

He was in too deep to let her go. She *was* worth it.

So this was what falling in love was like.

How was he going to convince her that this wasn't part of the game?

Frances was not surprised when no extravagant floral arrangement arrived the next day. No chocolates or champagne or jewels showed up, either.

They didn't arrive the day after that. Or the third, for that matter.

And why would they? She was not bound to Ethan. She had no claim on him, nor he on her. The only thing that remained of their failed, doomed "relationship" were several vases of withering flowers and an expensive necklace.

She had taken off the necklace.

But she hadn't been able to bring herself to return it. Not to him, not to the store for cash—cash she could use, now that the gallery was dead and she had no other job prospects, aside from selling her family's heirlooms on the open market.

The necklace sat on her bedside table, mocking her as she went to sleep every night.

She called Becky but didn't feel like talking except to say, "The funding is probably not going to happen, so plan accordingly."

To which Becky had replied, "We'll get it figured out, one way or the other."

That was the sort of platitude people said when the situation was hopeless but they needed to feel better. So Frances had replied, "Sure, we'll get together for lunch soon and go over our options," because that was the sort of thing rational grown-ups said all the time.

Then she'd ended the call and crawled back under the covers.

Byron had texted, but what could she tell him? That she'd done the not-rash thing for the first time in her life and was now miserable? And why, exactly, was she miserable again? She shouldn't be hiding under the covers in her cozy jammies! She'd won! She'd stopped Ethan in his tracks with a move he couldn't anticipate and he couldn't recover from. She'd brought him firmly down to where he belonged. He wasn't good enough for the Beaumonts, and he wasn't good enough for the Brewery.

Victory was hers!

She didn't think victory was supposed to taste this sour.

She didn't believe in love. Never had, never would. So why, when the next best thing had presented itself—someone who was fond of her, who admired her, and who could still make her shiver with need, someone who had offered to generously provide for her financial future in exchange for a year of her life even —*why* had she walked away?

Because he was only here for the company. And, fool that she was, she'd suddenly realized she wanted someone who was going to be here for her.

"I could love you." She heard his words over and over again, beating against her brain like a spike. He could.

But he didn't.

What a mess.

Luckily, she was used to it.

She'd managed to drag herself to the shower on the fourth day. She had decided that she was going to stop moping. Moping didn't get jobs, and it didn't heal broken hearts. She needed to get up and, at the very least, have lunch with Becky or go see Byron. She needed to do something that would eventually get her out of the Beaumont mansion because she was *done* living under the same roof as Chadwick. She was going to tell him that the very next time she saw him, too.

She'd just buttoned her jeans when she heard the doorbell. She ignored it as she toweled her hair.

Then someone knocked on her bedroom door. "Frannie?" It was Serena, Chadwick's wife. "Flowers for you."

"Really?" Who would send her flowers? Not Ethan. Not at this late date. "Hang on." She threw on a sweater and opened the door.

Serena stood there, an odd look on her face. She was not holding any flowers. "Um… I think you need to get these yourself," Serena said before she turned and walked down the hall.

Frances stood there, all the warning bells going off in her head at once.

Her heart pounding, she walked down the hallway and peered over the edge of the railing. There, in the middle of the foyer, stood Ethan, holding a single red rose.

She must have made a noise or gasped or something because he looked up at her and smiled. A good smile, the kind of smile that made her want to do something ridiculous like kiss him when she absolutely should not be glad to see him at all.

She needed to say something witty and urbane and snarky that would put him in his place, so that for at least a minute, she could feel like Frances Beaumont again.

Instead, she said, "You're here."

Damn. Worse, it came out breathy, as if she couldn't believe he'd actually ventured into the lair of the Beaumonts.

"I am," he replied, his gaze never leaving her face. "I came for you."

Oh. That was terribly close to a sweet nothing—no, it

wasn't a nothing. It was a sweet something. But what? "I'm here. I've been here for a few days now."

There, that was a good thing to say. Something that let him know that his apology—if this even was an apology—was days late and, judging by the single flower he was holding, dollars short.

"I had some things to do," he said. "Can you come down here?"

"Why should I?"

His grin spread. "Because I don't want to shout? But I will." He cleared his throat. *"Frances!"* he shouted, his voice ringing off the marble and the high-vaulted ceilings. *"Can you come down here? Please?"*

"Okay, okay!" She didn't know who else besides Serena was home, but she didn't need to have Ethan yelling at the top of his lungs.

She hurried down the wide staircase with Ethan watching her the entire time. She slowed only when she got to the last few steps. She didn't want to be on his level, not just yet. "I'm here," she said again.

He held out the lone red rose to her. "I brought you a flower."

"Just one?"

"One seemed…fitting, somehow." He looked her over. "How have you been?"

"Oh, fine," she tried to say lightly. "Just hanging out around the house, trying to avoid social media and gossip columns—the normal stuff, really. Just another day in the life of a Beaumont."

He took a step closer to her. It made her tense. "You don't have to do that," he said, his voice soft and quiet and just for her.

"Do what?"

"Put your armor on. I didn't come here looking for a fight."

She eyed him warily. What was this? A single rose? A claim that he didn't want to fight? "Then why did you come?"

He took another step in—close enough to touch her. Which he did. He lifted his hand and brushed his fingertips down her cheek. "I wanted to tell you that you're worth it."

She froze under his touch, the rose between them. "We aren't in public, Ethan. You don't have to do this. It's over. We made a scene. It's fine. We can go on with our lives now." Her words came out in a rush.

"Do you really believe that? That it's fine?"

"Isn't it?" Her voice cracked, damn it.

"It isn't. Three days without you has almost driven me mad."

"I drive you mad when we're together. I drive you mad when we're apart—you know how to make a woman feel special." The words should have sounded flippant. They didn't. No matter how hard she tried, she couldn't convince herself that this was no big deal. Not when Ethan was staring into her eyes with this odd look of satisfaction on his face, not when his thumb was now stroking her cheek.

"Why are you here?" she whispered, desperate to hear the answer and just as desperate to not hear it.

"I came for you. I've never met anyone like you before, and I don't want to walk away from you. Not now, not ever."

"It's all just talk, Ethan." Her voice was the barest of whispers. She was doing a lousy job convincing herself. She didn't think she was convincing him at all.

"Do you know how much you're worth to me?"

She shook her head. "Some diamonds, some flowers. A rose."

He stepped in another bit, bringing her body almost into contact with his. "As of yesterday, I am no longer the CEO of the Beaumont Brewery."

"What?"

"I quit the job. For personal reasons. My second in command, Finn Jackson, flew in today to take over the restructuring project. We're still dealing with a little fallout from AllBev, but it's nothing I can't handle." He said it as if it were just a little speed bump.

"You *quit*? The Brewery?"

"It wasn't my company. It wasn't worth it to me. Not like you are."

"I don't understand." He was saying words that she understood individually. But the way he was stringing them together? It didn't make sense. Not a bit.

Something in his eyes changed—deepened. A small shiver ran down Frances's back. "I do not need to marry you to solidify my position within the company because I no longer work for the company. I do not need to worry about unknown relations trying to overthrow my position because I have given up the position. The company was never worth more than you were."

She blinked at him. All of her words failed her. She had nothing to hide behind now.

"So," he went on, his eyes full of honesty and sincerity and hope. All of those things she hadn't believed she deserved. "Here I am. I have quit the Brewery. I have taken a leave of absence from my company. I could care less if anyone's listening to what we say or watching how we say it. All I care about is you. Even when you're messy and complicated and even when I say the wrong thing at the wrong time, I care about *you*."

"You can't mean that," she whispered, because what if he did?

"I can and I do. I truly never believed I would meet anyone I could care about, much less someone who would mean more to me than the job. But I did. It's you, Frances. I want you when your armor's up because you make sarcasm and irony into high art. I want you when you're feeling vulnerable and honest because I want to be that soft place where you can land after a hard day of putting the world in its place. And I want you all the times in between, when you challenge me and call me on my mistakes and push me to be a better man—one who can keep up with you."

Unexpectedly, he dropped to his knees. "So I'm asking you again. Not for the Brewery, not for the employees, not for the public. I'm asking you for me. Because I want to spend my life with you. Not a few months, not a year— my life. Our lives. Together."

"You want to marry me? *Me?*"

"I like you," he said simply. "I shouldn't, but I do. Even worse, I love you." He gave her a crooked grin. "I love you. I'd recommend you love me, too."

Her mouth opened, but nothing came out. Not a damn thing. Because what was she going to say? That he'd gotten better at sweet nothings? That he was crazy to have fallen for her? That...

That she wanted to say yes—but she was afraid?

"I've seen the real you," he said, still on his knees. "And that's the woman I love."

"Do we get—married? Next week?" That had been the deal, hadn't it? A whirlwind courtship, married in two weeks.

"I'm not making a deal, Frances. All I'm doing right now is asking a simple question. We can wait a year, if you want. You're worth the wait. I'm not going anywhere without you."

"It won't ever be simple," she warned him. "I don't have it in me."

He stood and pulled her into his arms as if she'd said yes, when she wasn't sure she had yet. The rose, she feared, was a total loss. "I don't want you simple. I want to know that every day, I've fought for you and every day, you've chosen me again."

Was it possible, what he was saying? Could a man love her?

"I expect to be wined and dined and courted," she warned him, trying to sound stern and mostly just laughing.

He laughed with her. "And what do I get out of this again?"

"A wife. A messy, complicated wife who will love you until the end of time."

"Perfect," he said, lowering his lips to hers. "That's *exactly* what I wanted."

* * * * *

If you loved Frances's story,
pick up the first four books in the
BEAUMONT HEIRS *series:*

NOT THE BOSS'S BABY
TEMPTED BY A COWBOY
A BEAUMONT CHRISTMAS WEDDING
HIS SON, HER SECRET

Available now from Mills & Boon By Request!

HIS ILLEGITIMATE HEIR

BY
SARAH M. ANDERSON

To Lisa Marie Perry,
who never ceases to shock and amaze me.
We'll always have Jesse Williams!

One

"You ready for this?" Jamal asked from the front seat of the limo.

Zeb Richards felt a smile pull at the corner of his mouth. "I was born ready."

It wasn't an exaggeration. Finally, after all these years, Zeb was coming home to claim what was rightfully his. The Beaumont Brewery had—until very recently—been owned and operated by the Beaumont family. There were a hundred twenty-five years of family history in this building—history that Zeb had been deprived of.

He was a Beaumont by blood. Hardwick Beaumont was Zeb's father.

But he was illegitimate. As far as he knew, outside of the payoff money Hardwick had given his mother, Emily, shortly after Zeb's birth, no one in the Beaumont family had ever acknowledged his existence.

He was tired of being ignored. More than that, he

was tired of being denied his rightful place in the Beaumont family.

So he was finally taking what was rightfully his. After years of careful planning and sheer luck, the Beaumont Brewery now belonged to him.

Jamal snorted, which made Zeb look at him. Jamal Hitchens was Zeb's right-hand man, filling out the roles of chauffeur and bodyguard—plus, he baked a damn fine chocolate chip cookie. Jamal had worked for Zeb ever since he'd blown out his knees his senior year as linebacker at the University of Georgia, but the two of them went back much farther than that.

"You sure about this?" Jamal asked. "I still think I should go in with you."

Zeb shook his head. "No offense, but you'd just scare the hell out of them. I want my new employees intimidated, not terrified."

Jamal met Zeb's gaze in the rearview mirror and an unspoken understanding passed between the two men. Zeb could pull off intimidating all by himself.

With a sigh of resignation, Jamal parked in front of the corporate headquarters and came around to open Zeb's door. Starting right now, Zeb was a Beaumont in every way that counted.

Jamal looked around as Zeb stood and straightened the cuffs on his bespoke suit. "Last chance for backup."

"You're not nervous, are you?" Zeb wasn't. There was such a sense of rightness about this that he couldn't be nervous, so he simply wasn't.

Jamal gave him a look. "You realize you're not going to be hailed as a hero, right? You didn't exactly get this company in a way that most people might call *ethical*."

Zeb notched an eyebrow at his oldest friend. With Jamal at his back, Zeb had gone from being the son of a hairdresser to being the sole owner of ZOLA, a private equity firm that he'd founded. He'd made his millions without a single offer of assistance from the Beaumonts.

More than that, he had proven that he was better than they were. He'd outmaneuvered and outflanked them and taken their precious brewery away from them.

But taking over the family business was something he had to do himself. "Your concern is duly noted. I'll text you if I need backup. Otherwise, you'll be viewing the properties?"

They needed a place to live now that they would be based in Denver. ZOLA, Zeb's company, was still head-quartered in New York—a hedge just in case his owner-ship of the Beaumont Brewery backfired. But buying a house here would signal to everyone that Zeb Richards wasn't going anywhere anytime soon.

Jamal realized he wasn't going to win this fight. Zeb could tell by the way he straightened his shoulders. "Right, boss. Finest money can buy?"

"Always." It didn't really matter what the house looked like or how many bathrooms it had. All that mattered was that it was better than anyone else's. Spe-cifically, better than any of the other Beaumonts'. "But make sure it's got a nice kitchen."

Jamal smirked at that bone of friendship Zeb threw him. "Good luck."

Zeb slid a sideways glance at Jamal. "Good luck hap-pens when you work for it." And Zeb? He *always* worked for it.

With a sense of purpose, he strode into the corporate headquarters of the Beaumont Brewery. He hadn't called to announce his impending arrival, because he wanted to see what the employees looked like when they weren't ready to be inspected by their new CEO.

However, he was fully aware that he was an unfamiliar African American man walking into a building as if he owned it—which he did. Surely the employees knew that Zebadiah Richards was their new boss. But how many of them would recognize him?

True to form, he got plenty of double takes as he walked through the building. One woman put her hand on her phone as he passed, as if she was going to call security. But then someone else whispered something over the edge of her cubicle wall and the woman's eyes got very wide. Zeb notched an eyebrow at her and she pulled her hand away from her phone like it had burned her.

Silence trailed in his wake as he made his way toward the executive office. Zeb fought hard to keep a smile off his face. So they did know who he was. He appreciated employees who were up-to-date on their corporate leadership. If they recognized him, then they had also probably read the rumors about him.

Zebadiah Richards and his private equity firm bought failing companies, restructured them and sold them for profit. ZOLA had made him rich—and earned him a reputation for ruthlessness.

He would need that reputation here. Contrary to some of the rumors, he was not actually heartless. And he understood that the employees at this brewery had undergone the ouster of not one but two CEOs in less than a year. From his reports on the company's filings, he understood that most people still missed Chadwick Beaumont, the last Beaumont to run the brewery.

Zeb had not gotten Chadwick removed—but he had taken advantage of the turmoil that the sale of the brewery to the conglomerate AllBev had caused. And when Chadwick's temporary replacement, Ethan Logan, had failed to turn the company around fast enough, Zeb had agitated for AllBev to sell the company.

To him, of course.

But what that really meant was that he now owned a company full of employees who were scared and desperate. Employee turnover was at an all-time high. A significant percentage of top-level management had followed Chadwick Beaumont to his new company, Percheron Drafts. Many others had taken early retirement.

The employees who had survived this long were holding on by the skin of their teeth and probably had nothing left to lose. Which made them dangerous. He'd seen it before in other failing companies. Change was a constant in his world but most people hated it and if they fought against it hard enough, they could doom an entire company. When that happened, Zeb shrugged and broke the business up to be sold for its base parts. Normally, he didn't care if that happened—so long as he made a profit, he was happy.

But like he told Jamal, he was here to stay. He was a Beaumont and this was his brewery. He cared about this place and its history because it was his history, acknowledged or not. Not that he'd wanted anyone to know that this was personal—he'd kept his quest to take what was rightfully his quiet for years. That way, no one could preempt his strikes or lock him out.

But now that he was here, he had the overwhelming urge to shout, "Look at me!" He was done being ignored by the Beaumonts and he was done pretending he wasn't one of them.

Whispers of his arrival must have made it to the executive suite because when he rounded the corner, a plump older woman sitting behind a desk in front of what he assumed was the CEO's office stood and swallowed nervously. "Mr. Richards," she said in a crackly voice. "We weren't expecting you today."

Zeb nodded his head in acknowledgment. He didn't explain his sudden appearance and he didn't try to reassure her. "And you are?"

"Delores Hahn," she said. "I'm the executive assistant to the—to you." Her hands twisted nervously in front of her before she caught herself and stilled them. "Welcome to the Beaumont Brewery."

Zeb almost grinned in sympathy. His assistant was in a tough spot, but she was putting on a good face. "Thank you."

Delores cleared her throat. "Would you like a tour of the facilities?" Her voice was still a bit shaky, but she was holding it together. Zeb decided he liked Delores.

Not that he wanted her to know that right away. He was not here to make friends. He was here to run a business. "I will—after I get settled in." Then he headed for his office.

Once inside, he shut the door behind him and leaned against it. This was really happening. After years of plotting and watching and waiting, he had the Beaumont Brewery—his birthright.

He felt like laughing at the wonder of it all. But he didn't. For all he knew, Delores had her ear to the door, listening for any hint of what her new boss was like. Maniacal laughter was not a good first impression, no matter how justified it might be.

Instead, he pushed away from the door and surveyed his office. "Begin as you mean to go on," Zeb reminded himself.

He'd read about this room, studied pictures of it. But he hadn't been prepared for what it would actually feel like to walk into a piece of his family's history—to know that he belonged here, that this was his rightful place.

The building had been constructed in the 1940s by Zeb's grandfather John, soon after Prohibition had ended. The walls were mahogany panels that had been oiled until they gleamed. A built-in bar with a huge mirror took up the whole interior wall—and, if Zeb wasn't mistaken, the beer was on tap.

The exterior wall was lined with windows, hung with heavy gray velvet drapes and crowned with elaborately hand-carved woodwork that told the story of the Beaumont Brewery. His grandfather had had the conference table built in the office because it was so large and the desk was built to match.

Tucked in the far corner was a grouping of two leather club chairs and a matching leather love seat. The wagon-wheel coffee table in front of the chairs was supposed to be a wheel from the wagon that his great-great-grandfather Phillipe Beaumont had driven across the Great Plains on his way to Denver to found the brewery back in the 1880s.

The whole room screamed opulence and wealth and history. Zeb's history. This was who he was and he would be damned if he let anyone tell him it wasn't his.

He crossed to the desk and turned on the computer—top-of-the-line, of course. Beaumonts never did anything by halves. That was one family trait they all shared.

He sat down in the leather office chair. From as far back as he could remember, his mother, Emily Richards, had told him this belonged to him. Zeb was only four months younger than Chadwick Beaumont. He should have been here, learning the business at his father's knee, instead of standing next to his mother's hairdressing chair.

But Hardwick had never married his mother—despite the fact that Hardwick had married several of his mistresses. But not Emily Richards—and for one simple reason.

Emily was black. Which made her son black.

Which meant Zeb didn't exist in the eyes of the Beaumonts.

For so long, he had been shut out of half of his heritage. And now he had the one thing that the Beaumonts had valued above all else—the Beaumont Brewery.

God, it felt good to come home.

He got himself under control. Taking possession of the brewery was a victory—but it was just the first step in making sure the Beaumonts paid for excluding him.

He was not the only Beaumont bastard Hardwick had left behind. It was time to start doing things his way. He grinned. The Beaumonts weren't going to see this coming.

He pressed the button on an antique-looking intercom. It buzzed to life and Delores said, "Yes, sir?"

"I want you to arrange a press conference for this Friday. I'm going to be announcing my plans for the brewery."

There was a pause. "Yes, sir," she said in a way that had an edge to it. "I assume you want the conference here?" Already Zeb could tell she was getting over her nervousness at his unannounced arrival.

If he had to guess, he'd say that someone like Delores Hahn had probably made the last CEO's life miserable. "Yes, on the front steps of the brewery. Oh, and Delores?"

"Yes?"

"Write a memo. Every employee needs to have an updated résumé on my desk by end of business tomorrow."

There was another pause—this one was longer. Zeb could only imagine the glare she was giving the intercom right about now. "Why? I mean—of course I'll get right on it. But is there a reason?"

"Of course there is, Delores. There is a reason behind every single thing I do. And the reason for the memo is simple. Every employee needs to reapply for their own job." He exhaled slowly, letting the tension build. "Including you."

"Boss?"

Casey Johnson jerked her head toward the sound of Larry's voice—which meant she smacked her forehead against the bottom of tank number fifteen. "Ow, dammit." She pushed herself out from under the tank, rubbing her head. "What?"

Larry Kaczynski was a middle-aged man with a beer gut, which was appropriate considering he brewed beer for a living. Normally, he was full of bluster and the latest stats on his fantasy football team. But today he looked worried. Specifically, he looked worried about the piece of paper in his hand. "The new guy... He's here."

"Well, good for him," Casey said, turning her attention back to her tank. This was the second new CEO in less than a year and, given recent history, he probably wouldn't make it past a couple of months. All Casey had to do was outlast him.

That, of course, was the challenge. Beer did not brew itself—although, given the attitude of the last CEO, some people thought it did.

Tank fifteen was her priority right now. Being a brewmaster was about brewing beer—but it was also about making sure the equipment was clean and functional. And right now tank fifteen wasn't either of those things.

"You don't understand," Larry sputtered before she'd rolled back under the tank. "He's been on the property for less than an hour and he's already sent this memo..."

"Larry," she said, her voice echoing against the body of the tank, "are you going to get to the point today?"

"We have to reapply for our jobs," Larry said in a rush. "By the end of the day tomorrow. I don't—Casey, you know me. I don't even have a résumé. I've worked here for the last thirty years."

Oh, for the love of everything holy... Casey pushed herself out from under the tank again and sat up. "Okay," she said in a much softer voice as she got to her feet. "Start from the beginning. What does the memo say?" Because Larry was like a canary in a coal mine. If he kept calm, the staff she was left with would also keep calm. But if Larry panicked...

Larry looked down at the paper in his hands again. He swallowed hard and Casey got the strangest sensation he was trying not to crack.

Crap. They were screwed. "It just says that by end of business tomorrow, every Beaumont Brewery employee needs to have an updated résumé on the new CEO's desk so he can decide if they get to keep their job or not."

Son of a... "Let me see."

Larry handed over the paper as if he'd suddenly discovered it was contagious, and he stepped back. "What am I going to do, boss?"

Casey scanned the memo and saw that Larry had pretty much read verbatim. Every employee, no exceptions.

She did not have time for this. She was responsible for brewing about seven thousand gallons of beer every single day of the year on a skeleton staff of seventeen people. Two years ago, forty people had been responsible for that level of production. But two years ago, the company hadn't been in the middle of the never-ending string of upstart CEOs.

And now the latest CEO was rolling up into *her* brewery and scaring the hell out of *her* employees? This new guy thought he would tell her she had to apply for her job—the job she'd earned?

She didn't know much about this Zebadiah Richards—but he was going to get one thing straight if he thought he was going to run this company.

The Beaumont Brewery brewed beer. No beer, no brewery. And no brewmaster, no beer.

She turned to Larry, who was pale and possibly shaking. She understood why he was scared—Larry was not the brightest bulb and he knew it. That was the reason he hadn't left when Chadwick lost the company or when Ethan Logan tried to right the sinking ship.

That was why Casey had been promoted over him to brewmaster, even though Larry had almost twenty years of experience on her. He liked his job, he liked beer and as long as he got regular cost-of-living increases in his salary and a year-end bonus, he was perfectly content to spend the rest of his life right where he was. He hadn't wanted the responsibility of management.

Frankly, Casey was starting to wonder why she had. "I'll take care of this," she told him.

Surprisingly, this announcement made Larry look even more nervous. Apparently, he didn't put a lot of faith in her ability to keep her temper. "What are you going to do?"

His reaction made it clear that he was afraid she'd get

fired—and then he'd be in charge. "This Richards guy and I are going to have words."

Larry fretted. "Are you sure that's the smart thing to do?"

"Probably not," she agreed. "But what's he going to do—fire the brewmaster? I don't think so, Larry." She patted him on the shoulder. "Don't worry, okay?"

Larry gave her a weak smile, but he nodded resolutely.

Casey hurried to her office and stripped off her hairnet. She knew she was no great beauty, but nobody wanted to confront a new boss in a hairnet. She grabbed her Beaumont Brewery hat and slid her ponytail through the back. And she was off, yelling over her shoulder to Larry, "See if you can get that drainage tube off—and if you can, see if you can get it flushed again. I'll be back in a bit."

She did *not* have time for this. She was already working ten-to twelve-hour days—six or seven days a week—just to keep the equipment clean and the beer flowing. If she lost more of her staff…

It wouldn't come to that. She wouldn't let it. And if it did…

Okay, so she'd promised Larry she wouldn't get fired. But what if she did? Her options weren't great, but at least she had some. Unlike Larry, she did have an updated résumé that she kept on file just in case. She didn't want to use it. She wanted to stay right here at the Beaumont Brewery and brew her favorite beer for the rest of her life.

Or at least, she had. No, if she was being honest, what she really wanted was to be the brewmaster at the old Beaumont Brewery, the one she'd worked at for the previous twelve years—the one that the Beaumont family had run. Back then the brewery had been a family business and the owners had been personally invested in their employees.

They'd even given a wide-eyed college girl the chance to do something no one else had—brew beer.

But the memo in her hand reminded her that this wasn't the same brewery. The Beaumonts no longer ran things and the company was suffering.

She was suffering. She couldn't remember the last time she'd strung together more than twenty-four hours of free time. She was doing the job of three people and, thanks to the hiring freeze the last CEO implemented, there was no relief in sight. And now this. She could not afford to lose another single person.

She was a thirty-two-year-old brewmaster—and a woman, at that. She'd come so far so fast. But not one of her predecessors in the illustrious history of the Beaumont Brewery had put up with quite this much crap. They'd been left to brew beer in relative peace.

She stormed to the CEO suite. Delores was behind the desk. When she saw Casey coming, the older woman jumped to her feet with surprising agility. "Casey—wait. You don't—"

"Oh, yes, I do," she said, blowing past Delores and shoving open the door to the CEO's office. "Just who the hell do you think you…are?"

Two

Casey came to a stumbling stop. Where was he? The desk was vacant and no one was sitting on the leather couches.

But then a movement off to her left caught her eye and she turned and gasped in surprise.

A man stood by the windows, looking out over the brewery campus. He had his hands in his pockets and his back turned to her—but despite that, everything about him screamed power and money. The cut of his suit fit him like a second skin and he stood with his feet shoulder-width apart, as if he were master of all he saw.

A shiver went through her. She was not the kind of girl who went for power suits or the men who wore them but something about this man—this man who was threatening her job—took her breath away. Was it the broad shoulders? Or the raw power wafting off him like the finest cologne?

And then he turned to face her and all she could see were his eyes—*green* eyes. Good Lord, those eyes—they held her gaze like a magnet and she knew her breath was gone for good.

He was, hands down, the most handsome man she'd ever seen. Everything—the power suit, the broad shoulders, the close-cropped hair and most especially the eyes—it was a potent blend that she felt powerless to resist. And this was her new boss? The man who'd sent out the memo?

He notched an eyebrow at her and let his gaze travel over her body. And any admiration she had for a good suit and nice eyes died on the vine because she knew exactly what he saw. Underneath her lab coat, she had on a men's small polo shirt with Beaumont Brewery embroidered over the chest—and she'd sweat through it because the brew room was always hot. Her face was probably red from the heat and also from the anger, and she no doubt smelled like mash and wort.

She must look like a madwoman.

A conclusion he no doubt reached on his own, because by the time he looked her in the eyes, one corner of his mouth had curved up into the kind of smile that said exactly one thing.

He thought she was a joke.

Well, he'd soon learn this was no laughing matter.

"Congratulations," he said in a voice that bordered on cold. "You're first." He lifted his wrist and looked down at a watch that, even at this distance, Casey could tell was expensive. "Thirty-five minutes. I'm impressed."

His imperious attitude poured cold water on the heat that had almost swamped her. She wasn't here to gawk at a gorgeous man. She was here to protect her workers. "Are you Richards?"

"Zebadiah Richards, yes. Your new boss," he added in a menacing tone, as if he thought he could intimidate her. Didn't he know she had so very little left to lose? "And you are?"

She'd worked in a male-dominated industry for twelve years. She couldn't be intimidated. "I'm Casey Johnson—your brewmaster." What kind of name was Zebadiah? Was that biblical? "What's the meaning of this?" She held up the memo.

Richards's eyes widened in surprise—but only for a second before he once again looked ice-cold. "Forgive me," he said in a smooth voice when Casey glared at him. "I must say that you are not what I was expecting."

Casey rolled her eyes and made no attempt to hide it. Few people expected women to like beer. Even fewer people expected women to brew beer. And with a name like Casey, everyone just assumed she was a man—and usually, they assumed she was a man like Larry. Middle-aged, beer gut—the whole nine yards. "It's not my problem if you made a set of erroneous assumptions."

The moment she said it, she realized she'd also made some erroneous assumptions herself. Because she had not anticipated that the new CEO would look quite like him. Oh, sure—the power suit was par for the course. But his hair was close-cropped to his head and his eyes... Damn, she just couldn't get past them.

He grinned—oh, Lord, that was not good. Well, it was—but in a bad way because that grin took everything hard and cold about him and warmed him up. She was certainly about to break out in another sweat.

"Indeed. Well, since you're the first person to barge into my office, I'll tell you the meaning of that memo, Ms. Johnson—although I'd hope the employees here at the brewery would be able to figure it out on their own. Everyone has to reapply for their jobs."

She welcomed his condescending tone because it pushed her from falling into the heat of his eyes and kept her focused on her task. "Is that a fact? Where'd you learn that management technique? Management 'R' Us?"

Something that almost looked like amusement flickered over his gaze and she was tempted to smile. A lot of people found her abrasive and yeah, she could rub people the wrong way. She didn't pull her punches and she wasn't about to sit down and shut up just because she was a girl and men didn't like to have their authority challenged.

What was rarer was for someone to get her sense of humor. Could this Richards actually be a real man who smiled? God, she wanted to work for a man she wouldn't have to fight every step of the way. Maybe they could get along. Maybe…

But as quickly as it had appeared, the humor was gone. His eyes narrowed and Casey thought, *You're not the only one who can be condescending.*

"The purpose is twofold, Ms. Johnson. One, I'd like to see what skill sets my employees possess. And two, I want to see if they can follow basic instructions."

So much for a sense of humor. Men as hot as he was probably weren't allowed to laugh at a joke. Pity. On the other hand, if he smiled, it might kill her with handsomeness and the only thing worse than a CEO she couldn't work with would be a CEO she lusted after.

No lusting allowed. And he was making that easier with every single thing he said.

"Let me assure you, Mr. Richards, that this company did not spring fully formed from your forehead yesterday. We've been brewing beer here for—"

"For over one hundred and thirty years—I know." He tilted his head to the side and gave her a long look. "And you've only been doing it for less than a year—is that correct?"

If she weren't so pissed at him, she'd have been terrified, because that was most definitely a threat to her job. But she didn't have time for unproductive emotions and anger was vastly more useful than fear.

"I have—and I earned that job. But before you question how a woman my age can have possibly surpassed all the good ol' boys who normally brew beer, let me tell you that it's also because all the more experienced brewers have already left the company. If you want to maintain a quality product line, you're stuck with me for the foreseeable future." She waved the memo in front of her. "And I don't have time to deal with this crap."

But instead of doing anything any normal boss would do when basically yelled at by an employee—like firing her on the spot—Richards tilted his head to one side and looked at her again and she absolutely did not shiver when he did it. "Why not?"

"Why not what?"

"Why don't you have time to respond to a simple administrative task?"

Casey didn't want to betray any sign of weakness but a trickle of sweat rolled out from under her hat and into her eye. Dammit. He better not think she was crying. She wiped her eyes with the palm of her hand. "Because I'm operating with a bare-bones staff—I have been for the last nine months. I'm doing the work of three people—we all are. We're understaffed, overworked and—"

"And you don't have time for this 'crap,' as you so eloquently put it," he murmured.

Was that a note of sympathy? Or was he mocking her? She couldn't read him that well.

Not yet, a teasing voice in the back of her mind whispered. But she pushed that voice away. She wasn't interested in reading him better. "Not if you want to fulfill production orders."

"So just hire more people."

Now she gaped at him. "What?"

He shrugged, which was an impossibly smooth gesture on him. Men should not be that smooth. It wasn't good for them, she decided. And it definitely wasn't good for her. This would be so much easier if he were at least 70 percent less attractive. "Hire more people. But I want to see their résumés, too. Why let the new people off easy, right?"

This guy didn't know anything, did he? They were screwed, then. This was the beginning of the end. Now she would have to help Larry write a résumé.

"But...there's been a hiring freeze," she told him. "For the last eight months. Until we can show a profit."

Richards stepped forward and traced a finger over the top of the conference table. It was an oddly intimate motion—a caress, almost. Watching his hand move over the wood...

She broke out in goose bumps.

"Tell me, Ms. Johnson, was it Chadwick Beaumont who put on the hiring freeze? Or Ethan Logan?"

There was something about his voice that matched his caress of the conference table. Casey studied him. She had the oddest feeling that he looked familiar but she was sure she would remember seeing him before. Who could forget those eyes? Those...everything?

"Logan did."

"Ah," he said, shifting so he wasn't silhouetted

against the window anymore. More light fell on him and Casey was startled to realize that the green eyes were set against skin that wasn't light but wasn't exactly deep brown, either. His skin was warm, almost tan, and she realized he was at least partly African American. Why hadn't she seen that right away?

Well, she knew why. First off, she was mad and when she was mad, she didn't exactly pay attention to the bigger picture. She hadn't noticed the fullness to his frowning lips or the slight flare of his nostrils. Second off, his eyes had demanded her total attention. They were striking, so gorgeous, and even…familiar?

His hand was still on top of the conference table. "So what you're telling me is that the only non-Beaumont to run this company instituted a series of policies designed to cut costs and, in the process, hamstrung the operations and production?"

"Yes." There was something about the way he said *the only non-Beaumont* that threw her for a loop.

And then—maybe because now she was paying more attention—it hit her like a ton of bricks.

This guy—this Zeb Richards who wasn't quite black and wasn't quite white—he looked vaguely familiar. Something in the nose, the chin…those eyes…

He looked a little bit like Chadwick Beaumont.

Sweet merciful heavens. He *was* a Beaumont, too.

Her knees gave in to the weight of the revelation and she lurched forward to lean on the coffee table. "Oh, my God," she asked, staring at him. "You're one of them, aren't you?"

Richards snatched his hand back and put it in his pocket like he was trying to hide something. "I can neither confirm nor deny that—at least, not until the press conference on Friday." He moved away from the conference table and toward his desk.

If he was trying to intimidate her, it wasn't working. Casey followed him. He sat behind the desk—the same place she had seen Chadwick Beaumont too many times to count and, at least three times, Hardwick Beaumont. The resemblance was unmistakable.

"My God," she repeated again. "You're one of the bastards."

He leaned back in his chair and steepled his fingers. Everything about him had shut down. No traces of humor, no hints of warmth. She was staring at the coldest man she'd ever seen. "The bastards?"

"Beaumont's bastards—there were always rumors that Hardwick had a bunch of illegitimate children." She blinked. It all made sense, in a way. The Beaumonts were a notoriously good-looking group of men and women—far too handsome for their own good. And this man... He was gorgeous. But not the same kind of blond handsomeness that had marked Chadwick and Matthew Beaumont. She knew he would stand out in a crowd of Beaumonts. Hell, he would stand out in *any* crowd. "He was your father, wasn't he?"

Richards stared at her for a long time and she got the feeling he was making some sort of decision. She didn't know what—he hadn't fired her yet but the day wasn't over.

Her mind felt like it was fizzing with information. Zeb Richards—the mysterious man who was rumored to have single-handedly driven down the brewery's stock price so he could force AllBev to sell off the company— was a Beaumont? Did Chadwick know? Was he in on it or was this something else?

One word whispered across her mind. *Revenge.*

Because up until about thirty-seven seconds ago, Beaumont's bastards had never been anything but a rumor. And now one of them had the company.

She had no idea if this was a good thing or a very, *very* bad thing.

Suddenly, Richards leaned forward and made a minute adjustment to something on his desk. "We've gotten off track. Your primary reason for barging into my office unannounced was about résumés."

She felt like a bottle of beer that had been shaken but hadn't been opened. At any second, she might explode from the pressure. "Right," she agreed, collapsing into the chair in front of his desk. "The problem is, some of my employees have been here for twenty, thirty years and they don't have a résumé ready to go. Producing one on short notice is going to cause nothing but panic. They aren't the kind of guys who look good on paper. What matters is that they do good work for me and we produce a quality product." She took a deep breath, trying to sound managerial. "Are you familiar with our product line?"

The corner of Richard's mouth twitched. "It's beer, right?"

She rolled her eyes at him, which, surprisingly, made him grin even more. Oh, that was a bad idea, making him smile like that, because when he did, all the hard, cold edges fell away from his face. He was the kind of handsome that wasn't fair to the rest of humanity.

Sinful. That was what he was. And she had been too well behaved for too long.

She shivered. She wasn't sure if it had anything to do with the smile on his face or the fact that she was cooling off and her sweat-soaked shirt was now sticking to her skin. "That's correct. We brew beer here. I appreciate you giving me the go-ahead to hire more workers but that's a process that will take weeks. Training will also take time. Placing additional paperwork demands on my staff runs the risk of compromising the quality of our beer."

Richards didn't say anything. Casey cleared her throat. "You *are* interested in the beer, right?"

He gave her another one of those measured looks. Casey sighed. She really wasn't so complicated that he had to stare at her.

"I'm interested in the beer," he finally said. "This is a family company and I'd like to keep it that way. I must say," he went on before Casey could ask about that whole "family" thing, "I certainly appreciate your willingness to defend your staff. However, I'd like to be reassured that the employees who work for this brewery not only are able to follow basic instructions," he added with a notch of his eyebrow that made Casey want to pound on something, "but have the skills to take this company in a new direction."

"A new direction? We're...still going to brew beer, right? We're not getting into electronics or apps or anything?"

"Oh, we'll be getting into apps," he said. "But I need to know if there's anyone on staff who can handle that or if I'm going to need to bring in an outside developer—you see my point, don't you? The Beaumont Brewery has been losing market share. You brew seven thousand gallons a day—but it was eleven thousand years ago. The popularity of craft breweries—and I'm including Percheron Drafts in that—has slowly eroded our sales."

Our sales? He was serious, she realized. He was here to run this company.

"While I understand Logan's cost-cutting measures,"

he went on, oblivious to the way her mouth had dropped open, "what we need to do at this point is not to hunker down and hope for the best, but invest heavily in research and development—new products. And part of that is connecting with our audience." His gaze traveled around the room and Casey thought there was something about him that seemed...hopeful, almost.

She wanted to like her job. She wanted to like working for Zeb Richards. And if he was really talking about launching new products—new beers—well, then she might like her job again. The feeling that blossomed in her chest was so unfamiliar that it took a second to realize what it was—hope. Hope that this might actually work out.

"Part of what made the Beaumont Brewery a success was its long family traditions," Richards went on in a quiet voice. "That's why Logan failed. The employees liked Chadwick—any idiot knows that. And his brother Phillip? Phillip was the brewery's connection with our target market. When we lost both Phillip and Chadwick, the brewery lost its way."

Everything he said made sense. Because Casey had spent the last year not only feeling lost but knowing they were lost. They lost ground, they lost employees, they lost friends—they lost the knowledge and the tradition that had made them great. She was only one woman—one woman who liked to make beer. She couldn't save the company all by herself but she was doing her damnedest to save the beer.

Still, Richards had been on the job for about two hours now—maybe less. He was talking a hell of a good game, but at this point, that was all it was—talk. All talk and sinful handsomeness, with a hearty dollop of mystery.

But action was what this company needed. His mesmerizing eyes wouldn't right this ship all by themselves.

Still, if Richards really was a Beaumont by birth—bastard or not—he just might be able to do it. She'd long ago learned to never underestimate the Beaumonts.

"So you're going to be the one to light the path?"

He stared her in the eyes, one eyebrow gently lifted. God, if she wasn't careful, she could get lost in his gaze. "I have a plan, Ms. Johnson. You let me worry about the company and you worry about the beer."

"Sounds good to me," she muttered.

She stood because it seemed like a final sort of statement. But Richards stopped her. "How many workers do you need to hire?"

"At least ten. What I need most right now is maintenance staff. I don't know how much you know about beer, but most of what I do is automated. It's making sure to push the right button at the right time and checking to make sure that things come together the right way. It doesn't take a lot of know-how to brew beer, honestly, once you have the recipes." At this statement, both of his eyebrows lifted. "But keeping equipment running is another matter. It's hot, messy work and I need at least eight people who can take a tank apart and put it back together in less than an hour."

He thought about that for a moment. "I don't mean to be rude, but is that what you were doing before you came in here?"

She rolled her eyes again. "What gave it away?"

He grinned. Casey took another step back from the desk—away from Zeb Richards smiling at her. She tried to take comfort in the fact that he probably knew exactly how lethal his grin could be. Men as gorgeous as he was didn't get through life without knowing exactly what kind of effect they had on women—and it usually made them jerks. Which was fine. Gorgeous jerks never went for women like her and she didn't bother with them, either.

But there was something in the way he was looking at her that felt like a warning.

"I'll compromise with you, Ms. Johnson. You and your staff will be excused from submitting résumés."

That didn't sound like a compromise. That sounded like she was getting everything she asked for. Which meant the other shoe was about to drop. "And?"

"Instead…" He paused and shot her another grin. This one wasn't warm and fuzzy—this one was the sharp smile of a man who'd somehow bought a company out from under the Beaumonts. Out from under his own family. "…you and your team will produce a selection of new beers for me to choose from."

That was one hell of a shoe—and it had landed right on her. "I'm sorry?"

"Your point that the skills of some of your employees won't readily translate into bullet points on a résumé is well taken. So I'd like to see their skills demonstrated in action."

She knew her mouth was open, but she didn't think she could get it closed. She gave it a shot—nope, it was still open. "I can't just…"

"You do know how to brew beer, don't you?"

He was needling her—and it was working, dammit. "Of course I know how to brew beer. I've been brewing Beaumont beer for twelve years."

"Then what's the problem?"

It was probably bad form to strangle your boss on his first day on the job. Tempting, though. "I can't just produce beer by snapping my fingers. I have to test new recipes—and some of them are not going to work—and then there's the brewing time, and I won't be able to do any of that until I get more staff hired."

"How long will it take?"

She grasped at the first number that popped into her mind. "Two months. At least. Maybe three."

"Fine. Three months to hire the workers and test some new recipes." He sat forward in his chair and dropped his gaze to the desk, as if they were done.

"It isn't that simple," she told him. "We need to get Marketing to provide us with guidance on what's currently popular and two—"

"I don't care what Marketing says." He cut her off. "This is my company and I want it to brew beers that I like."

"But I don't even know what you like." The moment the words left her mouth, she wished she could take them back. But it was too late. He fixed those eyes on her. Heat flushed down her back, warming her from the inside out. "I mean, when it comes to beer," she quickly corrected. "We've got everything on tap…" she added, trying not to blush as she motioned to the bar that ran along one side of the wall.

Richards leaned forward on his elbows as his gaze raked up and down her body again. Damn it all, he was a jerk. He only confirmed it when he opened his mouth and said, "I'd be more than happy to take some time after work and show you exactly what I like."

Well. If that was how it was going to be, he was making it a lot easier *not* to develop a crush on him. Because she had not gotten this job by sleeping her way to the top. He might be the most beautiful man she'd ever seen and those green eyes were the stuff of fantasy—but none of it mattered if he used his power as CEO to take advantage of his employees. She was good at what she did and she wouldn't let anyone take that away from her.

"Mr. Richards, you're going to have to decide what kind of Beaumont you are going to be—*if* you really are one." His eyes hardened, but she didn't back down. "Because if you're going to be a predator like your father instead of a businessman like your brother, you're going to need a new brewmaster."

Head held high, she walked out of his office and back to her own.

Then she updated her résumé.

Three

Zeb did not have time to think about his new brewmaster's parting shot. It was, however, difficult not to think about *her*.

He'd known full well there would be pushback against the memo. He hadn't lied when he'd told her he wanted to see who could follow directions—but he also wanted to see who wouldn't and why. Because the fact was, having the entire company divert work hours to producing résumés was not an efficient use of time. And the workers who already had up-to-date résumés ready to go—well, that was because they were a flight risk.

He couldn't say he was surprised when the brewmaster was the first person to call him on it.

But he still couldn't believe the brewmaster was a young woman with fire in her eyes and a fierce instinct to protect her employees. A woman who didn't look at him like he was ripe for the picking. A woman who

took one look at him—okay, maybe more than one—
and saw the truth.

A young woman with a hell of a mouth on her.

Zeb pushed Casey Johnson from his mind and picked
up his phone. He started scrolling through his contacts
until he came to one name in particular—Daniel Lee.
He dialed and waited.

"Hello?"

"Daniel—it's Zeb. Are you still in?"

There was a pause on the other end of the line. Daniel Lee was a former political operative who'd worked
behind the scenes to get several incumbents defeated.
He could manipulate public perception and he could
drill down into data. But that wasn't why Zeb called
him.

Daniel—much like Zeb—was one of *them*. Beaumont's bastards.

"Where are you?" Daniel asked, and Zeb didn't miss
the way he neatly avoided the question.

"Sitting in the CEO's office of the Beaumont Brewery. I scheduled a press conference for Friday—I'd like
you to be there. I want to show the whole world that they
can't ignore us anymore."

There was another pause. On one level, Zeb appreciated that Daniel was methodical. Everything he did
was well thought-out and carefully researched, with the
data to back it up.

But on the other hand, Zeb didn't want his relationship with his brother to be one based solely on how the
numbers played out. He didn't know Daniel very well—
they'd met only two months ago, after Zeb had spent
almost a year and thousands upon thousands of dollars
tracking down two of his half brothers. But he and Daniel were family all the same and when Zeb announced

to the world that he was a Beaumont and this was his brewery, he wanted his brothers by his side.

"What about CJ?" Daniel asked.

Zeb exhaled. "He's out." Zeb had tracked down two illegitimate brothers; all three of them had been born within five years of each other. Daniel was three years younger than Zeb and half-Korean.

The other brother he'd found was Carlos Julián Santino—although he now went by CJ Wesley. Unlike Zeb and Daniel, CJ was a rancher. He didn't seem to have inherited the Beaumont drive for business.

Two months ago, when the men had all met for the first time over dinner and Zeb had laid out his plan for taking control of the brewery and finally taking what was rightfully theirs, Daniel politely agreed to look at the numbers and weigh the outcomes. But CJ had said he wasn't interested. Unlike Zeb's mother, CJ's mother had married and he'd been adopted by her husband. CJ did not consider Hardwick Beaumont to be his father. He'd made his position clear—he wanted nothing to do with the Beaumonts or the brewery.

He wanted nothing to do with his brothers.

"That's unfortunate," Daniel said. "I had hoped…"

Yeah, Zeb had hoped, too. But he wasn't going to dwell on his failures. Not when success was within his grasp. "I need you by my side, Daniel. This is our time. I won't be swept under the rug any longer. We are both Beaumonts. It's not enough that I've taken their company away from them—I need it to do better than it did under them. And that means I need you. This is the dawn of a new era."

Daniel chuckled. "You can stop with the hard sell—I'm in. But I get to be the chief marketing officer, right?"

"I wouldn't have it any other way."

There was another long pause. "This had better work," Daniel said in a menacing voice.

Which made Zeb grin. "It already has."

It was late afternoon before Zeb was able to get a tour of the facilities. Delores, tablet in hand, alternated between leading the way and falling behind him. Zeb couldn't tell if she was humoring him or if she really was that intimidated.

The tour moved slowly because in every department, Zeb stopped and talked with the staff. He was pleased when several managers asked to speak to him privately and then questioned the need to have a résumé for every single person on staff—wouldn't it be better if they just turned in a report on head count? It was heartening, really. Those managers were willing to risk their necks to protect their people—while they still looked for a way to do what Zeb told them.

However, Zeb didn't want to be seen as a weak leader who changed his mind. He allowed the managers to submit a report by the deadline, but he still wanted to see résumés. He informed everyone that the hiring freeze was over but he needed to know what he had before he began to fill the empty cubicles.

As he'd anticipated after his conversation with Casey, the news that the hiring freeze was over—coupled with the announcement that he would prefer not to see his staff working ten-to twelve-hour days—bought him a considerable amount of goodwill. That was not to say people weren't still wary—they were—but the overwhelming emotion was relief. It was obvious Casey wasn't the only one doing the job of two or three people.

The brewhouse was the last stop on their tour. Zeb wasn't sure if that was because it was the logical conclusion or because Delores was trying to delay another confrontation with Casey.

Unsurprisingly, the brewhouse was warm, and emptier than he expected. He saw now what Casey had meant when she said most of the process was automated. The few men he did see wore white lab coats and hairnets, along with safety goggles. They held tablets and when Zeb and Delores passed them, they paused and looked up.

"The staffing levels two years ago?" Zeb asked again.

He'd asked that question at least five times already. Two years ago, the company had been in the capable hands of Chadwick Beaumont. They'd been turning a consistent profit and their market share was stable. That hadn't been enough for some of their board members, though. Leon Harper had agitated for the company's sale, which made him hundreds of millions of dollars. From everything Zeb had read about Harper, the man was a foul piece of humanity. But there was no way Zeb ever could've gotten control of the company without him.

Delores tapped her tablet as they walked along. The room was oddly silent—there was the low hum of machinery, but it wasn't enough to dampen the echoes from their footfalls. The noise bounced off the huge tanks that reached at least twenty feet high. The only other noise was a regular hammering that got louder the farther they went into the room.

"Forty-two," she said after several minutes. "That was when we were at peak capacity. Ah, here we are."

Delores pointed at the floor and he looked down and saw two pairs of jeans-clad legs jutting out from underneath the tank.

Delores gave him a cautious smile and turned her attention back to the legs. "Casey?"

Zeb had to wonder what Delores had thought of Casey bursting into his office earlier—and whether or not Casey had said anything on her way out. He still hadn't decided what he thought of the young woman. Because she did seem impossibly young to be in charge. But what she might have lacked in maturity she made up for with sheer grit.

She probably didn't realize it, but there were very few people in this world who would dare burst into his office and dress him down. And those who would try would rarely be able to withstand the force of his disdain.

But she had. Easily. But more than that, she'd rebuffed his exploratory offer. No, that wasn't a strong enough word for how she'd destroyed him with her parting shot.

So many women looked at him as their golden ticket. He was rich and attractive and single—he knew that. But he didn't want to be anyone's ticket anywhere.

Casey Johnson hadn't treated him like that. She'd matched him verbal barb for barb and *then* bested him, all while looking like a hot mess.

He'd be lying if he said he wasn't intrigued.

"...try it again," came a muffled voice from underneath the tank. This was immediately followed by more hammering, which, at this close range, was deafening.

Zeb fought the urge to cover his ears and Delores winced. When there was a break in the hammering, she gently tapped one of the two pairs of shoes with her toe. "Casey—Mr. Richards is here."

The person whose shoe she'd nudged started—which was followed by a dull *thunk* and someone going, "Ow, dammit. What?"

And then she slid out from under the tank. She was in a white lab coat, a hairnet and safety goggles, just like everyone else. "Hello again, Ms. Johnson."

Her eyes widened. She was not what one might call a conventional beauty—especially not in the hairnet. She had a small spiderweb scar on one cheek that was more noticeable when she was red in the face—and Zeb hadn't yet seen her *not* red in the face. It was an imperfection, but it drew his eyes to her. She was maybe four inches shorter than he was and he thought her eyes were light brown. He wasn't even sure what color her hair was. It had been under the hat in his office.

But she was passionate about beer and Zeb appreciated that.

"You again," she said in a tone that sounded intentionally bored. "Back for more?"

He almost laughed—but he didn't. He was Zeb Richards, CEO of the Beaumont Brewery. And he was not going to snicker when his brewmaster copped an attitude. Still, her manner was refreshing after a day of people bowing and scraping.

Once again, he found himself running through her parting shot. Was he like his father or like his brother? He didn't know much about either of them. He knew his father had a lot of children—and ignored some of them—and he knew his half brother had successfully run the company for about ten years. But that was common knowledge anyone with an internet connection could find out.

Almost everyone else here—including one prone brewmaster with an attitude problem—would have known what she meant by that. But he didn't.

Not yet, anyway.

Delores looked shocked. "Casey," she hissed in warning. "I'm giving Mr. Richards a tour of the facilities. Would you like to show him around the tanks?"

For a moment, Casey looked contrite in the face of Delores's scolding and Zeb got the feeling Delores had held the company together longer than anyone else.

But the moment was short. "Can't. The damned tank won't cooperate. I'm busy. Come back tomorrow." And with that, she slid right back under the tank. Before either he or Delores could say anything else, that infernal hammering picked up again. This time, he was sure it was even louder.

Delores turned to him, looking stricken. "I apologize, Mr. Richards. I—"

Zeb held up a hand to cut her off. Then he nudged the shoes again. This time, both people slid out. The other person was a man in his midfifties. He looked panic-stricken. Casey glared up at Zeb. *"What."*

"You and I need to schedule a time to go over the product line and discuss ideas for new launches."

She rolled her eyes, which made Delores gasp in horror. "Can't you get someone from Sales to go over the beer with you?"

"No, I can't," he said coldly. It was one thing to let her get the better of him in the privacy of his office but another thing entirely to let her run unchallenged in front of staff. "It has to be you, Ms. Johnson. If you want to brew a new beer that matches my tastes, you should actually know what my tastes are. When can this tank be back up and running?"

She gave him a dull look. "It's hard to tell, what with all the constant interruptions." But then she notched an eyebrow at him, the corner of her mouth curving into a delicate grin, as if they shared a private joke.

He did some quick mental calculating. They didn't

have to meet before Friday—getting the press conference organized had to be his first priority. But by next week he needed to be working toward a new product line.

However, he was also aware that the press conference was going to create waves. It would be best to leave Monday open. "Lunch, Tuesday. Plan accordingly."

For just one second, he thought she would argue with him. Her mouth opened and she looked like she was spoiling for a fight. But then she changed her mind. "Fine. Tuesday. Now if you'll excuse me," she added, sliding back out of view.

"I'm so sorry," Delores repeated as they hurried away from the hammering. "Casey is…"

Zeb didn't rush into the gap. He was curious what the rest of the company thought of her.

He was surprised to realize *he* admired her. It couldn't be easy keeping the beer flowing—especially not as a young woman. She had to be at least twenty years younger than nearly every other man he'd seen in the brewhouse. But she hadn't let that stop her.

Because she was, most likely, unstoppable.

He hoped the employees thought highly of her. He needed people like her who cared for the company and the beer. People who weren't constrained by what they were or were not supposed to be.

Just like he wasn't.

"She's young," Delores finished.

Zeb snorted. Compared to his assistant, almost everyone would be.

"But she's very good," Delores said with finality.

"Good." He had no doubt that Casey Johnson would fight him at every step. "Make sure HR fast-tracks her hires. I want her to have all the help she needs."

He was looking forward to this.

Four

"Thank you all for joining me today," Zeb said, looking out at the worried faces of his chief officers, vice presidents and departmental heads. They were all crammed around the conference table in his office. They had twenty minutes until the press conference was scheduled to start and Zeb thought it was best to give his employees a little warning.

Everyone looked anxious. He couldn't blame them. He'd made everyone surrender their cell phones when they'd come into the office and a few people looked as if they were going through withdrawal. But he wasn't about to run the risk of someone preempting his announcement.

Only one person in the room looked like she knew what was coming next—Casey Johnson. Today she also looked like a member of the managerial team, Zeb noted with an inward smile. Her hair was slicked back into a neat bun and she wore a pale purple blouse and a pair of slacks. The change from the woman who'd stormed into his office was so big that if it hadn't been for the faint spiderweb scar on her cheek, Zeb wouldn't have recognized her.

"I'm going to tell you the same thing that I'm going to tell the press in twenty minutes," Zeb said. "I wanted to give you advance warning. When I make my announcement, I expect each and every one of you to look supportive. We're going to present a unified force. Not only is the Beaumont Brewery back, but it's going to be better than ever." He glanced at Casey. She notched an eyebrow at him and made a little motion with her hands that Zeb took to mean *Get on with it.*

So he did. "Hardwick Beaumont was my father."

As expected, the entire room shuddered with a gasp, followed by a rumbling murmur of disbelief. With amusement, Zeb noted that Casey stared around the room as if everyone else should have already realized the truth.

She didn't understand how unusual she was. No one had ever looked at him and seen the Beaumont in him. All they could see was a black man from Atlanta. Very few people ever bothered to look past that, even when he'd started making serious money.

But she had.

Some of the senior employees looked grim but not surprised. Everyone else seemed nothing but shocked. And the day wasn't over yet. When the murmur had subsided, Zeb pressed on.

"Some of you have met Daniel Lee," Zeb said, motioning to Daniel, who stood near the door. "In addition to being our new chief marketing officer, Daniel is also one of Hardwick's sons. So when I tell the reporters," he went on, ignoring the second round of shocked murmurs, "that the Beaumont Brewery is back in Beaumont hands, I want to know that I have your full support. I've spent the last week getting to know you and your teams. I know that Chadwick Beaumont, my half brother," he added, proud of the way he kept his voice level, "ran this company with a sense of pride and family honor and I'm making this promise to you, here, in this room—we will restore the Beaumont pride and we will restore the honor to this company. My last name may not be Beaumont, but I am one nonetheless. Do I have your support?"

Again, his eyes found Casey's. She was looking at him and then Daniel—no doubt looking for the family resemblance that lurked beneath their unique racial heritages.

Murmurs continued to rumble around the room, like thunder before a storm. Zeb waited. He wasn't going to ask a second time, because that would denote weakness and he was never weak.

"Does Chadwick know what you're doing?"

Zeb didn't see who asked the question, but from the voice, he guessed it was one of the older people in the room. Maybe even someone who had once worked not only for Chadwick but for Hardwick, as well. "He will shortly. At this time, Chadwick is a competitor. I wish him well, as I'm sure we all do, but he's not coming back. This is my company now. Not only do I want to get us back to where we were when he was in charge of things, but I want to get us ahead of where we were. I'll be laying out the details at the press conference, but I promise you this. We will have new beers," he said, nodding to Casey, "and new marketing strategies, thanks to Daniel and his extensive experience."

SARAH M. ANDERSON 47

He could tell he didn't have them. The ones standing were shuffling their feet and the ones sitting were looking anywhere but at him. If this had been a normal business negotiation, he'd have let the silence stretch. But it wasn't. "This was once a great place to work and I want to make it that place again. As I discussed with some of you, I've lifted the hiring freeze. The bottom line is and will continue to be important, but so is the beer."

An older man in the back stepped forward. "The last guy tried to run us into the ground."

"The last guy wasn't a Beaumont," Zeb shot back. He could see the doubt in their eyes. He didn't look the part that he was trying to sell them on.

Then Casey stood, acting far more respectable—and respectful—than the last time he had seen her. "I don't know about everyone else, but I just want to make beer. And if you say we're going to keep making beer, then I'm in."

Zeb acknowledged her with a nod of his head and looked around this room. He'd wager that there'd be one or two resignations on his desk by Monday morning. Maybe more. But Casey fixed them with a stern look and most of his employees stood up.

"All right," the older man who had spoken earlier repeated. Zeb was going to have to learn his name soon, because he clearly commanded a great deal of respect. "What do we have to do?"

"Daniel has arranged this press conference. Think of it as a political rally." Which was what Daniel knew best. The similarities were not coincidences. "I'd like everyone to look supportive and encouraging of the new plan."

"Try to smile," Daniel said, and Zeb saw nearly everyone jump in surprise. It was the first time Daniel had spoken. "I'm going to line you up and then we're going to walk out onto the front steps of the building. I'm going to group you accordingly. You are all the face of the Beaumont Brewery, each and every one of you. Try to remember that when the cameras are rolling."

Spoken like a true political consultant.

"Mr. Richards," Delores said, poking her head in the room, "it's almost time."

Daniel began arranging everyone in line as he wanted them and people went along with it. Zeb went back to his private bathroom to splash water on his face. Did he have enough support to put on a good show?

Probably.

He stared at the mirror. He *was* a Beaumont. For almost his entire life, that fact had been a secret that only three people knew—him and his parents. If his mother had so much as breathed a word about his true parentage, Hardwick would've come after her with pitchforks and torches. He would've burned her to the ground.

But Hardwick was dead and Zeb no longer had to keep his father's secrets. Now the whole world was going to know who he really was.

He walked out to find one person still in the conference room. He couldn't even be surprised when he saw it was Casey Johnson. For some reason, something in his chest unclenched.

"How did I do?" The moment the words left his mouth, he started. He didn't need her approval. He didn't even want it. But he'd asked for it anyway.

She tilted her head to one side and studied him. "Not bad," she finally allowed. "You may lose the entire marketing department."

Zeb's eyebrows jumped up. Was it because of him or because he brought in Daniel, another outsider? "You think so?"

She nodded and then sighed. "Are you sure you know what you're doing?"

"Can you keep a secret?"

"If I say yes, is that your cue to say, 'So can I'?"

Zeb would never admit to being nervous. But if he *had* been, a little verbal sparring with Ms. Johnson would have been just the thing to distract him. He gave her a measured look. "I'll take that as a no, you can't keep a secret. Nevertheless," he went on before she could protest, "I am putting the fate of this company in the hands of a young woman with an attitude problem, when any other sane owner would turn toward an older, more experienced brewmaster. I have faith in you, Ms. Johnson. Try to have a little in me."

She clearly did not win a lot of poker games. One second, she looked like she wanted to tear him a new one for daring to suggest she might have an attitude problem. But then the compliment registered and the oddest thing happened.

She blushed. Not the overheated red that he'd seen on her several times now. This was a delicate coloring of her cheeks, a kiss of light pink along her skin. "You have faith in me?"

"I had a beer last night. Since you've been in charge of brewing for the last year, I feel it's a reasonable assumption that you brewed it. So yes, I have faith in your abilities." Her lips parted. She sucked in a little gasp and Zeb was nearly overcome with the urge to lean forward and kiss her. Because she looked utterly kissable right now.

But the moment the thought occurred to him, he pushed it away. What the hell was wrong with him today? He was about to go out and face a bloodthirsty pack of reporters. Kissing anyone—least of all his brewmaster—should have been the farthest thing from his mind. Especially considering the setdown she'd given him a few days ago.

Was he like his father or his brother?

Still, he couldn't fight the urge to lean forward. Her eyes widened and her pupils darkened.

"Don't let me down," he said in a low voice.

He wasn't sure what she would say. But then the door swung open again and Daniel poked his head in.

"Ah, Ms... Johnson, is it? We're waiting on you." He looked over her head to Zeb. "Two minutes."

Ms. Johnson turned, but at the doorway, she paused and looked back. "Don't let the company down," she told him.

He hoped he wouldn't.

Casey knew she should be paying more attention to whatever Zeb was saying. Because he was certainly saying a lot of things, some of them passionately. She caught phrases like *quality beer* and *family company* but for the most part, she tuned out.

He had faith in her? That was so disconcerting that she didn't have a good response. But the thing that had really blown her mind was that she had been—and this was by her own estimation—a royal bitch during the two times they'd met previous to today.

It wasn't that no one respected her. The guys she'd worked with for the last twelve years respected her. Because she had earned it. She had shown up, day in and day out. She had taken their crap and given as good as she got. She had taken every single job they threw at her, even the really awful ones like scrubbing out the tanks. Guys like Larry respected her because they knew her.

Aside from those two conversations, Zeb Richards didn't know her at all.

Maybe what he'd said was a load of crap. After all, a guy as good-looking as he was didn't get to be where he was in life without learning how to say the right thing at the right time to a woman. And he'd already hit on her once, on that first day when she'd burst into his office. So it was entirely possible that he'd figured out the one thing she needed to hear and then said it to soften her up.

Even though she wasn't paying attention, she still knew the moment he dropped his big bomb. She felt the tension ripple among her coworkers—but that wasn't it. No, the entire corps of reporters recoiled in shock. Seconds later, they were all shouting questions.

"Can you prove that Hardwick Beaumont was your father?"

"How many more bastards are there?"

"Did you plan the takeover with Chadwick Beaumont?"

"What are your plans for the brewery now that the Beaumonts are back in charge?"

Casey studied Richards. The reporters had jumped out of their chairs and were now crowding the stage, as if being first in line meant their questions would be answered first. Even though they weren't shouting at her, she still had the urge to flee in horror.

But not Richards. He stood behind his podium and stared down at the reporters as if they were nothing more than gnats bothering him on a summer day. After a moment, the reporters quieted down. Richards waited until they returned to their seats before ignoring the questions completely and moving on with his prepared remarks.

Well, that was impressive. She glanced at the one person who had thrown her for a loop this morning—Daniel Lee. The two men stood nearly shoulder to shoulder, with Daniel just a step behind and to the right of Richards. Richards had two inches on his half brother and maybe forty pounds of what appeared to be pure muscle. The two men shouldn't have looked anything alike. Lee was clearly Asian American and Richards wasn't definitively one ethnicity or another. But despite those differences—and despite the fact that they had apparently not been raised together, like the other Beaumonts had been—there was something similar about them. The way they held their heads, their chins—not that Casey had met all of the Beaumont siblings, but apparently, they all shared the same jaw.

As Richards continued to talk about his plans for restoring the Beaumont family honor, Casey wondered where she fit in all of this.

In her time, when she'd been a young intern fresh out of college and desperate to get her foot in the door, Hardwick Beaumont had been…well, not an old man, but an older man. He'd had a sharp eye and wandering hands. Wally Winking, the old brewmaster, whose voice still held a faint hint of a German accent even though he'd been at the brewery for over fifty years, had told her she reminded him of his granddaughter. Then he'd told her never to be alone with Hardwick. She hadn't had to ask why.

Three days ago, Richards had made a pass at her. That was something his father would have done. But today?

Today, when they'd been alone together, he'd had faith in her abilities. He made it sound like he respected her— both as a person and as a brewmaster.

And that was what made him sound like his brother Chadwick.

Oh, her father was going to have a field day with this. And then he was going to be mad at her that she hadn't warned him in advance. To say that Carl Johnson was heavily invested in her career would be like saying that NASA sometimes thought about Mars. He constantly worried that she was on the verge of losing her job—a sentiment that had only gotten stronger over the last year. Her dad was protective of his little girl, which was both sweet and irritating.

What was she going to tell her father? She hadn't told him about her confrontational first meeting with Richards—or the second one, for that matter. But she was pretty sure she would be on the news tonight, one face in a human backdrop behind Zeb Richards as he completely blew up everything people thought they knew about the Beaumont family and the brewery.

Well, there was only one thing to do. As soon as Daniel Lee gave her phone back, she had to text her dad.

Oh, the reporters were shouting again. Richards picked up his tablet to walk off the platform. Daniel motioned to the people in front of her as they were beginning to walk back up the front steps. The press conference was apparently over. Thank God for that.

Richards appeared to be ignoring the reporters but that only made the reporters shout louder. He'd almost made it to the door when Natalie Baker—the beautiful blonde woman who trafficked in local Denver gossip on her show, *A Good Morning with Natalie Baker*—physically blocked Zeb's way with her body. And her breasts. They were really nice ones, the kind that Casey had never had and never would.

Natalie Baker all but purred a question at Richards. "Are there more like you?" she asked, her gaze sweeping to include Daniel in the question.

It must've been the breasts, because for the first time, Richards went off script. "I've located one more brother, but he's not part of this venture. Now if you'll excuse me."

Baker looked thrilled and the rest of the crowd started shouting questions again. *That was a dumb thing to do*, Casey thought. Now everyone would have to know who the third one was and why he wasn't on the stage with Richards and Lee.

Men. A nice rack and they lost their little minds.

She didn't get a chance to talk to Richards again. And even if she had, what would she have said? *Nice press conference that I didn't pay attention to?* No, even she knew that was not the way to go about things.

Besides, she had her own brand of damage control to deal with. She needed to text her dad, warning him that the company would be in the news again but he shouldn't panic—her boss had faith in her. Then she had to go back and warn her crew. No, it was probably too late for that. She had to reassure them that they were going to keep making beer. Then she had to start the hiring process for some new employees and she had to make sure that tank fifteen was actually working properly today...

And she had to get ready for Tuesday. She was having lunch and beer with the boss.

Which boss would show up?

Five

Frankly, he could use a beer.

"Did you contact CJ?" Daniel asked. "He needs to be warned."

Here, in the privacy of his own office with no one but Daniel around, Zeb allowed himself to lean forward and pinch the bridge of his nose. Make that several beers.

"I did. He didn't seem concerned. As long as we keep his name and whereabouts out of it, he thinks he's unfindable."

Daniel snorted. "You found him."

"A fact of which I reminded him." Zeb knew that CJ's refusal to be a part of Zeb's vision for the brothers wasn't personal. Still, it bugged him. "I think it's safe to say that he's a little more laid-back than we are."

That made Daniel grin. "He'll come around. Eventually. Has there been any other…contact?"

"No." It wasn't that he expected the acknowledged

members of the Beaumont family to storm the brewery gates and engage in a battle for the heart and soul of the family business. But while the rest of the world was engaged in furious rounds of questions and speculation, there had been radio silence from the Beaumonts themselves. Not even a *No comment*. Just…nothing.

Not that Zeb expected any of them to fall over themselves to welcome him and Daniel into the family. He didn't.

He checked his watch.

"Do you have a hot date?" Daniel asked in an offhand way.

"I'm having lunch with the brewmaster, Casey Johnson."

That got Daniel's attention. He sat up straighter. "And?"

And she asked me if I was like my father or my brother and I didn't have an answer.

But that wasn't what he said. In fact, he didn't say anything. Yes, he and Daniel were in this together, and yes, they were technically brothers. But there were some things he still didn't want to share. Daniel was too smart and he knew how to bend the truth to suit his purposes.

Zeb had no desire to be bent to anyone's purposes but his own. "We're going over the product line. It's hard to believe that a woman so young is the brewmaster in charge of all of our beer and I want to make sure she knows her stuff."

His phone rang. He winced inwardly—it was his mother. "I've got to take this. We'll talk later?"

Daniel nodded. "One last thing. I had four resignations in the marketing department."

Casey had not been wrong about that, either. She had a certain brashness to her, but she knew this business.

"Hire whoever you want," Zeb said as he answered the call. "Hello, Mom."

"I shouldn't have to call you," his mother said, the steel in her voice sounding extra sharp today.

How much beer could one man reasonably drink at work? Zeb was going to have to test that limit today, because if there was one thing he didn't want to deal with right now, it was his mother.

"But I'm glad you did," he replied easily. "How's the salon?"

"Humph." Emily Richards ran a chain of successful hair salons in Georgia. Thanks to his careful management, Doo-Wop and Pop! had gone from being six chairs in a strip-mall storefront to fifteen locations scattered throughout Georgia and a small but successful line of hair weaves and braid accessories targeted toward the affluent African American buyer.

Zeb had done that for his mother. He'd taken her from lower middle class, where the two of them got by on $30,000 a year, to upper class. Doo-Wop and Pop! had made Emily Richards rich and was on track to make even more profit this year.

But that *humph* told Zeb everything he needed to know. It didn't matter that he had taken his mother's idea and turned it into a hugely successful woman-owned business. All that really mattered to Emily Richards was getting revenge on the man she claimed had ruined her life.

A fact she drove home with her next statement. "Well? Did you finally take what's yours?"

It always came back to the brewery. And the way she said *finally* grated on his nerves like a steel file. Still, she was his mother. "It's really mine, Mom."

Those words should have filled him with satisfaction.

He had done what he had set out to do. The Beaumont Brewery was his now.

So why did he feel so odd?

He shook it off. It had been an exceptionally long weekend, after all. As expected, his press conference had created not just waves but tsunamis that had to be dealt with. His one mistake—revealing that there was a third Beaumont bastard, unnamed and unknown—had threatened to undermine his triumphant ascension to power.

"They'll come for you," his mother intoned ominously. "Those Beaumonts can't let it rest. You watch your back."

Not for the first time, Zeb wondered if his mother was a touch paranoid. He understood now what he hadn't when he was little—that his father had bought her silence. But more and more, she acted like his siblings would go to extreme measures to enforce that silence.

His father, maybe. But none of the research he'd done on any of his siblings had turned up any proclivities for violence.

Still, he knew he couldn't convince his mother. So he let it go.

There was a knock on the door and before he could say anything, it popped open. In walked Jamal, boxes stacked in his hands. When he saw that Zeb was on the phone, he nodded his head in greeting and moved quietly to the conference table. There he began unpacking lunch.

"I will," Zeb promised his mother. And it wasn't even one of those little white lies he told her to keep her happy. He had stirred up several hornets' nests over the last few days. It only made good sense to watch his back.

"They deserve to pay for what they did to me. And you," she added as an afterthought.

But wasn't that the thing? None of the Beaumonts who were living today had ever done anything to Zeb. They'd just...ignored him.

"I've got to go, Mom. I have a meeting that starts in a few minutes." He didn't miss the way his Southern accent was stronger. Hearing it roll off Mom's tongue made his show up in force.

"Humph," she repeated. "Love you, baby boy."

"Love you, too, Mom." He hung up.

"Let me guess," Jamal said as he spread out the four-course meal he had prepared. "She's still not happy."

"Let it go, man." But something about the conversation with his mother was bugging him.

For a long time, his mother had spoken of what the Beaumonts owed *him*. They had taken what rightfully belonged to him and it was his duty to get it back. And if they wouldn't give it to him legitimately, he would just have to take it by force.

But that was all she'd ever told him about the Beaumont family. She'd never told him anything about his father or his father's family. She'd told him practically nothing about her time in Denver—he wasn't all that sure what she had done for Hardwick back in the '70s. Every time he asked, she refused to answer and instead launched into another rant about how they'd cut him out of what was rightfully his.

He had so many questions and not enough answers. He was missing something and he knew it. It was a feeling he did not enjoy, because in his business, answers made money.

His intercom buzzed. "Mr. Richards, Ms. Johnson is here."

Jamal shot him a funny look. "I thought you said you were having lunch with your brewmaster."

Before Zeb could explain, the door opened and Casey walked in. "Good morning. I spoke with the cook in the cafeteria. She said she hadn't been asked to prepare any— Oh. Hello," she said cautiously when she caught sight of Jamal plating up what smelled like his famous salt-crusted beef tenderloin.

Zeb noted with amusement that today she was back in the unisex lab coat with Beaumont Brewery embroidered on the lapel—but she wasn't bright red or sweating buckets. Her hair was still in a ponytail, though. She was, on the whole, one of the least feminine women he'd ever met. He couldn't even begin to imagine her in a dress but somehow that made her all the more intriguing.

No, he was not going to be intrigued by her. Especially not with Jamal watching. "Ms. Johnson, this is Jamal—"

"Jamal Hitchens?"

Now it was Jamal's turn to take a step back and look at Casey with caution. "Yeah… You recognize me?" He shot a funny look over to Zeb, but he just shrugged.

He was learning what Zeb had already figured out. There was no way to predict what Casey Johnson would do or say.

"Of course I recognize you," she gushed. "You played for the University of Georgia—you were in the running for the Heisman, weren't you? I mean, until you blew your knees out. Sorry about that," she added, wincing.

Jamal was gaping down at her as if she'd peeled off her skin to reveal an alien in disguise. "You know who I am?"

"Ms. Johnson is a woman of many talents," Zeb said, not even bothering to fight the grin. Jamal would've gone pro if it hadn't been for his knees. But it was rare that anyone remembered a distant runner-up for the Heisman who hadn't played ball in years. "I've learned it's best not to underestimate her. Ms. Johnson is my brewmaster."

It was hard to get the drop on Jamal, but one small woman in a lab coat clearly had. "What are you doing here?" Casey sniffed the air. "God, that smells good."

Honest to God, Jamal blushed. "Oh. Thank you." He glanced nervously at Zeb.

"Jamal is my oldest friend," Zeb explained. He almost added, *He's the closest thing I have to a brother*—but then he stopped himself. Even if it was true, the whole point of this endeavor with the Beaumont Brewery was to prove that he had a family whether they wanted him or not. "He is my right-hand man. One of his many talents is cooking. I asked him to prepare some of my favorites today to accompany our tasting." He turned to Jamal, whose mouth was still flopped open in shock. "What did you bring?" Zeb prodded.

"What? Oh, right. The food." It was so unusual to hear Jamal sound unsure of himself that Zeb had to stare. "It's a tasting menu," he began, sounding embarrassed about it. It was rare that Jamal's past life in sports ever intersected with his current life. Actually, Zeb couldn't remember a time when someone who hadn't played football recognized him.

Jamal ran through the menu—in addition to the salt-crusted beef tenderloin, which had been paired with new potatoes, there was a spaghetti Bolognese, a vichyssoise soup and Jamal's famous fried chicken. Dessert was flourless chocolate cupcakes dusted with powdered sugar—Zeb's favorite.

Casey surveyed the feast before her, and Zeb got the feeling that she didn't approve. He couldn't say why he thought that, because she was perfectly polite to Jamal at all times. In fact, when he tried to leave, she insisted on getting a picture with him so she could send it to her father—apparently, her father was a huge sports fan and would also know who Jamal was.

So Zeb took the photo for her and then Jamal hurried away, somewhere between flattered and uncomfortable.

And then Zeb and Casey were alone.

She didn't move. "So Jamal Hitchens is an old friend of yours?"

"Yes."

"And he's your…personal chef?"

Zeb settled into his seat at the head of the conference table. "Among other things, yes." He didn't offer up any other information.

"You don't really strike me as a sports guy," she replied.

"Come, now, Ms. Johnson. Surely you've researched me by now?"

Her cheeks colored again. He liked that delicate blush on her. He shouldn't, but he did. "I don't remember reading about you owning a sports franchise."

Zeb lifted one shoulder. "Who knows. Maybe I'll buy a team and make Jamal the general manager. After all, what goes together better than sports and beer?"

She was still standing near the door, as if he were an alligator that looked hungry. Finally, she asked, "Have you decided, then?"

"About what?"

He saw her swallow, but it was the only betrayal of her nerves. Well, that and the fact that she wasn't smart-mouthing him. Actually, that she wasn't saying whatever came to mind was unusual.

"About what kind of Beaumont you're going to be."

He involuntarily tensed and then let out a breath slowly. Like his father or his brother? He had no idea.

He wanted to ask what she knew—was it the same as the public image of the company? Or was there something else he didn't know? Maybe his father had secretly been the kindest man on earth. Or maybe Chadwick was just as bad as Hardwick had been. He didn't know.

What he did know was that the last time he'd seen her, he'd had the urge to kiss her. It'd been nerves, he'd decided. He'd been concerned about the press conference and Casey Johnson was the closest thing to a friendly face here—when she wasn't scowling at him. That was all that passing desire had been. Reassurance. Comfort.

He didn't feel comfortable now.

"I'm going to be a different kind of Beaumont," he said confidently because it was the only true thing he *could* say. "I'm my own man."

She thought this over. "And what kind of man is that?"

She had guts, he had to admit. Anyone else might have nodded and smiled and said, *Of course*. But not her. "The kind with strong opinions about beer."

"Fair enough." She headed for the bar.

Zeb watched her as she pulled on the tap with a smooth, practiced hand. He needed to stop being surprised at her competency. She was the brewmaster. Of course she knew how to pour beer. Tapping the keg was probably second nature to her. And there wasn't a doubt in his mind that she could also destroy him in a sports trivia contest.

But this was different from watching a bartender fill a pint glass. Watching her hands on the taps was far more interesting than it'd ever been before. She had long fingers and they wrapped around each handle with a firm, sure grip.

Unexpectedly, he found himself wondering what else she'd grip like that. But the moment the thought found

its way to his consciousness, he pushed it aside. This
wasn't about attraction. This was about beer.

Then she glanced up at him and a soft smile ghosted
across her lips, like she was actually glad to see him,
and Zeb forgot about beer. Instead, he openly stared at
her. Was she glad he was here? Was she able to look at
him and see not just a hidden bastard or a ruthless businessman but...

...him? Did she see *him*?

Zeb cleared his throat and shifted in his seat as Casey
gathered up the pint glasses. After a moment's consid-
eration, she set down one pair of glasses in front of the
tenderloin and another in front of the pasta. Zeb reached
for the closest glass, but she said, "Wait! If we're going
to do this right, I have to walk you through the beers."

"Is there a wrong way to drink beer?" he asked, pulling his hand back.

"Mr. Richards," she said, exasperated. "This is a tasting. We're not 'drinking beer.' I don't drink on the job—
none of us do. I sample. That's all this is."

She was scolding him, he realized. He was confident
that he'd never been scolded by an employee before.
The thought made him laugh—which got him some serious side-eye.

"Fine," he said, trying to restrain himself. When had
that become difficult to do? He was always restrained.
Always. "We'll do this your way."

He'd told Jamal the truth. He should never underestimate Casey Johnson.

She went back behind his bar and filled more half-
pint glasses, twenty in all. Each pair was placed in front
of a different dish. And the whole time, she was quiet.

Silence was a negotiating tactic and, as such, one that
never worked on Zeb. Except...he felt himself getting

twitchy as he watched her focus on her work. The next thing he knew, he was volunteering information. "Four people in the marketing department have resigned," he announced into the silence. "You were right about that."

She shrugged, as if it were no big deal. "You gave a nice talk about family honor and a bunch of other stuff, but you didn't warn anyone that you were bringing in a new CMO. People were upset."

Was she upset? No, it didn't matter, he told himself. He wasn't in this business for the touchy-feely. He was in it to make money. Well, that and to get revenge against the Beaumonts.

So, with that firmly in mind, he said, "The position was vacant. And Daniel's brilliant when it comes to campaigns. I have no doubt the skills he learned in politics will apply to beer, as well." But even as he said it, he wondered why he felt the need to explain his managerial decisions to her.

Evidently, she wondered the same thing, as she held up her hands in surrender. "Hey, you don't have to justify it to me. Although it might have been a good idea to justify it to the marketing department."

She was probably right—but he didn't want to admit that, so he changed tactics. "How about your department? Anyone there decide I was the final straw?" As he asked it, he realized what he really wanted to know was if *she'd* decided he was the final straw.

What the hell was this? He didn't care what his employees thought about him. He never had. All he cared about was that people knew their jobs and did them well. Results—that was what he cared about. This was business, not a popularity contest.

Or it had been, he thought as Casey smirked at him when she took her seat.

"My people are nervous, but that's to be expected. The ones who've hung in this long don't like change. They keep hoping that things will go back to the way they were," she said, catching his eye. No, that was a hedge. She already *had* his eye because he couldn't stop staring at her. "Or some reasonable facsimile thereof. A new normal, maybe. But no, I haven't had anyone quit on me."

A new normal. He liked that. "Good. I don't want you to be understaffed again."

She paused and then cleared her throat. When she looked up at him again, he felt the ground shift under his feet. She was gazing at him with something he so desperately wanted to think was appreciation. Why did he need her approval so damned bad?

"Thank you," she said softly. "I mean, I get that owning the company is part of your birthright, I guess, but this place..." She looked around as her voice trailed off with something that Zeb recognized—longing.

It was as if he were seeing another woman—one younger, more idealistic. A version of Casey that must have somehow found her way to the Beaumont Brewery years ago. Had she gotten the job through her father or an uncle? An old family friend?

Or had she walked into this company and, in her normal assertive way, simply demanded a job and refused to take no for an answer?

He had a feeling that was it.

He wanted to know what she was doing here—what this place meant to her and why she'd risked so much to defend it. Because they both knew that he could have fired her already. Being without a brewmaster for a day or a week would have been a problem, but problems were what he fixed.

But he hadn't fired her. She'd pushed him and challenged him and…and he liked that. He liked that she wasn't afraid of him. Which didn't make any sense— fear and intimidation were weapons he deployed easily and often to get what he wanted, the way he wanted it. Almost every other employee in this company had backed down in the face of his memos and decrees. But not *this* employee.

Not Casey.

"Okay," she announced in a tone that made it clear she wasn't going to finish her earlier statement. She produced a tablet from her lab-coat pocket and sat to his right. "Let's get started."

They went through each of the ten Beaumont beers, one at a time. "As you taste each one," she said without looking at him, "think about the flavors as they hit your tongue."

He coughed. "The…flavors?"

She handed him a pint glass and picked up the other for herself. "Drinking beer isn't just chugging to get drunk," she said in a voice that made it sound like she was praying, almost. She held her glass up and gazed at the way the light filtered through the beer. Zeb knew he should do the same—but he couldn't. He was watching her.

"Drinking beer fulfills each of the senses. Every detail contributes to the full experience," she said in that voice that was serious yet also…wistful. "How does the color make you feel?" She brought the glass back to her lips—but she didn't drink. Instead, her eyes drifted shut as she inhaled deeply. "What does it smell like—and how do the aromas affect the taste? How does it feel in your mouth?"

Her lips parted and, fascinated, Zeb watched as she

tipped the glass back and took a drink. Her eyelashes fluttered in what looked to him like complete and total satisfaction. Once she'd swallowed, she sighed. "So we'll rate each beer on a scale of one to five."

Did she have any idea how sensual she looked right now? Did she look like that when she'd been satisfied in bed? Or was it just the beer that did that to her? If he leaned over and touched his fingertips to her cheek to angle her chin up so he could press his lips against hers, would she let him?

"Mr. Richards?"

"What?" Zeb shook back to himself to find that Casey was staring at him with amusement.

"Ready?"

"Yes," he said because, once again, that was the truth. He'd thought he'd been ready to take over this company—but until right then, he hadn't been sure he was ready for someone like Casey Johnson.

They got to work, sipping each beer and rating it accordingly. Amazingly, Zeb was able to focus on the beer—which was good. He could not keep staring at his brewmaster like some love-struck puppy. He was Zeb Richards, for God's sake.

"I've always preferred the Rocky Top," Zeb told her, pointedly sampling—not drinking—the stalwart of the Beaumont product line. "But the Rocky Top Light tastes like dishwater."

Casey frowned at this and made a note on her tablet. "I'd argue with you, but you're right. However, it remains one of our bestsellers among women aged twenty-one to thirty-five and is one of our top overall sellers."

That was interesting. "It's the beer we target toward women and you don't like it?"

She looked up at him sharply and he could almost

hear her snapping, *Women are not interchangeable*. But she didn't. Instead, in as polite a voice as he'd ever heard from her, she said, "People drink beer for different reasons," while she made notes. "I don't want to sacrifice taste for something as arbitrary as calorie count."

"Can you make it better?"

That got her attention. "We've used the same formula for... Well, since the '80s, I think. You'd want to mess with that?"

He didn't lean forward, no matter how much he wanted to. Instead, he kept plenty of space between them. "There's always room for improvement, don't you think? I'm not trapped by the past." But the moment he said it, he wondered how true that was. "Perhaps one of your experiments can be an improved light-beer recipe."

She held his gaze, her lips curved into a slight smile. It was disturbing how much he liked her meeting his challenges straight on like that. "I'll do that."

They went through the rest of the beers and, true to her word, Zeb couldn't have said that he'd drunk enough to even get a slight buzz. Finally, as they'd eaten the last of their cupcakes, he leaned back and said, "So what are we missing?"

She surprised him then. She picked up what was left of her Rocky Top and took a long drink. "Look—here's the thing about our current product line. It's fine. It's... serviceable."

He notched an eyebrow at her. "It gets the job done?"

"Exactly. But when we lost Percheron Drafts, we lost the IPA, the stout—the bigger beers with bolder tastes. We lost seasonal beers—the summer shandy and the fall Oktoberfest beers. What we've got now is basic. I'd love to get us back to having one or two spotlight beers

that we could rotate in and out." She got a wistful look
on her face. "It's hard to see that here, though."

"What do you mean?"

"I mean, look at this." She swept her hand out, encom-
passing the remains of their lunch. *"This.* Most people
who drink our beer don't do so in the luxury of a private
office with a catered four-course meal. They drink a beer
at a game or on their couch, with a burger or a brat."

Suddenly, a feeling he'd gotten earlier—that she
hadn't approved of the setup—got stronger. "What about
you? Where do you drink your beer?"

"Me? Oh. I have season tickets to the Rockies. My
dad and I go to every home game we can. Have you done
that?" He shook his head. "You should. I've learned a
lot about what people like just standing in line to get a
beer at the game. I talk with the beer guys—that sort
of thing."

"A ball game?" He must have sounded doubtful, because she nodded encouragingly. "I can get a box."

"Really?" She rolled her eyes. "That's not how people drink beer. Here. I'll tell you what—there's a game
tomorrow night at seven, against the Braves. My dad
can't go. You can use his ticket. Come with me and see
what I mean."

He stared at her. It didn't sound like a come-on—
but then, he'd never gotten quite so turned on watching
another woman drink beer before. Nothing was typical
when it came to this woman. "You're serious, aren't you?"

"Of course."

He had a feeling she was right. He'd spent years learning about the corporate workings of the brewery from a
distance. If he was going to run this place as his own—
and he was—then he needed to understand not just the
employees but their customers.

Besides, the Braves were his team. And beyond that, this was a chance to see Casey outside work. Suddenly, that seemed important—vital, even. What was she like when she wasn't wearing a lab coat? He shouldn't have wanted to know. But he did anyway. "It's a da—" Casey's eyes got huge and her cheeks flushed and Zeb remembered that he wasn't having a drink with a pretty girl at a bar. He was at the brewery and he was the CEO. He had to act like it. "Company outing," he finished, as if that was what he'd meant to say all along.

She cleared her throat. "Covert market research, if you will." Her gaze flickered over his Hugo Boss suit. "And try to blend, maybe?"

He gave her a level stare, but she was unaffected. "Tomorrow at seven."

"Gate C." She gathered up her tablet. "We'll talk then."

He nodded and watched her walk out. Once the door was firmly closed behind her, he allowed himself to grin.

Whether she liked it or not, they had a date.

Six

Casey really didn't know what to expect as she stood near the C gate at Coors Field. She'd told Richards to blend but she was having trouble picturing him in anything other than a perfectly tailored suit.

Not that she was spending a lot of time thinking about him in a perfectly tailored suit. She wasn't. Just because he was the epitome of masculine grace and style, that was no reason at all to think about her boss.

Besides, she didn't even go for guys in suits. She usually went for blue-collar guys, the kind who kicked back on the weekend with a bunch of beer to watch sports. That was what she was comfortable with, anyway. And comfort was good, right?

And anyway, even if she did go for guys in suits—which she did not—she was positive she didn't go for guys like Richards. It wasn't that he was African American. She had looked him up, and one of the few pictures of him on the internet was him standing with a woman named Emily Richards in Atlanta, Georgia, outside a Doo-Wop and Pop! Salon. It was easy to see the resemblance between them—she was clearly his mother.

No, her not going for guys like Richards had nothing to do with race and everything to do with the fact that he was way too intense for her. The way he'd stared at her over the lip of his pint glass during their tasting lunch? Intensity personified, and as thrilling as it had been, it wasn't what she needed on her time off. Really. She had enough intensity at work. That was why she always went for low-key guys—guys who were fun for a weekend but never wanted anything more than that.

Right. So it was settled. She absolutely did not go for someone like Richards in a suit. Good.

"Casey?"

Casey whipped around and found herself staring not at a businessman in a suit—and also not at someone who was blending. Zeb Richards stood before her in a white T-shirt with bright red raglan sleeves. She was vaguely aware that he had on a hat and reasonably certain that he was wearing blue jeans, but she couldn't tear her eyes away from his chest. The T-shirt molded to his body in a way that his power suit hadn't. Her mouth went dry.

Good God.

That was as far as her brain got, because she tried to drag her eyes away from his chest—and made it exactly as far as his biceps.

Sweet mother of pearl was the last coherent thought she had as she tried to take in the magnitude of those biceps.

And when thinking stopped, she was left with nothing but her physical response. Her nipples tightened and her skin flushed—*flushed*, dammit, like she was an innocent schoolgirl confronted with a man's body for the first time. All that flushing left her shaken and sweaty and completely unable to look away. It took all of her self-control not to lean over and put a hand to that chest and feel what she was looking at. Because she'd be willing to bet a lot of money that he *felt* even better than he looked.

"...Casey?" he said with what she hoped like hell was humor in his voice. "Hello?"

"What?" Crap, she'd been caught gaping at him. "Right. Hi." Dumbly, she held up the tickets.

"Is there something wrong with my shirt?" He asked, looking down. Then he grasped the hem of the shirt and pulled it out so he could see the front, which had a graphic of the Braves' tomahawk on it. But when he did that, the neck of the shirt came down and Casey caught a glimpse of his collarbones.

She had no idea collarbones could be sexy. This was turning out to be quite an educational evening and it had only just begun. How on earth was she going to get through the rest of it without doing something humiliating, like *drooling* on the man?

Because drooling was off-limits. Everything about him was off-limits.

This was not a date. Nope. He was her boss, for crying out loud.

"Um, no. I mean, I didn't actually figure you would show up in the opposing team's shirt." Finally—and way too late for decency's sake—she managed to look up into his face. He was smiling at her, as if he knew exactly what kind of effect he had on her. Dammit. This was the other reason she didn't go for men like him. They were too cocky for their own good.

"That's all," she went on. "You don't exactly blend." She was pretty sure she was babbling.

"I'm from Atlanta, you know." He smirked at her and suddenly there it was—a luscious Southern accent that threatened to melt her. "Who did you think I was going to root for?" His gaze swept over her and Casey felt each and every hair on her body stand at attention. "I don't have anything purple," he went on when his gaze made it back to her face with something that looked a heck of a lot like approval.

She fought the urge to stand up straighter. She would not pose for him. This was not a date. She didn't care what he thought of her appearance. "We could fix that," she told him, waving at the T-shirt sellers hawking all sorts of Rockies gear. He scrunched his nose at her. "Or not," she said with a melodramatic sigh, trying to get her wits about her. "It's still better than a suit. Come on. We need to get in if we want to grab a beer before the game starts."

He looked around. People in purple hats and T-shirts were making their way inside and he was already getting a few funny looks. "This is literally your home turf. Lead on."

She headed toward the turnstiles. Zeb made a move toward one with a shorter line, but Casey put her hand on his arm. "This one," she told him, guiding him toward Joel's line.

"Why?"

"You'll see." At this cryptic statement, Zeb gave her a hard look. Oddly enough, it didn't carry as much weight as it might have if he'd been in a tie, surrounded by all the brewery history in his office. Instead, he looked almost...adorable.

Crap, this was bad. She absolutely couldn't be thinking of Zebadiah Richards as adorable. Or hot. Or... anything.

There might have been some grumbling following that statement, but Casey decided that she probably shouldn't get into a shouting match with him before they'd even gotten inside the stadium.

The line moved quickly and then Joel said, "Casey! There's my girl."

"Hey, Joel," she said, leaning over to give the old man a quick hug.

"Where's Carl?" Joel asked, eyeing Zeb behind her.

"Union meeting. Who do you think's going to win today?" She and Joel had the same conversation at nearly every game.

"You have to ask? The Braves are weak this season." Then he noticed Richards's shirt behind her and his easy smile twisted into a grimace of disapproval. He leaned over and grabbed two of the special promotion items—bobblehead dolls of the team. "Take one to your dad. I know he collects them."

"Aw, thanks, Joel. And give my best to Martha, okay?"

Joel gave a bobblehead to Richards, as well. "Good luck, fella," he muttered.

When they were several feet away, Richards said, "I see what you mean about blending. Do you want this?" He held out the bobblehead.

"I'm good. Two is my personal limit on these things. Give it to Jamal or something." She led him over to her favorite beer vendor. "Speaking of, where is Jamal? I thought you might bring him."

Honestly, she couldn't decide if she'd wanted Jamal to be here or not. If he had been, then maybe she'd have been able to focus on *not* focusing on Zeb a little better. Three was a crowd, after all.

But still…she was glad Zeb had come alone.

This time, he held back and waited until she picked the beer line. "He's still unpacking."

"Oh?" There were about six people in front of them. This game was going to be nowhere near a sellout. "So you really did move out here?"

"Of course." He slid her a side glance. "I said that at the press conference, you know."

They moved up a step in line. Casey decided that it was probably best not to admit that she hadn't been paying attention during the press conference. "So where are you guys at?"

"I bought a house over on Cedar Avenue. Jamal picked it out because he liked the kitchen."

Her eyes bugged out of her head. "You bought the mansion by the country club?"

"You know it?" He said it in such a casual way, as if buying the most expensive house in the Denver area were no biggie.

Well, maybe for him, it wasn't. Why was she surprised? She shouldn't have been. She wasn't. Someone like Zeb Richards would definitely plunk down nearly $10 million for a house and not think anything of it. "Yeah. My dad was hired to do some work there a couple years ago. He said it was an amazing house."

"I suppose it is." He didn't sound very convinced about this. But before Casey could ask him what he didn't like about the house, he went on, "What does your dad do? And I'm going to pay you back for his ticket. I'm sorry that I'm using it in his place."

She waved this away. "Don't worry about it. He really did have a union meeting tonight. He's an electrician. He does a lot of work in older homes—renovations and upgrading antique wiring. There's still a lot of knob-and-tube wiring in Denver, you know."

One corner of his mouth—not that she was staring at his mouth—curved up into a smile that was positively dangerous.

"What?" she said defensively—because if she didn't defend herself from that sly smile... Well, she didn't know what would happen. But it wouldn't be good.

In fact, it would be bad. The very best kind of bad.

"Nothing. I've just got to stop being surprised by you, that's all." They advanced another place in line. "What are we ordering?"

"Well, seeing as this is Coors Field, we really don't have too many options when it comes to beer. It's—shockingly—Coors."

"No!" he said in surprise. "Do they make beer?"

She stared at him. "Wait—was that a joke? Were you trying to be funny?"

That grin—oh, *hell*. "Depends. Did it work?"

No—well, yes, but *no*. No, she couldn't allow him to be a regular guy. If this "company outing" was going to stay strictly aboveboard, he could not suddenly develop a set of pecs *and* a sense of humor at the same time. She couldn't take it. "Mr. Richards—"

"Really, Casey," he said, cutting her off, "we're about to drink a competitor's beer outside of normal business hours at a game. Call me Zeb."

She was a strong woman. She was. She'd worked at the Beaumont Brewery for twelve years and during that time, she'd never once gotten involved with a coworker. She'd had to negotiate the fine line between "innocent flirting" and "sexual harassment" on too many occasions, but once she'd earned her place at the table, that had fallen away.

But this? Calling Richards by his first name? Buying beer with him at a ball game? Pointedly not staring at the way he filled out an officially licensed T-shirt? Listening to him crack jokes?

She simply wasn't that strong. This wasn't a company outing. It was starting to feel like a date.

They reached the cashier. "Casey!" Marco gave her a high five over the counter.

She could feel Zeb behind her. He wasn't touching her, but he was close enough that her skin was prickling. "Marco—what's the latest?"

"It happened, girl." Marco pointed to a neon sign over his head— one that proudly proclaimed they served Percheron Drafts.

Casey whistled. "You were right."

"I told you," he went on. "They cut a deal. You wanna try something? Their pale ale is good. Or is that not allowed? I heard you had a new boss there—another crazy Beaumont. Two of them, even!" He chuckled and shook his head in disbelief. "You think the Beaumonts knew their brother or half brother or whatever he is took over? I heard it might have been planned..."

It took everything Casey had not to look back over her shoulder at Zeb. Maybe she was reading too much into the situation, but she would put money on the fact that he wasn't grinning anymore. "I bet it was a hell of a surprise," she said, desperate to change the subject. "Give me the pale ale and—"

"Nachos, extra jalapeños?" He winked at her. "I'm on it."

"A *hell* of a surprise," Zeb whispered in her ear. The closeness of his voice was so unexpected that she jumped. But just then Marco came back with her order.

"Gotta say," Marco went on, ringing up her total, "it was good to see a brother up there, though. I mean...he was black, right?"

Behind her, Zeb made a noise that sounded like it was somewhere between a laugh and a choke. "It doesn't really matter," she said honestly as she handed over the cash, "as long as we get the beer right."

"Ah, that's what I like about you, Casey—a woman who knows her beer." He gave her a moony look, as if he were dazzled by beauty they both knew she didn't have. "It's not too late to marry me, you know that?"

Hand to God, Casey thought she heard Zeb growl behind her.

Okay, that was not the kind of noise a boss made when an employee engaged in chitchat with a— Well, Marco sold beer. So with a colleague of sorts. However, it was the sort of noise a man on a date made.

Not a date. *Not* a date.

For the first time, Marco seemed to notice the looming Braves fan behind her. "Come back and see me at the fifth?" Marco pleaded, keeping a cautious eye on Zeb.

"You know I will. And have Kenny bring me a stout in the third, okay?" She and Dad didn't have the superexpensive seats where people took her order and delivered it to her. But Kenny the beer vendor would bring them another beer in the third and again in the seventh—and not the beer he hawked to everyone else.

She got her nachos and her beer and moved off to the side. It was then she noticed that Zeb's eyes hadn't left her.

A shiver of heat went through her because Zeb's gaze was intense. He looked at her like…like she didn't even know what. She wasn't sure she wanted to find out, because what if he could see right through her?

What if he could see how much she was attracted to *him*?

This was a bad idea. She was on a date with her

brand-new CEO and he was hot and funny and brooding all at once and they were drinking their chief competitor's product and…

Zeb glanced over at her as he paid for his food and shot another warm grin at her.

And she was in trouble. Big, *big* trouble.

Seven

Zeb followed Casey to the seats. He tried his best to keep his gaze locked on the swinging ponytail that hung out the back of her Rockies hat—and not on her backside.

That was proving to be quite a challenge, though, because her backside was a sight to behold. Her jeans clung to her curves in all the right ways. Why hadn't he noticed that before?

Oh, yeah—the lab coat.

Which hadn't shown him the real woman. But this? A bright young woman with hips and curves who was friends with everyone and completely at home in the male bastion of a baseball stadium?

Who'd said—out loud—that it didn't matter if Zeb was black or not?

She turned suddenly and he snapped his gaze back up to her face. "Here," she said, notching an eyebrow at him and gesturing toward a nearly empty row. "Seats nine and ten."

They were eight rows off the first baseline, right behind the dugout. "Great seats," he told her. "I didn't bring my glove."

She snorted as she worked her way down the row. "Definitely keep your eyes on the ball here. You never know."

He made his way to seat nine. There weren't many people around, but he had a feeling that if there had been, they'd all have known Casey.

"What did you get?" she asked once they were seated.

"The Percheron lager."

"Oh, that's such a nice beer," she said with a wistful sigh.

"Yeah?" He held out his plastic collector's cup to her. "Have a drink."

She looked at him for a long moment and then leaned over and pressed her lips against the rim of his cup. Fascinated, he watched as her mouth opened and she took a sip.

Heat shot through his body, driving his pulse to a sudden pounding in his veins. It only got worse when she leaned back just enough that she could sweep her tongue over her lips, getting every last drop of beer.

Damn. Watching Casey Johnson drink beer was almost a holy experience.

Greedy was not a word he embraced. *Greedy* implied a lack of control—stupid mistakes and rash consequences. He was not a greedy person. He was methodical and detailed and careful. Always.

But right now he wanted. He wanted her lips to drink him in like she'd drunk the beer. He wanted her tongue to sweep over his lips with that slow intensity. God help him, he wanted her to savor him. And if that made him greedy, then so be it.

So, carefully, he turned the cup around and put his lips where hers had been. Her eyes darkened as he drank. "You're right," he said, the taste of the beer and of Casey mixing on his tongue. "It's a beautiful beer."

Her breath caught and her cheeks colored, throwing the spiderweb scar on her cheek into high relief. And then, heaven help him, she leaned toward him. She could have leaned away, turned away—done something to put distance between them. She could have made it clear that she didn't want him at all.

But she didn't. She felt it, too, this connection between them. Her lips parted ever so slightly and she leaned forward, close enough for him to touch. Close enough for him to take a sip.

The crack of a bat and the crowd cheering snapped his attention away. His head was buzzing as if he'd chugged a six-pack.

"Did they score?" Casey asked, shaking off her confusion. Then she did lean away, settling back into her chair.

Zeb immediately tamped down that rush of lust. They were in public, for God's sake. This wasn't like him. He didn't go for women like Casey—she was the walking embodiment of a tomboy. Women he favored were cultured and refined, elegant and beautiful. They were everything he'd spent his life trying to become.

Accepted. Welcomed. They belonged in the finest social circles.

Women he liked would never sit on the first-base side and hope to catch a fly ball. They wouldn't appreciate the finer points of an IPA or a lager. They wouldn't be proud of a father who was an electrician and they wouldn't be caught dead in a baseball hat—but Casey?

She was rough-and-tumble and there was a decent

chance she could best him in an arm-wrestling contest. There shouldn't have been a single thing about her that he found attractive.

So why couldn't he stop staring at her?

Because he couldn't. "Did you want to try mine? I helped develop it."

He leaned close to her and waited until she held the cup up to his lips. He couldn't tear his gaze away from hers, though. He saw when she sucked in a gasp when he ran his tongue over the rim before he reached up and placed his palm on the bottom of the cup, slowly tilting it back. The bitterness of the brew washed over him.

It wasn't like he'd never had an IPA before. But this was different. He could taste the beer, sure. But there was something about the brightness of the hops, the way it danced on his tongue—it tasted like...

Like her.

"It's really good," he told her. "You developed it?"

"I did. Percheron was, um…"

"It's all right," he said, leaning back. "I don't think if you say Chadwick's name three times, he magically appears. I understand the company's history."

"Oh. Okay." Damn, that blush only made her look prettier. "Well, Percheron was Chadwick's pet project and I'd been there for almost ten years by that point and he let me help. I was the assistant brewmaster for Percheron when he…" Her voice trailed off and she turned to face the field. "When he left."

Zeb mulled that over a bit. "Why didn't you go with him?"

"Because the brewmaster did and Chadwick wanted to actually make the beer himself. Percheron is a much smaller company."

He heard the sorrow in her voice. She'd wanted to go with her old boss—that much was clear.

Then she turned a wide smile in his direction. "Plus, if I'd left the brewery, I'd still be an assistant brewmaster. I'm the brewmaster for the third-largest brewery in the country because I outlasted everyone else. Attrition isn't the best way to get a promotion but it was effective nonetheless."

"That's what you wanted?"

She looked smug, the cat that had all the cream to herself. His pulse picked up another notch. "That's what I wanted."

Underneath that beer-drinking, sports-loving exterior, Zeb had to admire the sheer ambition of this woman. Not just anyone would set out to be the first—or youngest—female brewmaster in the country.

But Casey would. And she'd accomplished her goal.

Zeb took a long drink of his lager. It was good, too. "So, Percheron Drafts was your baby?"

"It was Chadwick's, but I was Igor to his Frankenstein."

He laughed—a deep, long sound that shocked him. That kind of laugh wasn't dignified or intimidating. Zeb didn't allow himself to laugh like that, because he was a CEO and he had to instill fear in the hearts of his enemies.

Except…except he was at a ball game, kicking back with a pretty girl and a beer, and his team was at the plate and the weather was warm and it was…

…perfect.

"So I want you to make Percheron—or something like it—your baby again."

Even though he wasn't looking at Casey, he felt the current of tension pass through her. "What?"

"I understand Chadwick started Percheron Drafts to compete with the explosion of craft breweries. And we lost that. I don't want to throw in that particular towel just yet. So, you want to try experimental beers? That's what I want you to do, too."

She turned to face him again, and dammit, she practically glowed. Maybe it was just the setting sun, but he didn't think so. She looked so happy—and he'd put that look on her face.

"Thank you," she said in a voice so quiet that he had to lean forward to hear it. "When you started, I thought…"

He smirked. She'd thought many things, he'd be willing to bet—and precious few of them had been good.

"Can you keep a secret?" he asked.

Her lips twisted in what he hoped was an amused grin. "How many times are you going to ask me that?"

"I'm not such a bad guy," he went on, ignoring her sass. "But don't tell anyone."

She mimed locking her lips and throwing the key over her shoulder.

Somewhere in the background, a ball game was happening. And he loved sports, he really did. But he had questions. He'd learned a little more about what kind of man his half brother was but that was just the tip of the iceberg.

But the spell of the moment had been broken. They settled in and watched the game. Sure enough, by the third inning, a grizzled older man came around with a stout for Casey. Zeb didn't warrant that level of personal service—certainly not in the opposing team's colors. As he sipped the flagship beer of his second-largest competitor, he decided it was…serviceable. Just as Casey had described their own beer.

A fact that was only highlighted when Casey let him sip her stout. "It's going to be tough to beat," he said with a sigh as she took a long drink.

For the first time, he had a doubt about what he was doing. He'd spent years—*years*—plotting and scheming to get his birthright back. He was a Beaumont and he was going to make sure everyone knew it.

But now, sitting here and drinking his half brother's beer…

He was reminded once again what he didn't have. Chadwick had literally decades to learn about the business of the brewery and the craft of beer. And Zeb—well, he knew a hell of a lot about business. But he hadn't learned it at his father's knee. Beer was his birthright—but he couldn't whip up his own batch if his life depended on it.

Casey patted his arm. "We don't have to beat it." She paused and he heard her clear her throat. "Unless…"

"Unless what?"

She looked into her cup. It was half-empty. "Unless you're out to destroy Percheron Drafts."

That was what she said. What she was really asking was, *Are you out to destroy the other Beaumonts?* It was a fair question.

"Because that's kind of a big thing," she went on in a quiet voice, looking anywhere but at him. "I don't know how many people would be supportive of that. At work, I mean." She grimaced. "There might be a lot of resignations."

She wouldn't be supportive of that. She would quit. She'd quit and go elsewhere because even though her first loyalty was to herself and then the beer, the Beaumont family was pretty high on her list.

Again, he wondered how she'd come to this point in

her life. The youngest female brewmaster at the third-largest brewery in the country. He might not know the details of her story, but he recognized this one simple truth: she was who she was in large part because the Beaumonts had given her a chance. Because she'd been Igor to Chadwick Beaumont's Frankenstein.

She'd give up her dream job if it came down to a choice between the Beaumont Brewery and Percheron Drafts.

This thought made him more than a little uncomfortable because he could try to explain how it was all business, how this was a battle for market share between two corporations and corporations were not people, but none of that was entirely true.

If he forced her to choose between the Beaumonts and himself, she'd choose them over him.

"There was a time," he said in a quiet voice, "when I wanted to destroy them."

Her head snapped up. "What?"

"I used to hate them. They had everything and I had nothing." Nothing but a bitter mother and a head for business.

"But…" She stared at him, her mouth open wide. "But *look* at you. You're rich and powerful and hot and you did that all on your own." He blinked at her, but she didn't seem to be aware of what she'd just said, because she went on without missing a beat, "Some of those Beaumonts— I mean, don't get me wrong— I like them. But they're more than a little messed up. Trust me. I was around them long enough to see how the public image wasn't reality. Phillip was a hot mess and Chadwick was miserable and Frances… I mean, they had everything handed to them and it didn't make them any happier." She shook her head and slouched back in her seat.

And suddenly, he felt he had to make her understand that this wasn't about his siblings, because he was an adult and he realized now what he hadn't known as a child—that his siblings were younger than he was and probably knew only what the rest of the world did about Hardwick Beaumont.

"Casey," he said. She looked at him and he could see how nervous she was. "I was going to say that I used to hate them—but I don't. How could I? I don't know them and I doubt any of them knew a thing about me before that press conference. I'm not out to destroy them and I'm not out to destroy Percheron Drafts. It's enough that I have the brewery."

She looked at him then—really looked at him. Zeb started to squirm in his seat, because, honestly? He didn't know what she saw. Did she see a man who made sure his mom had a booming business and his best friend had a good-paying job he loved? Did she see a son who'd never know his father?

Or—worse—would she see a boy rejected by his family, a man who wasn't black and wasn't white but who occupied a no-man's-land in the middle? Would she see an impostor who'd decided he was a Beaumont, regardless of how true it might actually be?

He didn't want to know what she saw. Because quite unexpectedly, Casey Johnson's opinion had become important to him and he didn't want to know if she didn't approve of him.

So he quickly changed the subject. "Tell me…" he said, keeping his voice casual as he turned his attention back to the field. He didn't even know what inning it was anymore. There—the scoreboard said fourth. The home team was at the plate and they already had two outs. Almost halfway done with this corporate outing. "Does that happen often?"

"What? Your boss admitting that he's not a total bastard?"

Zeb choked on his beer. "Actually, I meant that guy proposing to you."

"Who, Marco?" She snorted. "He proposes every time I see him. And since I have season tickets…"

"What does your dad think of that?"

That got him a serious side-eye. "First off, Marco's joking. Second off, my father is many things, but he's not my keeper. And third off—why do you care?"

"I don't," he answered quickly. Maybe too quickly. "Just trying to get a fuller picture of the one person responsible for keeping my company afloat."

She snorted as a pop fly ended the inning. "Come on," she said, standing and stretching. "Let's go."

Slowly, they worked their way out of the seats and back to the concession stands. He got a stout for himself and Casey got a porter. Marco flirted shamelessly but this time, Zeb focused on Casey. She smiled and joked, but at no point did she look at the young man the way she'd looked at him earlier. She didn't blush and she didn't lean toward Marco.

There was no heat. She was exactly as she appeared— a friendly tomboy. The difference between this woman and the one who'd blushed so prettily back in the seats, whose eyes had dilated and who'd leaned toward him with desire writ large on her face—that difference was huge.

With more beer and more nachos, they made their way back to their seats. As odd as it was, Zeb was having trouble remembering the last time he'd taken a night off like this. Yeah, they were still talking beer and competitors but...

But he was having fun. He was three beers in and even though he wasn't drunk—not even close—he was more relaxed than he'd been in a long time. It'd been months of watching and waiting to make sure all the final pieces of the puzzle were in place, and he was pretty sure he hadn't stopped to appreciate all that he'd accomplished.

Well, sort of relaxed. There was something else the beer vendor—Marco—had said that itched at the back of Zeb's mind.

"Did you mean what you said?" he blurted out. Hmm. Maybe he was a little more buzzed than he thought.

There was a longish pause before she said, "About?"

"That it didn't matter if I was black or not." Because it always mattered. *Always.* He was either "exotic" because he had an African American mother and green eyes or he was black and a borderline thug. He never got to be just a businessman. He was always a black businessman.

It was something white people never even thought about. But he always had that extra hurdle to clear. He didn't get to make mistakes, because even one would be proof that he couldn't cut it.

Not that he was complaining. He'd learned his lesson early in life—no one was going to give him a single damned thing. Not his father, not his family, not the world. Everything he wanted out of this life, he had to take. Being a black businessman made him a tougher negotiator, a sharper investor.

He wanted the brewery and the legitimacy that came with it. He wanted his father's approval and, short of that, he wanted the extended Beaumont family to know who he was.

He was Zebadiah Richards and he would not be ignored.

Not that Casey was ignoring him. She'd turned to look at him again—and for the second time tonight, he thought she was seeing more than he wanted her to.

Dammit, he should have kept his mouth shut.

"You tell me—does it matter?"

"It shouldn't." More than anything, he wanted it to not matter.

She shrugged. "Then it doesn't."

He should let this go. He had his victory—of sorts—and besides, what did it matter if she looked at him and saw a black CEO or just a CEO?

Or even, a small voice in the back of his mind whispered, *something other than a CEO? Something more?*

But he couldn't revel in his small victory. He needed to know—was she serious or was she paying lip service because he was her boss? "So you're saying it doesn't matter that my mother spent the last thirty-seven years doing hair in a black neighborhood in Atlanta? That I went to a historically black college? That people have pulled out of deals with me because no matter how light skinned I am, I'll never be white enough?"

He hadn't meant to say all of that. But the only thing worse than his skin color being the first—and sometimes only—thing people used to define him was when people tried to explain they didn't "see color." They meant well—he knew that—but the truth was, it *did* matter. He'd made his first fortune for his mother, merchandising a line of weave and braid products for upper-class African American consumers that had, thanks to millennials, reached a small level of crossover success in the mainstream market. When people said they didn't see color, they effectively erased the blackness from his life.

Being African American wasn't who he was—but it was a part of him. And for some reason, he needed her to understand that.

He had her full attention now. Her gaze swept over him and he felt his muscles tighten, almost as if he were in fight-or-flight mode. And he didn't run. He never ran.

"Will our beer suddenly taste black?" she asked.

"Don't be ridiculous. We might broaden our marketing reach, though."

She tilted her head. "All I care about is the beer."

"Seriously?"

She sighed heavily. "Let me ask you this—when you drink a Rocky Top beer, does it taste feminine?"

"You're being ridiculous."

That got him a hard glare. A glare he probably deserved, but still. "Zeb, I don't know what you want me to say here. Of course it matters, because that's your life. That's who you are. But I can't hold that against you, and anyway, why would I want to? You didn't ask for that. You can't change that, any more than I can change the fact that my mother died in a car accident when I was two and left me with this," she said, pointing to her scarred cheek, "and my father raised me as best he could—and that meant beer and sports and changing my own oil in my car. We both exist in a space that someone else is always going to say we shouldn't—so what? We're here. We like beer." She grinned hugely at him. "Get used to it."

Everything around him went still. He wasn't breathing. He wasn't sure his heart was even beating. He didn't hear the sounds of the game or the chatter of the fans around them.

His entire world narrowed to her. All he could see and hear and feel—because dammit, she was close enough that their forearms kept touching, their knees bumping—was Casey.

It mattered. *He* mattered. No conditions, no exceptions. He mattered just the way he was.

Had anyone ever said as much to him? Even his own mother? No. What had mattered was what he wasn't. He wasn't a Beaumont. He wasn't legitimate. He wasn't white.

Something in his chest unclenched, something he'd never known he was holding tightly. Something that felt like...

...peace.

He dimly heard a loud crack and then Casey jolted and shouted, "Look out!"

Zeb moved without thinking. He was in a weird space—everything happened as if it were in slow motion. His head turned like he was stuck in molasses, like the baseball was coming directly for him at a snail's pace. He reached out slowly and caught the fly ball a few inches from Casey's shoulder.

The pain of the ball smacking into his palm snapped him out of it. "Damn," he hissed, shaking his hand as a smattering of applause broke out from the crowd. "That hurt."

Casey turned her face toward him, her eyes wide. There was an unfamiliar feeling trying to make its way to the forefront of Zeb's mind as he stared into her beautiful light brown eyes, one he couldn't name. He wasn't sure he wanted to.

"You caught the ball bare-handed," she said, her voice breathy. Then, before Zeb could do anything, she looked down to where he was still holding the foul ball. She moved slowly when she pulled the ball out of his palm and stared at his reddening skin. Lightly, so lightly it almost hurt, she traced her fingertip over the palm of his hand. "Did it hurt?"

That unnamed, unfamiliar feeling was immediately buried under something that was much easier to identify—lust. "Not much," he said, and he didn't miss the way his voice dropped. He had a vague sense that he wasn't being entirely honest—it hurt enough to snap him out of his reverie. But with her stroking his skin...

...everything felt just fine.

And it got a whole lot better when she lifted his hand and pressed a kiss against his palm. "Do we need to go and get some ice or...?"

Or? Or sounded good. *Or* sounded great. "Only if you want to," he told her, shifting so that he was cupping her cheek in his hand. "Your call."

Because he wasn't talking about ice. Or beer. Or baseball.

He dragged his thumb over the top of her cheek as she leaned into his touch. She lifted her gaze to his face and for a second, he thought he'd taken it too far. He'd misread the signals and she would storm out of the stadium just like she'd stormed out of his office that first day. She would quit and he would deserve it.

Except she didn't. "I live a block away," she said, and he heard the slightest shiver in her voice, felt a matching shiver in her body. "If that's what you need."

What did he need? It should've been a simple question with a simple answer—her. Right now he needed her.

But there was nothing simple about Casey Johnson and everything got much more complicated when she pressed his hand closer to her cheek.

For the first time in a very long time, Zeb was at a loss for words. It wasn't like him. When it came to women, he'd always known what to say, when to say it. Growing up in a hair salon had given him plenty of opportunity to learn what women wanted, what they needed and where those two things met and when they didn't. *Smooth*, more than one of his paramours had called him. And he was. Smooth and cool and…cold. Distant. Reserved.

He didn't feel any of those things right now. All he could feel was the heat that flowed between her skin and his.

"I need to cool down," he told her, only dimly aware that that was not the smoothest line he had ever uttered. But he didn't have anything else right now. His hand was throbbing and his blood was throbbing and his dick— that, especially, was throbbing. Everything about him was hot and hard, and even though he was no innocent wallflower, it all felt strange and new. He felt strange and new because Casey saw him in a way that no one else did.

He didn't know what was going to happen. Even if all she did was take him back to her place and stick some ice on his hand, that was fine, too. He was not going to be *that* guy.

Still, when she said, "Come with me," Zeb hoped that he could do exactly that.

Eight

Was she seriously doing this? Taking Zeb Richards back to her apartment?

Well, obviously, she was. She was holding his not-wounded hand and leading him away from the stadium. So there really wasn't any question about what was happening here.

This was crazy. Absolutely crazy. She shouldn't be taking him back to her apartment, she shouldn't be holding his hand and she most especially shouldn't be thinking about what would happen when they got there.

But she was. She was thinking about peeling that T-shirt off him and running her hands over his muscles and...

His fingers tightened around hers and he pulled her a step closer to him. He was hot in a way that she hadn't anticipated. Heat radiated off his body, so much so that she thought the edges around his skin might waver like a mirage if she looked at him head-on.

She swallowed and tried to think of things she had done that were crazier than this. Walking into the brewery and demanding a job—that had been pretty bold. And there was that summer fling with a rookie on the Rockies—but he'd been traded to Seattle in the off-season and their paths didn't cross anymore. That had been wild and a hell of a lot of fun.

But nothing came close to bringing the new CEO of the Beaumont Brewery home with her. And the thing was, she wasn't entirely sure what had changed. One moment, they'd been talking—okay, flirting. They'd been flirting. But it seemed…innocent, almost.

And then she had told him about her mom dying in a car accident and he caught that ball before it hit her—she still didn't know how the hell he'd managed that—and everything had changed.

And now she was bringing her boss home with her.

Except that wasn't true, either. It was—but it also wasn't. She wasn't bringing home the ice-cold man in a suit who'd had the sheer nerve to call a press conference and announce that he was one of the Beaumont bastards. That man was fascinating—but that wasn't who was holding her hand.

She was bringing Zeb home. The son of a hairdresser who liked baseball and didn't look at her like she was his best friend or, worse, one of the guys.

She was probably going to regret this. But she didn't care right now. Because Zeb was looking at her and she felt beautiful, sensual, desirable and so very feminine. And that was what she wanted, even if it was for only a little while.

They made it back to her apartment. She led him to the elevator. Even standing here, holding his hand, felt off. This was the part she was never any good at. Sitting in front of the game with beers in their hands—yes. Then she could talk and flirt and be herself. But when she wanted to be that beautiful, desirable creature men craved...she froze up. It was not a pleasant sensation.

The elevator doors opened and they stepped inside. Casey hit the button for the fifth floor and the door slid shut. The next thing she knew, Zeb had pressed into the back of the elevator. His body held hers against the wall—but other than that, he didn't touch her and he didn't kiss her.

"Tell me I didn't read you wrong back there," he said, his voice low and husky. It sent a shiver down her spine and one corner of his mouth curved up into a cocky half smile. He lifted one hand and moved as if he were going to touch her face—but didn't. "Casey..."

This was her out—if she wanted it. She could laugh it off and say, *Gosh, how's your hand?* And that'd be that.

"You didn't," she whispered.

Then he did touch her. He cupped her cheek in his hand and tilted her head up. "Do I really matter to you?" he whispered against her skin. "Or are you just here for the beer?"

If Casey allowed herself to admit that she had thought of this moment before right now—and she wasn't necessarily admitting to anything—she hadn't pictured this. She assumed Zeb would pin her against the wall or his desk and seduce her ruthlessly. Not that there was anything wrong with being seduced ruthlessly—it had its place in the world and her fantasies.

But this tenderness? She didn't quite know what to make of it.

"At work tomorrow," she said, squinting her eyes shut because the last thing she wanted to think about was the number of company policies she was about to break, "it's about the beer." She felt Zeb tense and then there was a little bit of space between their bodies as he stepped away from her.

Oh, no. She wasn't going to let him go. Not when she had him right where she wanted him. She locked her arms around his neck and pulled him back into her. "But we're not at work right now, are we?"

"Right," he agreed. Her body molded to his and his to hers. "Nothing at work. But outside of work…"

Then he kissed her. And that? *That* bordered on a ruthless seduction because it wasn't a gentle, tentative touch of two lips meeting and exploring for the first time. No, when he kissed her, he *claimed* her. The heat from his mouth seared her, and suddenly, she was too hot—for the elevator, for her clothes, for any of it.

"Tell me what you want," he said again when his lips trailed over her jaw and down her neck.

This was crazy—but the very best kind of crazy. Carte blanche with someone as strong and hot and masculine as Zeb Richards? Oh, yeah, this was the stuff of fantasies.

She started to say what she always said. "Tell me—"

Just then, the elevator came to a stop and the door opened. Damn. She'd forgotten they weren't actually in her apartment yet.

Zeb pushed back as she fumbled around for her keys. Hopefully, that would be the last interruption for at least the next hour. Quickly, she led him down the hall. "It's not much," she explained, suddenly nervous all over again. Her studio apartment was certainly not one of the grand old mansions of Denver.

She unlocked the door. Zeb followed her in, and once the door was shut behind them, he put his hands on her hips. "Nice place," he said, and she could tell from the tone of his voice that he wasn't looking at her apartment at all. "Beautiful views," he added, and then he was pulling the hem of her shirt, lifting it until he accidentally knocked her hat off her head. The whole thing got hung up on her ponytail and, laughing, she reached around to help untangle it.

"What would you like me to tell you?" As he spoke, his lips were against the base of her neck, his teeth skimming over her sensitive skin.

She couldn't stop the shiver that went through her. "Tell me..." She opened her mouth to explain that she wanted to feel pretty—but stopped because she couldn't figure out how to say it without sounding lame, desperate even. And besides, wanting to feel pretty—it didn't exactly mesh with her fantasy about a ruthless seduction. So she hedged. She always hedged. "...what you're going to do to me."

In the past, that had worked like a charm. Ask for a little dirty talk? The cocky young men she brought home were always ready and willing.

But Zeb wasn't. Instead, he stood behind her, skimming the tips of his fingers over her shoulders and down her bare back. He didn't even wrench her bra off her, for crying out loud. All he did was...touch her.

Not that she was complaining about being touched. Her eyelids fluttered shut and she leaned into his touch.

"You still haven't told me what you want. I'm more than happy to describe it for you, but I need to know what I should be doing in the first place. For instance..." One hand removed itself from her skin. The next thing she knew, he wrapped her ponytail around his hand and pivoted, bringing her against the small countertop in her kitchen. "I could bend you over and take you hard and fast right here." He pulled her hair just enough that she had to lean back. "And I'd make sure you screamed when you came," he growled as he slipped his hand down over the seam of her jeans. With exquisite precision, he pressed against her most sensitive spot.

"Oh," she gasped, writhing against his hand. Her pulse pounded against where he was touching her and he used her ponytail to tilt her head so he could do more than skim his teeth over her neck. He bit down and, with the smallest movement of his hand, almost brought her to her knees. *"Zeb."*

And then the bastard stopped. "But maybe you don't like it rough," he said in the most casual voice she'd ever heard as he pulled his hands away from her ponytail and her pants. What the hell?

Then his hands were tracing the lines of her shoulders again.

"Maybe you want slow, sensual seduction, where I start kissing here…" he murmured against her neck. Then his lips moved down over her shoulder and he slid his hands up her waist to cup her breasts. "And there."

This time, both hands slid over the front of her jeans and maybe it was shameless, but she arched her back and opened for him. "And everywhere," he finished. "Until you can't take it."

And then he stopped *again*.

What was happening here? Because in the past, when she told someone to talk dirty to her, it got crude *fast*. And it wasn't like the sex was bad—it was good. She liked it. But it felt like…

It always felt like that was the best she could hope for. She wasn't pretty and she wasn't soft and she wasn't feminine, and so crude, fast sex was the best she could expect any man to do when faced with her naked.

And suddenly, she realized that wasn't what she wanted. Not anymore. Not from him.

"Maybe you want to be in charge," he went on, his voice so deep but different, too, because now there was that trace of a Southern accent coming through. It sounded like sin on the wind, that voice—honey sweet with just a hint of danger to it. He spun her around so he was leaning back on the counter and she had him boxed in. He dropped his hands and stared at her hungrily with those beautiful eyes. "Maybe I need to step back and let you show me what you want."

It was an intense feeling, being in Zeb Richards's sights.

"So what's it going to be?" But even as he asked it—sounding cool and calm and in complete control—she saw a muscle in his jaw tic and a tremor pass through his body. His gaze dipped down to her breasts, to her lucky purple bra that she wore to every home game, and a growl that she felt in her very center came rumbling out of his chest. He was hanging on to his control by the very thinnest of threads. Because of her.

He was waiting, she realized. It was her move. So that was what she did. She reached up and pulled his hat off his head and launched it somewhere in the middle of her apartment. He leaned toward her but he didn't touch her.

"What about you? What do you want?" she asked.

He shook his head in mock disappointment even as he smiled slyly at her. "I have this rule—if you don't tell me what you want, I won't give it to you. No mixed signals, no mind reading. I'm not going to guess and risk being wrong."

This wasn't working, she decided. At the very least, it wasn't what she was used to. All this…talking. It wasn't what she was good at. It only highlighted how awkward she was at things like seduction and romance, things that came naturally to other women.

She appreciated the fact that he wanted to be sure about her, about this—really, she did. But she didn't want to think. She didn't want each interaction to be a negotiation. She wanted to be swept away so she could pretend, if only for a little while, that she was soft and sultry and beautiful.

And she'd never get to hold on to that fantasy if she had to explain what she wanted, because explaining would only draw attention to what she wasn't.

Which left only one possible conclusion, really. She was done talking.

She leaned forward and grabbed the hem of his shirt. In one swift motion, she pulled it up and over his head and tossed it on the floor. And right about then, she not only stopped talking but stopped thinking.

Because Zeb's chest was a sight to behold. That T-shirt hadn't been lying. *Muscles*, she thought dimly as she reached out to stroke her hand over one of his packs. So many muscles.

"Casey..." He almost moaned when she skimmed her hand over his bare skin and moved lower. As she palmed the rippling muscles of his abs, he sucked in a breath and gripped the countertop so hard she could see his arms shaking. "You're killing me, woman."

That was better, she decided. She couldn't pull off seductive, but there was a lot to be said for raw sexual energy. That, at least, she could handle.

So she decided to handle it. Personally. She hooked her hands into the waistband of his jeans and pulled his hips toward her. As she did so, she started working at the buttons of his fly. His chest promised great, great things and she wanted to see if the rest of him could deliver on that promise.

"What do you want to hear?" he asked in that low, sensual voice that was summer sex on the wind.

Tell me I'm pretty.

But she couldn't say that, because she knew what would happen. She would ask him to tell her she was pretty and he would. He would probably even make it sound so good that she would believe him. After all, she thought as she pushed his jeans down and cupped him through his boxer briefs, what guy wouldn't find a woman who was about to sleep with him pretty?

She'd been here before, too. She might be pretty enough in the heat of the moment but the second the climactic high began to fade, so did any perceived beauty she possessed. Then she'd get her decidedly unfeminine clothes back on and before she knew it, she'd be one of the boys again.

She didn't just want him to tell her she was pretty or beautiful or sensual or any of those things. She wanted him to make her believe it, all of it, today, tomorrow and into next week, at the very least. And *that* was a trick no one had been able to master yet.

So she gave the waistband of his briefs a tug and freed him. He sprang to attention as a low groan issued from Zeb's throat.

Immediately, her jaw dropped. "Oh, Zeb," she breathed as she wrapped one and then the other hand around his girth, one on top of the other. Slowly, she stroked up the length of him and then back down. Then she looked up at him and caught him watching her. "I am *impressed.*"

He thrust in her hands—but even that was controlled. They were standing in her kitchen, both shirtless, and she was stroking him—and he wasn't even touching her. Sure, the look in his eyes was enough to make her shiver with want because she was having an impact. The cords of his neck tightened and his jaw clenched as his length slid in her grip.

But it wasn't enough. She needed more. "Feel free to join in," she told him.

"You're doing a pretty damn good job all by yourself," he ground out through gritted teeth. But even as he said it, he pried one hand off the countertop and gripped the back of her neck, pulling her into his chest. God, he was almost red-hot to the touch and all she wanted to do was be burned.

"Stop holding back." It came out as an order, but what was she supposed to do? If he was holding back out of some sort of sense of chivalry—however misguided—or consent or whatever, then she needed to get that cleared up right now.

She needed to tell him what she wanted—he'd already told her she had to, right? But she couldn't figure out how to say it without sounding sad about it, so instead, she fell back on the tried-and-true. "You've got what I want," she said as she gave him a firm squeeze. "So show me what you can do with it."

There was just a moment's hesitation—the calm before the storm, she realized. Zeb's eyes darkened and his fingers flexed against the back of her neck.

And then he exploded into movement. Casey was spun around and lifted up onto the countertop, her legs parted as he stepped into her. It happened so fast that she was almost dizzy. And *that* was what she needed right now. She needed his lips on her mouth, her neck, her chest. She needed his fingertips smoothly unhooking her lucky bra and she needed to hear the groan of desire when the bra fell to the ground.

"Damn, Casey—look at you," he said in a tone that was almost reverential.

Casey's eyes drifted shut as he stroked his fingertips over the tops of her breasts and then around her nipples.

"Yes," she whispered as he leaned down to take her in his mouth. His teeth scraped over her sensitive skin and then he sucked on her. "Oh, yes," she hissed, holding him to her.

His hand slid around her back and pulled her to the edge of the counter and then he was grinding against her, his erection hard and hot and everything she wanted— well, almost everything. There was the unfortunate matter of her jeans and the barrier they formed between the two of them.

"This is what you want, isn't it?" Zeb thrust against her. "You want me to take you here, on the countertop, because I can't wait long enough to get you into a bed?"

Every word was punctuated by another thrust. And every thrust was punctuated by a low moan that Casey couldn't have held if she'd tried.

"God, yes," she whimpered as her hips shimmied against his. This was better. Zeb was overpowering her senses, hard and fast. She didn't want to think. She just wanted to feel.

"I wonder," he said in a voice that bordered on ruthless, "if I should bite you here," he said as he traced a pattern on her shoulders with his tongue, "or here—" and he kissed the top of her left breast "—or...here." With that, he crouched down and nipped her inner thigh, and even though she could barely feel his teeth through the denim, she still shuddered with anticipation. This was better. This was things going according to script.

"D, all of the above." It was at that point that she discovered a problem. Zeb wore his hair close-cropped—there was nothing for her to thread her fingers through, nothing for her to hold on to as he rubbed along the seam of her jeans, over her very center.

But her hips bucked when he pressed against her. "Look at you," he growled as he came to his feet. "Just look at you."

She sucked in a ragged gasp when his hands moved and then he was undoing the button of her jeans and sliding down the zipper.

"I'd rather look at you," she told him as she lifted one hip and then the other off the countertop so he could work her jeans down. "You are, hands down, the most gorgeous man I've ever seen."

She let her hands skim over his shoulders and down his arms. It wasn't fair—there wasn't an ounce of fat on him. She was going to have to revise her opinion of men in suits, she thought dimly as he peeled her jeans the rest of the way off her legs.

"I can't wait," he growled in her ear, the raw urgency in his voice sending another shiver of desire through her body. He pulled the thin cotton of her panties to one side and then his erection was grinding directly against her. "Are you on something? Do you have something?"

"I'm on the Pill," she told him, her hips flexing to meet his. In that moment, she did feel desirable and wanted. His finger tested her body and she moaned into him. She might not be sensual or gorgeous, but she could still do this to a man—drive him so crazy with need that he couldn't even wait to get her undressed all the way.

"Now," she told him. "Now, Zeb. Please."

She didn't have to ask twice. He positioned himself at

her entrance. "You're so ready for me. God, just look at you." But he didn't thrust into her. Instead, it appeared he was actually going to look at her.

She pushed back against her insecurity as he studied her. She knew she couldn't measure up to his other lovers—a man that looked like him? He could have his pick of women. Hell, she wasn't even sure why he was here with her—except for the fact that she was...well, *available*. "Why are you stopping? Don't stop."

"Is that how you want it? Hard and fast?" Even as he asked, he moved, pushing into her inch by agonizing inch.

"Zeb." Even as she wrapped her legs around his hips and tried to draw him in farther. And when that worked only to a point, she wrapped her arms around his waist and dug her fingernails into his back.

That did the trick. With a roar of desire, he thrust forward and sank all the way into her. Oh, *God*. She took him in easily, moaning with desire. "Is that what you want?"

She heard his self-control hanging by a thread.

So she raked her nails up and down his back—not hard enough to break skin, but more than enough that he could feel it. He withdrew and thrust into her again, this time harder and faster.

"Yes," she whimpered. "More." She leaned her head back, lifting her chest up to him. "I need more."

Without breaking rhythm, he bent down and nipped at her breast again.

"More," she demanded because she was already so, so close. She needed just a little something to push her over the edge.

"I love a woman who knows what she wants." He sucked her nipple into his mouth—hard. There was just a hint of pain around the edges of the pleasure and it shocked her to her very core in the best way possible.

"Oh, God—" But anything else she would've tried to say got lost as his mouth worked on her and he buried himself in her again and again.

The orgasm snapped back on her like a rubber band pulled too tight, so strong she couldn't even cry out. She couldn't breathe—she couldn't think. All she could do was feel. It was everything she wanted and more. Everything she'd wanted since she'd stormed into his office that very first day and seen him. Ruthless seduction and mind-blowing climaxes and want and need all blended together into mindless pleasure.

Zeb relinquished his hold on her breast and buried his face in her neck, driving in harder and harder. She felt his teeth on her again, just as he promised. And then his hands moved between them and his thumb pressed against her sex as he thrust harder, and this time, Casey did scream. The orgasm shook through her and left her rag-doll limp as he thrust one final time and then froze. His shoulders slumped and he pulled her in close.

"God, Casey…" She took it as a source of personal pride that he sounded shaky. "That was *amazing*."

All she could do was sigh. That was enough. She'd take *amazing* every day of the week.

And then he had to go and ruin it.

He leaned back and shot her a surprised smile and said, "I should have guessed a girl like you would want it hard like that."

She didn't allow herself to be disappointed, because, really, what had she expected? She wasn't pretty or beautiful or sensual or sexy, damn it all. She was fun and cool, maybe, and she was definitely available. But beyond that? She was a good time, but that was it.

So she did what she always did. She put on her good-time smile and pushed him back so he was forced to withdraw from her body.

"Always happy to be a surprise," she said, inwardly cringing. "If you'll excuse me…"

Then she hurried to the bathroom and shut the door.

Nine

Jesus, what the hell had just happened? What had he just done?

Zeb looked down at Casey, mostly naked and flushed. Sitting on the edge of her kitchen counter. Staring at him as if she didn't know how they had gotten here.

Well, that made two of them. He felt like he was coming out of a fog—one of the thick ones that didn't just turn the world a ghostly white but blotted out the sun almost completely.

He had just taken her on her countertop. Had there even been any seduction? He tried to think but now that his blood was no longer pounding in his veins, he felt sluggish and stupid, a dull headache building in the back of his head. Hungover—that was how he felt. He didn't feel like he was in control anymore.

And he didn't like that.

He never lost control. *Ever*. He enjoyed women and sex, but this?

"If you'll excuse me," Casey said, hopping off the counter. She notched an eyebrow at him in something that looked like a challenge—but hell if he could figure out what the challenge was.

This was bad. As he watched her walk away, her body naked except for a pair of purple panties that might have matched her bra, his pulse tried to pick up the pace again. He was more than a little tempted to follow her back through her apartment, because if sex in the kitchen had been great, how good would sex in a bed be?

He was horrified to realize that he had not just had this thought but had actually taken two steps after her. He stumbled to a stop and realized that his jeans were still hanging off his butt. He tucked back into his boxer briefs and buttoned up, and the whole time, he tried to form a coherent thought.

What the hell was wrong with him? This wasn't like him. For God's sake—he hadn't even worn a condom. He had a dim recollection—she'd said she was on the Pill, right? How much had he had to drink, anyway? Three beers—that was all.

Even so, he'd done something he associated with getting plastered in a bar—he'd gone home with a woman and had wild, crazy, indiscriminate sex with her.

He scrubbed his hand over his face, but it didn't help. So he went to the sink and splashed cold water on his face. His hand—ostensibly the reason they'd come back to her place—throbbed in pain. He let the cold water run over it.

The indiscriminate sex was bad enough. But worse was that he'd just had sex with his brewmaster. An *employee*. An employee at the Beaumont Brewery, the very company he'd worked years to acquire. A company he was striving to turn around and manage productively.

And he…he couldn't even say he'd fallen into bed with Casey. They hadn't made it that far.

He splashed water on his face again. It didn't help.

He needed to think. He'd just done something he'd never done before and he wasn't sure how to handle it. Sure, he knew that employers and employees carried on affairs all the time. It happened. But it also created a ripple effect of problems. Zeb couldn't count the number of companies he'd bought that could trace their disintegration back to an affair between two adults who should have known better. And until this evening, he'd always been above such baser attractions. *Always.*

But that was before he'd met Casey. With her, he hadn't known better. And, apparently, neither had she.

Zeb found the paper towels and dried off his face. Then he scooped up his shirt and shrugged back into it. He had no idea where his hat had gone, but frankly, that was the least of his problems.

He'd lost control and gotten swept up in the moment with an employee.

It couldn't happen again.

That was the only reasonable conclusion. Yes, the sex had been amazing—but Zeb's position in the brewery and the community at large was tenuous at best. He couldn't jeopardize all of his plans for sex.

Hot, dirty, hard sex. Maybe the best sex he'd ever had. Raw and desperate and…

An involuntary shudder worked through his body. Jesus, what was *wrong* with him?

He heard the bathroom door open from somewhere inside the apartment. He could salvage this situation. He was reasonably sure that, before all the clothes had come off, she'd said…something about work. How they weren't going to do *that* at work. If he was remembering that right, then she also understood the tenuous situation they were in.

So he turned away from the sink to face her and explain, in a calm and rational way, that while what they shared had been lovely, it wasn't going to happen again.

He never got that far.

Because what he saw took his breath away and anything calm and rational was drowned out in a roar of blood rushing through his ears.

Casey had a short silk robe belted around her waist. Her hair was no longer pulled back into a ponytail—instead, it was down. Glorious waves brushed her shoulders and Zeb was almost overwhelmed with the urge to wind his fingers into that hair and pull her close to him again.

Last week, he wouldn't have called her beautiful. She still wasn't, not in the classic way. But right now, with the late-evening light filtering through the windows behind her, lighting her up with a glow, she was...

She was simply the most gorgeous woman he'd ever seen.

He was in so much trouble.

It only got worse when she smiled at him. Not the wide, friendly smile she'd aimed at every single person in the ballpark tonight. No, this was a small movement of the lips—something intimate. Something that was for him and him alone.

And then it was gone. "Can you hand me my bra?" she asked in the same voice she'd used when she'd been joking around with that beer guy.

"Sure," he said. This was good, right? This was exactly what he wanted. He didn't need her suddenly deciding she was in love with him or anything.

"Thanks." She scooped up her shirt and her jeans and

disappeared again. "Do you want to try and catch the end of the game?" she called out from somewhere deeper in the apartment. Which was *not* an invitation to join her.

Zeb stood there, blinking. What the hell? Okay, so he didn't want her to go all mushy on him. But she was acting like what had just happened…

…hadn't. Like they hadn't been flirting all night and hadn't just had some of the best sex of his life.

"Uh…" he said because seriously, what was wrong with him? First he lost control. Then he decided that this had to be a one-time-only thing. Then she appeared to be not only agreeing to the one-time thing but beating him to the punch? And that bothered him? It shouldn't have. It really shouldn't have.

But it did.

"I'll probably head back to the stadium," she said, reappearing and looking exactly the way she had when he'd first laid eyes on her this evening. Her hair was tucked back under her ball cap and she had his red cap in her hands.

It was like he hadn't left a mark on her at all.

But then he saw her swallow as she held his hat out to him. "This, um…this won't affect my job performance," she said with mock bravado.

Strangely, that made him feel better, in a perverse sort of way. He'd made an impact after all.

"It changes nothing," he agreed. He wasn't sure if his lie was any smoother than hers had been. "You're still in charge of the beer and I still want you to come up with a new product line."

And I still want you.

But he didn't say that part, because the signals she was sending out were loud and clear—no more touching. No more wanting.

"Okay. Good. Great." She shot him a wide smile that didn't get anywhere near her eyes.

In all his years, he'd never been in a postsex situation that was even half this awkward. Ever.

"I think I'm going to head home," he said, trying to sound just as cool as she did.

As his words hung in the air between them, something in her eyes changed and he knew that he'd hurt her.

Dammit, that wasn't what he wanted. At the very least, there'd been a moment when she'd made him feel things he hadn't thought he was capable of feeling and the sex had been electric. If nothing else, he was appreciative of those gifts she'd given him. So, even though it probably wasn't the best idea, he stepped into her and laced his fingers with hers.

"Thank you," he said in a low whisper. "I know we can't do this again—but I had a really good time tonight."

"You did?" Clearly, she didn't believe him.

"I did. The ball game and the beer and…" he cleared his throat. *And you.* But he didn't say that. "It was great. All of it." He squeezed her fingers and then, reluctantly, let go and stepped back. It was harder to do than he expected it to be. "I trust this will stay between us?"

That wasn't the right thing to say. But the hell of it was, he wasn't sure what, exactly, the right thing would be. There was no good way out of this.

"Of course," she replied stiffly. "I don't kiss and tell."

"I didn't—" He forced himself to exhale slowly. Attempting to bridge the divide between boss and lover wasn't working and he was better at being the boss anyway. "I look forward to seeing what you come up with," he said as he turned toward the door. "At work," he added stupidly.

"Right. See you at work," she said behind him as he walked out and shut the door behind him.

Just as the door closed, he thought he heard her sigh in what sounded like disappointment.

Well. He'd wondered what she'd seen when she'd looked at him.

He wished now he didn't know the answer.

All told, it could have been worse.

Her team had won and she'd gotten a bobblehead doll for Dad. She'd gotten to drink some Percheron Drafts, which were like memories in a cup. She'd gotten permission to do something similar—new, bold beers that would be hers and hers alone. None of that was bad.

Except for the part where she'd kind of, sort of, slept with her boss. And had some of the most intense orgasms of her life. And...and wanted more. She wanted more with him. More beers at the game, more short walks home, more time exploring his body with hers.

That part was not so good, because she was not going to get more.

Casey made sure to avoid the executive wing of the brewery as much as possible. It wasn't that she was avoiding Zeb, necessarily. She was just really focused on her job.

Okay, that was a total lie because she was avoiding him. But it was easy to do—in addition to overseeing the production lines, she was hiring new people and then training new people and resisting the urge to take a sledgehammer to tank fifteen because that damned piece of machinery had it coming and she had the urge to destroy something.

But underneath all of those everyday thoughts lurked two others that kept her constantly occupied. First, she had to come up with some new beers. She already had a porter in the fermenting tanks—she wanted to start with something that wasn't anywhere close to what the Beaumont Brewery currently had.

And then there was Zeb. He to be avoided at all costs. Besides, it wasn't like she wanted to see him again. She didn't. Really.

Okay, so the orgasms had been amazing. And yes, she'd had fun watching the game with him. And all right, he was simply the most gorgeous man she had ever seen, in or out of a suit.

But that didn't mean she wanted to see him again. Why would she? He had been everything she had expected—handsome, charming, great sex—and exactly nothing more than that.

She wanted him to be different. And he was—there was no argument about that. He was more intelligent, more ambitious and vastly wealthier than any other man she had ever even looked at. And that didn't even include the racial differences.

But she wanted him to be different in other ways, too. She felt stupid because she knew that, on at least one level, this was nothing but her own fault. The man had specifically asked her to tell him what she wanted—and she hadn't. Men, in her long and illustrious experience of being surrounded by them, were not mind readers. Never had been, never would be. So for her to have expected that Zeb would somehow magically guess what she needed was to feel gorgeous and beautiful and sultry—without her telling him—was unfair to both of them.

She didn't understand what was wrong with her. Why couldn't she ask for what she wanted? Why was it so hard to say that she wanted to be seduced with sweet nothings whispered in her ear? That instead of rough and dirty sex all the time, she wanted candlelight and silky negligees and—yes—bottles of champagne instead of beer? She wanted beautiful things. She wanted to *be* beautiful.

Well, one thing was clear. She was never going to get it if she didn't ask for it. Let this be a lesson, she decided. Next time a man said, *Tell me what you want*, she was going to tell him. It would be awkward and weird—but then, so was not getting what she wanted.

Next time, then. Not with her boss.

Casey wasn't sure what she expected from Zeb, but he seemed to be keeping his distance, as well. It wasn't that she wanted flowers or even a sweet little note…

Okay, that was another lie—she totally wanted flowers and the kind of love letter that she could hang on to during the long, dark winter nights. But the risk that came with any of those things showing up on her desk at work was too great. No one had ever sent her flowers at work before. If anything even remotely romantic showed up on her desk, the gossip would be vicious. Everyone would know something was up and there were always those few people in the office who wouldn't rest until they knew what they thought was the truth. And she knew damned well that if they couldn't get to the truth, they'd make up their own.

So it was fine that she avoided Zeb and he avoided her and they both apparently pretended that nothing had happened.

It was a week and a half later when she got the first email from him.

Ms. Johnson,
Status report?

Casey couldn't help but stare at her computer, her lips twisted in a grimace of displeasure. She knew she wasn't the kind of girl who got a lot of romance in her life, but really? He hadn't even signed the email, for God's sake. Four simple words that didn't seem very simple at all.

So she wrote back.

Mr. Richards, I've hired six new employees. Please see attached for their résumés. The new test beers are in process. Tank fifteen is still off-line. Further updates as events warrant.

And because she was still apparently mentally twelve, she didn't sign her email, either.

It was another day before Zeb replied.

Timeline on test beers?

Casey frowned at her email for the second time in as many days. Was he on a strict four-word diet or was she imagining things? This time, she hadn't even gotten the courtesy of a salutation.

This was fine, right? This was maintaining a professional distance with no repercussions from their one indiscretion.

Didn't feel any less awkward, though.

Still testing, she wrote back. It's going to be another few weeks before I know if I have anything.

The next day she got an even shorter email from him.

Status report?

Two words. Two stinking words and they drove her nuts. She was half-tempted to ask one of the other department heads if they got the same terse emails every day or so—but she didn't want to draw any attention to her relationship with Zeb, especially if that wasn't how he treated his other employees.

It was clear that he regretted their evening. In all reality, she should have been thankful she still had her job, because so far, she hadn't managed to handle herself as a professional around him yet. She was either yelling at him or throwing herself at him. Neither was good.

So she replied to his two-word emails that came every other day with the briefest summary she could.

Test beers still fermenting. Tank fifteen still not working. Hired a new employee—another woman.

But…

There were days when she looked at those short messages and wondered if maybe he wasn't asking something else. All she ever told him about was the beer. What if he was really asking about her?

What if *Status report?* was his really terrible way of asking, *How are you?*

What if he thought about her like she thought about him? Did he lie awake at night, remembering the feel of her hands on his body, like she remembered his? Did he think about the way he had fit against her, in her? Did he toss and turn until the frustration was too much and he had to take himself in hand—just like she had to stroke herself until a pale imitation of the climax he'd given her took the edge off?

Ridiculous, she decided. Of course he wasn't thinking about her. He'd made his position clear. They'd had a good time together once and once was enough. That was just how this went. She knew that. She was fun for a little while, but she was not the kind of woman men could see themselves in a relationship with. And to think that such a thing might be percolating just under the surface of the world's shortest emails was delusional at best. To convince herself that Zeb might actually care for her was nothing but heartache waiting to happen.

So she kept her mouth shut and went about her job, training her new employees, trying to beat tank fifteen into submission and tinkering with her new recipes. She caught evening games with her dad and added to her bobblehead collection and did her best to forget about one evening of wild abandon in Zeb Richards's arms.

Everything had gone back to normal.

Oh, no.

Casey stared down at the pack of birth control pills with a dawning sense of horror. Something was wrong. She hadn't been paying attention—but she was at the end of this pack. Which meant that five days ago, she should've started her period. What the hell? Why had she skipped her period?

This was *not* normal. She was regular. That was one of the advantages of being on the Pill. No surprises. No missed periods. No heart attacks at six fifty in the morning before she'd even had her coffee, for crying out loud.

In a moment of terror, she tried to recall—she hadn't skipped a dose. She had programmed a reminder into her phone. The reminder went off ten minutes after her alarm so she took a pill at exactly the same time every single day. She hadn't been sick—no antibiotics to screw with her system. Plus, she'd been on this brand for about a year.

Okay, so... She hadn't exactly had a lot of sex in the last year. Actually, now that she thought about it, there hadn't been anyone since that ballplayer a year and a half ago.

Unexpectedly, her stomach rolled and even though she hadn't had breakfast or her coffee, she raced for the bathroom. Which only made her more nervous. Was she barfing because she was panicking or was this morning sickness? Good Lord.

What if this was morning sickness?

Oh, God—what if she was…?

No, she couldn't even think it. Because if she was…

Oh, God.

What was she going to do?

Ten

"Anything else?" Zeb asked Daniel.

Daniel shook his head. "The sooner we know what the new beers are going to be, the sooner we'll be able to get started on the marketing."

Zeb nodded. "I've been getting regular status updates from Casey, but I'll check in with her again."

Which wasn't exactly the truth. He had been asking for regular status updates, and like a good employee, Casey had been replying to him. The emails were short and getting shorter all the time. He was pretty sure that the last one had been two words. Nothing yet. He could almost hear her sneering them. And he could definitely hear her going, *What do you want from me?*

Truthfully, he wasn't sure. Each time he sent her an email asking for a status report, he wondered if maybe he shouldn't do something else. Ask her how she was doing, ask if things were better now that she'd hired new people.

Ask her if she'd been to many more baseball games. If she'd caught any more foul balls.

He wanted to know if she ever thought of him outside the context of beer and the brewery. If he ever drifted through her dreams like she did his.

"Well, let me know. If you thought it would help," Daniel said as he stood and began to gather his things, "I could go talk to her about the production schedule myself."

"No," Zeb said too quickly. Daniel paused and shot him a hard look. "I mean, that won't be necessary. Your time is too valuable."

For a long, painful moment, Daniel didn't say anything. "Is there something I need to know?" he asked in a voice that was too silky for its own good.

God, no. No one needed to know about that moment of insanity that still haunted him. "Absolutely not."

It was clear that Daniel didn't buy this—but he also decided not to press it. "If it becomes something I need to know about, you'll tell me, right?"

Zeb knew that Daniel had been a political consultant, even something of a fixer—more than willing to roll around in the mud if it meant getting his opponent dirty, too. The thought of Daniel doing any digging into Casey's life made Zeb more than a little uncomfortable. Plus, he had no desire to give Daniel anything he could hold over Zeb's head. This was clearly one case where sharing was not caring, brotherly bonds of love be damned.

"Certainly," Zeb said with confidence because he was certain this was not a situation Daniel needed to know anything about. His one moment of indiscretion would remain just that—a moment.

"Right," Daniel said. With that, he turned and walked out of the office.

Zeb did the same thing he'd been doing for weeks now—he sent a short email to Casey asking for a status report.

She was exactly as she had been before their indiscretion. Terse and borderline snippy, but she got the job done and done well. He had been at the brewery for only about five weeks. And in that short amount of time, Casey had already managed to goose production up by another five hundred gallons. Imagine what she could do if she ever figured out the mystery that was apparently tank fifteen.

Then, just like he did every time he thought about Casey and the night that hadn't been a date, he forced himself to stop thinking about her. Really, it shouldn't have been this hard to *not* think about her. Maybe it was the brewery, he reasoned. For so long, taking his rightful place as the CEO of the Beaumont Brewery had occupied his every waking thought. And now he'd achieved that goal. Clearly, his mind was just at...loose ends. That was all.

This did not explain why when his intercom buzzed, he was pricing tickets to the next Rockies home game. The seats directly behind Casey's were available.

"Mr. Richards?" Delores's voice crackled over the old-fashioned speaker.

"Yes?" He quickly closed the browser tab.

"Ms. Johnson is here." There was a bit of mumbling in the background that he didn't understand. "She says she has a status report for you."

Well. This was something new. It had been—what—a little over three weeks since he'd last seen her? And also, she had waited to be announced by Delores? That wasn't like her. The Casey Johnson he knew would have stormed into this office and caught him looking at baseball tickets. She would've known exactly what he was thinking, too.

So something was off. "Send her in." And then he braced for the worst.

Had she gotten another job? And if so...

If she didn't work for him anymore, would it be unethical to ask her out?

He didn't get any further than that in his thinking, because the door opened and she walked in. Zeb stood, but instantly, he could see that something was wrong. Instead of the sweaty hot mess that she frequently was during work hours, she looked pale. Her eyes were huge and for some reason, he thought she looked scared. What the hell was she scared of? Not him, that much he knew. She had never once been scared of him. And it couldn't be the last email he'd sent, either. There hadn't been anything unusual about that—it was the same basic email he'd been sending for weeks now.

"What's wrong?" He said the moment the door shut behind her.

She didn't answer right away.

"Casey?" He came out from around the desk and began to walk to her.

"I have..." Her voice shook and it just worried him all the more. She swallowed and tried again. "I have a status report for you."

She was starting to freak him out. "Is everything okay? Was there an on-the-job accident?" He tried to smile. "Did tank fifteen finally blow up?"

She tried to smile, too. He felt the blood drain out of his face at the sight of that awful grimace.

"No," she said in a voice that was a pale imitation of her normal tone. "That's not what I have a status report about."

Okay. Good. Nothing had happened on the line. "Is this about the beers?"

She shook her head, a small movement. "They're still in process. I think the porter is going to be really good."

"Excellent." He waited because there had to be a reason she was here. "Was there something else?"

Her eyes got even wider. She swallowed again. "I—"

And then the worst thing that could have possibly happened did—she squeezed her eyes shut tight and a single tear trickled down her left cheek.

It was physically painful to watch that tear. He wanted to go to her and pull her into his arms and promise that whatever had happened, he'd take care of it.

But they were at work and Delores was sitting just a few feet away. So he pushed his instincts aside. He was her boss. Nothing more. "Yes?"

The seconds ticked by while he waited. It wasn't like whatever she was trying to tell him was the end of the world, was it?

And then it was.

"I'm pregnant," she said in a shattered voice.

He couldn't even blink as his brain tried to process what she had just said. "Pregnant?" he asked as if he had never heard the word before.

She nodded. "I don't understand... I mean, I'm on the Pill—or I was. I didn't miss any. This isn't supposed to happen." Her chin quivered and another tear spilled over and ran down the side of her face.

Pregnant. She was pregnant. "And I'm the…" He couldn't even say it. *Hell.*

She nodded again. "I hadn't been with anyone in over a year." She looked up at him. "You believe me, right?"

He didn't want to. The entire thing was unbelievable.

What the hell did he know about fatherhood? Nothing, that's what. Not a single damned thing. He'd been raised by a single mother, by a collective of women in a beauty shop. His male role models had been few and far between.

He wasn't going to be a father. Not on purpose and not by accident.

In that moment, another flash of anger hit him—but not at her. He was furious with himself. He never lost control. He never got so carried away with a woman that he couldn't even make sure that he followed the basic protocols of birth control. Except for one time.

And one time was all it took, apparently.

"You're sure?" Because this was the sort of thing that one needed to be sure about.

She nodded again. "I realized yesterday morning that I was at the end of my month of pills and I hadn't had my…" She blushed. Somehow, in the midst of a discussion about one-night stands and pregnancy, she still had the ability to look innocent. "After work yesterday, I bought a test. It was positive." Her voice cracked on that last, important word.

Positive.

Of all the words in the English language that had the potential to change his life, he had never figured *positive* would be the one to actually do it.

"We…" He cleared his throat. *We.* There was now a *we.* "We can't talk about this. Here." He looked around the office—his father's office. The man who had gotten his mother pregnant and paid her to leave town. "During work hours."

She looked ill. "Right. Sorry. I didn't mean to use work hours for personal business."

Dimly, he was glad to see that she still had her attitude. "We'll…we'll meet. Tonight. I can come to you."

"No," she said quickly.

"Right." She didn't want him back in her apartment, where he'd gotten carried away and gotten her into this mess. He wanted to use a less painful word—*situation, predicament*—but this was a straight-up mess. "Come to my place. At seven." She already knew where he lived. Hell, her father had done work in his house at some point.

"I don't… Jamal," she said weakly.

"Come on, Casey. We have to have this conversation somewhere and I'm sure as hell not going to have it in public. Not when you look like you're about to start sobbing and I can't even think straight."

Her eyes narrowed and he instantly regretted his words. "Of course. It's unfortunate that this upsets me," she said in a voice that could freeze fire.

"That's not what I—"

She held up her hand. "Fine. Seven, your place." She gave him a hard look—which was undercut by her scrubbing at her face with the heel of her hand. "All I ask is that you not have Jamal around." She turned and began to walk out of his office.

For some reason, he couldn't let her go. "Casey?"

She paused, her hand on the doorknob. But she didn't turn around. "What?"

"Thank you for telling me. I'm sure we can work something out."

She glanced back at him, disappointment all over her

face. "Work something out," she murmured. "Well. I guess we know what kind of Beaumont you are."

Before Zeb could ask her what the hell she meant by that, she was gone.

Eleven

"Hey, baby boy."

At the sound of his mother's voice, something unclenched in Zeb's chest. He'd screwed up—but he knew it'd work out. "Hey, Mom. Sorry to interrupt you."

"You've been quiet out there," she scolded. "Those Beaumonts giving you any trouble?"

"No." The silence had been deafening, almost. But he couldn't think about that other family right now. "It's just been busy. Taking over the company is a massive undertaking." Which was the truth. Taking over the Beaumont Brewery was easily the hardest thing he'd ever done. No, right now he had to focus on his own family. "Mom…"

She was instantly on high alert. "What's wrong?"

There wasn't a good way to have this conversation. "I'm going to be a father."

Emily Richards was hard to stun. She'd heard it all,

done it all—but for a long moment, she was shocked into silence. "A baby? I'm going to be a *grandma*?"

"Yeah." Zeb dropped his head into his hands. He hadn't wanted to tell her—but he'd needed to.

This was history repeating itself. "Just like my old man, huh?"

He expected her to go off on Hardwick Beaumont, that lying, cheating bastard who'd left her high and dry. But she didn't. "You gonna buy this girl off?"

"Of course not, Mom. Come on." He didn't know what to do—but he knew what he didn't want to happen. And he didn't want to put Casey aside or buy her off.

"Are you going to take this baby away from her?"

"That's not funny." But he knew she wasn't joking. Hardwick had either paid off his babies' mothers or married and divorced them, always keeping custody.

"Baby boy..." She sighed, a sound that was disappointment and hope all together. "I want to know my grandbaby—and her mother." Zeb couldn't think of what to say. He couldn't think, period. His mother went on, "Be better than your father, Zeb. I think you know what you need to do."

Which was how Zeb wound up at a jewelry store. He couldn't hope to make sense of what Casey had told him that morning but he knew enough to realize that he hadn't handled himself well.

Actually, no, that was letting himself off easy. In reality, he hadn't handled himself well since...the ball game. If he had realized that her getting pregnant was a legitimate outcome instead of a distant possibility...

He wanted to think that he wouldn't have slept with her. But at the very least, he wouldn't have walked out of her apartment with that disappointed sigh of hers lingering in his ears.

He'd hurt her then. He'd pissed her off today. He might not be an expert in women, but even he knew that the best solution here was diamonds.

The logic was sound. However, the fact that the diamonds he was looking at were set into engagement rings...

He was going to be a father. This thought kept coming back to him over and over again. What did he know about being a father? Nothing.

His own father had paid his mother to make sure that he never had to look at Zeb and acknowledge him as a son. Hardwick Beaumont might have been a brilliant businessman, but there was no way around the obvious fact that he'd been a terrible person. Or maybe he'd been a paragon of virtue in every area of his life except when it came to his mistresses—Emily Richards and Daniel's mother and CJ's and God only knew how many mothers of other illegitimate children.

"Let me see that one," he said to the clerk behind the counter, pointing to a huge pear-cut diamond with smaller diamonds set in the band.

Because this was where he'd come to in his life. He was going to be a father. He'd made that choice when he'd slept with Casey. Now he had to take responsibility.

He did not want to be a father like Hardwick had been. Zeb didn't want to hide any kid of his away, denying him his birthright. If he had a child, he was going to claim that child. He was going to fight for that child, damn it all, just like his father should have fought for him. His mother wanted to know her grandbaby.

He didn't want to have to fight Casey, though. Because the simplest way to stay in his child's life was to marry the mother.

Because, really, what were the alternatives?

He could struggle through custody agreements and legal arrangements—all of which would be fodder for gossip rags. He could pretend he hadn't slept with his brewmaster and put his own child through the special kind of hell that was a childhood divorced from half his heritage. He could do what Hardwick had done and cut a check to ensure his kid was well cared for—and nothing more.

Or he could ask Casey to marry him. Tonight. It would be sudden and out of left field and she might very well say no.

Married. He'd never seen himself married. But then, he'd never seen himself as a father, either. One fifteen-minute conversation this afternoon and suddenly he was an entirely different person, one he wasn't sure he recognized. He stared at the engagement ring, but he was seeing a life where he and Casey were tied together both by a child and by law.

No, not just that. By more than that. There was more between them than just a baby. So much more.

He'd spend his days with her watching baseball and discussing beer and—hopefully—having great sex. And the kid—he knew Casey would be good with the kid. She'd be the kind of mom who went to practices and games. She'd be fun, hands-on.

As for Zeb...

Well, he had two different businesses to run. He had to work. He'd made a fortune—but fortunes could be lost as fast as they'd been made. He'd seen it happen. And he couldn't let it happen to him. More than that, he couldn't let it happen to Casey. To their family.

He had to take care of them. Hardwick Beaumont had cut Emily Richards a check and the money had been enough to take care of him when he'd been a baby—but it hadn't lasted forever. His mother had needed to work to make ends meet. She'd worked days, nights, weekends.

There had been times when Zeb wondered if she was avoiding him. Emily Richards had always been happy to foist child care off on the other stylists and the customers. No one minded, but there'd been times he'd just wanted his mom and she'd been too busy.

He couldn't fault her drive. She was a self-made woman. But she'd put her business ahead of him, her own son. Even now, Zeb had trouble talking to her without feeling like he was imposing upon her time.

He didn't want that for his child. He wanted more for his family. He didn't want his baby's mother to miss out on all the little things that made up a childhood. He didn't want to miss them, either—but not only was the brewery his legacy, it would be his child's, as well. He *couldn't* let the brewery slide.

He'd work hard, as he always had. But he would be there. Part of his child's life. Maybe every once in a while, he'd even make it for a game or a play or whatever kids did in school. And he'd have Casey by his side.

"I'll take it," he said, even though he wasn't sure what he was looking at anymore. But he'd take that life, with Casey and their child.

"It's a beautiful piece." A deep voice came from his side.

Zeb snapped out of his reverie and turned to find himself face-to-face with none other than Chadwick Beaumont. For a long moment, Zeb did nothing but stare. It wasn't like looking in a mirror. Chadwick was white, with sandy blond hair that he wore a little long and floppy. But despite that, there were things Zeb recognized—the jaw-line and the eyes.

Zeb's green eyes had marked him as different in the African American community. But here? Here, stand-ing with this man he had never seen up close before, his eyes marked him as something else. They marked him as one of the Beaumonts.

Chadwick stuck out his hand. "I'm Chadwick."

"Zeb," he said, operating on autopilot as his hand went out to give Chadwick's a firm shake. "And who's this?" he asked, trying to smile at the little girl Chad-wick was holding.

"This is my daughter, Catherine."

Zeb studied the little girl. She couldn't be more than a year and a half old. "Hi there, Catherine," he said softly. He looked at Chadwick. "I didn't realize I was an uncle." The idea seemed so foreign to him that it was almost unrecognizable.

The little girl turned her face away and into Chad-wick's neck—then, a second later, she turned back, peek-ing at Zeb through thick lashes.

"You are—Byron has two children. Technically, Catherine is my wife's daughter from a previous re-lationship. But I've adopted her." Chadwick patted his daughter on her back. "I found that, when it comes to being a Beaumont, it's best to embrace a flexible defi-nition of the word *family*."

An awkward silence grew between them because Zeb didn't quite know what to say to that. He'd always thought that, at some point, he would confront the Beau-monts. In his mind's eye, the confrontation was not nearly this...polite. There wouldn't be any chitchat. He would revel in what he had done, taking the company away from them and punishing them for failing to acknowledge him and they would…cower or beg for forgiveness. Or something.

There was a part of him that still wanted that—but not in the middle of a high-end jewelry store and not in front of a toddler.

So instead, he didn't say anything. He had no idea what he was even supposed to say as he looked at this man who shared his eyes.

Suddenly, Zeb desperately wanted to know what kind of man this brother of his was. More specifically, he wanted to know what kind of man Casey thought Chadwick was. Because Zeb still didn't know if he was like his father or his brother and he needed to know.

"Who's the lucky woman?" Chadwick asked.

"Excuse me?"

Just then the clerk came back with the small bag that held an engagement ring. Chadwick smiled. "The ring. Anyone I know?"

It took a lot to make Zeb blush, but right then his face got hot. Instead of responding, he went on the offensive. "What about you?"

Chadwick smiled again, but this time it softened everything about his face. Zeb recognized that look—and it only got stronger when Chadwick leaned down and pressed a kiss to the top of his daughter's head. It was the look of love. "My wife is expecting again and the pregnancy has been…tiring. I'm picking her up something because, really, there's nothing else I can do and diamonds tend to make everything better. Wouldn't you agree?"

"Congratulations," Zeb said automatically. But he didn't tell this man that he'd had the exact same thought. He only hoped he wasn't wrong about the diamonds.

"Will there be anything else?" The clerk asked in a super-perky voice.

Zeb and Chadwick turned to see her looking at them with bright eyes and a wide smile. Crap. He needed to have a conversation with Chadwick—even if he wasn't exactly sure what the conversation should be about. But it couldn't happen here. How much longer before someone put two and two together and there were cameras or news crews and reporters or cell-phone-toting gossipmongers crowding them? Zeb didn't want to deal with it himself—he couldn't imagine that Chadwick wanted to put his daughter through it, either.

"No," he said just as another clerk approached and handed a small bag to Chadwick.

"Your necklace, Mr. Beaumont," the second clerk said. She and the first clerk stood elbow to elbow, grinning like loons.

They had to get out of here right now. "Would you like to…" *continue this conversation elsewhere?* But he didn't even get that far before Chadwick gave a quick nod of his head.

Both men picked up their small bags and headed out of the store. When they were safely away from the eager clerks, Zeb bit the bullet and asked first. "Would you like to go get a drink or something?"

"I wish I could," Chadwick said in a regretful voice. "But I don't think any conversation we have should be in public. And besides," he went on, switching his daughter to his other arm, "we probably only have another half an hour before we have a meltdown."

"Sure," Zeb said, trying to keep the disappointment out of his voice.

Chadwick stopped, which made Zeb stop, too. "You want answers." It was not a question.

Yes. "I don't want to intrude on your family time."

Chadwick stared at Zeb for a moment longer and his face cracked with the biggest smile that Zeb had ever seen. "You *are* family, Zeb."

That simple statement made Zeb feel as if someone had just gut-shot him. It took everything he had not to double over. This man considered *him* family? There was such a sense of relief that appeared out of nowhere—

But at the same time, Zeb was angry. If he was family, why hadn't Chadwick seen fit to inform him of that before now? Why had he waited until a chance meeting in a jewelry store, for God's sake?

Chadwick's eyes cut behind Zeb's shoulder. "We need to keep moving." He began walking again and Zeb had no choice but to follow. They headed out toward the parking lot.

Finally, Zeb asked, "How long have you known? About me, I mean."

"About six years. After my..." He winced. "I mean *our* father—"

Zeb cut him off. "He wasn't my father. Not really."

Chadwick nodded. "After Hardwick died," he went on diplomatically, "it took me a while to stabilize the company and get my bearings. I'd always heard rumors about other children and when I finally got to the point where I had a handle on the situation, I hired an investigator."

"Did you know about Daniel before the press conference?"

Chadwick nodded. "And Carlos."

That brought Zeb up short. CJ was not as unfindable as he liked to think he was. "He prefers CJ."

Chadwick smirked. "Duly noted. And of course, we already knew about Matthew. There was actually a bit of a break after that. I don't know if Hardwick got tired of paying off his mistresses or what."

"Are there more of us? Because I could only find the other two."

Chadwick nodded again. "There are a few that are still kids. The youngest is thirteen. I'm in contact with his mother, but she has decided that she's not interested in introducing her son to the family. I provide a monthly stipend—basically, I pay child support for the other three children." They reached a fancy SUV with darkened windows. "It seems like the least I can do, after everything Hardwick did." He opened up the back door and slid his daughter into the seat.

As he buckled in the little girl, Zeb stared at Chadwick in openmouthed shock. "You...you pay child support? For your half siblings?"

"They are family," Chadwick said simply as he clicked the buckle on the child seat. He straightened and turned to face Zeb. But he didn't add anything else. He just waited.

Family. It was such an odd concept to him. He had a family—his mother and the larger community that had orbited around her salon. He had Jamal. And now, whether she liked it or not, he had Casey, too.

"Why didn't you contact me?" He had so many questions, but that one was first. Chadwick was taking care of the other bastards. Why not him?

"By the time I found you, we were both in our thirties. You'd built up your business on your own, and at the time, I didn't think you wanted anything to do with us." Chadwick shrugged. "I didn't realize until later how wrong I was."

"What kind of man was he?" Zeb asked. And he felt wrong, somehow, asking it—but he needed to know.

He was getting a very good idea of what kind of man Chadwick was—loyal, dependable, the kind of man who would pay child support for his siblings because they were family, whether they liked it or not. The kind of man who not only cared about his wife but bought her diamonds because she was tired. The kind of man who knew how to put his own daughter into a safety seat.

Zeb knew he couldn't be like Chadwick, but he was beginning to understand what Casey meant when she asked if Zeb was like his brother.

Chadwick sighed and looked up at the sky. It was getting late, but the sun was still bright. "Why don't you come back to the house? This isn't the sort of thing that we can discuss in a parking lot."

Zeb just stared at the man. His brother. Chadwick had made the offer casually, as if it were truly no big deal. Zeb was family and family should come home and have a beer. Simple.

But it wasn't. Nothing about this was simple.

Zeb held up his small jewelry bag with the engagement ring that he somehow had to convince Casey to wear. "I have something to do at seven." He braced himself for Chadwick to ask about who the lucky woman was again, but the question didn't come.

Instead, Chadwick answered Zeb's earlier question. "Hardwick Beaumont…" He sighed and closed the door, as if he were trying to shield his daughter from the truth. "He was a man of contradictions—but then again, I'm sure we all are." He paused. "He was… For me, he was hard. He was a hard man. He was a perfectionist and when I couldn't give him perfection…" Chadwick grimaced.

"Was he violent?"

"He could be. But I think that was just with me, because I was his heir. He ignored Phillip almost completely, but then Frances—his first daughter—he spoiled her in every sense of the word." Chadwick tried to smile, but it looked like a thing of pain. "You asked me why I hadn't contacted you earlier—well, the truth is, I think I was a little jealous of you."

"What?" Surely, Zeb hadn't heard correctly. Surely, his brother, the heir of the Beaumont fortune, had not just said that he was—

"Jealous," Chadwick confirmed. "I'm not exaggerating when I say that Hardwick screwed us all up. I…" He took a deep breath and stared up at the night sky again. "He was my father, so I couldn't hate him, but I don't think I loved him, either. And I don't think he loved us. Certainly not me. So when I found out about you and the others, how you'd spent your whole lives without Hardwick standing over you, threatening and occasionally hitting you, I was jealous. You managed to make yourself into a respected businessman on your own. You did what you wanted—not what *he* wanted. It's taken me most of my life to separate out what I want from what he demanded."

Zeb was having trouble processing this information. "And I spent years trying to get what you have," he said, feeling numb. Years of believing that he had been cut out of his rightful place next to Hardwick Beaumont. It had never occurred to him that perhaps he didn't want to be next to Hardwick Beaumont.

Because he could see in Chadwick's eyes that this was the truth. His father had been a terrible man. Sure, Zeb had known that—a good man did not buy off his mistress and send her packing. A good man did not pretend like he didn't have multiple children hidden away. A good man took care of his family, no matter what.

Zeb suddenly had no idea if he was a good man or not. He took care of his mother, even when she drove him nuts, and he looked out for Jamal, the closest thing he'd had to a brother growing up.

But the Beaumonts were his family, too. Instead of looking out for them, he'd done everything he could to undermine them.

He realized Chadwick was staring. "I'm sorry," Chadwick said quickly. "You look like him."

Zeb snorted. "I look like my mother."

"I know." Chadwick moved a hand, as if he were going to pat Zeb on the shoulder—but he didn't. Instead, he dropped his arm back to his side. Then he waited. Zeb appreciated the silence while he tried to put his thoughts in order.

He knew he was running out of time. Chadwick's daughter would sit quietly for only so long—either that, or someone with a camera would show up. But he had so many questions. And he wasn't even sure that the answers would make it better.

For the first time in his life, he wasn't sure that knowing more was a good thing.

"I don't know how much of it was PR," Chadwick suddenly began. "But the press conference was brilliant and I wanted to let you know that we're glad to see that the brewery is back in family hands."

Really? But Zeb didn't let his surprise at this statement show. "We're still competitors," he replied. "Casey is formulating a line of beers to compete directly with Percheron Drafts as we speak."

Chadwick notched an eyebrow at him. "She'll be brilliant at it," he said, but with more caution in his voice. Too late, Zeb realized that he had spoken of her with too much familiarity. "And I expect nothing less—from both of you."

Inside the car, the little girl fussed. "I have to get going," Chadwick said, and this time, he did clap Zeb on the shoulder. "Come to the house sometime. We'll have dinner. Serena would love to meet you."

Zeb assumed that was Chadwick's wife. "What about the rest of your brothers and sisters?"

"You mean *our* brothers and sisters. They're…curious, shall we say. But getting all of us together in one room can be overwhelming. Besides, Serena was my executive assistant at the brewery. She knows almost as much about the place as I do."

Zeb stared at him. "You married your assistant?" Because that seemed odd, somehow. This seemed like something their father would've done. Well, maybe not the marrying part.

Had his brother gotten his assistant pregnant and then married her? Was history repeating itself? Was it possible for history to repeat itself even if Zeb hadn't known what that history was?

Chadwick gave him a look that might've intimidated a lesser man. But not Zeb. "I try not to be my father," he said in a voice that was colder than Zeb had heard yet. "But it seemed to be a family trait—falling for our employees. I married my assistant. Phillip married a horse trainer he hired. Frances married the last CEO of the brewery."

Oh, God. Had he somehow managed to turn into his father without ever even knowing a single thing about the man? He had gotten Casey pregnant because when he was around her, he couldn't help himself. She'd taken all of his prized control and blown it to smithereens, just as if she'd been blowing foam off a beer.

"Hardwick Beaumont is dead," Chadwick said with finality. "He doesn't have any more power over me, over any of us." He looked down at the small bag Zeb still clutched in his hand. "We are known for our control—both having it and losing it. But it's not the control that defines us. It's how we deal with the consequences."

Inside the car, the toddler started to cry in earnest. "Come by sometime," Chadwick said as he stuck out his hand. "I look forward to seeing how you turn the brewery around."

"I will," Zeb said as they shook hands.

"If you have any other questions, just ask."

Zeb nodded and stood aside as Chadwick got into his vehicle and drove away—back to the family home, to his assistant and their children. Back to where he could be his own man, without having to prove anything to his father ever again.

Hardwick Beaumont was dead. Suddenly, years of plotting and planning, watching and waiting for an opportunity to take revenge against the Beaumonts—was it all for nothing?

Because Zeb wasn't sure he wanted revenge—not on his brothers. Not anymore. How could he? If they'd known of him for only six years—hell, six years ago, Zeb had been just moving to New York, just taking ZOLA to the next level. What would he have done, six years ago? He wouldn't have given up ZOLA. He would've been suspicious of any overtures that Chadwick might've made. He wouldn't have wanted to put himself in a position where any Beaumont had power over him. And then he wouldn't have been in a position to take the brewery back from the corporation that bought it.

And now? Now Chadwick wanted him to succeed?

Even though they were competitors—and nowhere near friends—he hoped that Zeb would turn the brewery around?

It was damned hard to get revenge against a dead man. And Zeb wasn't sure he wanted revenge against the living.

He looked down at the small bag with an engagement ring in it.

What did he want?

Twelve

What did she want?

Casey had been asking herself that exact question for hours now. And the answer hadn't changed much.

She had no idea.

Well, that wasn't entirely the truth. What she wanted was... God, it sounded so silly, even in her head. But she wanted something romantic to happen. The hell of it was, she didn't know exactly what that was. She wanted Zeb to pull her into his arms and promise that everything was going to be all right. And not just the general promise, either. She wanted specific promises. He was going to take care of her and the baby. He was going to be a good father. He was going to be...

Seriously, they didn't have a whole lot of a relationship here. She didn't even know if she wanted to have a relationship—beyond the one that centered around a child, of course. Sometimes she did and sometimes she didn't. He was so gorgeous—too gorgeous. Zeb wasn't the kind of guy she normally went for; he was cool and smooth. Plus, he was a Beaumont. As a collective, they weren't known for being the most faithful of husbands.

That was unfair to Chadwick. But it wasn't unfair enough to Hardwick.

Fidelity aside, she had absolutely no idea if Zeb could be the kind of father she wanted her child to have. It wasn't that her own father, Carl Johnson, was perfect—he wasn't. But he cared. He had *always* cared for Casey, fighting for her and protecting her and encouraging her to do things that other people wouldn't have supported.

That was what she wanted. She wanted to do that for her and for this child.

Based on Zeb's reaction in the office earlier? She didn't have a lot of faith.

Casey had not been the best of friends with Chadwick Beaumont. They had been coworkers who got along well, and he'd never seen her as anything more than one of the guys. Which was fine. But she knew all of the office gossip—he had fallen in love with his assistant just as Serena Chase had gotten pregnant with someone else's baby. He had given up the company for her and adopted the baby girl as his own. Hell, even Ethan Logan—who had not understood a damned thing about beer—had given up the company for Frances Beaumont because they'd fallen in love.

Zeb's entire reason for being in Denver was the brewery.

Besides, she didn't want him to give it up. In fact, she preferred not to give it up, either. She had no idea what the company's maternity-leave policy looked like, though. She didn't know if Larry could handle the production lines while she was away. And after the leave was over, she didn't know how she would be a working mother with a newborn.

She didn't know if she would have to make it work herself or if she'd have help. And she still didn't know what she wanted that help to look like. But she didn't want to give up her job. She'd worked years to earn her place at the brewery's table. She loved being a brewmaster. It was who she was.

She was running a little bit late by the time she made it to the mansion where Zeb had set up shop. As she got out of her car, she realized her hands were shaking. Okay, everything was shaking. Was it too early to start blaming things on hormones? God, she had no idea. She hadn't spent a lot of time around babies and small children growing up. Other girls got jobs as babysitters. She went to work as an electrical assistant for her father. Small children were a mystery to her.

Oh, God. And now she was going to have one.

Stuck in this tornado of thoughts, she rang the bell. She knew she needed to tell Zeb what she wanted. Hadn't she resolved that she was going to do better at that? Okay, that resolution had been specifically about sex— but the concept held. Men were not mind readers. She needed to tell him what she wanted to happen here.

All she had to do in the next thirty seconds was figure out what that was.

It wasn't even thirty seconds before the door opened and there stood Zeb, looking nothing like the CEO she'd seen in the office just a few hours ago. But he didn't look like the sports fan that she'd gone on an almost date with, either. He was something in the middle. His loose-fitting black T-shirt hinted at his muscles, instead of clinging to them. It made him look softer. Easier to be around. God, how she needed him to be easier right now.

"Hi," she croaked. She cleared her throat and tried to smile.

"Come in," he said in a gentle voice. Which was, all things considered, a step up from this morning's reaction.

He shut the door behind her and then led her through the house. It was massive, a maze of rooms and parlors and stairs. He led her to a room that could best be described as a study—floor-to-ceiling bookcases, a plush Persian rug, heavy leather furniture and a fireplace. It was ornate, in a manly sort of way. And, thankfully, it was empty.

Zeb shut the door behind her and then they were alone. She couldn't bring herself to sit—she had too much nervous energy. She forced herself to stand in the middle of the room. "This is nice."

"Jamal can take the credit." Zeb gave her a long look and then he walked toward her. She hadn't actually seen him for several weeks—outside of this morning, of course. Was it possible she had forgotten how intense it was being in Zeb Richards's sights? "How are you?" he asked as he got near.

"Well, I'm pregnant."

He took another step closer and she tensed. Right about now it would be great if she could figure out what she wanted. "I don't mean this to sound callous," he said, lifting his hands in what looked a hell of a lot like surrender, "but I thought you said you were on the Pill?"

"I am. I mean, I was. I diagnosed myself via the internet—these things can…happen. It's something called breakthrough ovulation, apparently." He was another step closer and even though neither of them were making any broad declarations of love, her body was responding to his nearness all the same.

She could feel a prickle of heat starting low on her back and working its way up to her neck. Her cheeks were flushing and, God help her, all she wanted was for him to wrap his arms around her and tell her that everything was going to be all right.

And then, amazingly, that was exactly what happened. Zeb reached her and folded his strong arms around her and pulled her against the muscles of his chest and held her. "These things just happen, huh?"

With a sigh, she sank into his arms. This probably wasn't a good idea. But then, anything involving her touching Zeb Richards was probably a bad idea. Because once she started touching him, it was just too damn hard to stop. "Yeah."

"I'm sorry it happened to you."

She needed to hear that—but what killed her was the sincerity in his voice. Her eyes began to water. Oh, no—she didn't want to cry. She wasn't a crier. Really. She was definitely going to blame that one on the hormones.

"What are we going to do?" she asked. "I haven't seen you in weeks. We had one almost date and everything about it was great except that it ended…awkwardly. And since then…"

"Since then," he said as she could feel his voice rumbling deep out of his chest. It shouldn't have been soothing, dammit. She wanted to keep her wits about her, but he was lulling her into a sense of warmth and security. "Since then I've thought of you constantly. I wanted to see you but I got the feeling you might not have reciprocated that desire."

What? "Is that why you've been sending me emails every day?" She leaned back and looked up at him. "Asking for status reports?"

Oh, God, that blush was going to be the death of her. If there was one thing she knew, it was that an adorable Zeb Richards was an irresistible Zeb Richards. "You said at work that it was all about the beer. So I was trying to keep it professional."

Even as he said it, though, he was backing her up until they reached one of the overstuffed leather couches. Then he was pulling her down onto his lap and curling his arms around her and holding her tight. "But we're not at work right now, are we?"

She sighed into him. "No, we're not. We can't even claim that this is a corporate outing."

He chuckled and ran his hand up and down her back. She leaned into his touch because it was what she wanted. And she hadn't even had to ask for it. She let herself relax into him and wrapped her arms around his neck. "What are we going to do, Zeb?"

His hand kept moving up and down and he began rubbing his other hand along the side of her thigh. "I'm going to take care of you," he said, his voice soft and close to her ear.

God, it was what she needed to hear. She knew she was strong and independent. She lived her life on her own terms. She'd gotten the job she wanted and a nice place close to the ballpark. She paid her bills on time and managed to sock some away for retirement.

But this? Suddenly, her life was not exactly her own anymore and she didn't know how to deal with it.

"There's something between us," Zeb said, his breath caressing her cheek. She turned her face toward him. "I feel it. When I'm around you…" He cupped her face in his hands. "I could fall for you."

Her heart began to pound. "I feel it, too," she whispered, her lips moving against his. "I'm not supposed to go for someone like you. You're my boss and every-thing about this is wrong. So why can't I help myself?"

"I don't know. But I don't think I want you to."

And then he was kissing her. Unlike the first time, which had been hurried and frantic, this was everything she dreamed a kiss could be. Slowly, his lips moved over hers as he kissed the corner of her mouth and then ran his tongue along her lower lip.

If she'd been able to help herself, she wouldn't have opened her lips for him, wouldn't have drawn his tongue into her mouth, wouldn't have run her hands over his hair. If she'd been able to help herself at all, she wouldn't have moaned into his mouth when he nipped at her lip, her neck, her earlobe.

"I want you in a bed this time," he said when she skimmed her hands over his chest and went to grab the hem of his shirt. "I want to strip you bare and lay you out and I want to show you exactly what I can do for you."

"Yes," she gasped. And then she gasped again when he stood, lifting her in his arms as if she weighed next to nothing.

"Casey," he said as he stood there, holding her. His gaze stroked over her face. "Have I ever told you how beautiful you are?"

Thirteen

Whatever he'd just said, he needed to make sure he said it again. Often.

Because suddenly, Casey was all over him. She kissed him with so much passion he almost had to sit down on the couch again so he could strip her shirt off her and sink into her soft body and...

He slammed on the brakes. That wasn't what he'd promised her. Bed. He needed to get to a bed. And at the rate they were going, he needed to get there quickly.

It would be so tempting to get lost in her body. She had that ability, to make him lose himself. But it was different now. Everything was different. She was carrying his child. This wasn't about mindless pleasure, not anymore.

It wasn't like he wanted to be thinking about Chadwick Beaumont right now, but even as he carried Casey out of the office and up the wide staircase to his suite of rooms, he couldn't stop replaying some of the things his brother had said.

Casey took Zeb's hard-won control and blew it to smithereens, but that wasn't what made him a Beaumont. It was what he did after that.

He could turn her away. He could set her up with a monthly stipend and let her raise their child, just as Chadwick was doing with some of their half siblings.

But that was what his father would do. And Zeb knew now that he did not want to be like that man. And what was more, he didn't *have* to be like his father. He wasn't sure he could be as selfless as his brother was—but he didn't have to be that way, either.

He could be something else. Someone else. Someone who was both a Beaumont *and* a Richards.

A sense of rightness filled him. It was right that he take Casey to bed—a real bed this time. It was right that he make love to her tonight, tomorrow—maybe even for the rest of their lives. It was right that he become a part of the Beaumont family by *making* himself a part of it—both by finally taking his place as the head of the brewery and by starting his own family.

It was right to be here with Casey. To marry her and take care of her and their baby.

He kicked open the door to a suite of rooms and carried her through. Why was this house so damned big? Because he had to pass through another room and a half before he even got anywhere near his bed and each step was agony. He was rock hard and she was warm and soft against him and all he wanted to do was bury himself in her again and again.

Finally, he made it to his bed. Carefully, he set her down on top of the covers. He was burning for her as he lowered himself down on top of her—gently, this time. He knew that just because she was a few weeks along, didn't mean she was now some impossibly fragile, delicate flower who would snap if he looked at her wrong. But he wanted to treat her with care.

So, carefully, he slipped her T-shirt over her head. He smiled down at her plain beige bra. "No purple today?"

"I didn't wear my lucky bra, because I didn't think I was going to get lucky," she said in a husky voice. This time, when she grabbed at the hem of his shirt, he didn't stop her.

He wanted to take this slow, but when she ran her hands over his chest, her fingernails lightly grazing his nipples, she took what little self-control he had left and blew it away. Suddenly, he was undoing her jeans and yanking them off and she was grabbing his and trying to push them off his hips.

"Zeb..." she said, and he heard the need for him in her voice.

His blood was pounding in his veins—and other places—but he had to prove to her that he could be good for her. So instead of falling into her body, he knelt in front of the bed and, grabbing her by the hips, pulled her to the edge of it.

"I'm going to take care of you," he promised. He had never meant the words more than he did right now.

Last time, he hadn't even gotten her panties off her. Last time, he'd been more than a little selfish. This time, however, it was all about her.

He lowered his mouth to her sex and was rewarded as a ripple of tension moved through her body.

"Oh," she gasped as he spread her wide and kissed her again and again.

With each touch, her body spasmed around him. She ran her hand over his hair, heightening his awareness. Everything was about her. All he could see and taste and touch and smell and hear was her. Her sweetness was on his tongue and her moans were in his ears and her soft skin was under his hands.

Last time, he hadn't done this—taking the time to learn her. But this time? Every touch, every sigh, was a lesson—one he committed to memory.

This was right. The connection he felt with her—because that was what it was, a connection—it was something he'd never had before. He'd spent the last three weeks trying to ignore it, but he was done with that. He wasn't going to lie to himself anymore.

He wanted her. And by God, he was going to have her.

He slipped a finger inside her and her hips came off the bed as she cried out. "Zeb!"

"Let me show you what I can do for you," he murmured against her skin. "God, Casey—you're so beautiful."

"Yes, yes—don't stop!"

So he didn't. He stroked his tongue over her sex and his fingers into her body and told her again and again how beautiful she was, how good she felt around him. And the whole time, he got harder and harder until he wasn't sure he could make it. He needed her to let go so that he could let go.

Finally, he put his teeth against her sex—just a small nip, not a true bite. But that was what it took. Something a little bit raw and a little bit hard in the middle of something slow and sensual. She needed both.

Luckily, he could give her that. He could give her anything she wanted.

Her body tensed around him and her back came off the bed as the orgasm moved through her. Even he couldn't hold himself back anymore. The last of his control snapped and he let it carry him as he surged up onto the bed, between her legs. "You are so beautiful when you come," he said as he joined his body to hers.

Everything else fell away. His messy family history and their jobs, baseball and status reports—none of that mattered. All that mattered was that Casey was here with him and there was something between them and they couldn't fight it. Not anymore.

She cried out again as a second orgasm took her and he couldn't hold back anything else. His own climax took him and he slammed his mouth down over hers. If this was the rest of his life, he could be a happy man.

Suddenly exhausted, he collapsed onto her. She wrapped her arms around his back and held him to her. "Wow, Zeb," she murmured in his ear.

"I forgot to ask about birth control that time." She laughed at that, which made him smile. He managed to prop himself up on his elbows to look down at her. "Casey—" he said, but then he stopped because he suddenly realized he was about to tell her that he thought he was in love with her.

She stroked her fingertips over his cheek. "That…" she said, and he could hear the happiness in her voice. "That was everything I have ever dreamed." There was a pause. "And maybe a few things I hadn't thought of yet."

It was his turn to laugh. "Just think, after we're married, we get to do that every night." He withdrew from her body and rolled to the side, pulling her into his arms.

"What?" She didn't curl up in his arms like he thought she would.

"I'm going to take care of you," he told her again, pulling her into him. "I didn't have the chance to tell you, but I ran into Chadwick this afternoon and talking with him cleared up a couple of things for me."

"It…did?"

"It did. You've asked me if I'm like my father or my brother and I didn't know either of them. I only knew what was public knowledge. I knew that my father was not a good man, because he paid my mother to disappear. And I knew that everyone at the brewery liked Chadwick. But that didn't tell me what I needed to know."

"What did you need to know?" Her voice sounded oddly distant. Maybe she was tired from the sex?

That he could understand. His own eyelids were drifting shut but he forced himself to think for a bit longer. "When you asked me which one I was like, you were really asking me if I could be a good man. And not just a good man—a good man for you. I understand what that means now. You need someone who's loyal, who will take care of you and our child. You need someone who appreciates you the way you are."

Then she did curl into him. She slung her arm around his waist and held him tight. "Yes," she whispered against skin. "Yes, that's what I need."

"And that's what I want to give you." He disentangled himself long enough to reach over the side of the bed and retrieve his pants. He pulled out the small velvet-covered box with the ring inside. "I want to marry you and take care of you and our baby together. You won't have to struggle with being a single mother or worrying about making ends meet—I'll take care of all of that."

She stared at the box. "How do you mean?"

Was it his imagination or did she sound cautious? They were past that. He was all in. This was the right thing to do. He was stepping up and taking care of his own—her and their child.

"Obviously, we can't keep working together and you're going to need to take it easy. And your apartment was cute, but it's not big enough for the three of us." He hugged her. "I know I haven't talked about my childhood a lot—it was fine, but it was rough, too. My mom— she worked all the time and I basically lived at the salon, with a whole gaggle of employees watching over me. All I knew was that my dad didn't want me and my mom was working. And I don't want that kind of life for our baby. I don't want us to pass the baby off to employees or strangers. I want us to do this right."

"But…but I have to work, Zeb."

"No, you don't—don't you see? We'll get married and you can stay home—here. I'll take care of everything. We can be a family. And I can get to know Chadwick and his family—my family, I mean. All of the Beaumonts. I don't have to show them that I'm better than them. Because I think maybe…" He sighed. "Maybe they're going to accept me just the way I am, too."

He still couldn't believe that was possible. His whole life, he'd never felt completely secure in his own skin. He was either too light or too black, stuck in a no-man's-land in between.

But here in Denver? Chadwick wished him well and had invited him to be part of the family. And all Casey cared about was that he accepted her the exact same way he wanted to be accepted.

Finally, he had come home.

He opened the box and took the ring out. "Marry me, Casey. I know it's quick but I think it's the right thing."

She sat up and stared at him. "Wait— I— *Wait*."

He looked at her, confused. "What?"

A look of dawning horror crossed over her face—a look that was not what any man wanted to see after sex that good and a heartfelt offer of marriage. "You want to marry me so I can stay home and raise our kid?"

"Well…yes. I don't want to be the kind of father my own father was. I want to be part of my kid's life. I want to be part of your life. And I don't want you to struggle like my mom did. You mean too much to me to let that happen."

And then, suddenly, she was moving. She rolled out of the bed and away from him, gathering up her clothes.

"Are you serious?" she said, and he heard a decided note of panic in her voice. "That's not what I want."

"What do you mean, it's not what you want? I thought we agreed—there was something between us and you're pregnant and this makes sense."

"This does *not* make sense," she said as she angrily jabbed her legs into her jeans. "I am not about to quit my job so I can stay home and raise your baby."

"Casey—wait!" But she was already through the first door. She didn't even have a shirt on yet. She was running away as fast as she could.

Zeb threw himself out of bed, the engagement ring still in his hand. "Casey!" he called after her. "Talk to me, dammit. What is your problem here? I thought this would work. There's something here and I don't want to let that go." Unless…

Something new occurred to him. She had given him every indication that she wanted the baby, even if it was unexpected. But what if…?

What if she didn't? What if she didn't want to read stories at night and teach their kid how to ride a bike or throw a baseball? What if she didn't want to be the hands-on mom he'd imagined, coaching T-ball and playing in the park? The kind of mother he didn't have.

What if she was going to be like his mother—distant and reserved and…*bitter* about an unplanned pregnancy?

She swung around on him, her eyes blazing. "You don't know what you're talking about," she shot at him. The words sliced through the air like bullets out of a gun. "I don't want to quit my job. I've never wanted to be a stay-at-home mom."

"But you can't keep working," he told her, pushing against the rising panic in his chest. "You shouldn't have to."

That was the wrong thing to say. "I don't *have* to do anything I don't want to do. After I have this baby, I'm going to need help. If you think I'm going to give up my job and my life and fit myself into your world just because I'm pregnant with your baby, you've got another think coming."

She spun again and stalked away from him. "Casey!" He sprinted after her and managed to catch up to her—but only because she was trying to get her shirt on. "I'm trying to do the right thing here."

He was horrified to see tears spill over her eyelids. "Is this how it's going to be? Every time we're together, you make me feel so good—and then you ruin it. You just ruin it, Zeb." She scrubbed her hand across her face. "You'll be all perfect and then you'll be a total jerk."

What the hell was she talking about? "I'm trying not to be a jerk. I thought a marriage proposal and a commitment was the right thing to do. Obviously, we can't keep working together, because we can't keep our hands off each other." Her cheeks blushed a furious red. But then again, everything about her was furious right now. "So this is the obvious solution. I'm *not* going to raise a bastard. You *are* going to marry me. We *will* raise our child together and, damn it all, we *will* be a happy family. Unless..." He swallowed. "Unless you don't want me?"

She looked at him like he was stupid. Happiness seemed a long way off. She hadn't even put her bra on—it was hanging from her hand.

"You are trying so hard not to be like your father—

but this? Telling me what I want? Telling me what I'm going to do without giving me an option? You're essentially firing me. You're going to put me in this house and make me completely dependent upon you. You're going to hide me away here under the pretense of taking care of me because you somehow think that's going to absolve you of any guilt you feel. And that?" She jabbed at his chest with a finger. "That is *exactly* what your father would've done."

Her words hit him like a sledgehammer to the chest, so hard that he physically stumbled backward.

"I am not trying to hide anyone away. I'm not ashamed of you!" He realized too late he was shouting but he couldn't stop. "I just want my kid to have something I didn't—two loving parents who give a damn about whether he lives or dies!"

Her face softened—but only a little bit. She still looked fierce and when she spoke, it was in a low voice that somehow hurt all the more. "I am your brewmaster and I might be the mother of your child. I care about this baby and I could care very much for you—but not if you're going to spend the rest of our lives ordering me about. I am not your underling, Zeb. You don't get to decide that what you *think* you want is the same thing that I need. Because I'm only going to say this once. I'm sorry you had a miserable childhood. But it had nothing—not a damn thing—to do with the fact that you were raised by a single parent." A tear trickled down the side of her face and she scrubbed it away. "Don't you dare act like you're the only one raised by a single parent who had to work and sacrifice to survive."

"I never said that." But too late, he remembered her telling him how her mother had died in a car accident when she was two.

"Didn't you?" She moved in closer, and for a delusional second, he thought all was forgiven when she leaned in to kiss his cheek. But then she stepped back. "I give a damn, Zeb. Never think I don't. But I won't let your fears dictate my life."

She stepped around him, and this time, he didn't pull her back. He couldn't. Because he had the awful feeling that she might be right.

The door shut behind her, but he just stood there. Numbly, he looked down at the diamond ring in his hand. His father wouldn't have committed to the rest of his life with a woman he had gotten pregnant—he knew that.

But everything else?

He knew so little and the thing was, he wasn't sure he wanted to know more. He didn't know exactly what had happened between his parents. He couldn't be sure what made his mother the most bitter—the fact that Hardwick Beaumont had cast her aside? Or had it been something else? Had he forced her out of the company? Made her leave town and go back to Atlanta?

Why was this even a question? Hardwick had been married to a wealthy and powerful woman in her own right. Zeb was only four months younger than Chadwick. Of course Hardwick would've done everything within his power to hide Emily and Zeb.

And Zeb's mother…had she resented him? He was a living reminder of her great mistake—undeniable with his father's green eyes. Maybe she hadn't been able to love Zeb enough. And maybe—just maybe—that wasn't his fault.

Fourteen

She couldn't do this. Hell, at this point, she wasn't even sure what "this" was.

Could she be with Zeb? Could they have a relationship? Or would it always devolve into awful awkwardness? Could she work with him or was that impossible? If she didn't work at the brewery, what was she going to do?

It was hard enough to be a woman and a brewmaster. It wasn't like there were tons of jobs ripe for the picking at breweries conveniently located near her apartment. Plus, she was kind of pregnant. How was she supposed to interview at companies that might or might not exist and then ask for maternity leave after only a month or two on the job?

The entire situation was ridiculous. And she couldn't even think the whole thing over while drinking a bottle of beer. Somehow, that was the straw that was going to break her back. How was she going to brew beer without testing it?

There was a possible solution—she could go to Chadwick. He'd find a place for her at Percheron Drafts, she was pretty sure. And at least in the past, he had demonstrated a willingness to work around maternity leave. He knew what she was capable of, and frankly, his was the only brewery within the area that wouldn't force her to relocate. Plus...her child would be a Beaumont. Sort of. Chadwick would be her baby's uncle and the man was nothing if not loyal to the family name.

But even just thinking about going to Chadwick felt wrong. She wasn't six, running to her father to tattle. She was a grown woman. She'd gotten herself into this mess and she had to get herself out of it.

The worst part was, Zeb had been right. There *was* something between them. There had been since the very first moment she had walked into his office and locked eyes with him. There was chemistry and raw sexual attraction and the sex was amazing. And when he was doing everything right, he was practically... perfect.

But when he wasn't perfect, he *really* wasn't perfect.

Instead of going back to her apartment, Casey found herself heading toward her father's small ranch house in Brentwood. She'd grown up in this little house, and at one time, it had seemed like a mansion to her. She hadn't ever wanted to live in a real mansion. She didn't need to be surrounded by all the trappings of luxury—and she also did not need a diamond that probably cost more than a year's salary on her finger.

Instead, she wanted what she'd had growing up. A father who doted on her, who taught her how to do things

like change a tire and throw a baseball and brew beer.
A father who protected her.

She hadn't grown up with all the luxuries that money
could buy. But she'd been happy. Was it wrong to want
that? Was it wrong to *demand* that?

No. It wasn't. So that wasn't the right question.

The bigger question was, could she demand that of
Zeb?

She was happy to see that the lights were on at
home. Sometimes a girl needed her father. She walked
in the house, feeling a little bit like a teenager who had
stayed out past curfew and was about to get in trouble.
"Daddy?"

"In the kitchen," he called back.

Casey smiled at that. Any other parent who was in
the kitchen might reasonably be expected to be cooking. But not Carl Johnson. She knew without even seeing it that he had something taken apart on the kitchen
table—a lamp or doorbell, something.

True to form, a chandelier was sitting in the middle
of the table, wires strung everywhere.

The chandelier was a piece of work—cut crystal
prisms caught the light and made it look like the room
was glowing. It belonged in a mansion like Zeb's. Here,
in her father's house, it looked horribly out of place. She
knew the feeling.

It was such a comforting thing, sitting at this table
while her father tinkered with this or that. Casey slid
into her old seat. "How are you doing, Daddy?"

"Pretty good. How are you?" He looked at her and
paused. "Honey? Is everything okay?"

No. Things were not all right and she wasn't sure how
to fix them. "I think I've made a mistake."

He rested his hand on her shoulder. "Are you in trouble? You know I don't like you living in that apartment by yourself. There's still plenty of room for you here."

She smiled weakly at him. "It's not that. But I... I did something stupid and now I think I've messed everything up."

"Does this have something to do with work?" When Casey didn't reply immediately, her dad pressed on. "This is about your new boss?"

There was no good way to say this. "Yeah, it does. I'm... I'm pregnant."

Her father stiffened, his grip on her shoulder tight before he quickly released her. "Them Beaumonts—I never did trust them. Are you okay? Did he hurt you?"

Casey slumped forward, head in her hands and her elbows on the table. "No, it's not like that, Dad. I *like* him. He likes me. But I'm not sure that that's going to be enough." She looked at her father. He looked skeptical. "He asked me to marry him."

Her father sat straight up. "He did? Well, I guess that's the right thing to do—better than what his old man would've done." There was a long pause during which Casey went back to slumping against her hands. "Do you want to get married? Because you don't have to do anything you don't want to, honey."

"I don't know what to do. When he asked me, he made it clear that he expected me to quit my job and stay home and be a mother full-time." She sighed. It wasn't only that, though.

No, the thing that really bothered her had been the implication that she, Casey Johnson, wasn't good enough to be the mother to his child as she was. Instead, she needed to become someone else. The perfect mother. And what the hell did she know about mothering? Nothing. She'd never had one.

"And that's not what I want. I fought hard to get my job, Dad. And I like brewing beer. I don't want to throw that all away because of one mistake. But if I don't marry him, how am I going to keep working at the brewery?" Her father opened his mouth, but she cut him off. "And no, I don't think asking Chadwick for a job is the best solution, either. I have no desire to be the rope in Beaumont tug-of-war."

They sat quietly for a few moments, but it wasn't long until her father had picked up a few pieces of wire. He began stripping them in an absentminded sort of way. "This guy—"

"Zeb. Zeb Richards."

Another piece of copper shone in the light. "This Zeb—he's one of them Beaumont bastards, right?" Casey nodded. "And he offered to marry you so his kid wouldn't be a bastard like he was?"

"Yeah. I just… I just don't want that to be the only reason. I mean, I can see he's trying to do the right thing, but if I get married, I'd kind of like it to be for love."

Her dad nodded and continued to strip the wire. "I wish your mom were here," he said in an offhand way. "I don't know what to tell you, honey. But I will say this. Your mom and I got married because we had to."

"What?" Casey shot straight up in her chair and stared at him. Her father was blushing. Oh, *Lord*.

"I never told you about this, because it didn't seem right. We'd been dating around and she got pregnant and I asked her to marry me. I hadn't before then, because I wasn't sure I wanted to settle down, but with you on the way, I grew up—fast."

She gaped at him. "I had no idea, Dad."

"I didn't want you to think you were a mistake, honey.

Because you are the best thing that's ever happened to me." His eyes shone and he cleared his throat a few times—all while still stripping wire. "Anyway, that first year—that was rough. We had to learn how to talk to each other, how to live together. But you were born, and suddenly, everything about us just made more sense. And then when the accident came..." He shuddered. "The reason I'm telling you this," he went on in a more serious voice, as if he hadn't just announced that she was a surprise, "is that sometimes love comes a little later. If you guys like each other and you both want this kid, maybe you should think about it." He put down his wire trimmers and rested a hand on hers. "The most important thing is that you two talk to each other."

She felt awful because, well, there hadn't been a lot of talk. She'd gone over to his place tonight to do just that, and instead, they'd fallen into bed.

The one time she had sat down and had a conversation with the man had been at the ball game. She had liked him a great deal then—more than enough to bring him home with her. Maybe they could make this work.

No matter what Zeb had said, they didn't have to get married. Times had changed and her dad wasn't about to bust out a shotgun to escort them down the aisle.

She wasn't opposed to getting married. She didn't have anything against marriage. She just... Well, she didn't want their marriage to be on his terms only.

She knew who she was. She was a woman in her early thirties, unexpectedly pregnant. But she was also a huge sports fan. She could rewire a house. She brewed beer and changed her own oil.

She was never going to be a perfect stay-at-home

mom, baking cookies and wearing pearls and lunching with ladies. That wasn't who she was.

If Zeb wanted to marry her and raise their child as a family, then not only did he have to accept that she was going to do things differently, but he was going to have to support her. Encourage her.

That did not mean taking her job away under the pretext of taking care of her. That meant helping her find a way to work at the job she loved *and* raise a happy, healthy child.

She wanted it all.

And by God, it was all or nothing.

But men—even men as powerful as Zebadiah Richards—were not mind readers. She knew that. Hell, she was *living* that.

She needed to tell him what she wanted. Without falling into bed with him and without it devolving into awkward awfulness.

"I sure am sorry, honey," her dad went on. "I'd love to be a grandfather—but I hate that this has put you in an awkward position." He gave her fingers a squeeze. "You know that, no matter what you decide, I'll be here to back you up."

She leaned in to her dad's shoulder and he wrapped his arms around her and hugged her. "I know, Daddy. I appreciate it."

"Tell you what," Dad said when she straightened up. "Tomorrow's Friday, right? And the Rockies play a game at three. Why don't you play hooky tomorrow? Stay here with me tonight. We'll make a day of it."

She knew that this was not a solution in any way, shape or form. At some point, she was going to have to sit down with Zeb and hash out what, exactly, they were going to do.

Soon. Next week, she'd be an adult again. She would deal with this unexpected pregnancy with maturity and wisdom. Eventually, she needed to talk with Zeb.

But for right now, she needed to be the girl she'd always been.

Sometimes, fathers did know best.

Fifteen

"Where is she?"

The man Zeb had stopped—middle-aged, potbellied... He knew that he'd been introduced to this man before. Larry? Lance? Something like that. It wasn't important.

What was important was finding Casey.

"She's not here," the man said, his chins wobbling dangerously.

Zeb supposed he should be thankful that, since Casey was one of exactly two women in the production department, everyone knew which "she" he was talking about.

"Yes, I can see that. What I want to know," he said slowly and carefully, which caused all the blood to drain out of the guy's face, "is where she is now."

It wasn't fair to terrorize employees like this, but dammit, Zeb needed to talk to Casey. She had stormed out of his house last night and by the time he'd gotten dressed, she had disappeared. She hadn't been at her apartment—the security guy said he hadn't seen her. In desperation, Zeb had even stopped by the brewery, just to make sure she wasn't tinkering with her brews. But the place had been quiet and the night shift swore she hadn't been in.

Her office was just as dark this morning. He didn't know where she was and he was past worrying and headed straight for full-on panic.

Which meant that he was currently scaring the hell out of one of his employees. He stared at the man, willing himself not to shake the guy. "Well?"

"She said she wouldn't be in today."

Zeb took a deep breath and forced himself to remain calm. "Do you have any idea where she might be?"

He must not have been doing a good job at the whole "calm" thing, because his employee backed up another step. "Sometimes she takes off in the afternoon to go to a game. With her dad. But you wouldn't fire her for that, right?" The man straightened his shoulders and approximated a stern look. "I don't think you should."

The game. Of course—why hadn't Zeb thought of that? She had season tickets, right? She'd be at the game. The relief was so strong it almost buckled his knees.

"No, I'm not going to fire her," he assured the guy. "Thanks for the tip, though. And keep up the good work."

On the walk back to his office, he called up the time for the baseball game. Three o'clock—that wasn't her taking the afternoon off. That was her taking the whole day. Had he upset her so much that she couldn't even face him? It wasn't like her to avoid a confrontation, after all.

What a mess. His attempt at a marriage proposal last

night had not been his best work. But then, he had no experience proposing marriage while his brain was still fogged over from an amazing climax. He didn't have any experience in proposing marriage at all.

That was the situation he was going to change, though. He couldn't walk away from her. Hell, he hadn't even been able to do that before she had realized she was pregnant. There was something about her that he couldn't ignore. Yes, she was beautiful, and yes, she challenged him. Boy, did she challenge him. But there was more to it than that.

His entire life had been spent trying to prove that he was someone. That he was a Beaumont, that he belonged in the business world—that he mattered, regardless of his humble origins or the color of his skin.

And for all that Casey argued with him, she never once asked him to be anyone other than himself. She accepted him as who he was—even if who he was happened to be a man who sometimes said the wrong thing at the wrong time.

He had made her a promise that he would take care of her, and by God, he was going to do that.

But this time, he was going to ask her how she wanted him to take care of her. Because he should have known that telling her what to do was a bad idea.

Ah, the seats behind hers were still available for this afternoon's game. Zeb bought the tickets.

He was going to do something he had never done before—he was going to take the afternoon off work.

"You want me to go get you some more nachos, honey?" Dad asked for the third time in a mere two innings.

Casey looked down at the chips covered in gloppy

cheese. She was only kind of pregnant—wasn't it too soon for her stomach to be doing this many flips?

"I'm okay." She looked up and saw Dad staring at her. He looked so eager that she knew he needed something to do. "Really. But I could use another Sprite." Frankly, at this point, clear soda was the only thing keeping her stomach settled.

"I'll be right back," Dad said with a relieved smile, as if her problems could all be solved with more food. *Men*, Casey thought with another grin after he was gone.

Whereas she had no idea what she could do to make this better. No, it wasn't the most mature thing in the world to have skipped work today. It was just delaying the inevitable conversation that she would have to have with Zeb at some point or another.

There had been a moment last night—the moment before the kiss—where he'd told her that he was going to take care of her. That had been what she wanted. Hadn't that been why she'd gone to her dad after she had stormed out of Zeb's house? Because she wanted someone to take care of her?

But it wasn't a fair comparison. Her father had known her for her entire life. Of course he would know what she wanted—wasn't that why they were at this game today? It wasn't fair for her to hope and hope and just keep on hoping, dammit, that Zeb would guess correctly. Especially not when he'd gotten so close. There *was* a big part of her that wanted him to take care of her.

There was an equally big part of her that did not want to quit her job and be a stay-at-home mom. What if he couldn't see that? He was a hard-driving businessman who wasn't used to taking no for an answer. What if she couldn't convince him that she would be a better mom if she could keep her job and keep doing what she loved?

She was keeping her eye on the ball when she heard someone shuffling into the seat behind her. By instinct, she leaned forward to avoid any accidental hot dogs down the back of her neck. But as she did so, she startled as a voice came low and close to her ear. "It's a nice afternoon for baseball, isn't it?"

Zeb. She would recognize his voice anywhere—deep and serious, with just a hint of playfulness around the edge.

"Nice enough to skip work, even," he added when she didn't manage to come up with a coherent response.

Okay, now he was teasing her. She settled back in her chair, but she didn't turn around and look at him. She didn't want to see him in the suit and she didn't want to see him in a T-shirt. So she kept her eyes focused on the game in front of her. "How did you find me?"

"I asked Larry. I should've figured it out by myself. You weren't at your apartment and you weren't at work."

"I went home—I mean, my dad's home."

"I upset you. I didn't mean to, but I did." He exhaled and she felt his warmth against the back of her neck. "I shouldn't have assumed you would want to stay home. I know you and I know you're far too ambitious to give up everything you've worked for just because of something like this."

Now she did twist around. Good Lord—he was wearing purple. A Rockies T-shirt and a Rockies hat.

"You blend," she said in surprise. "I didn't think you knew how to do that."

"I can be taught." One corner of his mouth curved up in a small smile—the kind of smile that sent a shiver down her back. "I'm working on doing a better job of listening."

"Really?"

"Really. I have to tell you, I was frantic this morning when I couldn't find you at work. I was afraid you might quit on me and then where would I be?"

"But that's a problem, don't you see? How am I going to do my job? How am I going to brew beer if I can't drink it?"

Zeb settled back in his seat, that half smile still firmly on his face. "One of the things I've learned during my tenure as CEO of the Beaumont Brewery is that my employees do not drink on the job. They may sample in small quantities, but no one is ever drunk while they're at work—a fact which I appreciate. And I've also learned that I have extremely competent employees who care deeply about our brewery."

She stared at him in confusion. "What are you saying?"

He had the nerve to shrug nonchalantly. "I grew up in a hair salon, listening to women talk about pregnancies and babies and children. Obviously, we have to check with a doctor, but I think you taking a small sip every now and then isn't going to hurt anyone. And I don't want that to be the reason why you think you would have to leave a job you love."

She began to get a crick in her lower back. "Why are you here?" Because he was being perfect again and when he was perfect, he was simply irresistible.

"I'm here for you, Casey. I screwed up last night—I didn't ask you what you wanted. So that's what I'm doing now. What do you want to do?"

She was only vaguely aware that she was staring at him, mouth wide-open. But this was *the* moment. If she didn't tell him what she wanted right now, she might never get another chance.

"Come sit by me," she said. Obligingly, Zeb clambered down over the back of Dad's seat and settled in.

For a moment, Casey was silent as she watched the batter line out to right field. Zeb didn't say anything, though. He just waited for her.

"Okay," she said, mentally psyching herself up for this. Why could she defend her beer and her employees—but asking something for herself was such a struggle?

Well, to hell with that. She was doing this. Right now. "It's hard for me to ask for stuff that I want," she admitted. It wasn't a graceful statement, but it was the truth.

Zeb turned and looked at her funny. "You? Didn't you barge into my office and tell me off on my first day?"

"It's different. I defend my job and I defend my workers but for me to sit here and tell you what I want—it's... it's hard, okay? So just humor me."

"I will always listen to you, Casey. I want you to know that."

Her cheeks began to heat and the back of her neck prickled, but she wasn't allowing herself to get lost in the awkwardness of the moment. Instead, she forged ahead.

"The last time we were at a game together... I wanted you to tell me that I was beautiful and sensual and... and gorgeous. But it felt stupid, asking for that, so I didn't, and then after we..." She cleared her throat, hoping against hope that she hadn't turned bright red and knowing it way too late for that. "Well, afterward, what you said made me feel even less pretty than normal. And so I shut down on you."

Now it was his turn to stare at her, mouth open and eyes wide. "But...do you have any idea how much you turn me on? How gorgeous you are?"

God, she was going to die of embarrassment. "It's not

that—okay, maybe it is. But it's that I've always been this tomboy. And when we were together in my kitchen, it was good. Great," she added quickly when he notched an eyebrow at her. "But I don't want that to be all there is. If we're going to have a relationship, I need romance. And most people think I don't, because I drink beer and I watch ball games."

She had not died of mortification yet, which had to count for something.

"Romance," he said, but he didn't sound like he was mocking her. Instead, he sounded…thoughtful.

A small flicker of hope sparked to life underneath the heat of embarrassment. "Yes."

He touched her then, his hand on hers. More heat. There'd always be this heat between them. "Duly noted. What else? Because I will do everything in my power to give you what you want and what you need."

For a moment, she almost got lost in his gaze. God, those green eyes—from the very first moment, they had pulled her in and refused to let her go. "I don't want to give up my job. And I don't want to quit and go someplace else. I've worked hard for my job and I love it. I love everything about making beer and everything about working for the brewery. Even my new CEO, who occasionally sends out mixed signals."

At that, Zeb laughed out loud. "Can you keep a secret?"

"Depends on the secret," she said archly.

"Before I met you, I don't think I ever did anything but work. That's all I've known. It's all my mom did and I thought I had to prove myself to her, to my father— to everyone. I've been so focused on being the boss and on besting the Beaumonts for so long that…" He sighed and looked out at the game. But Casey could tell he wasn't seeing it. "That I've forgotten how to be me. Then I met you. When I'm with you, I don't feel like I have to be something that I'm not. I don't have to prove myself over and over again. I can just be *me*." The look he gave her was tinged with sadness. "It's hard for me to let go of that—of being the CEO. But you make me want to do better."

"Oh, Zeb—there's so much more to you than just this brewery."

He cupped her face. "That goes for you, too—you are more than just a brewmaster to me. You are a passionate, beautiful woman who earned my respect first and my love second."

Tears begin to prick at Casey's eyes. Stupid hormones. "Oh, Zeb…"

"There's something between us and I don't want to screw that up. Any more than I already have," he added, looking sheepish.

"What do you want?" She felt it was only fair to ask him.

"I want to know my child. I want to be a part of his or her life. I don't want my child to be raised as a bastard." He paused and Casey felt a twinge of disappointment. It wasn't like she could disagree with that kind of sentiment—it was a damn noble one.

But was it enough? She wanted to be wanted not just because she was pregnant but because she was… Well, because she was Casey.

But before she could open her mouth to tell Zeb this, he went on, "That's not all."

"It's not?" Her voice came out with a bit of a waver in it.

He leaned in closer. "It's not. I want to be with someone who I respect, who I trust to pull me back to myself when I've forgotten how to be anything but the boss. I want to be with someone who sparks something in me, someone I look forward to coming home to every single night." Casey gasped, but he kept going. "I want to be with someone who's just as committed to her work as I am to mine—but who also knows how to relax and kick back. I want to be with someone who understands the different families I'm a part of now and who loves me because of them, not in spite of them." His lips were now just a breath away from hers. She could feel his warmth and she wanted nothing more than to melt into him again. "But most of all, I want to be with someone who can tell me what she wants—what she needs—and when she needs it. So tell me, Casey—what do you want?"

This was really happening. "I want to know you care, that you'll fight for me and the baby—and for us. That you'll protect us and support us, even if we do things that other people don't think we should."

Oh, God—that grin on him was too much. She couldn't resist him and she was tired of trying. "Like be the youngest female brewmaster in the country?"

He understood. "Yeah, that. If we do this, I want to do this right," she told him. "But I want to meet you in the middle. I don't know if I want to live in the big house and I know we can't live in my tiny apartment."

His eyes warmed. "We can talk about that."

"That's what I want—I want to know that I can talk to you and know that you'll listen. I want to know that everything is going to work out for the best."

He pulled back, just the tiniest bit. "I can't guarantee anything, Casey. But I can promise you this—I will love you and our baby no matter what."

Love. That was the something between them—the thing that neither of them could walk away from.

"That's what I want," she told him. She leaned into him, wrapping her hand around the back of his neck and pulling him in closer. "I love you, too. That's all."

"Then I'm yours. All you have to do is ask." He gave her a crooked grin. "I won't always get it right. I'm not a mind reader, you know."

She couldn't help it—she laughed. "Did the all-powerful Zebadiah Richards just admit there was something he couldn't do?"

"Shh," he teased, his eyes sparkling. "Don't tell anyone. It's a secret." Then he leaned in closer. "Let me give you everything, Casey. We'll run the brewery together and raise our kid. We'll do it our way."

"*Yes.* I want you."

Just as his lips brushed against hers, she heard someone clearing his throat—loudly.

Dad. In all the talk, she'd forgotten that he'd left to fetch a soda for her. She jolted in her seat, but Zeb didn't let her go. Instead, he wrapped his arms around her shoulders.

"Everything okay?" Dad asked as he eyed the two of them suspiciously. "You want me to get rid of him, honey?"

Casey looked up at her dad as she leaned back into Zeb's arms and smiled. "Nope," she said, knowing that this was right. "I want him to stay right here with me."

Everything she'd ever wanted was hers—a family, her job and Zeb. He was all hers.

All she'd had to do was ask for him.

* * * * *

'05